# SAY YOU WILL

# SAY YOU WILL

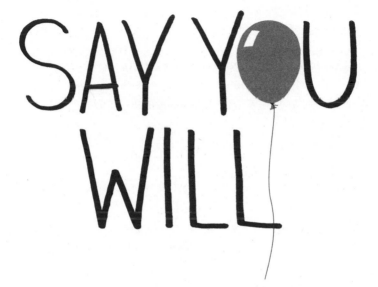

# ERIC WALTERS

DOUBLEDAY
CANADA

Doubleday Canada and colophon are registered trademarks of
Random House of Canada Limited

Library and Archives Canada Cataloguing in Publication

Walters, Eric, 1957-, author
    Say you will / Eric Walters.

Issued in print and electronic formats.
ISBN 978-0-385-68478-1 (pbk.).—ISBN 978-0-385-68479-8 (epub)

    I. Title.

PS8595.A598S293 2015      jC813'.54      C2014-907444-1
                                         C2014-907445-X

This book is a work of fiction. Names, characters, places and
incidents are products of the author's imagination or are used
fictitiously. Any resemblance to actual events or locales or
persons, living or dead, is entirely coincidental.

Printed and bound in the USA

Published in Canada by Doubleday Canada,
a division of Random House of Canada Limited,
a Penguin Random House Company

www.penguinrandomhouse.ca

10 9 8 7 6 5 4 3 2 1

Penguin
Random House
DOUBLEDAY CANADA

*For John Green—*
*for making me care enough about your characters to cry.*

# CHAPTER ONE

The bell rang, and instantly books were slammed shut and people started to get to their feet.

"Everybody sit down!" Mrs. Tanner yelled out.

The noise lessened but didn't stop.

She moved over to the door and took up a position directly in front of it. Nobody was leaving without going through her, and while she wasn't big, she was formidable. Nothing short of a truck was going to move her out of the way.

I slumped down into my seat. I knew this teacher well enough to understand that she wasn't going to be letting anybody out until she was good and ready.

"I've got all day!" she said. "Or at least all lunch period, so talk as long and as loudly as you want."

Kids shushed each other until the last people sat back down and closed their mouths.

"Just because the bell rings, that doesn't mean I'm ready to dismiss you. You so-called intelligent young people are acting more like Pavlov's dogs," Mrs. Tanner said.

"Are you calling us dogs, Mrs. Tanner?" Taylor asked with a playful smile.

Taylor—head cheerleader, perfect hair, perfect skin, perfect clothing, perfect everything else—was as far away from a dog as you could possibly imagine. Although, if she were a dog, I could see her as a well-coiffed white poodle wearing a sparkling, bejewelled collar.

"Of course I'm not calling any of you dogs. I have great respect for dogs. I'm referring to Pavlov and his famous experiment involving canines, bells, and salivation. A discussion of Pavlov certainly isn't out of place in a sociology course."

"Still not getting you," Taylor said, and there was supportive head-shaking and a chorus of murmured agreement.

"Nobody here knows about Pavlov and his dogs?" Mrs. Tanner asked.

Those paying attention just shook their heads, while the others were much more interested in the door, the clock, their pending lunch, and the grumbling in their stomachs. Or they were simply too busy looking at Taylor. That wasn't unusual.

Girls stared at her to find out how to act or what

to wear, while guys just plain stared at her, often with eyes and mouths wide open. Personally, I often looked at the people looking at her instead. That girl could cause guys to walk into each other, or into open lockers or closed doors, or trip and stumble up or down stairs.

Before this semester, Taylor had really been somebody I only knew *of* rather than knew. I guess everybody in the school knew who she was, but I'd never even thought of talking to her. That changed when we were partnered up for a project in Mrs. Tanner's class. We ended up spending a lot of time after school, mostly in the library, working together. She really was nice, and she was pretty smart, and she laughed at my stupid jokes and made me feel comfortable. I didn't get that feeling around most people. To top it off, we got a 97 on the assignment.

In the back of my mind I assumed that once the project was finished we'd be finished. But instead, she kept going out of her way to talk to me, or just say hello, and not just in class but around the school. I got the feeling that we'd really become friends. I liked that.

Watching Taylor—and people in general—was for me more than just idle curiosity. It was part of my ongoing quest to figure people out. Sometimes human interaction left me a bit confused. Sometimes it left me a lot confused. But I was working at it. That was part of my high school journey: to try to figure people out, and by doing so to become more like them, and, I guess, less like me.

"Samuel," Mrs. Tanner called out, startling me. I felt as though I'd been caught doing something I shouldn't—or, really, staring at somebody I shouldn't be staring at. I turned to face her, feeling I had to fight to break free from the magnetic north of Taylor.

"Yes?"

"Samuel, can you tell us about Pavlov's dogs?"

While I could have answered, I really didn't want to. It was embarrassing and show-offy, and it didn't exactly fit with the new and cooler persona I'd been working on this year, albeit with limited success. Knowledge might be king, but sometimes it only made you the king of the geeks, nerds, and dweebs. All I wanted to do was fit in, be known as something other than "that guy who knows everything." More and more I'd found that it's not so much what you know as who you know, and, on some levels, who you wear. And maybe even more important was what you *don't* know. People like other people who don't know the same things they don't know. That was one of the most important conclusions I'd reached and that made me feel even more alone and different.

"Well, Samuel?" she asked again. Mrs. Tanner was the only person who called me Samuel. To everybody else—except my Great-Auntie Mary—I was Sam or Sammy.

"What makes you think I'd know?" I asked.

"You're answering my question with a question.

4

*Do* you know the answer?" she asked. "Because now I've decided that I'm not letting *anybody* leave until *somebody* answers my question."

Instantly people pulled out their phones and started to search.

"Put those phones away immediately!" she ordered. "I'd much rather have a few smart students than a lot of smartphones. Doesn't *anybody* know?"

Ian, my best friend, reached over and put a hand on my shoulder. "Tell her, Sammy."

Reluctantly I put my hand up. Mrs. Tanner gave me a very satisfied smile and nodded. My desire to get out to lunch, coupled with my classical conditioned response to be correct—which would have greatly pleased Pavlov—overcame everything else.

"Ivan Petrovich Pavlov," I said, throwing in his middle name. Why did I do that? There was something that just made that irrelevant little piece of information jump out of me. In the past I would have done it to impress people. Now I knew it was more likely to impress them in the wrong way—in a way I didn't want to impress them any more.

"Do you know anything else?" Mrs. Tanner asked. "Because knowing his middle name won't be enough to free my students."

"Yes, of course," I said, shifting out of my thoughts. "He was a nineteenth-century Russian physiologist known for his work with classical conditioning and behavior modification."

"Go on," Mrs. Tanner said.

"His most renowned work, that for which he is best remembered, involved experiments he performed on dogs."

"He did experiments on dogs?" one of the girls asked. "That's awful. Nobody should experiment on animals. It should be illegal to harm animals for research."

I turned to her. "No, you don't understand. He didn't harm them, he *fed* them. He would always sound a bell before he fed the animals so they would learn to associate the sound of the bell with being fed. And eventually the ringing of a bell alone caused them to start to salivate, drool."

"And you think we drool like dogs when the lunch bell goes?" Taylor asked Mrs. Tanner.

"And that is the extension of the idea," Mrs. Tanner replied. "Congratulations to Taylor and Samuel for teaming up to free you all for lunch. You are now dismissed."

There was a spontaneous burst of applause—some for Taylor, some for me, but most of it for lunch. Chairs scraped against the floor, voices rose, and people bumped together as they pushed out through the newly vacated doorway.

Ian and a couple of the others congratulated and thanked me, but more of the class response was directed toward Taylor. She took it all in stride; she was used to approval and congratulations. With her, it was like water off a duck's back, or drool out of a dog's mouth. As she walked past she flashed one of her wonderful smiles in my direction.

"Hey, Sammy, nice work," she said.

I mumbled back a response.

Neither the wonderful, nor the smile, was a surprise. She was always friendly to me. In fact, she was always friendly to almost everybody.

Ian and I were among the last shuffling forward toward freedom and lunch.

"Samuel, a moment please," Mrs. Tanner said as we approached.

I stopped, and Ian hesitated.

"Meet you outside," I told him.

Ian filed out along with everybody else. Mrs. Tanner waited until we were alone and the room was silent. I didn't know what she wanted to talk about but I already knew I didn't want to talk about it.

"I assume you must surely understand that high school is designed to help students become smarter and wiser," she said.

"Yeah, of course."

"Then we must be failing you, because you seem to have become less smart and less wise during your years in our fine institution."

"I'm learning things. My marks are good," I said. They were actually, by almost anybody's standards, not just good but *very* good.

"This is the third year you've taken one of my courses. You must be aware that your marks have dropped from your first two years. Are your eleventh-grade courses so much more difficult than your freshman and sophomore classes?"

"I don't think so, not really." There was nothing hard about any of my classes.

"So how do you explain the lower marks?" she asked.

"There's nothing wrong with a 91 average."

"For most people, that would be excellent. For you, it's a drop of 8 percentage points. And that is a drop that could mean the difference between an Ivy League scholarship and having to go to a less-prestigious school."

"I can try to bring my marks back up next year," I offered.

"I'm sure you could do that, but universities look at both your junior *and* senior years," Mrs. Tanner said.

"And my SAT scores," I pointed out.

"Yes, they are important."

I wasn't going to say anything, but I knew that I could ace the SATs, and I wasn't worried at all about getting into the university I wanted.

"As I recall from a discussion we had in your freshman year, you are hoping to follow in your father's footsteps and become a doctor."

"I still think I'd like that," I said. Not nearly as much as my parents would like it, but it did seem like a pretty good goal.

"That's reassuring to know, because I had assumed you were now contemplating a career as either a professional surfer or beach bum."

"A surfer?"

She shrugged. "Just an assumption based on the recent changes to your haircut—or should I say hair*style*—and clothing."

"I'm just evolving," I explained.

On the one hand, I was pleased that she'd noticed and commented, but on the other, I still felt a little self-conscious about it all. There were times I'd catch a glimpse of my reflection in a mirror or store window and be surprised by how I looked. Over the last two years I'd grown, and I was now taller than average—as defined by the medical journals—and had, as my mother liked to say, "filled out."

Added to that was a calculated combination of longer hair, new clothes, the sprinkling of new words into my vocabulary—smaller words, combined with popular vernacular—and what would have appeared to be a much more relaxed attitude toward school. These were all factors that I had identified as being associated with students who occupied the "cooler" end of the social spectrum. Altogether, I didn't look half bad at all, and I certainly didn't look *that* different. Maybe you couldn't judge a book by its cover, but people still did judge a person by his appearance. I now looked like I fit in.

Regardless, "evolving" was the word I was using to explain to my parents and friends the changes I'd been implementing. Although these changes were visible for all to see, I hadn't really talked to anybody about the reasons behind them. It was hard for me to explain, because I didn't really fully understand them myself.

"Are you sure you're evolving and not devolving?" Mrs. Tanner asked.

"Lots of people dress like this," I said, gesturing to my clothing.

"I won't bore you with the 'if everybody was jumping off a building, would you?' argument, because unfortunately I know the answer and it involves a pile of bloody bodies on the pavement below."

I wouldn't jump off a building just because everybody else did, but I knew I'd at least go to the edge and see what all the fuss was about before I made my decision.

"For a smart person, Samuel, sometimes you can be rather stupid."

What was the correct response to that statement?

"I was just wondering when you decided it wasn't cool to be smart?" she asked.

"I didn't . . . I don't think it's not cool."

"Yet this semester you've stopped answering questions, even questions that you obviously know the answers to," she said.

"I answer questions."

"You seem to answer them only when given no choice, like today. You know, you can be smart and be cool as well. Stop hiding your light under a bushel."

I couldn't stop myself from laughing.

"You find that funny?" she asked. She didn't look amused.

"It's just that my grandmother used to say that."

"Your grandmother was a wise woman. And you are a wise young man. Show it, okay?"

I let out a big sigh. "I just want to fit in, to be like other people." I surprised myself when those words just flowed out like that. Not that I hadn't been thinking them—but saying them was different. And now, hearing them myself, they actually sounded rather pathetic, desperate.

"Do you know about Maslow's hierarchy of needs?" she asked. Before I could say either yes or no, she answered for me. "Of course you do, right?"

I reluctantly nodded.

"Explain it to me."

I hesitated.

"Please, humor me. There's nobody here but me and you, and I already know you're smart. I promise I won't think you're any less cool, and I won't tell anybody that you knew."

I guess there was no point in pretending ignorance.

"Abraham Maslow was—"

"You don't know his middle name?" she asked.

I paused a beat. "Harold."

"So, go on."

"He was a theoretical psychologist who first proposed his hierarchy of needs in 1943, and then elaborated on it in his seminal work *Motivation and Personality* in 1954."

Mrs. Tanner laughed. "Now, doesn't it feel good to let that out?"

It actually did.

"Go on, please."

"He proposed that basic physiological needs such as air, food, and sleep have to be satisfied before anything else could be pursued."

Mrs. Tanner grabbed a piece of chalk, drew a rough triangle on the board, and segmented it into four horizontal slices.

"Um, there are five parts to his pyramid," I said.

She looked surprised. "I can see where you knowing everything *could* be annoying," she said, and I recoiled slightly. "I'm joking! Don't look so hurt." She added another segment. "Here at the bottom are the physiological needs."

She wrote in "air," "food," "water," "sleep," which I'd said, and added "excretion" and "sex," which I'd just felt too embarrassed to say out loud.

Next she added the label "Safety" to the slice above that, and wrote in "security of body, resources, and family." She didn't write in "security of property," which should have gone there, but I made a point of not mentioning it, even though I had the strongest reflex to do so.

"And above that on the pyramid?" she asked.

"Love and belonging," I said.

"Fitting in."

I nodded.

"Funny, I see you as having some very good friends. Ian and Brooke from my afternoon class, for example. You three go way back, don't you?"

"Kindergarten."

They hadn't been just my best friends back then, basically they'd been my only friends. The three of us just sort of fit together. Because of them, I'd never really been alone. We'd all been different—looking back, we were definitely outsiders even then—but we were outsiders together. That made it so much less lonely. Maybe that was part of the problem. Because we had each other, we didn't work as hard as we might have to break through and become more like everybody else.

"And I've met your parents. They seem like good people . . . unless I'm misjudging them?"

"No, they're really good. They've always been there for me." Sometimes I thought my mother was there for me just a little bit too much.

"But you want more, correct?" Mrs. Tanner asked.

I reluctantly nodded. "I just want to be normal." Again, it was a shock to hear myself admit that to her, to hear my voice say it out loud.

"That, young man, is never going to be possible."

And that was a different kind of shock that she'd actually say that. "You don't think I'm normal?"

"'Normal' is a theoretical construct, Samuel. You have a remarkable mind that is different from other people's. You can try to hide it, but you can't change it with anything short of a major head injury. Are you expecting to experience a head injury?"

"That's not something I'm planning, but you never know."

"Then stop pretending that you're not smart."
She paused. "Do you think Taylor is 'normal'?"

"Um . . . yeah, sure she is."

"You've been fortunate enough to have partnered
with her on an assignment, so you'd know that. Besides,
you spend enough time observing her that I assumed
you would be able to answer that question easily."

I felt myself blush, badly, and looked down at the
floor.

"Don't be embarrassed. We're simply going back
to the bottom of Maslow's hierarchy, the physiological base of the pyramid. Half my class, the *male*
half, spends more time either thinking about her or
looking at her than they spend listening to anything
that I'm teaching. It's just part of human nature, the
whole evolutionary process. You know, you and
Taylor have a great deal in common."

"We do?"

"Yes, you are both defined by parts of you that
you have limited control over. For you it's your
mind, and for Taylor it's her looks. At least she has
embraced her gift and doesn't fight to hide it. The
sad part is that she's actually a very smart young
woman, but most people don't even notice that."

"So you're saying it's like a reverse halo effect,"
I said.

"You're familiar with Edward Thorndike?"

I shrugged.

"Explain to me what Thorndike meant by the
halo effect," she said.

I hesitated for a second before answering. "Thorndike stated that if an observer perceives somebody as possessing positive qualities it will be assumed that they also possess other positive qualities. The good qualities halo over other qualities."

"And the reverse effect?"

"It's like you said, because Taylor is good looking her appearance sort of blinds people to other good qualities she could have, like being smart."

"That was very well said," she said.

"I've read a bit."

"You've read more than a bit. The question is, why do you know so much about Pavlov and Maslow and Thorndike?"

"I guess I find human behavior interesting," I said. I'd been reading about it intensely for the past two years to try to understand it better.

"And do you find it puzzling as well?" she asked.

I nodded.

"Welcome to the club. Everybody is trying to figure people out."

I accepted that. It was just that for most people it seemed to come more naturally. For me, it was like trying to understand a language I wasn't fully fluent in.

"So, for Taylor, the reverse halo effect means that the glow of her good looks means that people overlook the intellect. And with you, the negative halo of your intellect means that people can't see you as possibly being cool or fitting in."

"There's more to it than that but I guess that's sort of it," I said.

"Don't be ashamed of being smart, even freaky-smart," she said.

Mrs. Tanner quickly wrote the words "Estem" and then "Self-Actualization" above it in the two top sections of the pyramid. In her haste she missed one of the "e's" in "esteem."

"We're all trying to get to the top of the pyramid and fulfill our own needs at all the different levels. I just think you have to be careful about how you try to get there. Being a teenager is the time to try on different clothing—not just literally but also psychologically speaking—to see what best suits you. At the same time it's important not to lose sight of who you are, the real, authentic, genuine you, as you make that climb to the top. Don't give in to the easy route to the top, okay?"

I nodded.

"You look as though you have something else you want to say," she said.

I did, but I didn't know if I should.

"Go ahead . . . please."

"Well, it's just that Maslow's hierarchy is really seen by modern psychologists as being rather simplistic and reductionist in nature, and it has been supplanted by more extensive and dynamic interactive models based on a more complex understanding of human needs and—"

"I was wrong," she said, cutting me off. "Sometimes

it might be better for you to hide it. Go for lunch."

I started for the door.

"Samuel."

I stopped and turned around. She pointed at my desk. My backpack, with my lunch, was still hanging over the back of the seat.

"Physiological needs first. Have a good lunch."

She left just ahead of me, but before I left the classroom there was one thing I needed to do. I went over to the board, picked up the chalk, and added another "e" to "esteem."

# CHAPTER TWO

I left the classroom behind and hurried down the hall, out the door, and onto the front steps. When the weather was good half the school ate lunch out on the front lawn. After a long, chilly, rainy winter the warmth just brought everybody out of hibernation. And like animals shedding their winter fur, everybody had traded their winter coats for far less clothing. In the case of many of the girls, it was far, *far* less clothing. Spring was good. Life was good.

I stopped atop the stairs and surveyed the scene. I couldn't help but think of that scene in *The Lion King* where Simba stands at the top of Pride Rock and looks out over his kingdom. Not that I was the king or this was my kingdom, but the image stuck in my mind.

The campus spread out before me. A long,

circular driveway framed an expanse of green grass
with trees and benches interspersed, criss-crossed
with walking paths. Below, rather than wildebeest
and giraffes or monkeys and hyenas, were freshmen,
sophomores, juniors, and seniors. Not wild animals,
but they were just as rigidly locked into species, fam-
ilies, prides, and packs.

I went down the stairs to join Ian and Brooke. I
didn't have to search for them because I knew where
they'd be. It was our spot, our little section of the campus. Everybody had their own little patch of ground.
Our spot had shifted since we'd first started high
school. That first year we'd been way off to the side, in
the sun, on worn grass, close to the exhaust fumes
from the cars on the driveway. Now we "owned" a
little patch of grass and shade close to the benches
where the seniors—the cool seniors—gathered. Next
year, after they migrated to university or college or
simply left, that spot would be ours!

My thoughts went back to what Mrs. Tanner had
said about me being freaky-smart. That was too close
to what I'd been called when I was young—a freak.
In grade school there were always lots of comments
about me having swallowed a calculator or a set of
encyclopaedias. Comments from kids were to be
expected because they were just kids, but lots of adults
seemed to have something to say as well. My mother
explained that you had to expect things like that from
people sometimes. "Different" made them nervous.
Great. I was different.

Of course, there was one person I was very similar to—my father. I got my able mind and my excellent memory from him. My father was a doctor. People called him a brilliant man. Funny how when you're a grown-up you're "brilliant," and when you're a kid you're a "freak." I just wanted to get old enough to stop being a freak.

Being compared to my father wasn't a bad thing. My father was a good guy. He saved people's lives. He never had an unkind word to say to or about anybody. He was a good husband and father. But it was obvious that he was a little odd at times. My mother kept him on the straight and narrow, helping him to navigate social waters, watching for the hidden reefs and rocks he still didn't seem to know existed. Maybe that was the big difference between the two of us. I knew about the hazards and was trying to understand how to avoid them. Shipwrecks are never pleasant.

Funny, I could remember a time when I didn't feel like a freak. Back then I knew I was different from other people, but I just figured we were all different in different ways. Then, as the grades passed, I became more aware of how people saw me. Being smart—freaky-smart—wasn't always a good thing, and sometimes it was a really bad thing. The comments that I hadn't heard or understood when I was little started to make more sense, and with that understanding came hurt. People said things that hurt.

In the ninth grade it became even more hurtful. I wasn't in school with just the kids I'd grown up with any more—there was a whole bunch of new kids. The kids I knew had sort of got used to me, but here, in the high school, my differentness became crystal clear. Even to me, the guy who didn't get social things all that well sometimes. It all finally started to make sense.

I plopped down on the grass beside Brooke and Ian. "Nice of you to join us," Brooke said. "I thought you'd found yourself somebody else to sit with."

"Who else would I sit with?" I asked. "And being late wasn't my choice. It was Mrs. Tanner's."

"Right. What was that whole thing with dogs and drooling about, anyway?" Ian asked.

"Was she talking about Pavlov's dogs?" Brooke asked.

"Yeah, that was it," Ian said. "You know about that?"

"Who doesn't?" she asked.

I wasn't surprised Brooke knew. She knew lots about lots. She was very smart. Normal very smart, not freaky-smart.

I zipped open my backpack and pulled out my lunch. I was hungry. I took a bite from my sandwich and—

"Eating meat is disgusting," Brooke said.

Brooke had become a vegetarian—a very vocal vegetarian. But at least she was just a normal vegetarian now. The year before she'd been a raw-food vegan. For raw-food vegans, not only were all forms of animal products out—including milk and eggs and even honey—but she wasn't allowed to cook or bake anything, even if it was a vegetable. That left her with very few food options, and even fewer that didn't taste bad. I had to give her credit, though, she was sticking to her guns about being a vegetarian— not that she believed in guns.

I took another bite of my sandwich.

"Meat is murder," she added.

I slowly swallowed the bite I was chewing. "I'm just eating it. I didn't kill it."

"If you had to kill it you probably would be a vegetarian," she said.

"If I had to grow my own food I would probably starve to death," I noted.

"If I had to make my own shoes I'd be barefoot," Ian said. "In fact, if I had to make my own clothes I'd be naked right now," he added.

"Thanks for that wonderful visual," Brooke said.

"I always thought you were picturing me that way anyway," Ian said. "Glad you can finally admit that you've been undressing me with your eyes. I guess it's only fair since I've pictured you—"

"Too much information," I said, cutting him off. "Sorry."

Brooke gave him a look. She was deadly with that look. I'd had it aimed at me more than a few times.

Ian had what his psychologist called a *filtration* problem. It sounded like something a water-treatment plant would have, but what it meant was that he said things without thinking them through. In fact, there were times when I was pretty sure he was just as shocked as the rest of the world by what came out of his mouth. It was like it just popped out. And while he instantly regretted it, there was no way to take it back.

Thank goodness his psychologist had agreed to a unique way to help re-channel his comments so that they wouldn't get him in so much trouble. It was something I'd suggested. His psychologist was the same one I used to see, Dr. Young.

"Hey, Sam."

I spun around, though I knew the voice without even looking. "Hey, Taylor . . . girls." Taylor was with her best friends, Brittney and Ashley.

"I was just telling Britt and Ash about Tanner going all crazy on us and how we defused her."

"That was cool that Tanner thought we made a nice team," I responded.

Brooke made a slight huffing sound but had the courtesy to make it soft enough that it wasn't obvious.

"Brookey," called Taylor, using the nickname she'd given her, "it's so wonderful that everybody has started using these water bottles." She held up a reusable water container with the school logo on it, as did Brittney and Ashley.

Brooke had spearheaded a drive to ban throw-away plastic water bottles on campus and replace them with reusable ones. The cheerleading squad, with Taylor leading the way, had bought into it, and shortly after that it had been approved by the Student Council and adopted by everybody in the school. It was sort of the halo effect for water bottles—the cheerleaders were cool, so everything they touched was cool too. That was pretty much the theory behind every beer and car commercial ever made.

"I guess you two make a great team as well," I commented.

The index finger on Ian's right hand started moving. Anybody who wasn't looking for it probably wouldn't have noticed. And even if somebody had noticed, they would have had no idea what he was doing. It came across as a nervous tap, or something a frustrated drummer might do. But I knew, and so did Brooke. He was tapping out a message in Morse Code. He used a short tap as a "dot" and a tap with a pause as a "dash." Each letter of the alphabet had different dot and dash combinations and basically he spelled out words. I watched as he tapped out, *Britt marry me*. Tapping it out was a much better idea than saying it out loud, and really, that was a much more socially acceptable message than a lot of what Ian tapped out.

"We'd better get going," Taylor said. "Take care, Sam, Ian, Brookey."

The three girls walked off, and Ian and I—and every other guy nearby—watched. Ian started another message. I made a point of not looking. The odds were that whatever he was trying to say wasn't going to be polite.

The three girls joined their friends at the benches

where the seniors and extremely popular juniors, like them, hung out. The three of us weren't cool, but in terms of our geographic location we were on the edge. I wondered if the halo effect applied to real estate.

"Apparently, it's not just dogs that get conditioned to drool," Brooke said.

"What?" Ian asked as he continued to stare in the girls' direction.

"Nobody's drooling," I said, defending both Ian and myself.

"Speak for yourself," Ian said. "That girl is hot."

"Do you mean *Tay* or *Britt* or *Ash*?" Brooke asked.

"Yes, yes, and yes, but mainly the last," Ian said.

"And just what crude thing did he tap out when they walked away?" Brooke asked.

She was one of the few people who knew what he was doing but she couldn't master the decoding, which frustrated her tremendously. He tapped things out pretty quickly and while she could decode some of it the whole message was too much for her to comprehend.

"Maybe I just had an itchy finger," Ian said.

"Better your finger than another part of your anatomy."

"It was nothing bad," I said. I was torn between wanting to keep Ian's comments confidential and being honest with Brooke. Dishonesty didn't wear well with me, and I was basically a terrible liar.

"If you'd like I could slow down, or use much smaller words," Ian offered—or rather taunted.

"Or shorten them," she added. "Just why do they have to shorten their names? Is two syllables too long?"

"Well, *Brookey*, she always gives you a second syllable, so you should be happy," I said.

"Shut up, Samuel, or should I say Sammy, or . . . oh, that's right, Sam, one syllable."

I pretended to zip my mouth closed. Winning an argument with Brooke was so rare it wasn't worth the attempt. It was amazing how I could have all the facts and she could have all the answers. That much hadn't changed since kindergarten. The biggest difference now was that she no longer punched me when she was in danger of losing an argument. That girl had a punch that was almost as strong as her opinions.

"Do you know what's really annoying about Taylor?" Brooke asked.

"That she calls you Brookey?" I asked.

"That she's too beautiful?" Ian questioned.

Brooke shook her head. "She's on Student Council. She's part of the Social Justice Club. She does volunteer work at a seniors' home. She does well at school. I've never seen her not being nice to anybody, *and*, to top it all off, she *is* too beautiful," Brooke said.

"And the annoying part?" I asked.

"Weren't you listening?" Brooke demanded.

"Listening, but not hearing. All I've heard is that she does lots of good things and she's nice."

"Then you *did* hear," Brooke said. "Despite being

that beautiful she's still nice, when she should be some sort of mean girl."

"Mean girl?"

"Don't you ever watch movies or read YA fiction?" Brooke asked. "The beautiful cheerleader is always supposed to be mean, or least conceited, and she's supposed to be dating the captain of the football team."

Taylor wasn't dating anybody. She was social and she went out in groups of friends all the time but she didn't actually date anybody. I'd heard people— well, guys who had asked her out and been turned down—say that maybe she thought she was "too good" for them. I figured she was just too busy. But, realistically, from a purely analytical perspective, looking at all the variables . . . she probably *was* too good for them.

"So, let me see if I have this right," Ian said. "You find Taylor annoying because she *isn't* mean."

"Exactly!" Brooke exclaimed.

I shook my head. How did you argue with that sort of logic?

Ian started to tap out a message.

"And you stop that right now!" Brooke yelled, and he stopped. "If you're going to say something about me, say it to my face!"

"I wasn't saying anything about you," Ian said, and then he looked over at me.

The first three letters he'd tapped out were *B-R-O*, so either he really was going to say something about

Brooke, or he was using dated street language and I was his *Bro*. I suspected the former.

A car horn sounded repeatedly and kept getting louder. I looked around—we all looked around—until the source of the noise came into view. It was a big, white stretch limo, and it was slowly moving along the school driveway. It slowed down even more as it got closer to us, the horn still blaring, every eye on it, a crowd gathering to watch. Then it stopped, right in front of the seniors' special territory, and a guy popped his head out of the sunroof. He was wearing a red-and-gold jersey—our school colors.

"It's Kevin!" Ian yelled.

Kevin *was* the captain of the football team—the guy Taylor would have been dating if this had been a movie instead of real life. As we watched, he climbed farther out of the sunroof. He must have been standing on the back of the seat.

"Can I have your attention, please?" he yelled out.

With the horn no longer blaring and the crowd waiting in hushed anticipation, his voice easily carried. People turned to face him or got up and moved toward him. The circle of people watching started growing. Kids who had been far away came running over, some sprinting. And it was all unfolding almost directly in front of us. There was a very large circle, three or four people deep, surrounding Kevin, the vehicle, and the select group of seniors.

"I have come here today on a mission!" Kevin

yelled out. "I have a very special request. Gentlemen, if you please."

Out of the crowd, members of the football team pushed their way forward. It looked like about a dozen of them, all in their jerseys. Even though the season had been over for months, I'd noticed earlier in the day that a lot of players were wearing them. Hey, if I had been on the football team—the pride of our school—I would have worn my jersey in the shower. But me being on the football team, or any team, was almost beyond comprehension. I could fully understand the mechanics of the game, the strategy, and all the statistics associated with it, but throwing and catching a ball wasn't within my genetic programming.

That was one of the things that Brooke, Ian, and I shared. Throughout our school lives we had always been the three people picked last for any team in gym. Of the three of us, Brooke was definitely the best, but her attitude was the worst. She had the ability to put bat to ball in baseball, but she was just as likely to run to third as she was to first. It wasn't that she didn't know the difference so much as she just hated being told what to do.

The football players assembled and lined up alongside the limo. All around us phones were popping up and pictures were being taken and texts were being tapped out. There was a lot of noise, laughing, talking, as the crowd buzzed as if they were watching a football game instead of watching a bunch of guys in football jerseys standing beside a car.

"I have a very special question for a very special person," Kevin called out, and the crowd quieted again, waiting for his next words.

Suddenly the football guys started to remove their jerseys. The buzz from the crowd got louder again as everybody tried to figure out what they were doing. Why would they . . . ? Then the answer appeared before our eyes. On their chests, each of them had a big letter painted in bright red. Together they read . . .

B-R-I-T-T-M-R-O-P-?

"What does 'Brittmrop' mean?" Brooke asked.

Judging by the expressions on the faces of the people around us and their mumbled comments, that was the question everybody was asking. Standing atop the limo, Kevin suddenly lost that look of confidence he almost always wore. He looked confused.

Then one of the football players stepped forward, looked down the row, and yelled something out. Two of them jumped forward and switched places, and suddenly it made sense. "BRITT PROM?" was what they now spelled out in their corrected order.

There was a squeal as Brittney jumped to her feet, and the crowd roared out its approval.

Turning back around, I saw that Kevin had pulled a bouquet of red roses from the car. He reached back in and, like a magic trick, out popped a bunch of red, helium-filled balloons!

"So, Brittney!" Kevin called out, silencing the crowd. "Will you accept my invitation to the prom by joining me?"

She rushed forward in response. Two of the football guys picked her up and passed her up to where Kevin was standing. She took the flowers and wrapped her arms around Kevin and gave him a big hug and then a long, long kiss—the sort of thing you see in movies—and the crowd started cheering and roaring again, even louder than before. They both looked so happy, so much like they belonged together. I wondered what that felt like.

Music started blaring from speakers—the limo had speakers on the outside of the vehicle. It was loud hip-hop, and the bass was so strong it felt as if the ground was shaking. The car started driving, slowly, parting the crowd, and Kevin suddenly released the balloons. They soared upward as the car started to edge its way forward, breaking through the inner circle. Some people started to chase after them, and the entire driveway seemed to be lined with people. Kevin and Brittney continued to stand and wave like they were the King and Queen of England. And really they *were* like the King and Queen of our school.

# CHAPTER THREE

The sound of the music faded as the limo turned onto the street, drove away, and then disappeared around the block. I looked up to see the balloons up in the sky. They were floating and fluttering, pushed by a wind up there that I couldn't feel down here. They rose higher and higher until they were nothing more than little red dots against the bright blue sky. Finally they were too high and too far away to see.

"Well, so much for me asking Britt to the prom," Ian said.

"What?" Brooke and I asked in unison.

"Yeah, she can't go with me now."

"You wanted to take Brittney to the prom?" There was a disbelieving tone in Brooke's voice.

"Well I can't now. Weren't you watching? She

just accepted an invitation to the prom from Kevin."

"I mean before Kevin asked her . . . you were thinking about asking her?" Brooke said.

"I think about Brittney a lot. Her and Ashley and Taylor, in different ways, with us doing different things and—"

"Filter," I said.

"Oh, yeah." He started to tap out a message.

"No, just tell us, were you really going to ask her to the prom?" I said.

He shook his head. "I hadn't really thought about the prom, to be honest. Besides, it costs a lot of money and I'm a little short on funds."

"That wouldn't be a problem if you still had your job," I pointed out.

"It is unfortunate that I was strategically re-deployed," Ian said.

"You were fired," Brooke said. "The manager told you to leave and never come back . . . not even when you have kids."

"I thought that was a little harsh," Ian said. "Although, with his poor people skills, I assume he'll still be the manager of Clown Town when I do have children."

"You're one to talk about poor people skills," Brooke said.

"It takes one to know one."

"And that whole kids thing. First you'd need to get a date before the concept of kids could even be entertained," Brooke said.

"Which does lead back to the whole prom thing. Maybe I should ask somebody to prom," Ian said.

"Which leads us even further back to the fact that you don't have money for prom because you were fired from your job," Brooke said.

"You know what the worst thing about being fired was? I thought the two of you would have walked out with me in solidarity." He held a fist in the air. "You should have both quit your jobs at Clown Town."

"Yeah, right, we should have followed you out the door."

"I don't see why you didn't. I *am* a natural leader," Ian countered. "People *want* to follow me."

"That's just to see what stupid thing you're going to do next."

"I admit I am an out-of-the-box thinker," Ian said.

"You're an out-of-your-mind thinker," Brooke added.

"Could you both just stop it?" I said. "Nobody is going to win this argument. Nobody ever wins these arguments. Let's talk about something important. What did you think of the promposal?"

"Important? Well, it wasn't bad. Some creativity was employed, which as an out-of-the-box thinker I can really appreciate," Ian said. "Of course, that means Brooke couldn't possibly appreciate it."

Brooke looked as though she was going to retaliate, and I held up my hands to stop her. I really got tired of the two of them fighting about things, but for them it was like a sporting event or a stage play.

"Brooke, what did you think about it?" I asked. I braced for her response.

"I'm of a mixed mind."

"You are?" I was more than a little surprised.

"Part of me *thinks* it's nothing more than just meaningless, wasteful decadence driven by mindless capitalism and our corporate culture that results in environmental degradation while pandering to teenage self indulgence."

I was impressed. She'd managed to tie in at least three of her favorite causes.

"And the other part of you?" I asked.

"That part *knows* it's all of those things. How ridiculous. I just don't believe in it."

"The promposal or the prom itself?" I asked.

"Both! The whole concept is ridiculous."

"What if it was a politically correct, green, carbon neutral, free range, fair trade, organic, peanut free, not tested on animals, global justice prom?" Ian asked.

"What?"

"You know, what if it was a prom that celebrated all the things that you believe in this week?" Ian explained.

Brooke did passionately believe in all those things, as well as vegetarianism, feminism, anti-racism, gluten-free food, the hundred-mile diet, and other assorted trends. The bounds of her social justice commitments were limitless.

She looked at me as if I was going to rescue her. I wasn't.

"Well, he's got a good question. What then?" I asked. "Would you go?"

She shook her head. "Why do I even listen to you two at all?"

"Because I am a source of inspiration, education, information, and amusement," Ian said.

Brooke turned to me again. "Sam, what do *you* think about this whole business?"

I hated it when the two of them put me in the middle, but I'd been asked . . . so . . . "I'm not sure Ian is that inspirational, but I certainly think he's amusing," I said.

"I meant what do you think of this whole promposal thing?" she asked.

"It certainly got my attention, and the attention of at least half of the other kids who go to this school, so I think it definitely was pretty interesting."

"You do?" Brooke questioned.

"Sure. I'd heard something about promposals, but seeing one was different. A guy would have to be pretty brave to do that."

"What part of that involved bravery: the balloons or the car ride?" she asked.

"Think about it. Kevin put himself out there, in front of everybody, and risked Brittney saying no to him," I explained.

"Do you really think it was that risky? They've been dating for months. What were the odds that she was going to turn him down?"

"Okay, maybe not brave, but he certainly gave it

a lot of thought and invested time and energy and—"

"And a massive amount of money that could have actually done some good in the world?" Brooke asked, cutting me off.

"Well, that too, but still, it was pretty cool."

"It sounds like *you* want to go to the prom," Brooke said.

I hadn't thought about it one way or the other. I *could* go to the prom if I wanted. I had enough money, and it was for seniors *and* juniors, so that wasn't a problem.

"I can't even picture you at a prom," Brooke said.

"Why not?"

"You in a fancy suit, drinking punch and dancing . . . do you even know how to dance?"

"I've danced."

"When have you ever danced?" she asked.

"I've danced at family weddings." A couple of times I'd been forced to by aunts. There really wasn't much more to it than shuffling your feet a little.

"I've never seen you dance," Ian said. "I just can't picture you being very good at it."

Great, the only thing worse than the two of them fighting was them ganging up on me.

"Look, I don't know why you two think it's so funny that I'd consider going to the prom. If I wanted to I could go."

"Wow, you've actually been thinking about it. You want to go to the prom! That's just unbelievable," Brooke said. She sounded almost disgusted, and looking at her face you'd think that she'd just bitten down on something awful.

"And if you did this, would you make some sort of stupid promposal?" Brooke demanded.

I didn't answer right away. I wanted to choose my words carefully.

"My God, now you're even thinking about making a promposal! That's even more unbelievable!"

"To be honest, up until a few minutes ago the idea had never crossed my mind."

"And now?"

"Well, if I was going to go to the prom, I think it might be interesting to make a promposal. Besides, it's not like I'd have a choice."

"No choice? What does that mean?" Brooke asked.

"If promposals are the new social norm, then I would have to follow that norm. Besides, I figure I'd have to do something pretty special to convince this particular girl to go with me."

"You have somebody in mind!" Ian said.

Brooke looked even less pleased than she had seconds before.

"I'm not saying yes or no. I was thinking purely theoretically that I'd need to do something pretty special or I'd be turned down."

"I just know that if this theoretical girl needs a big song and dance to convince her to go with you to the prom, maybe she isn't worth it," Brooke said.

"Isn't a prom just a big song and dance anyway?" Ian asked.

"That's not what I mean, it's just that . . . well . . . it's all just too stupid for words."

"Apparently," Ian said. "If you ask me, the whole thing involves way too much work and coordination for my short attention span . . . what was it we were talking about?"

First bell sounded, signaling ten minutes to get to afternoon classes. I started to gather up my stuff as people around us began to do the same. I was just grateful to get away from the conversation. Although that didn't mean I wasn't going to go on thinking about it. The whole thing—witnessing the promposal, and then talking about it—had got my mind racing away. If prom was part of the high school experience and fitting in, and I wanted to be part of that experience, shouldn't I go to the prom?

Besides, although I was barely able to admit it even to myself, I did have somebody in mind. As soon as I'd started thinking about the prom I'd started thinking about her. It was like I could picture the two of us there together—or perhaps more realistically I could picture her turning me down if I asked her. Probably. Maybe. But asking was the only way to have any chance, even a tiny one. Maybe being turned down would also be part of fitting in. Okay, that didn't make real sense, but that didn't mean it was wrong.

We headed back in with the rest of the herd. I listened to the buzz of conversation around us while Brooke and Ian continued to bicker. Almost everything I heard was about the promposal. Everybody was talking about it. I picked up little snippets of conversation. The girls—with the exception of a few like Brooke—seemed to be universally impressed. Kevin was suddenly every girl's dream prom date. However, that probably was as much a reflection of his previous status in the school culture as it was a result of today's efforts.

The boys, on the other hand, seemed to be expressing a variety of opinions and emotions. For sure, some of the guys were impressed. For a lot of them, everything Kevin did was golden. He was the popular, good-looking captain of the football team. I knew this was going to inspire a whole lot of promposals. There was a downside to all of that, though. Those who were thinking of asking somebody to the prom realized that the bar had now been set pretty high. Anything they were planning on doing would be judged against Kevin's elaborate show. And you had to think that the non-Kevins of the world would be scared of staging that kind of stunt only to receive a *very* public rejection.

Asking a girl out and being turned down would be bad enough. Well, at least I imagined it would be pretty awful, since I'd never asked anybody out. And how much would that be magnified, how much more humiliating and painful would it be to do what Kevin did today, in front of the whole student body, and get turned down? Actually, I couldn't even imagine that. I did have a freaky-smart mind, but it was

beyond even my ability to do that mathematical calculation. I pictured an algebraic equation like *money
spent* times *number of witnesses* divided by *emotional
stability*. Did I really want to risk being the casualty of
that equation?

"It's all over Instagram and Twitter," Ian said,
holding up his phone.

"I'm sure it's absolutely everywhere," Brooke said.

Ian continued to fiddle with his phone. "Here's
a video. Want to see it?"

"I just saw it happen in front of my eyes," Brooke
said.

"Yeah, but now it's been officially recorded. It
isn't real until it appears online."

"What you're saying is as stupid as the promposal
itself," Brooke said.

"There's nothing stupid about it. If a tree fell
in the forest and there was no social media to
record it, then it wouldn't make a sound. Seeing it
here on my phone makes the events I witnessed
become real."

"You are truly an idiot. I'm surprised it isn't you
instead of Sam thinking about a promposal."

How did this turn back around on me again?

"The Internet's only real purpose is social media,"
Ian said.

"Aren't you forgetting about business and commerce?" Brooke asked.

"Yeah, that and porn. I don't know what I'd do
without—"

"Filter!" we both yelled, and a bunch of other people turned around.

Instantly Ian began tapping his message on the side of his leg. I looked away. I didn't want to know what he was going to say next. All I know is it was a rather long, enthusiastic message.

# CHAPTER FOUR

"So, how was your day?" my mother asked my father.

"Any day I can be home to have dinner with my family is a great day," he answered.

He reached out and gave my mother's hand a little squeeze and she smiled. My parents actually liked each other, and it showed. I liked that a lot. And sort of envied it.

"And Sam, how was your day?" she asked.

"You know, just the same old same old."

"Nothing new or different?"

"Well . . . there was a big promposal today at lunch."

"I'm familiar with lunch, but I'm not sure what a promposal is," my father said.

"I've heard about them," my mother said. "That's when a boy asks a girl to the prom in some kind of public way?"

"Technically, it could be the other way around and a girl could make the promposal," I said. "Although, from what I've discovered, it's usually the guy doing the asking. I've been doing some research. They've become a big thing."

"I still don't get it. How could somebody asking somebody to the prom be a big thing?" my father asked.

"It's the public or creative part that makes it big," I said. I was going to explain what had transpired but I had a better, easier idea. "If a picture is worth a thousand words, then a video is worth a million," I said.

I pulled out my phone and searched YouTube for a link to the video of Kevin's promposal. Actually, I was looking for the *best* video because there were *dozens*. On top of that, I could have shown him photos, Facebook posts, Tweets, and enough comments to fill a short novel. If Ian was right and nothing was real until it had been on social media, then Kevin's promposal to Brittney was not only real but one of the most significant events that had taken place on planet Earth that day.

"Here it is," I said, turning my phone so that both my parents could see the scene.

"You filmed it?" my father asked.

"Not me. Other people, lots and lots of other people."

"That makes sense," my mother said. "Since it

seems like everybody over the age of six has a phone with them at all times, they also have a built-in ability to record every sight and sound around them."

My father said, "I read an article about how we now have to simply assume that every action we perform in a public space is recorded either by individuals or security cameras. It brings to mind the continual erosion of our privacy. It appears that Orwell wasn't wrong, though he was mistaken about the year when he suggested 1984. Similarly, in Aldous Huxley's *Brave New World*—"

"Dear," my mother said, putting a hand on my father's arm. "Let's watch the video."

This was one of the roles my mother played with my father, and I guess with me: trying to make us aware of things around us. The psychologist I used to see—the same one that Ian still saw—called these "social cues." My father often missed them. I could too, but I was better than him at picking them up. At least I knew I was missing them, while my father was completely oblivious. I was working hard to try to pick up more and miss less. That was part of my quest.

"Here it is," I said.

They watched as the image of the limo started to roll across the little screen of my phone. I'd seen it more than a dozen times myself and I still found it rather fascinating. Then little Kevin popped out of the top of the sunroof and started to speak.

"What is he saying?" my father asked.

"He said he has a special question for a very special person," I said.

"You mean he's going to ask her to the prom in front of all those people?" my father asked, incredulous.

"That's the public part of it," I said.

"I would never be brave enough to do that!" my father said.

"You cut people open with a knife for a living," I pointed out.

"Yes, but I don't do that in front of hundreds of people, and it's not like my patient is going to say no."

On the screen the guys who had come forward started to remove their football jerseys. I realized the letters on their chests were too small to read.

"It says 'Britt Prom?'" I explained.

They rearranged themselves to spell it correctly, and then came Brittney's squeal and the roar of the crowd. We continued to watch as she was passed up into the limo and it drove away, with Kevin releasing the red balloons. I liked the balloons being released.

"So that's a promposal," I said.

"And that's what's expected to ask a girl to the prom?" my father asked.

I was going to say no, but really, maybe it was. "It looks like that's the new normal." I knew my mother liked the word "normal." It was something she hoped I would continue to move toward. "That's what people are doing now."

"It was a lot simpler in my day," my father said. "Not that I went to the prom."

"Well, not many twelve-year-olds go to the prom," my mother said reassuringly.

Sometimes she still talked to him as though he were twelve—and I guess in some ways he did seem about that age. In other ways he was the smartest person I knew. Actually, he was the smartest person *most* people knew.

My father's IQ score was 160. That meant that he wasn't just a garden-variety genius, he belonged in the "high genius" category. He was, statistically, among the smartest people in the country. Following high school he graduated from university at fourteen and was a doctor by the time he was nineteen. Like me, he had a phenomenal memory. Strange, though, how he still couldn't remember to bring things home from the grocery store. He could be so lost in a medical problem he was trying to solve that nothing else seemed real to him.

There's a story about how Albert Einstein—whose IQ was the same as my father's—often had trouble finding his way home. People in his neighborhood in Princeton, New Jersey, would come home and find him sitting at their kitchen table, because not only had he walked into the wrong house, he hadn't even noticed. I didn't know if that story was true, but I could easily see my father doing that.

My parents had never allowed anyone to give me an IQ test. They were able to quote lots of studies that showed the tests to be faulty and inaccurate and biased. I had read some of those and mostly agreed. Still, it would have been nice to know my number. Numbers were always comforting to me. Quantitative over qualitative data made so much more sense.

I guess I had to be grateful that my parents—especially my mother—worked to protect me from things like that. What she wanted for me was to lead a normal life. That was why I had never been allowed to skip grades but instead stayed in class with people who were my own age. Being different was hard. Skipping a grade or two wouldn't have taken away my difference, it would only have added the difference in age as well. Besides, staying in the same grade meant that I still had Ian and Brooke with me. What would I have done without them?

"Did you go to your prom?" I asked my mother.

"Yes, though my date just asked me over the phone."

"*Who* was your prom date?" my father asked.

"His name was Marc. He was very nice."

"Whatever happened to him?" my father asked.

"He went to a different university, on a volleyball scholarship. I heard he ended up playing professionally in France."

"You always were a sucker for us athletic types," my father said, and we all burst into laughter.

My father was one of the few people I knew—along with Ian—who were even less athletic than me.

It was unfortunate that I'd got both his brains *and* his utter lack of coordination.

"So if you want to go to the prom, you have to come up with something like what this boy did, some kind of promposal?" my father asked.

"I guess that's the assumption."

"Good thing you have a whole year to think about it," he said.

"The prom is in six weeks."

My father got a confused look. "You're in your junior year, aren't you?"

"Yes, but the prom is for both juniors and seniors."

"Are you thinking of going?" my mother asked.

I knew that this was more than just a random question. If I said yes, she would be a jumbled mess of happy, hopeful, worried, and scared. If I said no, she would be relieved, disappointed, and worried in a whole different way. The happy part would come from my desire to do something that "normal" high school kids did. The worried part would be that I wasn't actually capable of doing it.

"Not that I expect you to go, or not go, or anything. It's all your decision, and I wouldn't want you to think that there was any pressure or expectation that you *should* or *shouldn't*—"

"Mom, it's okay. I understand."

"So *are* you thinking of going?" my father asked, wading back into the dangerous waters my mother had just retreated from.

They both waited for the answer.

"I was thinking about it."

My mother looked as though she might scream out in joy or cry out in worry, but she managed to restrain herself. "That's very nice."

"And you're going to do that, with a limo and everything?" my father asked.

"No, that's been done. I'd have to come up with something else, something original. But really, I'm not positive I'm going to do anything. I'm just thinking about it, that's all."

"Again, whatever you do or don't do is just fine," my mother said. "You know we support your—"

"Mom, no worries. I understand."

"Good. I just didn't want you to think that there was any pressure from us."

"Pressure?" my father said. "A public declaration in front of all those people with the risk of utter and complete rejection is all the pressure you could possibly—"

My mother squeezed his arm again to silence him.

"Not that it's our business, but have you thought about who you might invite?" she asked.

"I have somebody in mind, but I can't tell you."

"We wouldn't dream of prying," my mother said.

I gave her a look of total disbelief.

"I'm not *trying* to pry, but if we do, it's only because we care," she said.

"It's okay, really, but thanks."

"And, of course, if you want, we'd be willing to help you with your proposal," she added.

"I'm not asking somebody to marry me. It's a promposal."

"Of course it is!"

"But I do appreciate your support. I was wondering, would you and Dad be willing to paint letters on your chests?"

My father laughed almost immediately, and my mother looked a little hurt.

"I'm sorry. Listen, it's just . . . there's nothing for you to do or to worry about. I'll take care of everything . . . if I do it at all," I said.

I thought about all the help Kevin had—ten football players. If I needed help there were only two people I could ask. One of them wasn't going to be particularly helpful, and the other wasn't going to be particularly happy, and it was probably wrong to get her to help me do it anyway.

# CHAPTER FIVE

"Here's your Clown Town jumbo pepperoni pizza!" I announced as I set down the extra-large pizza on the table and the birthday party kids gave an extra-large cheer.

Instantly they tore into it, grabbing at pieces like a pack of hyenas at a kill. I did a quick check of my fingers, pleased that they all had come away from the carnage. You'd have thought the birthday boy and his guests were starving to death, when in reality it was their third pizza and, judging from their general appearance, none of them had ever missed a meal, a dessert, or even a snack.

I left the party room, trying not to stumble over my large clown feet, and closed the door that sealed off their squealing, only to be engulfed by the general noise of the big activity room. It was a combination of loud music, video games clanging and ringing, yelling and running kids, and the desperate voices of adults trying to control and corral the yelling and running kids. It was a typical Saturday at Clown Town, which was sort of like Chuck E. Cheese on steroids.

The place was so packed and overbooked that the party rooms were all filled, and some of the groups who hadn't made reservations had been shuffled and set up out in the activity room. A woman at a large table waved me over. There were four or five women and a couple of dozen kids sitting there.

"We're ready to order!" she yelled over the noise.

"Okay, go ahead."

There was a lot of debate, yelling, and changes, but finally the last kid gave his order.

"Okay, thanks," I said, and turned to walk away.

"Wait, aren't you going to write this down?" one of the women asked.

"No."

"It's a big order."

"I got it. Your food and drinks will be out shortly," I said.

She still looked skeptical.

There were only two ways she was going to believe me, and one of them could be almost instantaneous. I repeated the entire order, pointing to each person as I recited it all back.

"That's amazing," she said.

I shrugged. "I think everybody at Clown Town can do that. I'll bring your order out soon." I reached into one of the pockets of my big red pants, pulled out a handful of game tokens, and handed them to her. "A game for everybody—on the house."

A cheer went up from the kids.

"Thank you so much!" the women said.

I went off to the kitchen to place the order.

Every shift, each Clown Town employee was given a pocketful of game tokens to hand out. Most people used them when an order was screwed up, or took too long to arrive, or when they wanted to encourage a better tip. I gave them out just for fun.

Lots of the staff—and a lot of our grown-up customers—found that they could only take a certain amount of Clown Town before they got a headache, got upset, or needed to step outside. It was the strangest thing for me that, in spite of the utter chaos and noise, I somehow found the place calming. It was completely counterintuitive that this would work, but it did. I thought it might be similar to the way they gave children with attention deficit disorder medications that were stimulants, and somehow that slowed them down. For some reason, all of the outside noise and movement caused the thoughts in my head to settle, and I could relax and become calm.

I'd spent the last day thinking a lot about making a promposal. I wasn't sure what scared me more, actually doing it, or telling Brooke that I was going to do it and asking for her help. For better or worse, she was essential to my plan succeeding, so I needed to get her onside. We were co-workers at Clown Town, so between birthday parties, when the two of us met in the kitchen area, I'd been talking to her— and during two of those conversations I'd started to bring up the topic of promposals. Both times she'd made gagging sounds and wandered off to pick up more pizza. Not the encouraging reaction I'd been hoping for.

I thought it was probably best not to try to talk about it at all any more in the midst of birthday party insanity. I'd wait until we could go to a quiet place where I could logically, rationally, and reasonably explain my plan and respectfully request her help. Really, though, it didn't matter. Either place, either way, I was sure any discussion would result in her giving me a very unreasonable, very illogical, very emotional reaction. So, maybe there really wasn't much point in waiting. I'd bring it up again as soon as I had a chance.

I went into the kitchen. The swinging door swung shut behind me, blocking out at least some of the activity room noise. Brooke was leaning against the counter. She must have been waiting for her next order to come up.

"You look ridiculous," she said.

Red pants, checked shirt, and the matching flaming red fright wig were all part of the compulsory Clown Town staff costume that I was wearing.

"You know you're wearing the same outfit, right?" I asked.

"Yes, but I'm wearing it *ironically*."

"You're ironically wearing a clown costume? Can you explain that to me?"

"If I have to explain it then clearly you must be incapable of understanding. Perhaps if you'd worked here as long as I have, you'd get it."

"You've only been here two weeks longer than me!" I protested.

"It's actually fifteen days. And you should be grateful to me. You wouldn't even be working here if it weren't for me," she said.

"Thank you," I offered. She was right about the job. She had recommended me to the manager, but more significantly, if she hadn't been working here there was no way I would have even applied.

"Brookey!" Mel yelled out from behind the counter. "Your order is up!" Mel was the only person, other than Taylor, who called her that.

"Excuse me," she said. "I've got birthday pizza to deliver." The two pizzas on her tray were decorated with little candles. That meant that the clown waiters would all gather around to sing a birthday song.

"Is it a boy or girl?" I asked.

"It's going to be one of the two, I'm pretty sure. Does it matter? Do you only sing for girls?"

"Of course not. I sing for everybody! Let me put in my order while you round up the clowns—and don't you dare start without me!"

"No guarantees on that," Brooke said as she left.

I had an order to place and I had to do it fast.

"Mel, can I have three jumbo Clown Town pizzas, one just cheese, one with cheese and pepperoni, and the third deluxe. Can I also have three orange sodas, two with ice, five diet colas, two iced teas, one of them extra-sweet, and five waters—two of them flat, two sparkling, and one straight tap water with a slice of lemon."

Mel slid a pad across the counter. "I'm surprised you can remember all that, but can't remember that I can't keep it straight even if you can. Write it down."

"But I have to get out there or I'll miss the birthday song!"

"Kid, in the history of Clown Town, you're the only employee who's ever enjoyed singing the birthday song," Mel said. "Don't worry, it's going to take Brookey a while to find enough clowns to make a choir. You have time."

Letting out a big sigh, I took a pen and scribbled down the order. After all, I didn't really have a choice, but also, he was right. When I rushed out to find Brooke, I caught sight of the tail end of a bunch of unhappy-looking clowns entering one of the party rooms.

Technically, a group of clowns is called a "troop." That just never seemed right to me. Baboons and kangaroos came in troops. It sounded so military—I pictured a group of clowns with big bow ties and red fright wigs dressed in camouflage costumes, mud smeared on their faces, tripping over their oversized shoes as they stormed a beach. Clowns were the farthest thing from troops. I needed to come up with something better, more descriptive. Other groups got names they deserved: a crash of rhinos, a leap of leopards, a barrel of monkeys, a bloat of hippos, a tower of giraffes, and a cackle of hyenas. Those all made perfect sense. And then, it came to me— a bunch of clowns should be known as "a hilarity." That was it—a hilarity of clowns!

I shuffled into the party room to join the hilarity. That did sound *so* right. I'd mention it to the manager and to Brooke later. I was sure the manager would like it. And I was sure that Brooke would simply tell me that I continued to spend way too much of my brain power on very stupid things. She was, of course, mostly right about that.

I squeezed into the middle of the hilarity. There were nine of us. Not big, but big enough. Brooke, as the hostess clown of this party, had to lead. She started clapping her hands and we all joined in with her. I worked hard to try to keep in rhythm. That was hard for me. That and singing on key.

"Who's the Clown Town birthday boy?" she asked.

A little boy who looked like he matched the six candles on the pizzas practically jumped into the air, smiling and laughing and waving his hands to make sure nobody else could be mistaken for the man— boy—of the hour. I couldn't understand why anybody wouldn't want to be part of this!

"Happy Clown Town Birthday!" Brooke yelled, and we all started singing.

*Clown Town, birthday time,*
*Clown Town, birthday time,*
*Happy Clown Town birthday to you,*
*Happy, happy Clown Town birthday to you!*

At first, I'd found the Clown Town birthday song a bit pointlessly awkward, but then it was explained to me that, due to copyright laws, Clown Town had to make the words and music just different enough to avoid any messy and unnecessary lawsuits involving the *real* birthday song.

As we continued to sing our version I looked at the party guests. It wasn't just the birthday boy who was off-the-wall happy. Every single one of the party guests was singing along and smiling manically. If they hadn't been a bunch of six-year-olds I would have questioned whether they'd been drinking, but really, a sugar high was almost as potent as alcohol.

Behind the birthday boy stood a couple who I assumed were his parents. They seemed almost as happy as the kids. I liked it when the birthday parents were happy. Most were, but not all. They seemed to fall into two types—those who appeared to genuinely enjoy the experience, either directly or through the eyes of their child, and those who looked as though they'd rather be anywhere else in the world. But this was Clown Town, not a visit to the dentist!

I guess even the staff fell into those two categories. Some people couldn't stand the noise and confusion and chaos. But for other people it was a happy place because every day was a birthday party—or, like today, forty or fifty birthday parties. I really just liked being here, and I guess it showed. I had been the employee of the month the last three months in a row. And just before my shift today, the manager had told me in confidence that he had decided to give me the award again. He was going to announce it at the end of the day.

Unless I was mistaken, with each additional month I'd won there had been less polite applause from my co-workers. I was pretty sure that they were not especially interested in the honor, but they would have liked the fifty-dollar bonus that went along with it. My fourth picture would soon proudly adorn the wall that led to the employee change area, and I'd be receiving another small, framed certificate.

The money was one thing, but it wasn't everything. I was actually rather proud of my accomplishments. It wasn't as though I had a mantel full of trophies from my many sports accomplishments, so Employee of the Month certificates from Clown Town helped to fill the void. I'd won awards regularly for academics, and a few medals for chess tournaments before I'd got bored with chess, but it wasn't the same. Nobody proudly wore the medals they got from a chess tournament around their necks the next day at school. I'd learned that the hard way in grade four when my chess medal was ripped off my neck and thrown over the fence by one of the older kids. I didn't climb after it. I didn't even tell anybody what he'd done. Not the teachers or my parents. When my mother asked, I just said I'd "lost it," which was completely easy to believe. How strange. I'd done nothing except win a tournament, and yet I'd been made to feel ashamed. Part of me still felt that way.

My Clown Town honors were starting to feel like the yin to the yang of my school accomplishments—opposite but complementary. At school, I was working hard to not let people know I was the "student of the month," the smartest kid in the building. But at Clown Town I was working as hard as I could to be recognized for doing a great job. It was actually a lot harder than school. Here I really had to *try*. Carrying heavy trays and dodging the running, screaming kids on sugar highs while wearing oversized clown shoes, dealing with a lot of anxious or overbearing parents—these things were different and difficult. While remembering orders was easy, understanding social interaction wasn't always. Being employed here gave me more experience in doing that.

Ian and I had started at Clown Town on the same day, but he had lasted only a few shifts. It was a bad combination, the noise of the place and the noise in his head that kept spilling out. It wasn't that he didn't like the job so much as the job didn't like him. His lack of filtration system got him in trouble time and time again. He questioned whether certain kids really needed extra-large ice cream floats when they already looked as though they'd eaten too much and were too, shall we say, stocky. He asked parents why they couldn't control their "little monsters" better. Sometimes the wall of noise at Clown Town worked in his favor. Either he wasn't heard at all or people assumed they must have misheard him. But by his third shift, one too many complaints to the manager meant he was fired.

Of course, a lot of what he was saying was factually correct—many of these kids did need a salad more than a triple scoop of ice cream, and there were a lot of kids who did need to be controlled. However, I'd learned that there was a difference between being right and knowing the right thing to say. Ian probably knew that as well, but he couldn't control his words, and that was why he was asked to leave. In protest he'd kept the clown costume. It hung in his closet like an animal skin.

The song finished to thunderous applause and lots of cheering, and the birthday boy blew out the candles, a smattering of food particles riding out on his breath. Then, at the far end of the table, another kid added an unexpected party favor as he lurched forward and vomited up a colorful combination of ice cream, hot dogs, fudge, and potato chips, which splattered across the table and bounced onto the birthday pizzas!

I rushed over to the phone that served as an intercom and picked up the receiver.

"Attention please, attention please," I called out, my words loud enough to cut through the noise of the activity room. "Can we please have a Clown

Cleaning Crew come to Party Room Eleven, Clown Cleaning Crew to Party Room Eleven. Thank you!"

"There we go, one more party room finished," I said as I dumped the rest of the torn-down streamers and swept-up confetti into the big garbage can. Confetti cannons were a lot of fun to shoot but a lot of work to clean up after.

"I hate this part of the job," Brooke said.

"It's amazing how much debris is left behind."

"I just can't ever get over how much plastic and paper, stuff that could be recycled, gets tossed out in the garbage. It's just not right."

Brooke—environmental activist—had spoken to Mr. Myers, the manager, about doing more recycling, but her pleas had landed on deaf ears. He said that it was Clown Town corporate office that made those decisions, and he trusted they knew what they were doing.

I pictured that office. In my mind, everybody was sitting around in little cubicles, working on their computers, answering phones, having meetings in the conference room. All of them dressed in full Clown Town costume. Somehow it was hard to have confidence in any decision made by a bunch—correction, a *hilarity*—of clowns.

Brooke tossed an entire pizza—missing one piece—into the garbage can. "And this is such a waste as well. People are starving in the world and this is what we do with food. It's so decadent!"

She was right, of course, but there was no point in either agreeing with her or defending it in any way. When you had an abundance of anything—whether it was food, money, good looks, or athletic ability—it stopped meaning as much. I'd figured out that was how we humans were hard-wired.

"At least we didn't have any food fights today," I offered.

"Those are even worse!" she snapped. "In most of the world there are fights because there isn't enough food, and here we use food as a weapon!"

"Well, technically, in many conflict zones, food *is* used as a weapon, through systematic distribution or withholding of food, by gathering people into refugee camps where they can be controlled, or—"

"Are you trying to get me annoyed?" she asked.

"Not really trying."

"Then you are truly a self-taught or natural genius when it comes to annoying me. Can you imagine how effective you would be if you put your considerable intellect into being deliberately annoying?"

"I hadn't really thought about that, but I guess if—"

"That was a joke!" she snapped.

"Oh . . . I understand. Could I ask you a question?"

"Of course."

"If what you were saying was a joke, shouldn't it be at least a little bit funny?"

Brooke screamed and tossed a piece of pizza at me, missing me by a mile and hitting the wall instead.

"Nice throw."

"Do you think you could have done better?" she asked.

"Of course not. You know I can't throw."

I picked up the piece of pizza and tossed it toward the garbage can. Of course it missed and hit the floor. I bent over, picked it up, and dropped it in the can. It was helpful that the pizza here was so plastic that it stayed in one piece, the pepperoni topping seemingly glued onto the cheese. I used a cloth to wipe up the grease mark it had left on the wall and then on the floor.

"You know, with the kids all gone you don't have to wear the clown costume any more," Brooke said. She had changed into her normal street clothes, as had most of the other employees.

"I'm not wearing *all* of my costume," I countered. I'd taken off the fright wig, which always made my scalp itchy, and the oversized shoes. I could trip over my own feet easily enough without adding to the problem. "I figure it's better to get my clown outfit dirty than my regular clothes," I said, although the real reason was that in my rush to get to work I'd forgotten to pack pants. The oversized red clown pants were all that I had.

Forgetting things was part of the puzzling way my mind seemed to work. I could remember obscure facts, complicated orders, and insignificant details, but I would often forget my backpack, shoes, books, and this time even my pants. Although, to my credit, I *was* wearing pants when I left the house. It wasn't like I'd wandered outside in my boxers.

"Your mother's picking us up today, right?" she asked.

"Yeah."

"Good, because the last thing I want to do is ride home on the bus with you dressed like that."

"I think it would be okay. Because some big, mean biker dude could come up to me and say, 'Hey you, kid, what are you, some kind of clown?' And I'd answer, 'Isn't it obvious?'"

Brooke laughed. I loved when she laughed.

"You really are funny, and I don't mean just the times you don't mean to be funny."

"I guess I'll take that as a compliment," I said. "You know, there are worse places to work than Clown Town."

"I know. Part of me is disgusted by the waste, gluttony, and general degradation of the environment wrought by the blatant consumerism of this establishment."

"And the other part of you?"

"Well, who doesn't like an unlimited ice cream bar with fifteen flavors and forty different types of toppings and sprinkles?"

"How about we finish cleaning up and have a sundae before our ride gets here?" I suggested.

"It sounds like you're asking me out on a date," Brooke said.

I felt a rush of blood into my face and knew I was glowing almost as red as the fright wig I was no longer wearing. I was hoping Brooke hadn't noticed, and I was relieved to see that she was looking away, continuing to gather party trash.

The fact that even joking around about going on a date with somebody got me blushing made me realize just how insanely hard doing a promposal would be. I was going to need help, and not from my mother. Now I just needed to change the subject.

"Not as many kids vomited today as usual," I said.

"I hadn't really noticed."

"The Clown Cleaning Crew was called only nineteen times today, so the maximum number of incidents was less than ten when you factor in spilled drinks."

"Are you sure . . . ? Wait . . . of course you're sure. You're always right when it comes to *that* sort of thing."

The unstated part of her statement was, "And so wrong about other things," and really, she wasn't saying anything I could argue with. I was working at getting better, but it was still very much a work in progress.

"This place was made to produce vomit," Brooke said. "Insert piles of greasy pizza, unlimited ice cream sundaes, and bottomless pitchers of carbonated beverages into small human containers and then take those containers and have them shaken and spun on bouncy castles, in ball pits, and on indoor slides and swings and it's a recipe for regurgitation."

"I guess it's inevitable."

"All they really need to do is add a couple of troughs by the ice cream bar and we'd have ourselves a regular little vomitorium," she said.

"Yes, it would be enough to make Caligula proud," I added, before I could help myself, naming the man who had ruled the Roman Empire from August 31, 12 C.E., until January 22, 41 C.E.

Brooke looked up and smiled. "Do you know what I love about you?" she asked.

"My clown costume?"

"Even more than your clown costume. Who else would get my vague reference to the decadence and decay of the Roman Empire and put it in context?"

"I guess just me, or maybe a history professor," I answered.

What I *didn't* say was that I not only caught the reference but realized that there was a common error in it. Her use of "vomitorium" betrayed a misunderstanding, one that was promoted most famously by Aldous Huxley in his 1923 novel *Antic Hay*, in which he used the word to describe large troughs being constructed so that the Romans could binge-eat and then puke to empty their systems before returning to the banquet to gorge on more food. In reality, a vomitorium was a passage in a Roman amphitheatre or stadium that allowed the crowd to disperse quickly at the end of a performance. The base word, *"vomo,"* was Latin for "spewing forth," and that was where the misunderstanding of the word had arisen.

I had decided it would be wise of me not to correct her and *spew forth* all the additional information. Like Ian and his unfiltered comments, it was really hard for me to hold it in when I knew I was right. Maybe I really was making progress.

I'd discovered over the years that people— especially adults, and especially, *especially* teachers— didn't like to be corrected. Most of the time people would rather be unwittingly wrong than be corrected. I was learning. My psychologist and my mother had both helped me to understand that being right often meant that other people had to be wrong, and they didn't like to be wrong. I'd have to make a point of telling my mother about this little incident and my triumph. For a split second I regretted that I wasn't going to see my psychologist any more. She would have been proud too.

The decision not to see the psychologist any more was mine. I knew that neither my mother nor Dr. Young agreed with it, but there were some things that just needed to be done on your own. It was kind of like swimming. I'd had the lessons, and now I had to either sink or swim. Wearing a life jacket would only make me look different. No life jacket for me.

"By the way, the ice cream sundae you were talking about is my treat," Brooke said.

"But we get it for free."

"Yeah, I know, and that's why I'm treating. Heck, you can even have a double or triple if you promise not to vomit it up on the ride home, because it's not like your car has a mobile vomitorium."

"That it doesn't," I agreed. Even better, twice in a row I didn't correct her—although the urge was definitely getting stronger.

# CHAPTER SIX

My father pulled the car up to the front of Clown Town and inadvertently bumped the passenger-side front wheel up onto the sidewalk.

"I thought it was going to be your mother," Brooke said.

"So did I. You could always take the bus. It's not too late."

"I guess I'll chance it. He hasn't killed us yet."

I went to climb into the front seat, but when I pulled the door open I realized it was piled high with Home Depot bags. My father was attempting to rebuild our back deck. So far the effort had been only moderately productive—although my mother proclaimed the fact that he hadn't cut off any fingers yet was a sign of true success. Instead of finishing the project, it seemed, he was amassing a wealth of tools.

I slammed the door shut and jumped into the back seat with Brooke, landing partly on top of her.

"A little personal space would be nice, you big clown," she said.

"Sorry." I shuffled over and fumbled with my seatbelt.

"I thought Mom was going to pick us up," I said. She always tried to be the one who drove because she actually *could* drive.

"I volunteered," he explained. "I told her that since I was out picking up some more tools it was practically on the way for me."

"How's the deck coming?" Brooke asked.

"Technically it's coming along very well. I have the plan, and I now have the tools necessary to execute that plan. Although I'm starting to understand that a Skilsaw is a very complex piece of equipment."

We started off, bumping off the curb. Another car honked and swerved, the driver giving us the finger as we re-entered traffic.

For somebody who made his living saving lives by doing precision surgical cuts with a scalpel or laser scalpel, my father was really, really uncoordinated. Driving was a skill he hadn't mastered. Worse still, this was yet another aspect in which I was taking after him. I'd taken driving lessons—like almost every sixteen-year-old in the world—and had failed my test. It wasn't that I didn't know the answers to the written portion. Of course I could quote those word for word. I just couldn't actually make the vehicle do the things I asked it to do. My instructor said I didn't so much drive the car as aim it.

Brooke had declined to work toward a driver's license, as she felt that cars were "killing the planet." Of course, that didn't seem to stop her from taking advantage of riding in one. It was sort of like her comment about how I wouldn't eat meat if I had to kill an animal myself. From that I could also extrapolate that if there were ever a car that ran on meat as fuel she'd really be outraged.

Ian was always teasing Brooke about her causes, and sometimes I'd join in. Really, though, I admired her. She was so passionate about so much, when most people were just plain apathetic. That was something nobody could ever accuse her of. She believed what she believed and was fearless in letting people know. Fearless—that was probably one of the words that best described her.

"So, how are my two favorite clowns doing today?" my father asked.

"Pretty good, Dr. Davies. At the end of the shift your son was named the Clown of the Month again."

"That's Employee of the Month," I said.

"It's Clown Town. All the employees are clowns, so what are you arguing about? You're simply the best clown around," Brooke said.

"I'm not arguing, just noting."

"Either way, congratulations," my father said as he reached over the seat to offer me his hand.

"Eyes on the road, Dad!" I yelled as our car leaned into the lane beside us. He turned the wheel and we jerked back into the correct lane, aided by another car honking out encouragement.

"Sorry about that," he said. "So, did you get another certificate?"

"And another bonus," Brooke added. "How much money have you saved up?"

"I don't know," I mumbled.

"You don't know?" both my father and Brooke said together.

"Are you telling me you don't remember the number of dollars in your savings account?" Brooke asked.

That was, of course, ridiculous. I could recite the closing balance for each month since I'd opened the account.

"I remember. It's just not polite to ask people things like that," I said.

"Now I know I'm in trouble when *you* start to give lessons on the proper things to say. What's next, Ian telling me I have to filter my comments?" Brooke asked.

"Look, it's personal. Besides, we've both worked the same shifts so the only difference in what I've earned and what you've earned is my bonus money. And since you've been working there longer, our earnings should probably be almost identical."

"Yes, but I have expenses," Brooke said.

"From what I know, most females want to spend money on clothes and makeup," my father said.

Both Brooke and I laughed. That was okay because my father would have figured we were just laughing along with his little joke instead of the foolish reference to how Brooke was spending her money.

Brooke hardly ever wore any makeup. And on the rare occasion she did wear a bit, she made sure that she bought only non-animal-tested, fair trade, environmentally conscious brands. And as for clothes, almost everything she wore was either a hand-me-down, or from some thrift shop, or something she'd made herself. Nothing Brooke wore ever had a label. She'd long ago read a book about the pervasive evils of advertising, and she'd been a one-woman no-logo zone ever since. It had nothing to do with a lack of money and everything to do with her commitment to social justice. And to being her usual quirky self.

"Most of Brooke's money is committed to social justice endeavors," I explained to my father.

"Very commendable," my father said. "Is there anything special you need a contribution for right now?"

"I'm part of a group that's building water projects in Africa. And I'm also supporting a local food bank," she said.

"How about if I give a donation and you split it between the two causes?" my father suggested.

"Thanks, Dr. Davies. I'm also doing some volunteer work at a women's shelter. Could I split it three ways?"

"Completely your decision," my father said.

"I'm going to be there tonight."

"You're working Saturday night at the shelter?" I asked.

"And what are you doing that's so great?" she asked.

"Nothing much, I guess." What I'd been hoping was to be doing that "nothing much" with her and Ian so we could talk.

"As I recall, Sam, you're going to be doing some work from the SAT study guide tonight," my father chipped in.

Brooke laughed. "Now that sounds *much* better."

Putting in extra work with the SAT study guide was a trade-off I'd made with my parents that allowed me to continue working at Clown Town. They had blamed my part-time job for my marks falling and wanted me to quit. They didn't understand why the job was so important to me, and that was hardly surprising. I had enough trouble understanding it completely myself, much less articulating my reasons to somebody else. But it had a lot to do with wanting to have my own income, my own money, even though there was nothing I really wanted to buy and nothing I needed that my parents wouldn't buy for me.

"Maybe I could donate my Employee of the Month bonus to help with your causes as well," I suggested.

"You'd do that?"

"Why not? If you believe in them, then they must be worth donating to. The money is yours, or I guess theirs."

Brooke threw an arm around me and gave me a little kiss on the cheek. I was too shocked and stunned to react or say anything.

"Hey, hey!" my father called out. "Maybe the two of you should get yourselves a room or—"

He stopped mid-sentence as even he realized how inappropriate that was.

"Not that I meant that you two really *should* get a room, or *need* to get a room, or *want* to get a—"

"Dad, we understand, it was just a joke."

Thank goodness his awkwardness had somehow covered up mine.

"Besides," I went on, trying to get back to the relative safety of the original subject, "it's not such a big deal to donate a few dollars to a worthy cause."

"I guess not," he said, "but remember, limos don't come cheap."

"Limos?" I asked.

"Yes, if you decide to use a limo like that Kevin fellow for your own promposal then you're going to need a fair bit of money," my father added.

So much for subtle, or the right time, or easing into it. My father had dropped the P-bomb.

"Wait, you've actually decided? You're really going ahead with this promposal idiocy?" Brooke shot me a look of total and utter disgust. I'd seen that look before, but it was even more shocking now as she'd managed to make a complete 180 turn from the approving look she'd given me just seconds before. She probably would have taken back the peck on my cheek if she could have.

"I was just thinking about the *concept* of promposals."

"Why else would you think about them if you weren't going to make one?" Brooke asked.

"She has a point there," my father added.

Great. Wasn't it bad enough that he was talking about what he shouldn't be talking about without him also agreeing with what he shouldn't be agreeing with?

"I was thinking. The boys in that video had school football jerseys," my father said.

"You've seen the video?" Brooke asked.

"Half a dozen times. Sam showed it to us. So, getting back to what I was saying. You don't have a football jersey, but you do have a really nifty clown costume, and your two best friends, Brooke and Ian, also have clown costumes, so what would you think about having them help you and asking somebody to the prom dressed like a clown and—?"

"That is a terrible idea!" Brooke said. "Nobody, I repeat, nobody wants to go to a prom with a clown."

"Well, perhaps another clown might," my father said, tentatively.

"I wasn't thinking about wearing my clown suit," I said. "Honestly."

"But you were thinking of going ahead with this

promposal thing, right?" Judging by her tone of voice, there was no question what she thought of the whole idea.

"I think about a lot of things," I argued.

"You know what I think of promposals, and proms in general," Brooke said.

"I know, I know."

"But if you are in fact insane enough to decide to do this, you know you'll need my help so that you don't make a complete and utter fool of yourself."

"Wait . . . you mean, if I decided to do this, you'd actually be okay with it? You'd help me?"

"What choice would I have?" she asked. "I don't believe in proms or anything to do with them, but I do believe in friendship, and believe me, if you were even remotely thinking of wearing your Clown Town suit then you couldn't possibly pull this off without my help." She paused. "So, do you want my help or not?"

This was quickly going from the abstract to the real, and from the real to the absurd.

"Well? Last chance . . ." she said.

"Yes, I would really like your help. I'd like it a lot." I suddenly felt a wave of confidence flow into me. For the first time, I thought I had a real chance of making this work.

"I figure with my help you won't be *totally* humiliated," Brooke said. "Only humiliated."

And the wave flowed out.

# CHAPTER SEVEN

The waitress refilled our cups. We were meeting Sunday morning at a little independently owned coffee shop that Brooke liked because it featured nothing but free-trade coffee and gluten-free baked goods made on the premises.

"Just so I understand," Ian said, "you're going to stage a promposal."

"Yes, that's what I'm going to do."

"And you want my help because I'm so skilled in understanding the female mind."

Brooke scoffed. "You are out of *your* mind."

"Agreed, but he does want my help, correct?"

She nodded.

"And you've agreed to help him too?" Ian asked.

Again she nodded.

"I know I'm used to being somewhat confused—"

"Somewhat?" Brooke asked.

"Okay, a lot confused, but why are you, the anti-prom queen, helping Sam with a promposal?"

"Because I'm being a good friend and trying to save him from embarrassment."

"I don't see how anything to do with this project could fail to bring down a great deal of very public embarrassment and humiliation."

"Well then maybe I just want a front-row seat," Brooke said.

"Hello! I'm right here!" I said, holding up my hand.

"We're aware. Stop interrupting while I'm negotiating," Brooke said. "So, Ian, are you in?"

"One condition. If I help Sam with a promposal, then he has to help *me* with one."

"You want to go to the prom too?" I exclaimed.

"I'm not saying I'll do it for sure, but if I decide to, I will, like my good friend here, also need of a lot of help."

"And a girl with incredibly low expectations and standards," Brooke added.

"Again, no argument from me. But my mind has instantly jumped to a potential strategy," Ian said.

"You're going to ask your mother?" Brooke asked.

"Okay, that's not a strategy as much as a fall-back plan. Do you want to hear my original thought?"

"I think we both want to hear this," I said, and Brooke nodded in agreement.

"You know how they say timing is everything," Ian said. "I figure it's not so much who asks or who is asked as *when* they're asked."

"You've lost me," I said.

"What do you think would happen if I asked Ashley to go to the prom tomorrow?" Ian asked.

"You'd be turned down," Brooke said.

"Of course I would. But what if nobody asks her to the prom, and I wait until a few days before the prom to pop my proposal? What do you think would happen then?"

"She'd still turn you down," Brooke said.

"Hold on, I think I understand what he's saying. Let's say we accept the very unlikely premise that no one else asks her first. Ashley probably would turn him down, but maybe she wouldn't," I said. "Ian is banking on the fact that she wants to go to the *prom* more than she doesn't want to go with *him*."

Ian smiled and nodded his head enthusiastically.

"Amazing. That actually makes sense," Brooke said. "Congratulations, Ian, for not only understanding your limitations, but figuring out a potential way around them. You're going to be much more helpful in this than I would have imagined."

"I'll take that as a compliment. So, who are you going to ask to the prom?" Ian asked.

I shook my head. "Sorry, but that's got to be my secret."

"That doesn't make sense," Ian said. "You have to tell us."

"Obviously," Brooke chimed in. "We can't very well be your personal consultants on this if we don't even know who you're asking!"

"I get what you're saying, but I'm still not going to tell you. I'll tailor it to—"

"You're going to ask Taylor to the prom?" Ian questioned.

"I said *tailor*, as in design or fit, not Taylor, the girl."

"But who wouldn't want to ask Taylor?" Ian said. "She isn't dating anybody and she's practically perfect and you share some classes and she's in your study group and she talks to you all the time and—" He stopped himself and started tapping out the inappropriate comments to follow.

"Just stop," I said, grabbing Ian's hand and silencing his message.

"You can't be serious," Brooke said. "Taylor is, well, Taylor. You'd be asking for failure. It's not just that she's out of your league, the two of you are hardly even the same species."

"You never know," Ian said. "They say opposites attract."

"They do appear to be completely opposite, so I'll give you that much."

"And, if I'm not missing anything, I think Taylor does like our Sammy," Ian said. "She smiles at him and shares little jokes, and I remember she once touched you on the arm, Sam, and—"

"Look, can you both just stop?"

"So it's Taylor?" Ian asked.

"I didn't say I was asking her," I argued.

"But, curiously, you didn't say you weren't," Ian added.

"Look, we'll help you. We both promised. But you have to be realistic. If you want to sweep Taylor off her feet and make her forget that you're an incredibly unsuitable prom date long enough for her to say yes, you're going to have to stage a pretty dazzling promposal to even think about that one," Brooke said.

"And that would mean you'd have to spend millions," Ian added.

"I'm not a millionaire but I do have money to do some things."

"How much?" she asked.

"Nine hundred and forty-three dollars and seventy-two cents, with the potential for another two hundred before the prom comes."

"You'll need at least half of that for the prom itself, so let's say you have about five hundred for the promposal. Are you willing to spend that much?"

"I am. I think it's worth it. And I think you're right—it's going to take one spectacular promposal to make this work," I said.

Brooke didn't look pleased. "The only thing harder to believe than you doing this is that I'm your accomplice."

"You promised, and I'm not letting you out of it. I need your help."

"You need the help of a team of psychiatrists, but I'm going to keep my word." She paused. "I just wish I *could* talk you out of this."

"You can't. I want to do this."

"No matter what the consequences?" she said.

"If I don't try, I can't succeed."

"Even if you do try, you're probably not going to succeed," she added. Her expression changed. "Look, Sam, you're my friend, and it's just that I don't want to see you set yourself up for something that's going to, well, probably hurt you."

"I thought the word was *humiliation* and you wanted a front-row seat for it," I said.

"Not so much want as will be there. You're completely sure you want to do this?"

I nodded my head.

She let out a big sigh. "Then let's get going. There's work to be done."

# CHAPTER EIGHT

I looked over my test again—for the fifth time. I'd finished within five minutes, but my unofficial protocol now called for me to never hand in a test until at least one other person did. It had been explained to me, repeatedly, that going up after just a few minutes was distressing to other students, because I was basically telling them that the test was ridiculously easy and implying that they weren't very bright, or that I was much brighter, or both. Once again, there were times when the truth was not necessarily a helpful thing.

Besides, no matter what, I never wanted to call other people stupid, and I never would. I knew enough about being called names and other nasty things that I never wanted to do that to anybody else, ever. Sometimes words hurt a lot more than punches, and I had lots of comparison points to make that calculation. Being hit only stung for a while. Some things that had been said to me still hurt ten years later.

I put my head back into the test. It was multiple choice and that was, without a doubt, the easiest type of test for me. While some of the choices were nuanced versions of the same idea, it was usually crystal clear to me which was the best answer. I'd filled in all the boxes, marking the correct answers, but I went back a second time to rub out four of them, changing correct to incorrect. Ninety-six percent was good enough to satisfy teachers and parents. I'd found that perfect was considered pretentious and made you the target of comments. Pretentious, perfect, and a target were the last things I wanted to be. Now, even more than usual. They might get in the way of a prom date.

While I waited, I thought about my promposal. Ian and Brooke and I had spent a good chunk of Sunday morning going through our strategy. I liked strategy. Basically, I'd decided to consider the whole thing as nothing more than a mathematical problem or a video game—things I was good at. If I plugged in all the right variables I'd be able to come up with a solution, leading to a successful promposal and a prom date. At least, that's what I kept telling myself. In a video game you usually had more than one life to lose, but here there was only one chance. Not that

I thought I was going to die—unless rejection could cause you to die of embarrassment.

Surprisingly, both Ian and Brooke seemed to be into doing this. I appreciated their support and help, especially Brooke's. Not surprisingly, my mother was pretty enthusiastic about this whole idea too, so of course my father came along for the ride. I think my mother considered this another successful step on my road to normalization. So be it.

There was a pencil tip pressed into my back. Ian was going to push out a message to me. It was a welcome distraction, although if he'd finished the test, why didn't he just hand it in so I could as well?

He pushed the end of the pencil into my back: four short and one long, the number four. Was he asking about fourth period? There was a break, and then he repeated it. What could he possibly mean? Wait . . . he was asking for the answer to question four. Was that it? There was only one way to find out.

I looked at my test. It was a difficult question. The answer was A, and I had put down B as one of my deliberate misses. It was best to get the hard ones wrong to avoid suspicion.

Slowly and quietly, pencil against the desk, I tapped out one short and one long for the letter A.

A few seconds later there was another message pressed into my back: a series of dots and dashes—twenty-three. That was at the bottom of the page. The correct answer—the one I'd filled in—was B.

I tapped back one long followed by three short to give him the answer.

Slowly I looked up to see if what we were doing was being noticed. Most eyes were glued to their tests, and Mrs. Tanner was at her desk, head down, scribbling something on a piece of paper.

Twice more he asked for answers. Twice more I gave them: question forty-four was B, and the answer to question seventy-five was A.

Finally a girl walked to the front and handed in her paper. It was now okay for me to turn mine in as well. I went to get up and realized that I'd failed to answer one question—"NAME"—and I printed mine in the space. I got up and walked to the front, dropping the paper on Mrs. Tanner's desk.

She looked up. "You need to stay after class."

"Why?"

"Because I told you to. Don't worry, Ian isn't going to be going anywhere either."

I had a rush of fear. Somehow she'd figured out what we were doing . . . No, that wasn't possible.

I turned and headed back to my desk and waited.

The class emptied out, leaving just Ian, Mrs. Tanner, and me. Mrs. Tanner motioned for us to come to the front as she remained at her desk. Just after Ian had handed in his paper—and was asked to stay behind as well—he'd pressed the word "why" into my back. I'd been smart enough not to answer, but I certainly had my suspicions.

We stood in front of her desk. I noticed that she was holding my test in her hand.

"I guess you're both wondering why I asked you two to stay behind," she said.

"Kinda curious," Ian said calmly.

For somebody with filtration issues he certainly could be cool in the face of danger. I guess in some ways he'd managed to get himself in so much trouble over the years that he'd become used to dealing with it. Practice makes perfect.

With her finger, Mrs. Tanner started to tap out her answer. She had what Morse Code operators called a "clumsy handle," but it was pretty clear what she was spelling out: M–O–R–S–E.

Ian looked as though he'd been punched in the gut, which was how I felt as well.

"So you two were communicating in Morse Code, is that correct?" she asked.

"Yeah, we do that all the time. It's just us talking," I lied. "We do it so nobody knows what we're talking about."

"I knew," she said.

"How did you know?" I asked.

"Girl Scouts. It was a long time ago but I remember things," she said.

"My therapist encourages me to do it so I don't say so many stupid things out loud and get in trouble,"

Ian explained. "You can talk to her if you want and she'll tell you."

"It wasn't you tapping out the message. It was Sam. I looked at your test," she said, holding it up. "Nowhere is there a sequence of four questions with the correct answers being A, B, B, A. What exactly were you trying to communicate to Ian?"

Ian laughed, which seemed to surprise both of us. "You caught us," he said. "This is sort of embarrassing. Do you want to tell her, Sam, or should I?"

"Why don't you," I suggested, since I had no idea what he was going to say.

"Sure. You know all about the promposals that are going around, right?" Ian asked Mrs. Tanner.

"I don't know all about them, but I certainly know of them. It's hard not to notice. Go on."

"Sam is going to be making one—"

"You are?" Mrs. Tanner sounded surprised.

"Yeah, Ian and Brooke are helping me arrange it."

"Strange, but continue," she said. "Explain how this relates to what we're talking about."

"Well, most of them come with musical accompaniment, and before class I asked Sam to tell me which group he thinks should be featured, and he told me he was thinking it over. We were having this discussion about whether it should be something current or something retro. During the test he told me which group he wanted. It's ABBA."

"ABBA, as in the Swedish group from the '70s?" Mrs. Tanner asked.

"Whose music, while retro, has been made *eternal* through one of the finest movies ever made, *Mamma Mia*, starring both Meryl Streep and Pierce Brosnan. It's one of Sam's personal favorite movies, and I must admit that I find it catchy as well. Have you seen it?"

"Of course I have."

"Then you can probably make the same guess I have as to what song he must have chosen," Ian said. "Well, what's your guess?"

Mrs. Tanner looked flustered. "Um . . . I don't know," she said, shaking her head.

"Of course you do, just think about it. What is the perfect song from that movie to use to ask somebody to a prom?"

Mrs. Tanner looked even more uncomfortable.

"Come on, I expect better from you," Ian scolded. "Think about it. Proms, dancing, party, king and queen of the dance. Well?"

"'Dancing Queen'?" Mrs. Tanner asked.

"That's what I was thinking!" Ian exclaimed, and then he turned to me. "Well, is that the song you have in mind, Sam?"

Rather than answer I tapped out one long, one short, and two long—Y—followed by one short—E—followed by three short—S.

Mrs. Tanner let out a huge sigh. "That's wonderful. Thank goodness you two weren't cheating, because you know I'd have no choice but to have you both suspended."

"Good to know," Ian said. "But I guess it's time

for a little confession. The reason Sam's marks have gone down this year is that I refuse to give him the answers. I said to him last year that I was tired of carrying him on my back."

"Very noble of you," Mrs. Tanner said, with a small smile. "And Sam, if there's anything I can do to offer assistance with your little promposal adventure, please feel free to ask."

"That's nice of you, very nice," I said.

"And it's very brave of you," she responded. "Of course, there's a fine line between brave and foolish."

"Boy, do I know that line!" Ian exclaimed.

"I'm sure you do. Now, you both need to go for lunch."

We quickly gathered our things and headed out the door.

"That was incredibly close," I said once we were safely out of earshot.

"Not to mention incredibly clever."

"ABBA? How did you come up with that?" I asked.

"Sheer genius. Do you think you're always the smartest guy in the room? Wait, don't answer that. Of course, the only down side is that no matter what you finally arrange for your promposal you'll have no choice but to use 'Dancing Queen' as the theme music."

"It could be worse," I agreed.

"It could be much worse, depending on whether Taylor likes ABBA or not. Do you know?"

"I don't know that, any more than you know that it's Taylor I'm asking to the prom."

"Fine, fine, stay all mysterious. I just know that if you're going to ask her you'd better do it quickly. Do you think she's going to remain unasked for very long?"

"I hadn't thought of that, but you're probably right."

"So it *is* her you're going to invite!"

"I didn't say that either. I just said I hadn't thought about her being invited quickly."

"It goes without saying. Britt's been asked, so Ash and Tay are not going to be far behind. I can almost see the line starting to form on the left. If it's going to happen, it had better happen soon."

Of course he was right. There was going to be somebody asking her out soon, and that could ruin everything I had planned.

# CHAPTER NINE

Brooke was already waiting for us, and we slumped down onto the grass beside her. She pulled a tablet from her backpack.

"I've been doing some research. I spent all of last night surfing and searching and screening ideas about promposals, and I've consolidated, organized, and categorized them," she said.

"It sounds like you're really getting into this whole promposal thing," Ian said.

"It sounds like I'm keeping my word to help. Besides, I'd rather do almost anything than study for Thursday's math test."

She spun the tablet around so I could read the page. In big letters it read "Operation Promposal—Mission Impossible."

"So you want to do a *Mission Impossible* theme? A Tom Cruise kind of thing?" I asked.

"Tom Cruise? Oh, no, you could *never* pull that off."

"Then why is it called 'Mission Impossible'?" I asked, though I had a sinking feeling I knew.

"Just think about it for a minute, genius," she said.

Ian chuckled. "I get it. Good one."

"Oh, I wouldn't laugh if I were you, Ian. Don't even get me started about what I think the chances are of *you* ever getting somebody to accept your invitation. Is there even a word that means less than impossible?"

"I don't know what you mean," Ian said. "My mother tells me I'm special."

"Yes, you are. In fact, you are so special that your mom would probably be the only date you could get to the prom," Brooke said.

"I've already told you, that's my fall-back plan. She is a pretty good dancer, and my father says she's a good kisser, so—"

"Filter! Filter!" we both screamed together.

"Okay, even I know that was over the top," Ian admitted.

Brooke scrolled to the next page. "There are three main characteristics of a classic promposal, and I've listed them, along with examples," she said.

On the first page was a large heading, "Elements of a Promposal—The Three *P*s." I scrolled to the next page. There was one word written, a title.

"Public."

"I guess this first one is fairly obvious, but it is the very essence of a promposal," Brooke said. "A successful invitation must be done in a very public way."

"Like Kevin's promposal," I said.

"Exactly, and the more people there to witness it the better. Beyond that, it needs to be videoed and put online."

"So I was right," Ian said, "it isn't real until it's on social media."

"I hate to admit it, but yes. Ideally it goes viral. After I go through these initial points, we can look at some of the most successful ones."

"I'm good for a few hundred views of Kevin's all by myself," Ian said.

"Hundreds is a joke. There's one video of this guy who organized a flash mob dance for his promposal, and it's at over 1.1 million views and still climbing," she said.

"That must have been some flash mob," I said.

"I've got the link. You can see for yourself and decide."

I made a note to look at that one. Not that I was any good at dancing, but I could always get people to dance for me if it came to that.

"Some of these are even more public than Kevin's. Airplanes dragging banners across a whole city, or big-screen messages on the Jumbotrons at stadiums."

"I've seen marriage proposals like that," I said. "I remember they flashed the couple's faces up on the screen, and I couldn't tell for sure but I didn't think she looked very happy."

"Of course, that's the danger. The bigger the audience, the bigger the risk," Brooke said.

"I hadn't really thought about that equation," I said.

"You, with your lengthy history of successful interactions with females, hadn't thought about being rejected?" Brooke asked.

Okay, I understood the reasons for the sarcasm. "No, of course I'd thought about being rejected."

"You should give that concept some real thought," Brooke said. "Getting rejected is bad. Getting rejected in front of hundreds of people is really bad, but you have to think of the long-lasting implications. Your humiliating rejection will be recorded and posted so countless people can view it again and again, across the country and basically forever."

I shuddered.

"And it's like they say, nothing that's up on the Internet ever really comes down," Ian pointed out, helpfully. "Twenty years from now there it will be, online for everybody to see. Until the Internet virtually crashes and burns, everybody with a computer will be able to see *you* crash and burn, over and over and over again."

"I get it."

"Do you?" Brooke asked. "The videos with the most views are the ones of somebody getting rejected."

"Do you have statistics on how often somebody is turned down?" I asked.

"The good news is it's not that often. It looks like less than 10 percent of the time."

"That's good to know." I sighed, relieved.

"But you have to understand that you're dealing with a biased sample," Brooke said.

"Okay, now I'm lost. Do you understand what she means?" Ian asked me.

"In general terms, a biased sample refers to a survey in which the sample, rather than being randomly selected and neutral in nature, is chosen to reflect or generate a predetermined preference or outcome."

"And in this case, that would mean what?" Ian asked.

"I think Brooke is implying that in most of the promposals there was a pre-understanding, an unstated—"

"Or stated," Brooke said.

I nodded. "Or stated agreement that the promposal was coming, and there was a tacit—"

"Or explicit," Brooke said.

"Okay, or explicit understanding that the promposal was going to be accepted even before it was made . . . right?"

"Yes. In some cases the promposal was nothing more than a public announcement of what had already been agreed to in private," Brooke said.

"Okay, I get it. So, the question is, does this mystery lady, the subject of your promposal—just for the sake of argument we'll call her Taylor— know that you're going to invite her?" Ian asked.

"My mystery lady has no idea. As far as I can tell, she doesn't even suspect."

"Then I believe that the failure rate is much, much higher than 10 percent," Brooke said. "The 10 percent rejection rate is with most of them already agreeing to go before the promposal is made."

"Then you think he might want to consider sort of feeling her out, to see if she's interested, before we go any further," Ian suggested.

"Sorry. Can't do that. I'm just going to take the risk."

"Fine, don't say I didn't warn you," Brooke said.

"Warning noted. What's the next point?"

Brooke scrolled through a bunch of pages that featured blue-colored web links to what I assumed were the examples she'd mentioned. She stopped at the next heading.

"Pompous."

"That sounds a little negative all by itself, don't you think?" I asked.

"Sorry, but I was working with the theme of all three starting with the letter *P*. I could have gone with something else. Perhaps overblown, or over- consumption, or show-offy, or excessive, or pretentious."

"Pretentious starts with a *P*. You could have gone with that and it would have worked," Ian said.

"Actually, at one point I was thinking of going with four *P*s and including that as a separate cate-gory, but I thought it might appear that I have a prejudice against promposals and proms."

"Is it still called a biased sample if the person doing the sampling is actually biased against it?" Ian asked.

"I'm not hiding how I feel," Brooke said. "I gathered the information without bias no matter how I feel about the subject itself."

"I believe you, although it might have been better if you'd tried to find at least one word for this section that wasn't quite so negative," I commented.

"It's not about negative or positive, it's about facts. The best promposals—by which I mean the promposals that seem to succeed and get the most social media attention—are all way over the top and feature massive outlays of money and material goods."

"So limos are good," Ian said.

"And stretch limos are better, and limos with hot tubs are best. Balloons are only good if there are too many of them—hundreds of them. A dozen roses doesn't make nearly the statement that five dozen or sixteen dozen makes."

"Sixteen dozen roses? You're joking, right?"

"No, I have the link for you. And with balloons we're not just talking hundreds but even more than a *thousand*. I can show you the guy who had fifteen hundred balloons, all in the potential date's favorite color."

"Where do you even put fifteen hundred balloons?" Ian asked.

"It filled the atrium of the school. I have to admit, it did look pretty impressive. Then there are signs, billboards—"

"Billboards?"

"It's one of the more common methods of making a promposal. That, and signs on the sides of buses or bus shelters, skywriting, planes towing signs, dozens of signs stuck in the front lawn, and singing telegrams."

"A Strip-O-Gram might be unique," Ian said. "It would send a message."

"The wrong message," I said.

"Just remember, with everything you're thinking of doing, that more is always better, bigger is always better, and completely outrageous is the very, very best. So, shall we go on to the next *P*?"

I felt my head spinning but I waved her onward. She scrolled forward over some more pages and stopped at a page with a new heading.

"Personal."

"It is important to design your promposal to match the person you're making the promposal to," Brooke said. "Again, this is very obvious, but difficult for us to assist you with if you won't tell us who it is."

"You don't need to know."

"Fine, but do you know some basic things about her that could help us?" Brooke asked.

"I know things."

"Things," Brooke said, shaking her head. "Do you know her favorite color, the flowers she likes the best, her favorite song?"

"I know the color and I think the flowers but I'm going to have to check the song."

"Ideally it would be 'Dancing Queen' by ABBA," Ian said.

"What?" Brooke demanded.

"It's a long story," I told her. "I know lots of things about her, and what I don't know I can try to find out."

"You'd better. Much depends on the very specific nature of the promposal. It's not just that she's more likely to say yes if the promposal fits her, but that she'll be impressed that you went to the trouble to find out what she likes. Does that all make sense?"

"It does."

"You can even probably find out the dress she's hoping to wear to the prom," Brooke said.

"How do I do that?" I asked.

"Midnight break-ins, checking bedroom closets, hiding in dress store dressing rooms, and stalking would all work," Ian suggested.

We both laughed, and Ian laughed along. I knew he was just joking about all of that . . . well, at least I was pretty sure he was just joking.

"Not stalking but trolling. There are websites where girls post their prom dresses. Not necessarily what they did buy but what they will buy. Basically, they're calling dibs on their dress."

"You're the one joking now," I said.

"I wish I were. There's one specifically for our school. Over thirty seniors, and a few of the more ambitious or hopeful juniors, have all posted pictures of their chosen dresses."

"That could be incredibly helpful," Ian said. "At least for me. I can do some scouting to see who's already bought a dress, and figure out who's getting more desperate as the prom approaches."

"And that's your plan, to chart their increasing desperation?" Brooke asked.

"That's *part* of my plan."

"You'll also notice when you do your cyber-stalking that there are very specific warnings about dresses—these girls are not just claiming specific dresses or styles, they'll even claim colors. There are comments like 'Nobody is allowed to wear this shade of blue.'"

"That is so intense. I had no idea it was like that," I said.

"Apparently, the greatest ill that can ever befall somebody is to have the same prom dress as somebody else," Brooke explained.

"I guess the best way around that would be to make your own dress," I said. "You made the one you're wearing today, didn't you?"

"Yes, I did."

"It's very nice," I said. It was a long, flowing blue dress that matched her eyes.

"It's very nice and unusual and remarkably socially appropriate of you to notice," she said.

"You know I'm working on socially appropriate."

"Me too," Ian said, and he started to tap out a message.

"Well, one of you is obviously more successful with your socially appropriate behavior than the other. And by the way, Ian, I don't care what you think about my dress."

"And I don't want to hear that," I said.

Ian stopped tapping. Well, at least he stopped where I could see it. I knew there was a possibility he was still tapping out the message with his big toe. What Brooke didn't know was that he wasn't making a comment about her dress but rather what was *under* her dress. I was hoping this was kind of like the tree falling in the forest with nobody to hear it—if she couldn't seem him tapping, his comments wouldn't exist.

Brooke didn't care what Ian thought. She didn't care what I thought, or what anybody else thought. At least, that was the attitude she worked on projecting to the world. I really didn't believe her. Everybody cared. She wasn't nearly as tough and unconcerned about what people thought as she liked to make out. We'd been friends long enough for me to know when something hurt her, even if she didn't want to show it.

"So, how are you three doing?"

I looked up. It was Taylor, along with Brittney and Ashley. Standing there, staring down at us and the promposal page on the tablet.

# CHAPTER TEN

Brooke reached over, and flipped the tablet over so that the page wasn't visible.

"That was a pretty tough test," Taylor said.

"It wasn't easy," I fibbed.

"I noticed you weren't even the first one finished this time," she said.

"I wanted to double- and triple-check my answers," I explained. Of course, I didn't say anything about needing the time to deliberately mark some of the answers wrong, and how I could have finished in five minutes if I'd really wanted to.

"Would you ladies like a chocolate?" Ian offered.

"What kind?" Ashley asked.

"Only the best." He dug into his backpack and pulled out a very fancy, very expensive box of chocolates. Where had they come from?

"They're Belgian truffles," Ian said.

He offered the box and each girl made a selection.

"These are amazing!" Ashley said as she took a bite.

"Incredible!" Brittney agreed.

"Thank you so much," Taylor added.

"I think all three of you should take a second."

"I don't know if I can afford another one," Brittney said. "I have to fit into my prom dress."

"That isn't going to be a problem," Taylor said. "You're so super-fit."

Ian started to tap out something but I shot him a dirty look and he stopped himself. That was very encouraging. On the other hand, he had probably just relocated his message to his shoe.

"I was wondering if you've thought about us forming a study group for final exams," Taylor said.

"Sure, that would be great." I'd be part of it, even though I never actually studied for anything.

"I was thinking that a few of us who have Mrs. Tanner could get together and study for the final," she explained. "Ian, are you in?"

"I could do that," Ian said.

"Brooke's taking that course with Mrs. Tanner, only she's in the afternoon class. Could she be part of the study group too?" I asked.

"Of course!" Taylor said. "Would you be willing to join us?"

"Sure, it couldn't hurt," Brooke said.

"It'll be a much better group with you in it. I'm sorry I didn't think of it . . . hope you didn't feel excluded?"

"No worries."

"I could even bring chocolates," Ian said.

Okay, that was a little awkward.

"If you girls ever need a little chocolate fix, you come and find me."

They all flashed their smiles at him.

"Remember, when you think of me you should think of chocolate, the *finest* chocolate in the world. When you want a chocolate—the world's best—come and find me."

Okay, this was now starting to make a bizarre kind of sense—the kind that only Ian could have thought of and only I could have figured out.

The three girls said their goodbyes and Ian, to his credit, neither said nor tapped out anything inappropriate.

After they left, Brooke reached out to take a chocolate and Ian pulled the box away.

"They're not for you," he said.

She looked shocked, and then confused, and then angry.

"You gave them two chocolates each but you don't have one for me?"

"Or for Sam. I'm not planning on asking either of you to the prom," Ian said.

"Oh, how disappointing, yet another dream of

mine that will never come true. Are you planning on asking all three of them to the prom?"

"Don't be silly. Britt already has a date, and Taylor is Sam's."

"She's not mine."

"Not yet," Ian said.

"So you're going to ask Ashley? She's your potential prom date?" Brooke asked.

"She's probably out of my league."

"Probably?" Brooke asked. "*Probably?*"

"Look, I get it. I heard people saying that Ashley's hoping to be Prom Queen, and I just don't think I'm King material. I wouldn't fit into her equation."

"You're right there. You're way more like the Court Jester than the King. So, if you're not planning on asking any of those girls to the prom, why did you give them all chocolates?" Brooke asked.

"Don't get me wrong, I'm not ruling Ashley out completely. Who knows, extreme desperation on her part could still tip the scales in my favor. I'm going to be giving out chocolates to girls who might be potential dates. I only gave chocolates to Britt and Taylor because it would have been difficult to explain excluding them. I would have looked weird, or like a creep."

"You would have looked *more* weird or *more* creepy," Brooke said.

"Okay, point taken," Ian agreed.

"So, you think if you give a girl a chocolate she'll go to the dance with you?" Brooke said.

"That's the ultimate goal."

"Do you really think that any girl is going to trade a date for a hunk of chocolate?" Brooke asked.

"Not *trade*, but *associate*."

"You've lost me again, and perhaps it would be better if I stayed lost," Brooke said.

She might have been lost, but I could read Ian like a road map. "I understand what you're doing. You're practicing basic behavior modification through association with a pleasurable stimulus—you're teaching them to associate something they love, chocolate, with you," I said.

"Exactly! I read up on that Pavlov guy and thought I'd try a little experiment of my own. Doesn't that make perfect sense?" he asked.

"Textbook perfect," I agreed.

"Except this isn't a textbook and girls aren't dogs," Brooke pointed out.

"I didn't imply that they were, but it should still work. I want girls—attractive, potential prom dates—to associate me with delicious chocolate. Hey, maybe they'll even start to drool when they see me."

"Or get sick to their stomachs, or get lots of pimples," Brooke said. "Would you like them to associate you with pimples?"

"I'm prepared to take that chance."

"Ian, you are truly amazing. Well, at least Sam still has a shot at getting to the prom."

"I do?" I asked. "What happened to 'Mission Impossible'?"

"Taylor just came over to talk to you—again. She seems to actually like you."

"I think she does," I agreed.

"Besides, you really aren't *bad* looking. Some people might even describe you as having a quirky kind of cuteness."

"I have been called quirky before."

"I've gotten creepy, which is sort of like quirky," Ian said.

"No it isn't," Brooke said, then she turned back to me. "With the new haircut, the clothes you're wearing, well, if I didn't know what a dork you are, I wouldn't know what a dork you are. Not that you should let that go to your head."

"I'll try not to. So you think I have a chance?"

"I've definitely upgraded this project from 'Mission Impossible' to 'Mission Improbable.' Let's work on a plan tonight and start assembling the pieces. But first things first," she said. "I've got that test with Tanner right after lunch. Any questions I'm going to have trouble with?"

"It was pretty straightforward," I said. "Basic multiple choice."

"As easy as an A, then a B, followed by a second B, and ending with an A," Ian said.

The ten-minute warning bell sounded, saving me from trying to explain Ian any further.

# CHAPTER ELEVEN

As we started toward the school, my attention was caught by the sound of music. But it wasn't coming from a car or a stereo. It sounded live, and it was getting closer. And then I saw the source—the whole school marching band was coming around the side of the building toward the front steps, where the three of us and most of the lunch crowd were headed. The music got louder and louder as more band members, all in uniform, turned the corner of the building and we all merged toward the same place. They were being led by the drum major and a trio of baton-throwing majorettes.

"Strange time and place to practice," Brooke said.

"Even though it sounds like they need it," Ian said.

He was right. They usually sounded much better.

"Can you even figure out what song they're playing?" Ian asked.

I listened hard. I couldn't, but it did sound familiar.

"I think they're playing 'Happy,'" Brooke said.

"Are you sure?" Ian questioned.

"Not positive, but listen."

It got louder and louder and the melody line became clearer. That was definitely the song, although it didn't quite sound right coming from a bunch of tubas, trumpets, and trombones.

"Even this version makes my feet tap," Ian said. He did a little slide dance.

"I've heard of people busting a move," Brooke said, "but that move looked more like it was busted."

I laughed but didn't want to admit that I couldn't have done one even that good.

The band came to a stop directly in front of the steps, blocking the entrance, and continued to play as a crowd gathered round. Some of the people in the crowd started clapping along with the beat. I tried to join in, but realized I was half a beat behind and stopped myself. Rhythm was not in my programming. No point in advertising to a potential prom date that I couldn't dance. I was already trying to overcome a steep uphill battle without putting another obstacle in my path.

A few people—those with even better rhythm and coordination—started to dance along. They were very good. Then, seeing how good they were, a few more joined the first. They were also good. The crowd of dancers grew until there were fifteen or twenty of them. And, unlike Ian, they were all amazing. I realized then that what they were doing wasn't random, it was choreographed. This wasn't just some spontaneous act, it was a planned, coordinated effort—a dance flash mob.

Now it looked as though every second person in the crowd had pulled out a phone and was either filming the dancers and the marching band or trying to take a selfie with all of that in the background.

Suddenly, out of nowhere, there were balloons. Only a few at first, but then there were dozens and dozens of yellow and blue balloons floating down and being kicked around or bopped back up into the air by the crowd. I looked up—they were being tossed off the roof of the school!

The crowd continued to grow. There were hundreds and hundreds of people now. It wasn't just those of us who had been out on the lawn for lunch. There was a gigantic crowd gathering on the steps behind the marching band, and people were looking down or pushing out through the main doors. I could just imagine the texts and photos flying across the campus and everybody rushing here in response, finding a reason to leave classes behind. Up above, it looked as though every window in the school had been thrown open, and heads popped out to watch.

"Do you know what's happening?" Brooke yelled over the horns.

"Hardly ever!" Ian yelled back.

"It's gotta be a promposal!"

Of course she was right. What else could it be? I scanned the crowd trying to figure out who might be making it or who it could be for, but there was no way of knowing.

Kevin's promposal had been big. But this one was already much bigger. There were more people involved, and more coordination of effort. This wasn't just a limo and ten guys who had painted their chests. Kevin set the bar high, but this person, whoever this was, was raising it way, way up. Here we were with a whole marching band, dancers, and balloons—hundreds and hundreds of balloons raining down, all of them yellow and blue. There had to be a reason for that. Were those the favorite colors of the person on the receiving end of this promposal?

I thought about Brooke's promposal guide. I tried to evaluate this one based on the three *P*s that Brooke had outlined.

First, there was no question this was Public. It seemed like everybody who went to our school, and probably even people who didn't, was gathered here. If potential social media hits could be predicted by the number of cameras present and the inherent attractiveness of the event, then this indicated it would go public far and wide. If that other flash mob promposal Brooke was describing had got over a million hits, then this was worth more than that.

Full marks for public.

Was it Pompous or Pretentious? I didn't know if a marching band could ever be considered either of those things, but it couldn't have been either easy or cheap to arrange. Whoever staged this would either have had to convince that many people, or paid all of them to participate. Add in the dancers, some of whom I was sure were professionals, and the cost of all of those balloons, and this must have cost a fair amount of money.

There was no question that it was big. I sometimes had difficulty qualifying things but I could always quantify. There were fifty members of the marching band, lots of dancers, and a number of people up on the roof who continued to toss down balloons. This was much bigger than the crew that had helped Kevin. The only question was whether, in the high school social hierarchy equation, ten football players were worth more than fifty marching band members.

"Something this over the top has to be for somebody high on the food chain," Brooke said.

I looked around to try to locate Taylor and her friends. They were at the top of the pecking order. Brittney was gone but that still left Ashley and Taylor. I couldn't think of that. I had to focus on evaluating it.

The final criteria in Brooke's book was just how Personal the attempt was. I couldn't possibly know until the reveal, and even then how would I know what the person liked? I could only assume that the decision to go with this music and these colored balloons was very strategic—that the "promposer" knew those things about the "promposee."

All at once the song ended, and after a second of silence a gigantic cheer went up from the crowd. That noise was punctuated by the sound of the bell. Afternoon classes had officially begun and we were all supposed to be in class. Nobody was going anywhere. Not even the teachers. We all just stood and stared and waited and wondered. Who was the promposal for, who was making the promposal, and, most important, was it going to be accepted?

There was a flash of white, and from the top of the roof a banner came unfurling down. There, in big letters, were these words: *ASHLEY, WOULD YOU GO TO THE PROM WITH ME?*

Brooke had been right that a big promposal like this was for somebody with status.

"I guess I have to take Ashley off my list," Ian said.

"She was never on any list that you should have been keeping," Brooke said. "But don't strike her off yet. Continue to enjoy your delusional fantasy until she accepts."

"Who wouldn't accept this?" Ian asked.

The crowd seemed to part slightly to reveal Ashley, flanked by Taylor and Brittney. Then the other two girls stepped back so that Ashley stood alone in the middle of the massive crowd. She had to be wondering what everybody else was wondering— who was making the proposal, and why hadn't he stepped forward yet? It had to be somebody she knew or had dated. I also wondered if she'd seen this coming. Was this going to be one of those cases of a public acceptance of a predetermined promposal, or was she in the dark like the rest of us?

I could only see her face in profile so it was hard to read her look, but it certainly wasn't the look of joy I'd witnessed with Brittney. Instead, Ashley seemed perplexed, and confused, and worried. Maybe that was the answer to my question. She had not known this was going to happen.

In answer to the collective question, one of the members of the marching band stepped forward, a bouquet of long-stemmed red roses in his hand. He removed his peaked band cap and walked toward where Ashley stood.

"Who is that?" Ian asked.

"I don't know," Brooke said. "I don't recognize him. Is he a member of the band, or has he just borrowed a uniform?"

"Why would he borrow a band uniform?" I asked.

"Maybe he couldn't get his hands on a Clown Town clown costume."

Even I knew that was a shot.

"Wait, I recognize him," Ian said. "It's Trevor. He lives down the street from me. He's a senior."

The guy stopped directly in front of Ashley and then dropped to one knee.

"Ashley, I know you don't know me well," he began.

"Oh, this does not look good," Brooke said, and I felt it.

"But I know you," Trevor continued. "Would you do me the great, great honor of being my date to the prom?"

The silence now was complete. You could have heard a pin drop. Everybody waited. I couldn't imagine how he must have felt, because I could hardly breathe just watching him.

Ashley suddenly turned and ran away, pushing past people and disappearing into the crowd. There was a collective gasp. Nobody moved for just a second, and then Taylor and Brittney turned and chased after her. The people in their way, no longer so stunned, separated to allow them to follow.

My eyes turned back to the guy, the promposer, Trevor. He'd managed to get back to his feet, but other than that he hadn't moved. Of course, where was he going to go? He must have just wanted the earth to swallow him up. I felt for him, right in the pit of my stomach.

That could be me. But it didn't have to be. I didn't have to do this. Was the chance of success worth the risk of humiliation?

# CHAPTER TWELVE

I looked at the video again. There were his brave words, the invitation to the prom, the silence that followed, and then Ashley running away in answer. It was hard to watch, but the hardest was what came next.

From where I'd been standing I'd seen only Trevor's back. But whoever was working the camera had zoomed in on his face and stayed right on him, so tight and so focused that I could see deep into his eyes. He looked as though he was dying, or felt like he was dying, or wanted to die, or all of the above rolled into one. And the camera just stayed on him.

In the background of the shot I could see the crowd dissipating as everybody rushed off to the class they were already late for. He just stood there, not moving, not blinking, and, thank goodness, not crying. I felt like crying for him. If it was this painful to watch, how painful must it have been to live through?

We'd rushed off too. It wasn't like I was going to go over to say something to him. I didn't know him. Besides, it seemed like the right thing to do to give him some privacy. Privacy. What a concept! His face and his reaction were already spread out across the Internet. Privacy did not exist.

Maybe I'd walked away not just because I didn't know him but because I didn't know what to say to him. This was like watching someone die, but not a peaceful death from natural causes. It was a public execution. And worst of all, he'd pulled the switch himself, and spent a small fortune doing it.

Scanning through the comments that followed the video I discovered his full name, Trevor Brady. Before this, the name meant nothing to me. I'd never heard of him. Now he was a phenomenon. A couple of the comments even talked about "pulling a Trevor."

Ian had mentioned that he was a senior and I knew we'd never shared a class together. I'd probably seen him hundreds of times in the halls or the cafeteria, and of course dozens of times as he marched on the field, just another one of the trumpet players in identical hats and uniforms. Tonight, he probably would have given anything to be anonymous.

The story going around was that Ashley had known absolutely nothing about Trevor's intentions. Before the two of them being linked together forever on the Internet by a promposal, they had only spoken casually a few times. Of course, as a member of the marching band, he would have always been at the games, and Ashley would have been there along with the other cheerleaders, dancing and cheering on the team. The band members had seats right in the front row, closest to the cheerleaders. I wondered if he felt that being close to Ashley physically meant he was close to her in other ways.

In three years I'd never missed a football game. Just because I couldn't throw or catch a football to save my life didn't mean I didn't love the game. There was a statistical purity to football that was surpassed only by baseball, the other sport I loved to watch and couldn't play to save my life.

There were now over eleven thousand views for the video, in less than five hours. I'd contributed eight of those myself. It was like watching a car accident. No, far worse than that—a car fatality.

I scrolled down through the comments again. They continued to grow, and they continued to be mainly nasty. Both guys and girls were making fun of Trevor, calling him a "band geek" and saying that he got what he deserved for trying to date "out of his zip code."

I could only imagine the comments that would go up about me. I wasn't even a band geek. I would have *loved* to have been in the marching band. If I could have either played an instrument or marched without tripping over my feet I would have tried out.

A few of the comments were kinder—well, kinder to Trevor. Those were mainly from girls who called Ashley all sorts of bad things. Apparently Brooke wasn't the only one who bought into the stereotype that all cheerleaders are dumb, mean girls. I sort of knew Ashley, and she wasn't as smart as Taylor but she was almost as kind. She certainly wasn't mean.

I scrolled back to the top to the image of Trevor's face, frozen there on my screen. I wished I knew more about him. Maybe I could do an Internet search. There were probably people at school, and from across the country, doing the same thing right now. That made it even creepier. I closed up my laptop. Really, I didn't need any more information. I wanted to say something, and I figured it was better to do it in person.

I stood on the sidewalk in front of the house. Now that I was here, I was thinking maybe I shouldn't have come. I didn't even know for sure it was the right place. I'd dropped by Ian's place and he'd given me directions. He'd even offered to go with me, but that was not going to make this any better or easier for either of us. Three was a crowd, and the last thing Trevor needed right now was another crowd.

There was a car in the driveway and a light in the front window so I assumed that somebody was home.

That eliminated the possibility of a noble gesture: knocking and leaving because nobody was there—doing "the right thing" without actually having to pay the price. Then again, just because somebody was there didn't mean they'd answer the door. That was a small but cold comfort.

I walked up to the front door and listened. There was no sound from inside. I took a deep breath and knocked. It echoed back at me. I wanted to knock, not attack. Within a few seconds the door opened and a woman—a mom-aged woman—was standing there.

"Hello," she said, and she offered a sad little smile.

"Hello. I was hoping to speak to Trevor. Is he in?"

"He's home, but I think he might be too, um, busy to come to the door."

"It won't take long, I promise. I just want to tell him something."

She looked hesitant. "I know my son's friends. I don't know you."

"I'm not really a friend. I'm just a guy from school. My name is Sam Davies. I wanted to say something to your son."

"I'm not sure he's in the mood for a conversation."

"It's not a conversation. I just wanted to tell him . . . maybe it will make him feel better . . . at least a little."

"So this is about the . . . the thing that happened at school today?" she asked.

"Yes. I was there."

She looked as though she might start to cry.

"He really tried hard to do the right thing. He didn't do anything wrong," I said.

She let out a loud sigh. "It's nice of you to say that. Wait a bit and I'll tell him you're here," she said.

She closed the door and I stood there on the stoop, waiting, and thinking. If Trevor was as upset as she was suggesting, maybe this plan of mine had gone from a possibly-not-good idea all the way to a really-bad idea. So far the smartest part of my plan had been not bringing Ian, but that didn't mean the rest wasn't stupid. Was coming here wrong, a socially inappropriate gesture?

I heard footsteps and the door opened and Trevor appeared. His eyes looked red. Either he'd been crying or peeling onions or he had bad allergies. Maybe all of them, because they certainly weren't mutually exclusive, but if I had to bet I knew which explanation I'd choose.

"Hello, Trevor, I'm Sam Da—"

"I know you, well, know *of* you. You're that really smart kid in eleventh grade."

"That's me."

"And you now know me as the stupidest."

"I don't think so. I didn't read any comment that said that."

He looked a little shocked. Obviously I'd said something I shouldn't have.

"I looked at some of the stuff online," I said.

"You and everybody else in the school, the city, and across the country."

"Probably lots of people from other countries as well," I added, before realizing that was not exactly what he wanted to hear.

"My mom said you had something you wanted to say to me. What is it?" he asked.

I tried to get my words in the right order. "I was there today."

"Everybody was there today."

"I guess most people in the school were but probably not everybody. There would have been a few people, maybe more than two hundred, who weren't, although I'm sure they've all seen a video of it by now."

"Is that what you wanted to say to me?" he asked. He didn't sound or look happy.

"No, I just wanted to tell you that I was really doing a lot of thinking about maybe doing a promposal. I was even going to do it in a big public way, like yours, and I wanted to thank you."

"Because now you realize that it can lead to total humiliation and you're not going to do it?"

"No, you don't understand. Now I'm not just *thinking* about it. I'm *going* to do it."

"What are you talking about? You realize that she turned me down."

"I think everybody knows she turned you down. That's not the reason. What you did today, out there in front of everybody, was probably the bravest thing I've ever seen anybody do."

"Brave. You thought I was brave?"

"It was like leaping out of an airplane not knowing if your parachute was going to open, or if you were even wearing one. That is incredibly brave."

"Stupid and brave can get confused," he said.

"Those two things are distinctly separate. And while there might possibly be a slight overlap in a Venn diagram, they're very different."

"Okay, now you're just confusing me."

"I do that a lot. Look, do you know the biggest difference between your promposal and the one that Kevin made?" I asked.

"He got a yes, a hug, and a kiss, and he rode away in a limo with his prom date, while mine ran away sobbing after rejecting and humiliating me?" he asked.

"Well, there are those differences as well," I admitted. "But the biggest thing is that he already knew she was going to say yes."

"You know that for sure?"

"I know that."

I'd asked Taylor and she'd confirmed it for me. I couldn't explain that to Trevor, though, without breaking her confidence, and I'd learned over the years that that was a bad thing.

"But you, what you did, that was just brave. You were willing to risk it all. If you'd asked me I would have gone with you."

"Wait, are you here to ask *me* to the prom?"

"What?"

"Because I understand, and you know, respect people's right to date whoever they want and even take that date to the prom. But I like girls . . . I like girls a lot, and that's why I did what I did."

It suddenly dawned on me what he was saying. "No, no, I'm going to ask a girl, I just meant that if I *were* a girl, and I'm not and I don't want to be a girl, I would have said yes, because what you did was a brave and thoughtful thing. Lots of girls are saying that."

"They are?" he asked.

"In the comments that are being left. Have you looked at them?"

"I stopped reading them after an hour or so. Too painful."

"Not all of them are mean and nasty," I explained. "Some of them are very positive toward you, girls saying what a great guy you were to do that."

"I guess I didn't look that far," Trevor said.

"And there are some that have great things to say about you and nasty things to say about Ashley," I added.

"She doesn't deserve that," he said.

"You still think that even though she turned you down?"

"Why wouldn't I? She had every right in the world to turn me down. I shouldn't have ambushed her like that."

"That's really good of you to say that. You're not just brave but you must really be a good person," I said.

"I am . . . just not good enough for her."

"No," I said, shaking my head. "That's the only thing you've said that's wrong. I just want you to know that, because of you, I'm going to go out there and do a promposal."

"And does this girl know you're going to do it?" Trevor asked.

"She has no idea whatsoever."

"But you're pretty sure she's going to say yes, right?"

"I'm almost certain that she's going to say no."

"I don't understand. If you're so certain that she's going to say no, then why are you going to do it?" Trevor asked.

"It's just that, win or lose, sometimes you have to take a chance. Like you did."

"And if you get shot down like me?" Trevor asked.

"Then at least you'll have company. We can even see which goes more viral, my rejection or yours."

He laughed. I think that surprised him.

"Of course you have a head start, so it's not really a fair competition," I said. "Maybe I can make up an equation to factor that in."

"You have pretty high expectations if you really think you can compete with me in terms of big, public humiliation," Trevor said.

"I'll give you credit, you really did set the bar incredibly high!"

"Or really low, depending on who you talk to."

"Could I ask you a question?"

"Sure, why not?" he said.

"When it happened—you know, when she ran away—that look in your eyes . . . well, did it feel like somebody had punched you in the stomach?"

"Actually, it felt more like a kick, and it was about a foot lower than my stomach. I wonder how it felt to Ashley."

"Not good, I'm sure," I said.

"I just feel so bad for her. It's not her fault I did something stupid in front of everybody."

"She'll get over it. So will you. And so will I if I get shot down. That's all I wanted to say. Thanks for coming to the door and speaking to me, it meant a lot," I said.

"No, thank you," he said. "See you around school."

I started to walk away and he called out my name. I stopped and turned around.

"Sam, is she worth it? Is she worth getting publicly humiliated over?"

That I didn't need to think about. "Oh, yes. Yes, she is."

# CHAPTER THIRTEEN

I took a towel and dried off my hair. It felt good to have the final traces of vomit washed away. Another fine shift at Clown Town completed, and this time the kid had projectile-vomited so hard that it had somehow seeped around and through the fright wig and got to my real hair underneath. In true Clown Town tradition, I'd made it to the washroom and washed off as much as possible and managed to finish up my shift. Brooke thought I was a big clown shoe-in for Employee of the Month again.

I heard the doorbell ring and knew it was going to be either Ian or Brooke. I threw on a clean pair of jeans, pulled a polo shirt over my head, and grabbed a pair of socks from the drawer. I did a quick color-match check. The shirt was a similar shade of blue to the jeans and the socks were black. Black and blue went together okay.

By the time I got downstairs Brooke and Ian were already at the kitchen table with my mother, all of them huddled over a tablet. I didn't need to hear the conversation to know what they were looking at. They were all so engrossed that they didn't even acknowledge—or basically even notice—my approach. I slipped in behind them to watch what was now known online as the "crash and burn" video.

It was coming to the end, and my mother made a sound like she'd been kicked in the stomach when Ashley turned and ran away. As the camera zoomed in on Trevor I looked away, down to the count on the bottom. It was now at over seventy-five thousand views.

"That poor boy," my mother said. "I wonder how he is."

"He's doing a lot better today," I said, and everybody looked at me curiously.

"I can't imagine that's possible," she said.

"He didn't think it would be either. Yesterday he was feeling *really* awful, but today he's only feeling awful."

"And you would know this how?" Brooke asked.

"Trevor just sent me a text message a few minutes ago. We've been texting all day."

"You know him?" my mother asked.

"Not well. We formally met yesterday," I explained.

"But yesterday was his crash and burn. When yesterday?" Brooke asked.

"Yesterday evening. I went to his house and we—"

"Hold on, you went to his house?" my mother asked.

I nodded. "He lives down the street from Ian and I went over to see him. That's when we met."

Brooke looked shocked. My mother looked worried.

"So, let me understand this," my mother began. "After the most humiliating episode of his life—"

"Possibly *any* life," Ian added.

"All right, any life," my mother agreed. "After that, you walked up to the door of a boy you didn't know and asked to speak to him. Is that right?"

"Yeah, that's about it."

"But . . . why?" Brooke asked.

"I just wanted to talk to him, ask him how he was feeling."

"I think that was pretty obvious," Brooke said.

"Yeah, even I got that," Ian added.

"But I also wanted to tell him that I thought he was brave. And I wanted his advice about what he did, because, really, it got me wondering whether my promposal was such a smart idea."

My mother let out a sigh of relief. "Thank goodness you've decided not to do it."

"Good call," Brooke said.

"I have to agree with the ladies on this one," Ian agreed.

"No, you don't understand. It has made me decide. I am going to do it. If we can work out the details, I'm thinking Friday afternoon toward the end of the day. Trevor and I talked about that."

"You're getting advice from the guy who crashed and burned?" Ian asked.

"Who better? He said that the rest of that day after he was turned down was the hardest time in his life, so going at the very end of the afternoon is better. And a Friday is good because then you have the weekend to stay home and recover. Oh, by the way, I'm going to be walking to school with Trevor on Monday morning."

"You are?" Brooke asked.

"Yes. Me and some of his other friends. We just wanted him to feel like we support him."

"Who arranged all of that?" Brooke asked.

"One of his friends put it up on Facebook."

"I like it," Ian said. "By the way, you might want to get everybody's names and cell numbers."

"Why?"

"I have a terrible feeling that you're going to need some extra company yourself next Monday."

Nobody said a word, which meant they all had been thinking the same thing. And so had I.

Brooke, Ian, and I spent the next few hours viewing, searching, surfing, and making notes. Every half
hour or so, my mother would pop her head into the
room with an offer of snacks or refreshments. I knew
those were legitimate offers, but only half the story.
She really wanted to know what we were planning.
This was more than just being nosey or pushy. She
was worried about me.

She was always worried about me, and she'd been
there to witness many of my social stumbles over the
years. It went without saying that whatever bothered
me, bothered her more. I wasn't so much worried
about how I was going to handle the rejection as I was
about how much it was going to hurt her. I'd have to
help her understand that this was what I wanted to do.
Maybe even needed to do.

"So you're definitely going to go with balloons,"
Brooke said.

"Everybody likes balloons."

"How many balloons?" Ian asked.

"I was thinking five hundred."

"That's a lot of air," Ian said.

"Not air. Helium. I don't want them to fall down
but float up. It's more symbolic."

"Since when have you been into symbolism?"
Brooke asked.

"It's a recent change. Interested in symbolism,
thoughtful, somewhat romantic, and aware of social
cues—those are the characteristics that best describe
me now."

"Surprisingly, that's how I've always seen you," Brooke said.

"Really?"

"Of course not. Have you chosen a color for the balloons?" she asked.

"I'm pretty sure they should be red, which is her favorite color."

"Better be more than just pretty sure," she warned. "You have to know 100 percent."

"I'll check and double-check."

"You are certain about the flowers, though, right?"

"Certain. Roses. Who doesn't love roses?" I asked.

"Well, me," Brooke said. "There's a decadence to them, but more than that they have thorns. Shouldn't love be without thorns?"

"Oh, I get it," Ian said. "Love shouldn't hurt."

"Exactly, although from what I've heard it almost always does," she said. "Now, you need to settle on a tux."

"Already done."

"Which one?" she asked.

"It's a surprise. You'll see it when I make the promposal."

"You're going to wear it that day?" she asked.

"I have to reveal it that day. Some kid puked on my Clown Town uniform, so it still has that lingering aroma to it so I can't wear that for the promposal."

"Point taken. And your final decision on the vehicle. Are you going with the limo?"

"Limo is out. Too pretentious and too eco-unfriendly."

"That's right, Taylor is in the Social Justice Club so the environment is probably important to her," Brooke said.

"Isn't it important to everybody?" I asked.

"It *should* be. So, it is Taylor?" she said.

"I'm still not saying."

"Your chances of success would increase greatly if we could help make the promposal fit the person. Wouldn't it be better if you just admitted that it was Taylor?" She turned to Ian. "Don't you want to know?"

"I do know."

"I think it's Taylor too, but that's still just a guess. You really can't know for sure," she said.

"No, you don't understand. Sam told me who he was asking," Ian said.

She looked shocked. She looked from Ian to me and I nodded.

"You told him, but you didn't tell me?"

"I need his help with a couple of details," I explained.

"I could have taken care of those details. You can't tell me I'm not better at details than *he* is," she said.

"He can handle these details. I trust him."

"I trust him too . . . I trust him to screw up. You can't think he's not going to tell somebody, just blurt it out."

"He hasn't yet."

"How long have you known?" Brooke asked.

"Since he texted me, hours and hours ago," Ian said, holding up his phone.

In one quick motion Brooke grabbed his phone and—

"Don't bother. I deleted the text," he said.

She looked up at him, confused, disbelieving. "Sure you did." She went back to looking at the phone, checking things out. Satisfied, or maybe frustrated, she made a puffing noise and then handed it back.

"It doesn't matter, I know it's Taylor," she said.

"Believe what you want," I said. "You'll find out soon enough."

"I'll find out sooner than soon. Ian will tell me, or somebody else, or he'll tap it out or sing a song or something before you have a chance to make the promposal. Wait, is that why you told him? So she'll find out before you do it and maybe tell you not to bother so you don't get humiliated in public?"

"Of course not."

"Because that's the only reason I can think of for telling him and not me. You trust him *not* to keep the secret!"

"I'm not going to blow it," Ian said. "I'm not going to tell her. It's all going to work out and Sammy and I are going to double-date to the prom. Sam with his date and me with Ashley."

"Ashley, the girl who turned down Trevor in front of the world?"

"It wasn't the whole world. I doubt it went farther than a few English-speaking countries," Ian said.

"Ian, the only thing dumber than Sam confiding in you is you thinking Ashley is going to be your prom date. Do you really want what happened to Trevor to happen to you?"

"It's because of what happened to him that it's not going to happen to me."

"Because the best indicator of future behavior is past behavior?" Brooke said.

"Exactly!" Ian said. "Her past behavior of turning down Trevor increases the odds of her going to the prom with me. Right, Sam?"

"I think those are independent variables at best. Probably Brooke is right."

"Let me explain," Ian said. "Do you think Ashley turning Trevor down that way scared off other potential 'promposers'?"

"Definitely," Brooke said, and I nodded in agreement.

"And because there's less completion I've got a greater chance of success. Ashley has become low-hanging fruit. I can pluck her and then I can—"

"Filter! Filter!" I screamed.

"I was going to say take her to the prom. Honestly."

For whatever reason, I believed him.

"I just have to wait a bit longer," Ian said. "I'm counting on her really wanting to go to the prom and I would become the solution."

"You know she could still just go to the prom with her friends and without you," Brooke said.

"I guess that's a possibility, but only if her friends aren't already going with somebody. Britt has a date and once Taylor has committed to going to the prom then that would be the best time for me to ask Ashley."

"So it *is* Taylor you're asking!" Brooke exclaimed. "Ian gave it away!"

Ian shook his head. "I didn't say Sam was asking her. Doesn't it just make sense that somebody is going to ask Taylor?"

Brooke didn't look quite so pleased with herself all of a sudden.

# CHAPTER FOURTEEN

I watched as a mother, holding her daughter's hand, walked by on the path that ran between the edge of the pond and the bench on which I was sitting. The girl, about three years old or so, pulled at her mother's hand, trying to get closer to the edge of the water, closer to the ducks. She squealed in delight and the ducks quacked back. Both mother and daughter looked happy.

"How are you and the ducks doing on this fine Sunday afternoon?" Brooke said as she sat down on the park bench beside me. She was wearing a flowery dress and a big floppy hat.

"The ducks are fine."

"And you?" she asked.

"Probably not as fine as the ducks, but okay, I guess. How did you find me?"

"I called your house and your mother said you weren't home," she said.

"Not home doesn't exactly narrow down the possibilities. I could have been anywhere in the world."

"You're right, and that's why I checked the Antarctic first, then the Galapagos Islands, and this was my third choice."

"Seriously," I said.

"She said you took a loaf of bread with you so I figured either you were really hungry or you were coming to feed the ducks."

"They are not mutually exclusive categories," I said.

"Probably not, but I know how much you like to feed the ducks."

"They ate the whole loaf. They were even hungrier than me."

"So how long have you been sitting here?" she asked.

"About an hour and a half."

"Feeding the ducks would take five minutes, so what have you been doing besides that?"

"Just thinking," I said.

"Knowing you, you weren't just thinking but overthinking."

"Strange you should say that. I was thinking that I've been overthinking a lot lately."

"You're the only person I know who would spend too much time thinking about the fact that he's thinking too much!"

She was right, but I wasn't going to admit that.

"I was watching the people going by," I said.

"You couldn't have picked a better spot. I love watching people."

The path right in front of our bench ran the length of the park. There was a pretty constant stream of people walking, running, biking, and skate boarding.

"And, of course, you being you, you probably had a theme or a theory you were working out," Brooke said.

"I was trying to pick out who looks happy."

"And your conclusion?" she asked.

"Little kids are happy. Look at the playground," I said.

The nearby playground was small—a couple of slides, some swings, a climbing apparatus. There were a dozen kids of assorted ages playing, and some parents hovering over them, or sitting on a little bench close at hand. As we watched, a little girl fell from the swings and burst into tears, and her parents rushed to her side to help.

"She doesn't seem too happy," Brooke said.

"She has a reason. She's hurt. But it probably won't last. Little kids are like the express elevators in a skyscraper. They're either at the top or the bottom, and they can move from one to the other in seconds."

"So, who else do you think looks happy?" Brooke asked.

"Parents of small children and pregnant women. Pregnant women practically glow with happiness."

"That glow could be nausea, but I think you're probably right. Who else?" she asked.

"People feeding ducks are almost always happy," I said.

"So you think doctors should be prescribing duck-feeding for people who are suffering from depression."

"Depression is different, although I read somewhere that many people who are diagnosed as depressed are really just unhappy," I said.

"Isn't it natural that if you're depressed you're unhappy?" Brooke asked.

"You probably are, but they're still distinct phenomena, and their treatment is different, too. Depression requires medication, and unhappiness requires finding a way to get happy. Giving unhappy people an antidepressant isn't going to help them because they're not depressed, they're unhappy. What they need is to find a way to get happy."

"I get it," she said. "It actually makes sense. How about these two?" Brooke asked, motioning to a couple, holding hands, about our age, coming along the path.

I studied them. "They both look sort of happy, but not the same *level* of happy."

"Now you're just confusing me."

"Look, doesn't one of them look *more* happy than the other?" I asked, pointing at them.

She took my hand and pulled it down. "First off," she said, "don't point, or talk so loudly when the people are almost standing in front of you."

"Sorry," I whispered.

They walked past us.

"He did look happier than her," Brooke said.

"I thought so too. With some couples they both look happy, but with others there's definitely a difference between the two," I said.

"It looked sort of like he was more pleased to be with her than she was to be with him," Brooke said.

"That's what I was thinking. I wish I could interview them and find out."

Brooke laughed. "I'm sure that would go over just wonderfully. 'Excuse me, would you mind telling me which one of you is more into the other?' You wouldn't get answers but you might just make yourself a lot less happy when somebody punched you."

"Socrates said that all men naturally desire happiness," I told her.

"All *people*, not just men," Brooke said.

"My apologies to both you and all the women in the world. Socrates was the first person in western civilization who believed that happiness could be obtained by human effort. Before his time, it was accepted that happiness could only be granted by the gods."

"Is that what this whole promposal thing is about, you trying to be happy?"

"Isn't that what everything everybody does is about?" I asked. "Socrates and Plato asserted that every activity is connected to our quest for happiness."

"And your quest leads through the prom?"

"In *The Republic*, Plato said—"

"Enough of dead Greeks and their philosophy. The only classical thing about all of this is you over-thinking things again. Is that why you want to go to the prom?"

"Couples look happy. Dancing people look happy. Why wouldn't I want to be part of a happy dancing couple?" I asked. "Why wouldn't I want that, too?"

"No reason. But if you get turned down, does that mean you will be unhappy?"

"Probably very unhappy . . . at least at first. Although not trying might make me unhappy and knowing that I tried and failed still might make me happy."

Brooke shook her head. "You know, back in the day, when we were young, you were just about the happiest person I knew."

"I was?"

"You were. And then you started to think too much."

"Come on, I've always thought too much. Nothing new there."

"Yes there is. You started thinking too much about what other people think about you." She paused. "Do you know what? I have a way, guaranteed, to make you happier right now, right here."

"You do?"

She unzipped her purse and pulled out a bag half filled with bread. She got up and walked toward the pond. I followed, pulling out my phone. I wanted to take a few pictures of her and of happy.

# CHAPTER FIFTEEN

"How about if we take a short break?" Taylor asked.

The rest of the group—Ian, Brooke, and Josh, who was in Brooke's class—all readily agreed. We'd been working for the entire lunch period, eating as we worked. I got up and stretched. The library was almost empty so it was like having the place to ourselves. I wondered if the entire school population was out on the front lawn waiting to see if something exciting would happen today.

"I hear that Tanner's finals are really tough, but I think we're going to do well," Taylor said.

"I'm not worried because we're getting such an early start," Ian said. "Taylor, can I ask you and Brooke a question?"

"Of course."

"My mother's birthday is coming up," he said, putting out the agreed-upon lie, "and I was thinking about buying her flowers. What do you think about me getting her roses?"

"I think that would be so sweet!" Taylor said.

"And roses would be good, right?" Ian persisted.

"Who doesn't like roses?"

"So, they're your favorite flowers?" he asked.

"No, I love daisies," Taylor said. "I know they're not fancy but they're just so, I don't know, pure and simple, and I like that about them."

That sounded like something Taylor would say— or Brooke.

"Brooke, what are your favorite flowers?"

"Nothing really fancy, just flowers from a regular garden. Even wildflowers."

"Any color of flowers in particular?" I asked.

"Red. You know red is my favorite color," she said.

"That's right. I forgot."

"And Taylor, what's your favorite color?" Ian asked.

"Red as well." She reached out and she and Brooke exchanged a high-five.

"Just out of curiosity, are blue and yellow Ashley's favorite colors?" Ian asked.

"No, pink."

I knew Ian was noting that for his own potential purposes.

"I just thought with all those yellow and blue balloons at the promposal . . ." Ian said.

Taylor shook her head. "I guess Trevor didn't even know her well enough to know her favorite color. Ash is still feeling bad about the whole thing. She actually likes Trevor."

"She has a funny way of showing it," Josh said.

"That was harsh," Taylor responded.

"Sorry," he said. He looked like a kid who'd been scolded by a parent.

"It's just that she didn't want to go to the prom with him and she felt so . . . so trapped," Taylor explained.

"Did Britt feel that way when Kevin asked her?" I asked.

"No, but that was different . . . she's different. She didn't know the details but she knew Kevin was going to do something."

"I saw my favorite movie last night," Ian said.

He was following the script we'd agreed on to get information, but it was a jarring change in direction.

"It's *True Lies*, with Arnold and Jamie Lee Curtis, a young and incredibly hot Jamie Lee Curtis," Ian said. "I can't watch that movie without thinking about—"

"How about you, Brooke?" I asked, cutting him off.

"Mine is a classic too. *Pretty in Pink*, with Molly Ringwald."

"That's a wonderful movie!" Taylor exclaimed. "I love that she makes her own prom dress."

"Brooke makes a lot of her own clothes," I said. "Didn't you make the dress you're wearing?"

Brooke nodded. She looked a little bit proud and a little bit embarrassed.

"It's so beautiful, and so personal, because there's only one. I wish I could learn how to do that," Taylor said.

"I could teach you. It's not hard."

"Thank you so much Brookey, let's do that."

"Taylor, just out of curiosity, what's your favorite movie?"

"It's an old one too," she said. "*Ten Things I Hate About You*. You know there's this one scene in particular—"

"Heath Ledger singing 'Can't Take My Eyes Off You'?" Brooke asked.

Taylor sighed. "Yes, that was so romantic. Him being there in front of everybody like that and singing that song to Kat. Who wouldn't fall for that?"

"So, if he had sung that song for you, would you have gone to the dance with him?" Brooke asked.

"Wouldn't you?"

Brooke nodded ever so slightly. "Probably."

I looked past them to see Mrs. Tanner walk into the library and drop a couple of books in the return book slot. She saw us as well and came over.

"What an interesting gathering, some of my favorite students from both of my classes," she said. "So, what's happening here?"

"Study group," Ian said.

"Good for you. I wish all of my students would take my course so seriously. Is there anything I can do to help?"

"You could give us the answers to the final exam," Josh suggested.

"I could, but Sam could probably do the same thing."

"He knows the . . . oh, I get it," Ian said.

"Well, I'll let you get back to studying."

"Could I talk to you for a minute, Mrs. Tanner . . . in private?" I asked.

"Of course. Walk me back to class."

I got up and left with her.

"This is convenient since I wanted to talk to you as well," she said as we walked down the hallway.

"About what?" Was this about our Morse Code conversations again? Had she somehow figured out that we really were cheating after all?

"You first."

I wished I'd practiced what I was going to say so the words would come more easily. "I think I need your help with something."

She skidded to a stop, and turned to face me. "Okay, now there's a first, you needing help from a teacher. So, tell me, what can I do for you?"

I swallowed hard. "You know I'm going to make a promposal."

"I certainly remember that conversation. I must admit that you surprised me with that, but then again, you are a continual series of things I didn't see coming. So, how can I help you?"

Other students were streaming by us in the narrow hall and I was getting nervous about being overheard.

"Could we go somewhere we could talk more privately?" I asked.

"Of course."

We continued to her class, she unlocked the door, and we went inside, closing the door behind us.

"This is much better," she said. "Well, what's the plan and how can I help?"

There were still some details to be worked out but I quickly outlined the part of my plan that was set and what I needed from her.

"Impressive and different, but again, I'd expect nothing less. I can easily arrange my part, so you can count on me."

"Thanks so much, I really appreciate it."

"Actually, I'll help you on one condition—no, make that two. And this ties in nicely with what I wanted to talk to you about. You got 96 percent on that last test."

"That's great. I've almost brought my marks back to where they were before."

"But, of course, I'm not telling you anything you didn't already know. You knew you had a 96."

"How would I know that?"

"Because that's what you wanted, a 96, so that was what you got. Why didn't you want to get perfect?"

"Why would you think I didn't?"

"Please, your IQ is well beyond mine but I'm a reasonably smart person. I went back and looked at your four mistakes. In each case you had originally marked in the correct answer, and then erased it to mark an incorrect one."

"I guess I should have gone with my first guess," I said, looking down at the desk.

"I went through the whole test and those are the only four questions where you changed the answer. What an amazing coincidence that the only four you changed were the only mistakes you made. It pushes probability to believe that could just be a coincidence."

"I guess those things happen. Somebody has to win the lottery even though the odds are astronomically against it. They say that truth is stranger than fiction," I suggested, grasping at straws.

"In this case your explanation is the fiction. My first condition for helping you is that you tell me the truth about the test," she said. "If you lie to me, then you're on your own. Now, did you deliberately get those questions wrong so that you could have a lower mark?"

Slowly I nodded.

"You may be the only student in the history of education who basically cheated to get a lower mark."

"It's not really cheating, is it?"

"It's cheating yourself, which might be the

worst thing you could do. So tell me, why did you do it . . . why do you want to get lower marks?"

"It's hard to explain," I said. "It's just that sometimes it's difficult when teachers make a fuss about it, tell everybody how well I do."

"So you'd be okay with a perfect mark as long as nobody knew about it?"

"That would probably be better," I said.

"But still, on some level you really did want to get them all right. Why else would you have filled them in correctly to begin with?"

I didn't know what to say, but I knew she was right.

"And the other condition?" I asked.

"You have to get 100 percent on the final exam."

"But the exam doesn't happen until after the prom," I said.

"That doesn't matter. If you promise me you'll do it, then I know you'll do it, or at least I know you won't deliberately get answers wrong. Well?"

"Deal."

We shook hands to make it official.

# CHAPTER SIXTEEN

"Welcome," Dr. Young said. "Have a seat."

She sat down in her swivel chair while I settled into one of the big, comfy leather armchairs. I always liked sitting in these chairs because I felt like they were giving me a hug. They were safe and warm and I'd missed them. Not that I'd tell her or anybody else that.

"It's been a while since our last session," she said.

"Thirty-seven weeks."

"Not that you were counting."

"You know I don't have a lot of control over remembering things," I said.

"Of course. So, how are you doing?"

"I'm doing very well. Probably a lot better than my mother thinks I am."

"She did seem distressed when she called to

arrange for the session. I'm glad you agreed to see me."

"She means well. She must be more worried than I thought," I said.

"She is worried. Is this all about your planned promposal?"

"She told you about it."

"Actually, I've had a running account of it from Ian."

Ian still saw Dr. Young on a regular basis, and back when I was seeing her too, we had given permission for her to talk to either of us about the other. Sometimes we'd even had sessions together— sort of like couples therapy, except of course we were just a couple of friends.

"He was so proud of you trusting him with the name of your potential prom date. That was very caring of you to share that information with him."

"He is my best friend. Well, he and Brooke."

"But you didn't tell Brooke. You told the person who has a lengthy history of not being able to keep anything secret."

"He's doing much better," I said.

"It would appear. He made a point of not even telling me. By the way, I wanted to thank you again for coming up with the idea for him to tap out his comments in Morse Code. That was a stroke of genius on your part," she said.

"You know, he doesn't even do that as much as he used to."

"He's had some breakthroughs, and, as I understand it, so have you. So tell me, what is upsetting your mother so much about you asking this girl to the prom?"

"She doesn't want me to get hurt."

"And this could cause you to be hurt."

"If I get turned down it will be in front of everybody at the school, and very likely it will also be put online and go viral. Did Ian tell you about a guy called Trevor and what happened to him?"

"Yes, he did," Dr. Young said. "That must have been very hard on him."

"It was hard enough just to watch it."

"But still, you want to do the same thing," Dr. Young said.

"Not exactly the same thing. I'd like my promposal to be accepted."

"And do you think it will be?"

I hesitated. I didn't want to give her a simple, flip answer. I wanted to answer the question using the variables and data available.

"You're doing math in your mind right now, aren't you?" she asked.

I nodded.

"I don't want math, I want your opinion."

"Well, when this started Brooke labeled it 'Mission Impossible.'"

"That's her opinion. And yours?"

I let out a big sigh. "Initially it was, at best, a long shot."

"Ten percent chance of success?" she asked.

"That sounds like mathematics to me, but yes, about that, or maybe less."

"But with the odds that bad, you still wanted to do it."

"Yes."

"Some people would consider that admirable, maybe even noble. Don Quixote tilted at windmills," Dr. Young said.

"Hopefully, I'm of sounder mind than that, but I think I'm on a quest just the same."

"A quest for what?"

"To ask a girl to the prom."

"I see," she said.

I hated "I see" because most of the time it meant that I didn't see and she didn't either. It was like somebody saying "honest" or "trust me," which always meant you had to worry.

"And do you think that going to the prom will make you more 'normal'?" she asked.

I laughed. "Aren't you the one who always says there's no such thing as 'normal,' that all people are made up more or less of a number of different but common attributes?"

"It's good to know you remember some of what we talked about."

"I remember *everything* we talked about because I remember, well, everything. Besides, what's wrong with wanting to be more normal?"

"Nothing. Do you still feel like Pinocchio?" Dr. Young asked.

"So we've gone from seventeenth-century Spanish writers to nineteenth-century Italian writers. Is that progress?" I asked.

"Pinocchio is *your* reference, not mine. I remember the things we talk about too. You were the one who said you were on a journey to become a real boy. Is the prom part of it?"

"Part of growing up. Did you go to your prom?"

"I did."

"And do you regret going?"

"I think you're trying to change the subject," she said.

"I thought proms were the subject. Tell me about your prom. I really want to know."

Dr. Young looked as though she was thinking. I wasn't sure if she was going to answer or not.

"I was taken to the prom by a young man named Bruno. It was different back then. He just asked me and I said yes." She laughed. "I had no idea he was going to ask me, and I really wasn't so sure that I wanted to go with him."

"But you said yes."

"I felt I couldn't say no. Unlike that young lady, her name was Ashley, right?"

I nodded.

"She not only had the right to say no, but she had the strength to do it. I wasn't that strong. Besides, I did want to go to the prom. Doesn't everybody?"

"I guess 'normal' people do. So, tell me about it," I said.

"The night of the prom Bruno showed up at my house with a dozen red roses and a corsage for my wrist. He was dressed in a black tux and he had a fancy white car waiting for us outside."

"That all sounds very good."

"In the beginning he was such a gentleman, running to open doors and pulling out my chair and getting me drinks."

"Can I assume you said 'in the beginning he was such a gentleman' because he was less so as the night went on?"

"I'm impressed that you'd pick that out. I'm afraid that's correct. As the night went on he snuck a few drinks, and that led to a few more, until he was rip-roaring drunk. One of the most memorable moments of that evening involves my date and one of his friends having a contest in the parking lot to see who could leave the longest trail as they walked and urinated. They actually had a literal pissing contest!"

"I didn't see that one coming," I said.

"Neither did I." She stopped and got a far-away look in her eyes. "You know, despite the lack of a storybook ending to the evening I never regretted going."

"So why do you think I'm going to regret it?" I asked.

"I didn't say I thought that you would."

"So you're not going to try to talk me out of going any more?"

"I was never going to try to talk you out of any-thing. I just want to make sure you know why you're going. Do you?"

"I do know."

"And are you going to share that with me?"

"Well, there's this girl, and I like her a lot, and I thought that she and I could get dressed up and go and have a meal and dance."

Dr. Young smiled. "That sounds like a very good reason to ask somebody to the prom. But why the elaborate promposal?"

"It's the way it's done these days. Besides, I want her to know that I'd be willing to go to a lot of trouble for her."

"Even if she turns you down?"

"Especially if she turns me down. 'It is better to have loved and lost than never to have loved at all.'"

"So now you're quoting Tennyson," she said. "Just remember that his best known poem is 'The Charge of the Light Brigade.' 'Into the valley of Death' and all that. No one lived."

"I'm not going to die," I said. "Although I'm aware of the possibility that I might feel like I want to if she turns me down."

"And what are the odds now of getting a yes?"

"Still not good, but better than they were. I think it might be a thirty-seventy split."

"And the yes, the acceptance of your promposal, is represented by the thirty in that fraction?"

"Yes, and that might still be wildly optimistic."

"And knowing all of that, you're still prepared to take the chance?" Dr. Young asked.

"I am."

"Even if her turning you down not only makes you feel terrible but might alienate you from her for all time?" she asked.

Wait . . . I'd thought about the first part a lot, but not the second. Her turning me down could change everything forever. Regardless, I knew I had to do what I had to do.

"I'm going to do it. So, do I have your blessing?"

"You don't need my blessing or my permission. Or that of your parents. Maybe you're tilting at windmills. Maybe you're just trying to evolve, like Pinocchio. Maybe this is the charge into the valley of Death, but you have every right to try."

"You'll tell my parents, my mother?"

"No, that's something you have to do. After all, anybody brave enough to do what you're going to do is brave enough to talk to his parents. Will you do me a favor, though, and come back and tell me what happens, so I'll know?"

"You'll know within two days. Especially if I crash and burn. I'll have a video to prove it!"

# CHAPTER SEVENTEEN

I was going over the details one more time. I was actually obsessing over the details, trying to read them the way a fortune-teller reads tea leaves. I'd have had better luck with the tea leaves.

It was almost one in the morning. Lack of sleep was not going to increase the odds in my favor.

My phone vibrated and I picked it up. It was a text from Brooke.

*R u still up?*

*No I'm sleep texting. Why r u up?* I tapped back.

*Can't sleep. Worried.*

*Why r u worried? U making a promposal tomorrow?* I tapped out and sent.

Almost instantly my phone rang and I grabbed it before the first ring had finished.

"You know you're not nearly as funny as you think you are," she said.

"I wasn't trying to be funny. I just thought I'd inspired you to ask somebody to the prom. It's not too late if you're going to ask me."

"You? I was thinking about asking Ian," she replied.

"I always thought there was something between the two of you."

"I'm hoping there will always be something between us, maybe a wall, a restraining order, or a continent."

"She doth protest too much."

"What?"

"Shakespeare. Be relieved that at least it's not from *Romeo and Juliet*," I said.

"*Romeo and Juliet* might come in handy tomorrow, when you make the promposal. The outcome might be equally tragic."

"Like I said to Dr. Young, nobody is going to die. I can live with embarrassment. I've had lots of practice at it."

"Exactly, past tense, you *had* lots of practice. You hardly ever say or do anything stupid any more."

"That's probably the nicest thing you've ever said to me in the whole time I've known you."

"Come on, I must have said something nice to you back in the day," she said.

"I don't know about that, but I do remember the very first thing you ever said to me."

"You do?"

"Of course. It was 'Give me the Lego.' And then you punched me."

She laughed. "I remember the punch."

"I've been punched harder . . . by you."

"Are you going to bring that up again?" she asked. "That last punch was more than four years ago. Not that I haven't thought of punching you since then."

"I appreciate your restraint."

"Just out of curiosity, if I threatened to beat you up if you went ahead with this, would it stop you?"

"If I was worried about being beaten up I wouldn't do it to begin with. I have to do this."

"You don't *have* to do anything. You don't *need* to go to the prom at all. Just hang out with me and Ian the night of the prom," Brooke said.

"What if Ashley actually accepts Ian's promposal?"

"Okay, I was wrong, you are funny. Seriously, you don't have to do this."

"It's too late to back out," I said.

"It's not too late until the second before you cue the music." She paused . . . for a long time. "Is she really worth it?"

"I think so."

"Okay, then there's nothing more I can say, is there?"

"Just be there. I couldn't do this without you being there," I said.

"I'll be there. I promise."

"Thank you, Brooke. Now go to bed. You know how cranky you get when you don't get enough sleep."

# CHAPTER EIGHTEEN

The bell sounded to signal the end of the morning and the start of lunch. I let out a loud, long sigh as people filed out.

I got up and turned to Ian. "Lunch, thank goodness."

"Yeah, I won't be coming with you today."

"You're not going to have lunch?"

"I'm going to eat, just not with you and Brooke. I can't risk talking to her or somebody else in case I just blurt things out. I'm going to eat by myself. It's too close, and my mind is going too fast. See you, you know, when it's time."

"I understand, and thanks for thinking of that."

"No, thank you for trusting me."

"There's nobody I trust more."

To my complete surprise he reached out and gave me a hug, a big long hug. The few people still in the room reacted—twittering and giggling. I started to feel a rush of embarrassment and then stopped myself. There was nothing wrong with a guy hugging his best friend. I hugged him back.

"See you later," he said as he released me. "I'm going to go behind the scenes and make sure things work out."

He left. Now it was just me and Mrs. Tanner in the room.

"For a minute there I thought you'd made your promposal to Ian," she said.

"No, you don't understand! We were—"

She started to laugh. "I know, I know . . . not that there would be anything wrong with that. So you're ready, things are in place?"

"Things are in place, but I'm not sure if I'm ready."

"It's not too late to back out."

"Everybody keeps saying that to me."

"I'm not trying to convince you to back out, Samuel. I think your plan is, well, sweet. Now we'd both better get to lunch."

Brooke was waiting in our usual place. She looked worried, and instead of sitting on the grass she was standing.

"Where were you?" she asked.

"Class."

"And where's Ian?" she demanded.

"Busy."

She looked all around. "Is it happening now? At lunch? I don't even see her so you can't—"

"Slow down, please. It's all right. Ian is just taking care of a few details. That's all he's doing."

"Okay, sure."

I sat down, and she sat down beside me.

"I have to hand it to him. He hasn't told me, or, as far as I know, anybody."

"I knew he wouldn't," I said.

"Knew or hoped?"

"Both. You have to have hope . . . I still have hope."

"Sometimes it's better to travel hopefully than to arrive," Brooke said.

"I've always liked that saying. Do you know who wrote it?"

"I'm not sure . . . wait . . . you don't know?" she questioned.

"There are lots of things I don't know."

Our thoughts were cut off by the sound of loud music and a black BMW that drove slowly along the curved driveway. I didn't have to think twice to know what was happening. This had certainly become the prime place for public promposals.

The music was easy to pick out. Ed Sheeran, "Give Me Love."

"Nice choice," Brooke said.

"It's no 'Dancing Queen,' but I like it too."

The car came to a stop as the music ended. Change the song and the car and this looked a lot like Kevin's promposal. A guy got out—thank goodness he wasn't wearing a football jersey. I recognized him immediately. His name was Carlos. He and his girlfriend Eva had been together forever and it was rare to see one without the other.

Before she was even asked Eva came forward, slipping through the circling crowd. He said something that was too quiet for me to hear. Eva squealed—that I could hear! He reached into the car and pulled something out. What was it? It was white and . . . it was a pair of white wings, like the ones worn by the angel or the cupid in the Sheeran video. He turned her around and helped her put them on. Nice touch. Very nice touch.

They hugged and kissed and then waved as they tried to climb into the car. Her wings got in the way and she had to bend one of them a bit as she finally pushed inside. The music came on again as the car started to drive off.

"Well, on the three-*P* scale, that was Public, but not especially Pompous. Maybe it was really Personal, depending on just how much she loves that Ed Sheeran song."

"And it wasn't exactly brave," Brooke said. "Although it would have really been something if he had asked somebody else."

"Or if she'd turned him down," I added. "Now that would have been brave of her."

"I don't think you should even joke about a girl turning somebody down today."

"I guess it's like whistling past a cemetery."

In the background I heard more music—big marching band music. I wasn't completely caught by surprise.

"Is this yours, did you arrange for this?" Brooke questioned.

"Not me," I said, holding up my hands.

"Because if this is your promposal then it is a terrible idea. It's just bad, bad karma to repeat what happened to Trevor."

"Maybe they're just practicing."

"Even you can't believe that. I recognize the song—'Stay With Me' by Sam Smith . . . it's a promposal for sure."

Brooke wasn't the only person thinking that. The band was like the Pied Piper and the crowd came along with them, everybody anticipating what—and who—this was going to involve.

It wasn't the whole band this time, maybe half. I could understand why Trevor wouldn't want to be part of this . . . wait . . .

"There's Trevor," I gasped. He and his trumpet were in the first row of the band.

"That is one incredible way to handle this, returning to the scene of the crime, or in this case the scene of the rejection."

"It's okay, his friends are with him," I said.

The marching band came to a stop directly in front of where we were sitting—and in front of Taylor, Brittney, and Ashley, as well. I had a terrible fear. He wasn't asking her again, was he? Then another thought. Was somebody going to ask Taylor, right now, right here, in front of our eyes?

The band stopped playing and there was a moment of silent anticipation. Out of the crowd a girl came forward, and she was carrying a bouquet of roses.

"Who is that?" Brooke asked.

"You think I would know?"

"I'm here today," the girl began, "because I want to make a promposal."

The crowd roared with approval and a couple of people yelled out her name—Lucy. "Way to go, Lucy!"

She held up her arms to silence everybody. "I should have done this earlier. I almost lost my chance." She turned so she was facing the marching band. "You are the kindest, nicest boy I ever met. I knew that. Over the past week I've learned that you are even more amazing than I thought. Trevor, could you please come forward?"

There was a second of stunned silence as everybody processed what she'd just said, and then an explosion of applause and cheering.

I scanned the band, finding Trevor. He stumbled forward, one of his band mates holding his trumpet and two others taking him by the arms and leading him out of the pack.

The cheering got louder and louder as he came forward and Lucy dropped to one knee. She was saying something—I could just see her lips moving. Trevor reached down, pulled her to her feet, and they kissed. It was a big, lean her over backwards movie kiss, and the crowd just went crazy! People were screaming, jumping up and down, cheering and clapping, and it kept going on and on and on.

I turned. There was one person's reaction I wanted to see. There she was—Ashley—and she was cheering as loudly as anybody. Lucy hadn't only freed Trevor.

Brooke leaned in close so that she could say something to me over the wall of sound.

"That was beautiful," she said.

"It was."

"But it leaves you in a bind. How do you possibly top that?"

"I'm not sure I can," I admitted.

"Did you think somebody was asking Taylor?" she yelled.

"I thought about it."

"That would have ruined everything you planned!"

"It would have put a dent into things," I agreed.

"So it is Taylor!"

I shook my head. "Just wait. You'll find out soon enough!"

# CHAPTER NINETEEN

We shuffled into the auditorium, along with every other student in the school. It was always a game for some students to see if they could sneak out a door or hide out somewhere to avoid having to go to the assembly. Unfortunately for them, the teachers were just as good at that game and they'd been playing it for longer. They knew all the hiding places and positioned themselves at all the exits, herding everybody into the auditorium, where they then stood at the doors.

Brooke and I settled into seats at the front. There was never much competition for the front row. The farther back the better for most people, and I understood that. For me, being with Brooke was more important than blending into the crowd, and she always wanted to be up front. Her excuse was that she was often called up on stage to deliver reports on the various clubs and activities she was part of. The truth, though, was that she had made us sit there in our freshman year as well, when her only extra-curricular activity was trying to find her way around the school. She just liked to be close to the action.

"Still no Ian," she said.

"He's still occupied with *very* last-minute details."

"So this is it. You're going to do it here, in front of every single student and teacher in the school."

I nodded my head. Hearing her say it made it more real.

"I've got to give you marks for Public. This is a true act of bravery."

"Or stupidity," I said.

"Or both. At least when it goes wrong you won't have long to wait before the end of school."

"Thanks for the vote of confidence."

"I shouldn't have said that. I know it's going to go right, one way or another."

That was a little cryptic. It could only go one way or the other, and one way was very, very wrong. There weren't a lot of variables in this equation.

"So, where are the balloons?" she asked.

"You'll see soon enough."

"Is Ian with the balloons?"

"It's all taken care of."

"And aren't you supposed to be dressed, you know, better than this? Isn't that the plan?"

"Don't worry," I said.

"And your transportation. Is it waiting outside?" she asked.

"It's waiting. Don't worry about a thing."

"How can you possibly be this calm?"

"I'm not that calm. My armpits are practically floating I'm in such a flop sweat."

"Too much information," she said. "And by the way, try not to work that into your promposal, okay?"

I laughed. Against all odds, I laughed.

Our vice-principal came onstage and called out for everybody to be quiet. It took a few seconds, and he silenced the last few rumbles by simply raising his arms above his head. Other people in the audience saw it and silenced the noisy ones.

Mr. Roberts had a reputation for not taking any disrespect. In one of the first assemblies of the year, at the end of a school day, he'd stood on stage silently waiting for the audience to settle down. When they didn't, he just continued to stand there, waiting, and, I noticed, looking at his watch. Almost ten minutes passed before it was quiet enough for him to start. He then kept the whole school in for ten minutes at the end of the assembly. He'd never had to do that again.

The usual collection of school announcements and pronouncements began. Assorted students and staff came to the front and gave nervous little blurbs about their clubs or teams. Some people appeared to be quite calm, casual, almost matter-of-fact, as though they were just talking to a couple of friends instead of standing in front of 1,500 people.

For others it was more like they were standing naked in front of the entire world, and the people in the audience were carrying the weapons of their execution and the cameras to record it. I'd never been up there before so I didn't know what it was going to feel like for me.

Mrs. Tanner was introduced and walked across the stage toward the podium. I was going to find out how it felt soon enough.

"Good afternoon," she began. "I'm here to introduce a very special part of our day. Could Samuel Davies please come up to the stage."

I got up and headed toward the stage accompanied by a scattering of awkward applause. The clapping trailed off as I walked up the steps and across the stage in silence, surprised by the glare of the lights and the imagined glare of the audience. I couldn't see anyone. I reached the podium and took refuge behind it, using it as a shield.

"It's all yours," Mrs. Tanner said quietly to me. "You're going to do great."

"Thanks," I mumbled. My tongue felt thick and my mouth suddenly was very, very dry.

I gave a gesture to the invisible Ian in the booth at the back of the auditorium. Instantly, right in front of the curtains in the center of the stage, a screen dropped down from the ceiling and a bright beam from the digital projector came on.

I reached behind the podium and pulled free one red balloon. I held onto it as it tried to float away. I understood how it felt. I wanted to escape too.

The lights dimmed, putting most of the auditorium into darkness. There was no escape for me, though, as a spotlight came on aimed directly at me and the podium.

"Good afternoon," I said and my words bounced around the room. I backed away a little from the microphone. "I'm here today to make a special invitation."

The silence in the room was replaced by a loud buzz of conversation—everybody knew what was going to happen next, although, of course, they didn't know the who or the how. I raised my arms the way Mr. Roberts had. To my surprise, it worked.

I picked up a little remote off the top of the podium and clicked to my first slide. In big letters it read simply "The Promposal."

I thought through to the next step. The whole plan, all of the words were in my head, as clear as if I were reading them. That was one of those advantages that was built into my hard-wiring.

"I'm standing here in front of everybody, but you need to know that I'm only speaking to one person."

A low-level rumbling started up again. I was sure people were talking about who it was, who it could be.

"This balloon is for you," I said. I raised my arm to let it fly just a little higher.

I used the remote to move to the next slide. It was filled with balloons.

"These are the 499 red balloons that I'm not giving to you," I said.

I hit the next slide. Two white horses were hitched to an intricate, elaborate white carriage.

"This is the horse-drawn carriage that we won't be going to the prom in."

I clicked for the next slide.

"Here is the bicycle built for two that will get us there. Not only is it environmentally friendly, but we'll get some exercise along the way."

I clicked the slide again and a beautiful corsage appeared. "This is the expensive, exotic corsage made up of flowers found only in the Amazon jungle . . . that I'm not going to give you."

I clicked to the next slide.

"And here are the flowers from my mother's garden that she said I could pick for you."

A swell of sound went up from the audience. For a second I thought it was disapproval, but I soon realized it was a bunch of female voices going "*Aaaawwww!*" all at once. That gave me confidence that what I was doing wasn't completely stupid.

I advanced one more slide to show a man wearing a tuxedo.

"This is an exact replica of the midnight-blue tuxedo James Bond wore in *Skyfall*."

It did look awfully good.

"But I'm not, as you know, James Bond."

I clicked it forward again. It was a picture of my father with big hair wearing a bright baby-blue tuxedo. Laughter replaced the "*Aaaawwww*"s.

"For better or worse, I'm my father's son, and this is the tuxedo he wore at his wedding to my mother. It fits me. It may not be stylish, but you'll be able to pick me out across the room. Even in total darkness. I think it glows."

There was more laughter and some hooting as I forwarded to the next slide. It was a picture of a female model wearing a very fancy prom dress made of ribbons, sequins, and ostrich feathers.

"This is the dress I'm positive you'd never be caught dead in." I clicked again to a slide that showed a bolt of cloth—red—and a pair of tailoring shears. "If you need any assistance in making your own dress, I can get you some help."

I clicked on the next slide. There was a check made out for $973.

"That is the amount of money it would have cost me to buy all the things in the slides that I didn't buy. That's the amount of money I donated toward building a well in Kenya, because I know that's important to you."

I clicked on a slide showing a well being constructed. I could feel the reaction of the crowd.

I advanced it again and it simply said: "Will you go to the prom with me?"

"I've thought about this for a long time. I want you to know that there's no pressure. Whether you say yes, or you say no, I won't think anything less of you. You're a wonderful person, and you're the only person I want to be with for prom."

I advanced to the last slide. It was a picture of Brooke, the picture I'd taken the day we were feeding the ducks, wearing her floppy hat and flowery dress.

"Brooke, I know you don't believe in proms, but I hope you believe in me more than you don't believe in them. Would you do me the great honor of being my prom date?"

The audience erupted in cheers. A smaller spotlight appeared from the rafters and searched the front rows of the audience until it located her. In the light I could now see her face—she looked completely and utterly stunned.

"Brooke? Could you please come up to the stage?" I asked.

She got up, climbed the steps, and crossed the stage. The cheers from the audience were louder with each step, and the noise got so loud that I could almost feel it blowing my hair back. She stopped right beside me.

I suddenly realized that she'd come up onto the stage but she hadn't actually said yes. That realization made my heart almost stop beating.

"Well, Brooke?" I asked.

She pulled me closer so she could speak into my ear. "Before I answer, I need to know, when did you decide to invite me instead of Taylor?"

"It was never Taylor."

"Never?" she asked.

"It always *was* you. It always *has* been you. It always *will* be you."

"Why didn't you say something before this?" she demanded.

"It is supposed to be a surprise, isn't it? Well?"

"You are such an idiot." She paused. "And this is my answer."

She reached over and gave me a kiss—my first kiss. I felt thrilled and embarrassed and shocked all at once. The audience screamed even louder, but it didn't matter at all.

Two members of the AV crew walked onto the stage pushing the bicycle built for two from my slide show. I took the bike and gestured for Brooke to take the front seat.

"I thought you'd like to steer."

She took a piece of paper out of her pocket and handed it to me.

"What's this?" I asked.

"It's the promposal I was going to make to you."

"What?"

"I didn't know what Taylor was going to say, but if she said no I was going to ask you to the prom, right there and then."

"But if you wanted to go, why didn't you just ask me?"

"I wanted you to be happy, and I thought Taylor would make you happy."

"I am happy, and you are amazing," I said.

"Yes, I *am* amazing."

We climbed on the bike—Brooke in front and steering—and started to wobble until we picked up speed. The audience jumped to their feet, screaming and yelling. The stage wasn't that wide so the bike ride would have to end soon. That was okay. I was pretty sure we had a longer, even happier ride ahead of us.

**ERIC WALTERS**, a former elementary school teacher, began writing as a way to encourage his students to become more enthusiastic about literature. His young adult novels have won numerous awards, been translated into more than a dozen languages and are available around the world. He is the driving force behind The Creation of Hope (www.creationofhope.com)—an organization that serves orphans and needy children in Kenya.

In 2014 Eric was named a Member of the Order of Canada "for his contribution as an author of literature for children and young adults whose stories help young readers grapple with complex social issues."

For more information go to www.ericwalters.net.

# Conglomerate Enterprise
## and
### Public Policy

# Conglomerate Enterprise and Public Policy

JESSE W. MARKHAM
*Charles E. Wilson Professor of Business Administration*
*Harvard University*

**Division of Research**
Graduate School of Business Administration
Harvard University

**Boston**

Library of Congress Catalog Card No. 73-75882
ISBN 0-87584-104-X

*Faculty research at the Harvard Business School is under-
taken with the expectation of publication. In such publication the Faculty member responsible for the research
project is also responsible for statements of fact, opinions,
and conclusions expressed. Neither the Harvard Business
School, its Faculty as a whole, nor the President and Fel-
lows of Harvard College reach conclusions or make rec-
ommendations as results of Faculty research.*

Printed in the United States of America

# Foreword

THIS STUDY OF THE LARGE DIVERSIFIED FIRM by Professor Jesse W. Markham has been directed primarily at the antitrust implications of those corporate acquisitions known variously as a "conglomerate" or "diversifying" acquisition. There has been a wave of this type of merger or acquisition during the 1960s, and it has stirred up a major controversy as to whether such acquisitions were or were not circumventing the competitive forces of the market and, if so, whether they could be curbed by existing legislation or would require new legislation. This study was designed to provide a factual foundation relating to diversifying acquisitions and the conglomerate corporation which would bear on this controversy.

Until the last few years the enforcement of the antimerger legislation (the 1950 amendment of Section 7 of the Clayton Act) had been aimed at horizontal and vertical acquisitions. In these cases the change in market structure resulting from the acquisition could be assessed directly for a possible substantial lessening of competition in a given market. A variety of measurable tests had been devised to analyze such acquisitions. In the case of a conglomerate acquisition, however, there is no immediate change in market structure in any line of commerce. The identity of the competitors would have changed, and there would probably be a change in the financial strength of one of the competitors, but whether competition itself would have been injured cannot be ascertained by the usual criteria.

The wave of conglomerate acquisitions and the rise of a substantial number of giant conglomerate corporations in the 1960s, however, became a key issue for those concerned with the functioning of the market economy. Some feared that this movement would increase aggregate concentration in the hands of the largest 100 or 200 largest corporations. Others believed that the increased financial strength of the acquiring firm would lead to relatively more rapid growth of that firm and increased concentration in the particular markets involved. Finally, still others were concerned with behavioral patterns of the conglomerate corporation and feared that the acquisition wave was eliminating significant potential competitors, substituting asset growth by acquisition for new capital formation, providing fertile ground for reciprocity and for subsidizing weak products with the excess profits of stronger products, and for entrenching the strong competitive position of leading firms.

Many of these concerns were speculative in nature. There was no generally accepted economic theory of the behavior of such diversified firms and there was no generally accepted theory of corporate management practice which would support such concerns. In addition, there was no body of empirical case studies to provide the foundation for a solid theory of the expected behavior of the conglomerate firm and for the market effects of such diversification. Basically there was a scarcity of relevant facts and analyses relating to the conglomerate or diversified corporation problem.

This was the situation when Professor Markham proposed this research project in December 1968. Professor Markham had only recently joined the Faculty of the Harvard Business School, and he saw an opportunity to supplement his earlier work as an economist in this field with the more intimate knowledge of and interest in the management practices of American business organizations of his colleagues here. He hoped to enrich our knowledge of these problems by a blend of the approaches of economics and business administration.

His research plan called for starting with a set of intensive case studies of several conglomerates or diversified corporations to examine especially the acquisition patterns of such firms and the decision-making processes of such firms. He then planned to conduct a survey of approximately the 1,000 largest United States corporations which would include a large number of diversified firms to check some of the more important findings from the intensive sample, to test the validity of certain hypotheses generated from the initial analysis, and to establish possible differences in patterns of practices between diversified and nondiversified companies.

This volume reports the results of this research program. It clearly adds to our knowledge of the nature of the wave of diversifying acquisitions in the decade of the 1960s and its effects on the structure of the economy. It examines and sheds light on many of the alleged harmful effects on competition which are feared to result from this type of acquisition and it discusses the public policy implications of such findings. Finally, it relates the findings to the economic theory of the firm and comments on the applicability of existing economic theory to this more complex type of business organization.

The research itself has been spread over the last three years and has been supported by two generous grants from the United States Chamber of Commerce Foundation. The School is deeply indebted to the Foundation for this support of an important project in its research program.

Soldiers Field                                  Bertrand Fox
Boston, Massachusetts                         Formerly Director
July 1973                                   Division of Research

# Preface

THE ACCELERATED PACE AT WHICH DIVERSIFYING ACQUISITIONS occurred in the 1960s set off a new wave of speculation over the implications the new and more numerous "conglomerates" held for the functioning of the market economy. Given the nation's long-standing public policy of maintaining competition, and the more vigorous prosecution of business mergers in recent years as a particularly manifest expression of that policy, most of the speculation has understandably evolved around the antitrust significance of conglomerates.

On the one hand, those who equate the newly created conglomerates with a distinctive form of monopoly power have viewed their emergence with predictable apprehension. This power, it is urged, derives from the conglomerate's unique capacity to engage in cross-product subsidization, to exploit its wider opportunities for reciprocity dealings, and to profit from the atmosphere of competitive forebearance it engenders. Such tactics eventually lead to increased market concentration and its consequent enfeeblement of the competitive process. These concerns have loomed large in the emerging public policy toward diversifying acquisitions—those consummated in the 1960s, and those now in progress.

Others, viewing the broad contours of essentially the same phenomenon, have found less cause for disquietude; some even reasons for subdued approval. Hence, they contend that conglomerates not only confront disincentives for engaging in the alleged anticompetitive practices, they are moved to such desirable economic ends as more efficient resource allocation, greater economic stability, and a larger commitment to technological progress.

Those who would have occasion to review the vast and

growing body of literature on conglomerate enterprise would, I believe, find most of these conflicting hypotheses equally plausible. They all turn ultimately on how conglomerate firms are managed. The factual evidence on this important matter is not only woefully meager, but that which does exist (developed largely by students of business management) does not address the policy issues. The primary objective of this study has been to close, or at least to narrow, this factual void. Concomitantly, it sought to integrate certain aspects of the economic theory of the firm with the pertinent research output on business management in the hope of modest benefit to both. The result makes no pretense of being a giant step for mankind, but I believe it represents progress along a path that merits additional traffic, even pedestrian traffic.

Since the scope and plan of the research, along with the variety of data used to implement it, are described fully in Chapter 3, there would appear to be no reason to reproduce a condensed version of this descriptive material here. However, I wish to acknowledge my special indebtedness to the management of several large diversified companies (all but ITT and Textron prefer to remain anonymous) who advised me during the initial stages of the project on the form and structure of the detailed data request eventually sent to 600 large corporations, and to the 211 companies that supplied all or most of the requested data. A list of the responding companies, except for the 36 preferring not to be identified by name, appears in Appendix E.

In the two years while this project was in progress, I have had the invaluable help of several research assistants: Marilyn Stewart of the faculties of Mount Ida Junior College and the Boston Conservatory; Jon Didrichsen and John Dory, both doctoral students at the Harvard Graduate School of Business Administration; and Sandy Cole, who for the past two years has doubled as my research assistant and secretary.

In the formulation of the various regression models appearing in Chapter 6, and in the interpretations of their solutions in the form of what impresses me as an incredibly large stack of computer printouts, I have benefited greatly from the guidance and counsel of my colleagues in managerial economics. Mr. Bing Sung provided me with a thorough critical review of an earlier draft of Chapter 6, and he, Dr. Betty Bock, and Earle Birdzell, offered helpful comments on the entire manuscript.

I should like also to acknowledge the generous financial assistance that made the project possible. A grant from the General Electric Foundation enabled me to convert some preliminary ideas on how one might approach this very large subject and work it into a reasonably specific research proposal. A United States Chamber of Commerce Foundation grant to the Harvard Business School supported the two years of research that went into the project.

Finally, I should like to acknowledge help received from a very special and much cherished source. A small but dedicated group of Harvard College students—in the case of some with senior theses in mind——have with some frequency initiated discussions with me on the subject with which this study is concerned; sometimes in my office, occasionally over lunch in their respective Houses. My son Jesse, Jr., served as the unabashed traffic manager. The enthusiastic interest displayed in their probing questions, perceptive observations, and critical comments has throughout sustained my view that this has been a subject worth exploring.

Soldiers Field           JESSE W. MARKHAM
Boston, Massachusetts
December 1972

# Table of Contents

# List of Tables

Conglomerate Enterprise
and
Public Policy

# 1. Conglomerate Mergers: An Overview

## THE POLICY SETTING

MERGERS, MORE THAN ANY OTHER SINGLE BUSINESS activity, have excited the interest and absorbed the energies of students of industrial organization. The merger wave of the late nineteenth century gave birth to a stream of books and articles on trusts and consolidations, and to the creation of courses bearing this or a similar title. The waves of the 1920s and the immediate postwar period of 1947–1950 rekindled the interest and absorbed the research efforts of another generation of students and scholars. The relevant data, and the public pronouncements they have prompted, suggest that we are currently experiencing, or may have just experienced, still another wave of merger activity — a wave that differs in important respects from those of earlier periods in that it is being generated very largely by diversifying, or more popularly "conglomerate," acquisitions. As a consequence, the current merger wave presumably is registering a new and distinctive impact on the structure and functioning of the market economy, and is confronting public policy toward the

1

private sector with a new and distinctive set of policy issues.

Recurrent upsurges in merger activity have, again more than any other business activity, shaped the course and substantive content of our antitrust policy. Congress enacted the Sherman Act in 1890, the nation's parent antitrust statute, in response to the trust and combination movement in progress at that time. The Federal Trade Commission Act and the Clayton Act of 1913 were Congress's legislative responses to the continuation of business mergers the Sherman Act seemed incapable of arresting. And the 1950 amendment of Section 7 of the Clayton Act, the Celler Kefauver Amendment, was fashioned to check the postwar merger wave.

A central issue in the recent investigations of mergers by the Federal Trade Commission and Congress is whether the current "conglomerate" merger wave makes new legislation necessary. On this point officials in high office responsible for administration of our antitrust laws have held different opinions. Until Richard W. McLaren assumed his duties as Assistant Attorney General for Antitrust in January 1969, spokesmen for the Antitrust Division had held that the accepted tests of a "substantial lessening of competition or a tendency toward monopoly" (the tests laid down in Amended Section 7) were not clearly applicable to diversifying acquisitions. In the application of these tests to horizontal and vertical acquisitions, measures of increases in concentration, the reduction in the number of competitors, or the likelihood of foreclosure in the relevant market, all had been used as pertinent statistical evidence of probable competitive injury. Once the relevant market had been defined, the measurable *change* in market structure attributable to the merger at bar became critical to an assessment of the merger's probable competitive effects.

Diversifying acquisitions have no immediate effect on market structure; the market shares before and after such an acquisition are precisely the same, only the *identity* of the firms comprising the market undergoes change. Except in the rather unusual circumstances where this change in the identity of firms itself would result in a probable lessening of competition, it was contended, "conglomerate" mergers were beyond the reach of the existing antimerger statute.[1] Hence, a general attack on conglomerate mergers, comparable in effectiveness to that waged against horizontal and vertical mergers under existing law, and employing the familiar economic tests of competitive injury, would require new legislation.

The Department of Justice leadership under President Nixon's administration has held a different view. As former Assistant Attorney General McLaren put it:

> We did not agree with the prior administration that it was up to Congress to amend Section 7 if it wanted something done about this conglomerate merger trend. We felt that the legislative history of the 1950 amendment to Section 7, together with the Supreme Court's opinions in several conglomerate merger cases up to that time, made it abundantly clear that Section 7, as it now stands, would reach a great many conglomerate mergers. And contrary to the opinions of a number who have written on the subject, we relied on the Supreme Court-approved theories that mergers having the reasonable probable effect of eliminating potential competition, of entrenching a leading firm, of creating reciprocity power, or of contributing to and proliferating a merger trend — given the necessary degree of substantiality — violated the law.[2]

---

[1] *Cf.* Donald F. Turner, "Conglomerate Mergers and Section 7 of the Clayton Act," *Harvard Law Review*, Vol. 78 (May 1965) p. 1,313.

[2] "Antitrust — The Year Past and the Year Ahead," an address by Richard W. McLaren before the New York State Bar Association, Antitrust Law Section, New York, New York, January 29, 1970.

Mr. Kauper, the new Antitrust Chief, has stated that he proposes to prosecute conglomerate mergers under the same standards.[3]

The tests to be applied to conglomerate acquisitions then are whether they eliminate potential competition, entrench a leading firm, create reciprocity power, or contribute to and proliferate a merger trend. Often the overriding, and to some extent overlapping, test of cross-product subsidization is either expressed or implied.

While stated in reasonably familiar language, these tests necessarily lean on less precise and less conventional standards of evaluation than those employed in the past in horizontal and vertical merger litigations. This is not to say that conglomerate mergers may not, in certain circumstances, lead eventually to one or more of the anticompetitive effects on one-time Assistant Attorney General McLaren's list. However, there is neither a generally accepted theory of market behavior nor a body of empirically established economic propositions that determine what these circumstances are. For example, what particular conditions attend those conglomerate acquisitions that may eliminate potential competition? Is it sufficient to show that the acquiring firm might logically have been expected eventually to move into the acquired firm's product market to further round out a full line? Or is it sufficient simply to show that this expectation was held by the existing actual competitors and this fact alone made the acquiring firm a potential competitor?

The difficulties that attend the determination of the anticompetitive effects of conglomerate acquisitions need not be extended or belabored here. The essential point is that this determination must obviously rely more heavily on judg-

---

[3] "Antitrust Strategist," *The New York Times*, Financial Section, November 12, 1972, p. 7.

ments concerning managerial behavior than on the more
familiar, and in general the more widely accepted, quantitative measures of market structure. This constitutes a more
radical departure from the evidentiary rules by which the
anticompetitive consequences of mergers have historically
been determined than might appear on initial inspection.
As the House Committee Report spelling out the intent of
Congress in amending Section 7 of the Clayton Act (1950)
made clear, the tests prescribed "are intended to be similar
to those which the courts have applied in interpreting the
same language as used in other Sections of the Clayton Act.
Thus it would be unnecessary for the Government to speculate as to what is in the 'back of the minds' of those who
promote a merger. . . ." [4] The newly enunciated conglomerate merger tests pertaining to potential competition, the
entrenchment of a leading firm and reciprocity, would appear
to require that the government not only speculate on the
cerebrations of those who promote the merger, but on what
is in the "back of the minds" of those firms who may have
regarded the promoter as a potential competitor and of those
to whom it has been both a supplier and customer as well.
The tests pertaining to the proliferation of a merger trend
are no less speculative, but are of a different sort.

It is not to be inferred from the above, however, that the
managerial aspects of large diversified companies have been
neglected. The increasing importance of such companies has
attracted the attention of students of business management
no less than that of students of public policy.[5] As Professor

---

[4] H. R. Rep. 1191, 81st Congress, 1st Sess. (August 4, 1949), p. 8.

[5] *Cf.* Alfred D. Chandler, Jr., *Strategy and Structure; Chapters in the
History of the American Industrial Enterprise* (Cambridge: Massachusetts
Institute of Technology Press, 1962); Peter Hilton, *Planning Corporate
Growth and Diversification* (New York: McGraw-Hill Book Co., 1970);
Joseph L. Bower, *Managing the Resource Allocation Process: A Study of*

Alfred Chandler has pointed out, there is considerable evidence to support the proposition that management decentralization and diversification tend to go hand in hand.[6]  Decentralized multiproduct organizations are not only more complex than centralized single-product organizations, they may very well be managed *differently* from single-product organizations. Students of business management have noted, for example, that in large diversified companies corporate and division management may hold discernibly different attitudes toward risks; and, as an added complexity, the distribution of managerial functions may differ perceptibly between such "diversified majors" as General Electric and such large financially based collections of separate operating units as Textron, generally considered to be a prototype of the modern "conglomerate." [7]

While the synergism of factual studies of business management and firm and industry models of economic theory may be readily apparent, the two are all too infrequently joined for purposes of formulating and administering public policies toward business enterprise. In assessing the issues precipitated by contemporary conglomerates, the need for joining the two is especially compelling, a point already intimated and one that is given considerable emphasis later on. Determination of the anticompetitive effects of diversifying acquisitions, as discussed at some length above, must rely more heavily on judgments concerning how diversified firms are managed than on the logic underlying the traditional economic models of industrial organization as applied to

---

*Corporate Planning and Investment* (Boston: Division of Research, Harvard Graduate School of Business Administration, 1970); Norman A. Berg, "Strategic Planning in Conglomerate Companies," *Harvard Business Review* (May–June 1965), pp. 79–92.

[6] Alfred D. Chandler, Jr., *Strategy and Structure*, pp. 14–17.
[7] For a synthesis of recent research on the management of diversified com-

the familiar quantitative measures of monopoly and market structure; the latter being the essential ingredients of an anti-merger policy shaped almost entirely out of contemplation of horizontal mergers and acquisitions. Since the newly enunciated test of legality for conglomerate acquisitions reflect this greater reliance on judgments concerning the managerial aspects of conglomerates it would appear axiomatic that such judgments should ultimately rest on generalizations drawn from factual analyses of how large diversified companies are managed.

## THE CONGLOMERATE MERGER WAVE: ITS STATISTICAL DIMENSIONS

The importance of the policy issues raised by the new tests of legality has derived largely from what has been popularly designated the new "conglomerate merger wave," the scope and magnitude of which have been judged largely from the only publicly available compilation of mergers and acquisitions by type published periodically by the Federal Trade Commission (Table 1-1). It is apparent from these data, and from other data to be observed later, that the timing and composition of the wave are greatly affected by how a conglomerate acquisition is defined. The FTC's more encompassing definition includes all acquisitions that extend the operations of the acquiring firm beyond its present product or geographical markets; its more restrictive definition includes only those acquisitions where, in the language of the recently issued Federal Trade Commission's *Report*, the two companies "have neither a buyer-seller relationship nor a

panies see Joseph L. Bower, "Management Decision Making in Large Diversified Firms," Draft of Paper Presented to the Large Diversified Firm Conference, Harvard Graduate School of Business Administration (November 14–16, 1971).

## TABLE 1-1

### Acquisitions of Manufacturing and Mining Firms with Assets of $10 Million or More, by Type of Acquisition, 1926–1971

| Type of Acquisition | 1926–1930 (Percent) | | 1940–1947 (Percent) | | 1948–1951 (Percent) | | 1952–1955 (Percent) | | 1956–1959 (Percent) | |
|---|---|---|---|---|---|---|---|---|---|---|
| | Number | Assets | Number | Assets | Number | Assets | Number | Assets | Number | Assets |
| Horizontal | 68 | — | 62 | — | 36.4 | 40.5 | 36.1 | 39.2 | 22.2 | 24.0 |
| Vertical | 5 | — | 17 | — | 18.2 | 18.2 | 11.3 | 11.9 | 14.0 | 16.1 |
| Conglomerate | 27 | — | — | — | | | 52.6 | 48.9 | 63.7 | 59.9 |
| Product Extension | 19 | — | 21 | — | 41.0 | 38.6 | 36.1 | 35.8 | 41.5 | 36.6 |
| Market Extension | 8 | — | —a | — | —a | —a | 4.5 | 2.5 | 6.4 | 4.7 |
| Other | —b | — | —b | — | 4.4 | 2.7 | 12.0 | 10.6 | 15.8 | 18.6 |
| Total | 100 | — | 100 | — | 100.0 | 100.0 | 100.0 | 100.0 | 100.0 c | 100.0 |

## TABLE 1-1 (*continued*)

| Type of Acquisition | 1960 (Percent) Number | 1960 (Percent) Assets | 1961 (Percent) Number | 1961 (Percent) Assets | 1962 (Percent) Number | 1962 (Percent) Assets | 1963 (Percent) Number | 1963 (Percent) Assets | 1964 (Percent) Number | 1964 (Percent) Assets | 1965 (Percent) Number | 1965 (Percent) Assets |
|---|---|---|---|---|---|---|---|---|---|---|---|---|
| Horizontal | 17.0 | 18.0 | 20.4 | 8.3 | 16.7 | 23.4 | 9.4 | 8.3 | 14.7 | 11.3 | 14.9 | 9.7 |
| Vertical | 10.6 | 12.5 | 18.2 | 22.3 | 16.7 | 23.0 | 15.1 | 29.6 | 13.2 | 20.2 | 11.9 | 7.6 |
| Conglomerate | 72.4 | 69.5 | 61.4 | 69.4 | 66.7 | 53.6 | 75.5 | 62.1 | 72.1 | 68.5 | 73.1 | 82.7 |
| Product Extension | 49.0 | 53.7 | 34.1 | 31.5 | 43.4 | 31.4 | 49.0 | 44.7 | 61.8 | 48.8 | 47.7 | 36.8 |
| Market Extension | 8.5 | 5.2 | 9.1 | 10.1 | 5.0 | 8.8 | 5.7 | 4.2 | 1.5 | 0.8 | 7.5 | 25.9 |
| Other | 14.9 | 10.6 | 18.2 | 27.8 | 18.3 | 13.4 | 20.8 | 13.2 | 8.8 | 18.9 | 17.9 | 20.0 |
| Total | 100.0 | 100.0 | 100.0 | 100.0 | 100.0 c | 100.0 | 100.0 | 100.0 | 100.0 | 100.0 | 100.0 c | 100.0 |

## TABLE 1-1 (*continued*)

| Type of Acquisition | 1966 | | 1967 | | 1968 | | 1969 | | 1970 | | 1971 [d] | |
|---|---|---|---|---|---|---|---|---|---|---|---|---|
| | Number (Percent) | Assets (Percent) | Number (Percent) | Assets (Percent) | Number (Percent) | Assets (Percent) | Number (Percent) | Assets (Percent) | Number (Percent) | Assets (Percent) | Number (Percent) | Assets (Percent) |
| Horizontal | 10.5 | 8.2 | 5.3 | 12.1 | 4.8 | 2.8 | 9.5 | 19.5 | 8.9 | 15.4 | 7.3 | 19.8 |
| Vertical | 11.9 | 6.8 | 9.7 | 4.9 | 8.4 | 6.8 | 8.8 | 7.4 | 3.3 | 4.2 | 1.8 | 0.5 |
| Conglomerate | 77.7 | 85.0 | 85.0 | 83.0 | 86.8 | 90.4 | 81.6 | 73.1 | 87.8 | 80.4 | 90.9 | 79.7 |
| Product Extension | 51.4 | 52.1 | 60.2 | 48.2 | 58.5 | 36.8 | 45.6 | 33.0 | 40.0 | 34.1 | 43.6 | 32.2 |
| Market Extension | 2.6 | 15.6 | 0.8 | 8.4 | 0.6 | 6.0 | 4.4 | 3.1 | 7.8 | 14.1 | 5.5 | 2.3 |
| Other | 23.7 | 17.3 | 24.0 | 26.4 | 27.7 | 47.6 | 31.6 | 37.0 | 40.0 | 32.2 | 41.8 | 45.2 |
| Total | 100.0 c | 100.0 | 100.0 | 100.0 | 100.0 | 100.0 | 100.0 c | 100.0 | 100.0 | 100.0 | 100.0 | 100.0 |

a Included under "Horizontal."
b Included under "Product extension."
c Percentages do not add to 100.0 due to rounding.
d Figures for 1971 are preliminary.
SOURCES: Bureau of Economics, FTC, *Current Trends in Merger Activity*, 1969, 1970, 1971, and 1972, annual issues; and FTC Report, *Economic Report on Corporate Mergers* (1969). The computations for 1948–1971 are based on acquisitions for which the assets involved are public information; they represent 80 percent of all acquisitions of $10 million or more known to have occurred between 1948 and 1971.

functional relationship in manufacturing or distribution, such as a shipbuilder and an ice cream manufacturer."[8] Disaggregated data on such acquisitions, which the Commission designates as "other" conglomerates in its tabular presentations, are available only for 1952–1955 and on an annual basis thereafter; for earlier years they were included in market extending acquisitions.

Whether one uses the FTC's broad definition or the narrow one, it is obvious that diversifying acquisitions are not a new business phenomenon. As far back in the history of business mergers as the 1926–1930 period, when the merger wave of 1919–1931 reached its crest, conglomerate acquisitions accounted for 27 percent of all acquisitions of $10 million or more in mining and manufacturing, most of which were either product extending or the more obvious diversifying acquisitions.

It is also very likely that such acquisitions became both absolutely and relatively more significant around the mid-1950s. According to the FTC data, in the four-year period 1952–1955 diversifying acquisitions accounted for 52.0 percent of all assets acquired in large mergers. From the mid-1950s on, the trend in diversifying acquisitions was sharply upward until by 1970 they accounted for 84 percent of all large mergers and for 72 percent of all assets that exchanged hands through acquisition. Meanwhile, the actual number of recorded acquisitions increased from around 535 per year (1954–1955) to 2,346 per year (1968–1969), and the number of large acquisitions of $10 million or more increased from almost 50 per year to almost 200 (Table 1-2). In the three-year period 1967–1969, $32.5 billion in assets changed hands

---

[8] Staff Report to the Federal Trade Commission, *Economic Report on Corporate Mergers* (Washington, D.C.: U.S. Government Printing Office, 1969), p. 60. Hereafter cited as FTC *Report* (1969).

through acquisition,[9] nearly 80 percent of which was accounted for by diversifying acquisitions. Clearly, diversifying acquisitions, broadly defined, have increased discernibly

### TABLE 1-2
#### Number of Manufacturing and
#### Mining Concerns Acquired, 1940–1971

| Period | Large [a] | All | | Period | Large [a] | All |
|---|---|---|---|---|---|---|
| 1940 | | 140 | | 1955 | 67 | 683 |
| 1941 | | 111 | | 1956 | 55 | 673 |
| 1942 | | 118 | | 1957 | 51 | 585 |
| 1943 | | 213 | | 1958 | 37 | 589 |
| 1944 | | 324 | | 1959 | 64 | 835 |
| 1945 | | 333 | | 1960 | 62 | 844 |
| 1946 | | 419 | | 1961 | 55 | 954 |
| 1947 | | 404 | | 1962 | 72 | 853 |
| 1948 | 6 | 223 | | 1963 | 71 | 861 |
| 1949 | 5 | 126 | | 1964 | 89 | 854 |
| 1950 | 4 | 219 | | 1965 | 89 | 1,008 |
| 1951 | 9 | 235 | | 1966 | 99 | 995 |
| 1952 | 14 | 288 | | 1967 | 167 | 1,496 |
| 1953 | 23 | 295 | | 1968 | 207 | 2,407 |
| 1954 | 35 | 387 | | 1969 | 155 | 2,307 |
| | | | | 1970 | 98 | 1,351 |
| | | | | 1971 [b] | 66 | 1,011 |

[a] Acquired company had assets of $10 million or more; not available for years prior to 1948.

[b] Preliminary.

SOURCES: Bureau of Economics, Federal Trade Commission, *Current Trends in Merger Activity,* Statistical Report No. 10 (May 1972). Data limited to mergers and acquisitions reported by Moody's Investors Service, Inc., and Standard & Poor's Corporation. Comparable totals for the years 1919 to 1939 were published in the Commission's *Report on Corporate Mergers and Acquisitions* (May 1955), p. 33.

---

[9] Bureau of Economics, Federal Trade Commission, *Statistical Report No. 5, Large Mergers in Manufacturing and Mining, 1948–1969* (February 1970), p. 6.

in recent years, the upswing having become evident by the mid-1950s.

If the Federal Trade Commission's more restricted definition of a conglomerate acquisition is used (namely, the bringing together of two firms functionally unrelated in either marketing or production), conglomerate mergers have been numerically much less significant, but the pronounced upward trend since the mid-1950s has been unmistakable. In the 1952–1955 period such "genuine" conglomerate acquisitions accounted for only 3.6 percent of total assets involved in acquisitions of firms having assets of $10 million or more; by 1956–1959 this percentage had risen to 14.2 percent, and by 1968 had reached 42 percent. In 1969 the assets involved in such acquisitions declined to 38 percent of total acquired assets, the year in which the total number of acquisitions, the number of large acquisitions, and the total assets acquired, also began to register significant declines.

The FTC data show that as the volume and economic importance of diversifying acquisitions have increased, assets involved in such acquisitions have also become a larger component of total corporate investment (Table 1-3). In 1954 the ratio of acquired assets to total corporate investment rose to 11.1 percent, or to slightly more than double the comparable ratio of 5.5 percent for 1953. Since diversifying acquisitions accounted for about one-half of all acquired assets in 1954, they accounted for assets amounting to $0.7 billion, or 5.7 percent of total investment. However, the more strictly defined diversifying acquisitions accounted for assets amounting to only $274 million, or only slightly more than 2.0 percent of total investment. In 1967–1969, the three-year period for which total acquired assets suddenly increased to 35 percent of total investment, the assets involved in diversifying acquisitions of all types rose to 28 percent of total investment and those involved in the more strictly defined conglomerate

# TABLE 1-3

## Assets Acquired in All Acquisitions and in Diversifying Acquisitions by Type, Compared with New Investment in Manufacturing and Mining, 1948–1971

| | | Acquired Assets [b] *(Billions of Dollars)* | | | | | | | | | |
| | | Total Acquisitions | | Total Diversifying Acquisitions | | Product Extension | | Market Extension | | Other | |
| Year | Total Investment [a] *(Billions of Dollars)* | Amount | Percent of Total Investment | Amount | Percent of Total Investment | Amount | Percent of Total Investment | Amount | Percent of Total Investment | Amount | Percent of Total Investment |
|---|---|---|---|---|---|---|---|---|---|---|---|
| 1948 | 9.94 | .063 | 0.6 | .035 | 0.4 | .035 | 0.4 | — | — | — | — |
| 1949 | 8.00 | .066 | 0.8 | .053 | 0.7 | .053 | 0.7 | — | — | — | — |
| 1950 | 8.23 | .186 | 2.2 | .020 | 0.2 | .020 | 0.2 | — | — | — | — |
| 1951 | 11.82 | .189 | 1.6 | .100 | 0.8 | .086 | 0.7 | — | — | .013 | 0.1 |
| 1952 | 12.66 | .531 | 2.6 | .202 | 1.6 | .144 | 1.1 | .010 | 0.1 | .048 | 0.4 |
| 1953 | 13.11 | .725 | 5.5 | .306 | 2.3 | .234 | 1.8 | .034 | 0.3 | .038 | 0.3 |
| 1954 | 12.52 | 1.336 | 11.1 | .688 | 5.5 | .369 | 3.0 | .044 | 0.4 | .274 | 2.2 |
| 1955 | 13.20 | 2.101 | 15.9 | 1.001 | 7.6 | .863 | 6.5 | .022 | 0.2 | .116 | 0.9 |
| 1956 | 17.04 | 1.782 | 10.5 | .764 | 4.5 | .567 | 3.3 | .066 | 0.4 | .131 | 0.8 |
| 1957 | 18.20 | 1.102 | 6.1 | .852 | 4.7 | .642 | 3.5 | .069 | 0.4 | .141 | 0.8 |
| 1958 | 13.81 | 1.111 | 8.0 | .590 | 4.3 | .441 | 3.2 | — | — | .149 | 1.1 |
| 1959 | 14.13 | 1.293 | 9.1 | .962 | 6.8 | .286 | 2.0 | .112 | 0.7 | .564 | 4.1 |
| 1960 | 16.39 | 1.428 | 8.7 | .994 | 6.1 | .768 | 4.7 | .074 | 0.5 | .150 | 0.9 |
| 1961 | 15.62 | 1.926 | 12.3 | 1.336 | 8.5 | .605 | 3.9 | .195 | 1.2 | .534 | 3.4 |
| 1962 | 16.46 | 1.998 | 12.1 | 1.072 | 6.5 | .628 | 3.8 | .175 | 1.1 | .268 | 1.6 |
| 1963 | 17.49 | 2.553 | 14.6 | 1.588 | 9.1 | 1.143 | 6.5 | .108 | 0.6 | .337 | 1.9 |
| 1964 | 20.68 | 2.179 | 10.5 | 1.494 | 7.2 | 1.053 | 5.1 | .018 | 0.1 | .412 | 2.0 |
| 1965 | 24.90 | 3.191 | 12.8 | 2.640 | 10.6 | 1.175 | 4.7 | .825 | 3.3 | .639 | 2.6 |
| 1966 | 29.82 | 3.201 | 10.7 | 2.722 | 9.1 | 1.669 | 5.6 | .499 | 1.7 | .553 | 1.9 |
| 1967 | 30.16 | 8.417 | 28.0 | 6.986 | 23.2 | 4.052 | 13.5 | .706 | 2.3 | 2.227 | 7.4 |
| 1968 | 30.00 | 12.387 | 41.1 | 11.196 | 37.2 | 4.557 | 15.2 | .749 | 2.5 | 5.890 | 19.6 |
| 1969 | 33.54 | 10.849 | 32.3 | 7.933 | 23.6 | 3.580 | 10.7 | .338 | 1.0 | 4.015 | 12.1 |
| 1970 | 33.84 | 5.846 | 17.2 | 4.698 | 13.8 | 1.992 | 5.9 | .825 | 2.4 | 1.880 | 5.6 |
| 1971 [c] | 32.34 | 2.340 | 7.3 | 1.865 | 5.8 | .752 | 2.3 | .052 | 0.2 | 1.060 | 3.3 |

[a] Total expenditures for new plant and equipment plus acquired assets.

[b] Acquired firms with assets of $10 million or more.

[c] Figures for 1971 are preliminary.

SOURCE: Bureau of Economics, FTC, *Current Trends in Merger Activity, 1971* (May 1972), and *Large Mergers in Manufacturing and Mining,* Bureau of Economics, Federal Trade Commission, Statistical Report No. 9 (May 1972).

acquisitions ("other") rose to 12 percent of total investment.

These quantitative relationships between acquired assets in various types of acquisitions and total corporate investment are, of course, purely descriptive; they show only that toward the end of the 1960s acquired assets became a significantly more important component of total corporate capital outlays. It does not necessarily follow from this that the acquisition of assets through diversifying mergers, or that mergers generally, has increasingly been substituted for new investment. [10] As the Federal Trade Commission *Report* points out, an understanding of the full significance of the recent increase in assets acquired, relative to those entered on corporate balance sheets as new investment, requires further analysis.[11]

Nevertheless, the data do suggest that acquisition and new investment are alternative means to company growth. For example, between 1966 and 1970 total investment in mining and manufacturing fluctuated within the narrow range of $29.8 billion and $33.8 billion. The relative stability in total investment resulted from offsetting fluctuations in the volume of new investment and acquired assets. Between 1965 and 1968, while the annual rate of acquired assets rose from $3.8 billion to $13.3 billion, that of new investment declined from $21.1 billion to $16.7 billion; and between 1968 and 1971, while the annual rate of acquired assets declined to $2.5 billion, that of new investment rose to $29.8 billion. Although these offsetting movements in the acquired assets and new investment series strongly suggest that they are alternative means of company growth, it does not follow that they are substitute means for expanding in, or entering into, the same

---

[10] This substitution has sometimes been implied, leading to the conclusion that growth through merger reduces the growth in the Gross National Product by reducing net new investment, a principal source of economic growth.

[11] FTC *Report* (1969), p. 42.

industries. On the contrary, as subsequent analysis will show, companies seldom regard entry by new investment as a feasible alternative to entry by acquisition in particular industries.

The scope, magnitude, and, by implication, the overall structural consequences of the recent merger wave have, up to this point, been measured entirely in terms of FTC data. In the FTC compilations all acquisitions were assigned to one of the three classifications of horizontal, vertical, or conglomerate. Aside from the obvious fact that some degree of arbitrariness must inevitably attend attempted delineations of acquisitions by mutually exclusive classes, many acquisitions involve elements of two, and in some cases all three, classes. That is, a given acquisition may not be horizontal *or* conglomerate, but horizontal *and* conglomerate. Consider, for example, a hypothetical merger[12] of two companies, X and

### TABLE 1-4
#### A Hypothetical Merger of X and Y
#### with Different Product Mixes

| Product Line | Company X | | Company Y | | Company XY |
| --- | --- | --- | --- | --- | --- |
|  | *Output* | *Purchases* | *Output* | *Purchases* | *Output* |
| A | $30M | 0 | $20M | 0 | $50M |
| B | 20M | 0 | 0 | $10M | 20M |
| C | 30M | 0 | 0 | 0 | 30M |
| D | 20M | 0 | 0 | 0 | 20M |
| E | 0 | 0 | 10M | 0 | 10M |

Y, with different mixes of products A, B, C, D, and E (Table 1-4). In terms of company X's production, the merger is 30 percent horizontal, 20 percent vertical, and 50 percent conglomerate; for company Y it is 50 percent horizontal, 25 per-

---

[12] This illustration is adapted from Dr. Betty Bock, "Notes on Problems of Identifying Merger Patterns" (Unpublished, 1968).

cent vertical, and 25 percent conglomerate; and for the combined company XY the merger is 38.5 percent horizontal, 15.4 percent vertical and 46.1 percent conglomerate. Obviously, the merger defies unequivocal classification, even if one confines his attention to the acquiring firm, as is customarily done. As a practical matter the merger would probably be classified as conglomerate, although it at best is only half-conglomerate; successive assignments of such acquisitions to the conglomerate class, or to any single class, lead eventually to substantial statistical aberration.

Fortunately, the FTC published the list of acquisitions used in compiling its various series on mergers and acquisitions of $10 million or more by type, identifying the principal 3-digit SIC industry of both the acquiring and the acquired firm. From information contained in various issues of *Fortune's Plant and Product Directory* and *News Front*, and from information available on an unsystematic basis from other sources, it was possible to compile lists of 4-digit, 3-digit and 2-digit SIC industries in which most of the acquired and acquiring firms operated in the year of, or in one to two years immediately preceding, the acquisition. In a reasonably large number of instances the information permitted a determination of whether a given acquiring or acquired firm was an important factor in such industries.[13]

The FTC conglomerate acquisitions were reclassified according to whether they were significantly horizontal (or, conversely, conglomerate) at the 4-digit, 3-digit and/or 2-digit level (Table 1-5). Of the 593 acquisitions the FTC defined as conglomerate, additional information as described above

---

[13] For example, *News Front* (Leading U.S. Corporations) publishes the rank of firms in 3-digit SIC industries. A detailed description of the Standard Industrial Classification (SIC) Code used by the Census Bureau of the U.S. Department of Commerce may be found in *1967 Census of Manufactures*, U.S. Department of Commerce, Bureau of the Census, pp. 1–3.

**TABLE 1-5**

**Reclassification of Conglomerate Mergers
of $10 Million or More in Assets Reported by the
Federal Trade Commission, 1961–1969, Under
Alternative Definitions of "Conglomerate"**

| Year | Number of Conglomerate Mergers Reported by FTC | Number of Reported Conglomerates on Which Additional Information Was Available | Reported Number of Conglomerates Partly Horizontal at Various SIC Levels | | |
|---|---|---|---|---|---|
| | | | 4-digit | 3-digit | 2-digit |
| 1961 | 32 | 32 | 10 | 15 | 23 |
| 1962 | 32 | 32 | 9 | 20 | 24 |
| 1963 | 48 | 48 | 17 | 29 | 36 |
| 1964 | 48 | 48 | 17 | 24 | 33 |
| 1965 | 49 | 49 | 17 | 22 | 31 |
| 1966 | 104 | 104 | 36 | 58 | 77 |
| 1967 | 119 | 119 | 40 | 53 | 84 |
| 1968 | 100 | 97 | 18 | 26 | 49 |
| 1969 | 61 | 60 | 18 | 26 | 36 |
| | | | Subtotal | 91 | 120 |
| Total | 593 | 589 | Total 182 | 273 | 393 |

was available on 589. It is immediately evident from the reclassification results that the size of the 1961–1969 conglomerate merger wave varies greatly according to whether one employs a broadly inclusive or highly restrictive definition of a conglomerate acquisition. Of the 589 acquisitions classified as conglomerate by the FTC, 182 (well over one-fourth of the total) brought together firms operating in at least one identical, and often several identical, 4-digit industries; an additional 91 operated in the same 3-digit (but not in the same 4-digit) industry; and still an additional 120 operated in the same 2-digit (but not in the same 4-digit or 3-digit) industry. Stated another way, of the 589 FTC conglomerate acquisitions on which sufficient information for reclassification was available, 196 (considerably less than two-fifths) involved firms in entirely different 2-digit industries, and a little more than one half involved firms in entirely different 3-digit (but not in different 2-digit) industries.

There is, of course, no readily available objective test by which one may reconstruct the Federal Trade Commission series for the 1960s by employing an unequivocally rational definition of a conglomerate acquisition. What the data in Table 1-5 bring out clearly, however, is that considerably less than half of the acquisitions classified by the FTC as conglomerate probably involved firms in totally unrelated production and marketing activities. In fact, the data suggest that more often than not an acquisition recorded as conglomerate extended the operations of the acquiring firm within some broad industry group in which it already operated.

Data on acquisitions by type supplied by reporting corporations in the Harvard Business School Diversified Firm Survey[14] corroborate this conclusion. The relevant data on acquisitions are presented in Table 1-6. Out of a total of 1,967 acquisitions reported by 211 corporations, only 683, or 34.7 percent, added a new 4-digit industry to the acquiring firm's operations.[15] This percentage is dramatically lower than the approximately 75 percent reported by the FTC for several reasons: (1) it is based on all acquisitions, irrespective of size, whereas the FTC data are for only those acquisitions of $10 million or more in assets; (2) a large percentage of the FTC "conglomerate" acquisitions fall in the "product extension" and "market extension" subclassifications; some of the former, and many of the latter, very likely represented

---

[14] The HBS Survey is described in detail in Chapter 3.

[15] Since the calculated correlation coefficient between the number of acquisitions and the value of acquisitions is 0.80, this percentage should be a reasonably good proxy for the value of acquisitions as well.

## TABLE 1-6

### Total Number of All Acquisitions Compared with Total Number of Diversifying Acquisitions, 204 Reporting Corporations, 1961–1970

| Year | Number of Acquisitions | Number of Diversifying Acquisitions [a] | Percent Diversifying of Total |
|------|------------------------|------------------------------------------|-------------------------------|
| 1961 | 116 | 32 | 27.5% |
| 1962 | 98 | 35 | 35.7 |
| 1963 | 122 | 40 | 32.8 |
| 1964 | 139 | 43 | 30.9 |
| 1965 | 217 | 53 | 24.4 |
| 1966 | 219 | 67 | 30.6 |
| 1967 | 227 | 88 | 38.8 |
| 1968 | 314 | 117 | 37.2 |
| 1969 | 302 | 125 | 41.4 |
| 1970 | 213 | 83 | 39.0 |
| Total | 1,967 | 683 | 34.7% |

[a] A diversifying acquisition was defined as one that added at least one significant new 4-digit industry to the acquiring firm's operations.
SOURCE: HBS Diversified Firm Survey data.

mergers among firms in the same 4-digit industries; and (3) the FTC and the Survey corporate universes are not identical; hence, it would not be expected that the ratio of diversifying acquisitions to all acquisitions for the two universes would be the same. In view of the large number of reporting corporations in the survey, however, it would be expected that the difference in the ratios would be much less than it actually is. A reasonable inference is that a large proportion of those acquisitions the FTC classified as conglomerate were not considered to be diversifying acquisitions by the acquiring companies. But whatever the explanation for the difference may be, conglomerate mergers in the 1960s appear to have been less characteristic of acquisitions generally, and of relatively less importance, than previous studies have implied.

Moreover, comparisons of recent diversifying acquisition activity with that of the 1950s, and with such components of the Gross National Product as new investment, are likely to give an exaggerated picture of its size, scope, and economic significance. The $7.7 billion corporations spent on all diversifying acquisitions in 1969, and the $4 billion they spent on the more strictly defined diversifying acquisitions, amounted respectively to only 0.8 percent and 0.4 percent of the Gross National Product, to less than two-thirds and less than one-third of the total annual corporate outlays on research and development, and to only one-quarter and one-eighth of the annual business outlays on advertising. Hence, while it is readily apparent that corporate management, more accurately the management of some corporations, has unquestionably become more actively engaged in diversifying through acquisition, this activity apparently has fallen far short of absorbing the energies of corporate management generally.

## THE ISSUES

Some, after viewing essentially the foregoing statistical terrain, have made somber pronouncements on its economic impact. For example, in his statement before the Committee on Ways and Means, U. S. House of Representatives, on March 12, 1969, Dr. Willard F. Mueller stated that:

> There is much that we do not know about the causes and ultimate consequences of the current conglomerate merger movement. There no longer can be any doubt, however, that we are in the midst of an exceptional period of our economic history. Future economic historians will surely say that the late 1960's marked a critical turning point in our free enterprise system. For good or ill, what future historians write will

depend largely on the public policy actions of the next year
or two.[16]

The public policy actions will not only affect what histo-
rians write, they will also affect what business managers do,
and how they do them. Evidence abounds that corporate
managements regard growth, diversification, and the extension of product and geographical markets as important goals
for their respective companies. These activities have long
been considered the indispensable means of continuing,
stable, and growing profits, but it has also been stated, and
on both logical and empirical grounds, that firm growth, to
which other activities are clearly related, is itself a goal of
the firm. As Professor Baumol has pointed out, businessmen
have many impelling reasons for showing concern about their
sales and sales growth. Declining sales, or even nongrowth
in sales, create difficult managerial problems: limitations on
managerial and personnel advancement, the loss of distribu-
tors, deterioration in credit rating, and the loss in relative —
or possibly in absolute — market position, among others.[17]

It is clear that business management considers merger and
acquisition important means of growth, and in recent years
has turned increasingly to diversifying acquisitions for this
purpose. The imposition of new policy constraints on this
means of growth would significantly affect the managements
of corporations who participate in the acquisition process.
While this scarcely supports a conclusion that policy constraints should not be imposed, it does argue strongly for
more searching inquiry into the form the constraints should
take and the antitrust objectives they may logically be ex-

[16] Bureau of Economics, Federal Trade Commission, *Economic Papers,
1966–69* (Washington, D.C.: U.S. Government Printing Office, 1970) p. 262.
[17] William J. Baumol, *Business Behavior, Value and Growth* (Rev. ed.;
New York: Harcourt, Brace & World, Inc., 1967), pp. 45–46.

pected to serve. In short, policy innovations based solely on untested hypotheses concerning the diversified firm and cross-product subsidization, potential competition, reciprocity dealings, and the level of economic concentration, would clearly be ill-advised, as would the failure to introduce such policy changes because of the equally untested counter-hypotheses.

Central to the issue of reconciling through the instruments of public policy the corporate objectives of growth and diversification and the public objectives of preserving a reasonably competitive and efficiently functioning market economy, lie those managerial techniques and strategies especially identified with, although not necessarily the unique properties of, diversified enterprise. Do large diversified firms, more than other large firms, seek dominance in their various markets? Do they, again more than other large firms, employ the tactics of cross-product subsidization or reciprocity dealings in their pursuit of company objectives? Do conglomerates tend to be more or less profitable than corporate enterprise generally? And, if so, what evidence is there that those management properties (distinctively conglomerate) explain the discernible difference? At a more global level of inquiry is the growth in both number and size of large diversified companies in recent years attributable to "honestly industrial" responses of management to opportunities provided in the market place? And does the resulting conglomerate "merger wave" mark a critical turning point in our free enterprise system in terms of its measurable effects on the structure of the markets involved and on the level of overall concentration in the corporate economy? It is to these and related issues that this study is addressed.

# 2. The Theory and Policy Issues

## THE CONGLOMERATE AND CONVENTIONAL MICROTHEORY

THE ACCELERATED PACE AT WHICH CORPORATE enterprise has diversified through acquisition, as indicated earlier, represents a significant reordering of the means of corporate growth on the part of business management. As diversified firms have become more numerous, more conglomerate in scope, and relatively more important subsets of the economy's firm population, they have generated new management techniques, new organizational structures, and have presented a new challenge to traditional public policy. The large diversified firm has also placed an unusually heavy strain on the explanatory capabilities of the theory of the firm.

The inadequacies of microeconomic theory, even without explicitly introducing the additional complexities of diversity, in explaining the behavior of contemporary corporate enterprise have been dealt with at length in the literature, the details of which scarcely need repeating here.[1] The inten-

---

[1] The several pages that follow were adapted from an earlier article: Jesse W. Markham, "Antitrust and the Conglomerate: A Policy in Search of a Theory," *Conglomerate Mergers and Acquisitions: Opinion and Analysis, St. John's Law Review*, Special Edition, Vol. 44 (Spring 1970), p. 282.

24

sity of the debate over the relevancy of marginal analysis, the cornerstone of the theory of firm behavior, ushered in by the well-known articles of Lester, Machlup, and Hall and Hitch, may have diminished, but the debate itself has not been completely resolved.[2] A. A. Berle's inquiries into the modern large corporation led him to conclude that that institution has rendered the traditional theory of the firm obsolete.[3] Professor Galbraith has contended that the discernible disparity between the observable behavior of business firms and the behavior contemporary theory would predict has created a gap in our understanding of the operative mechanics of our industrial economy, a gap he then attempted to close with his concept of countervailing power.[4] In a more recent assessment, Galbraith virtually eschews the conventional theory of the firm altogether, not so much on the grounds of its inadequacies but because of its irrelevancy.[5]

The deficiencies and impertinencies of microeconomic theory can easily be exaggerated. Embedded in the recent rejections of the theory of the firm is the factual observation, sometimes expressed but more often implied, that the relatively simple assumptions underlying the economic models of firms and markets do not accord with the "real world."

---

[2] *Cf.* R. A. Lester, "Shortcomings of Marginal Analysis for Wage-Employment Problems," *American Economic Review,* Vol. 36 (March 1946), pp. 63–82; F. Machlup, "Marginal Analysis and Empirical Research," *American Economic Review,* Vol. 36 (September 1946), pp. 519–554; R. L. Hall and C. J. Hitch, "Price Theory and Business Behavior," *Oxford Economic Papers,* Vol. 2 (May 1939), pp. 12–45. For a recent review of the debate, see F. Machlup, "Theories of the Firm: Marginalist, Behavioral, Managerial," *American Economic Review,* Vol. 52 (March 1967), pp. 1–33.

[3] See A. A. Berle, *The Twentieth Century Capitalist Revolution* (New York: Harcourt, Brace & World, Inc., 1954).

[4] John K. Galbraith, *American Capitalism; The Concept of Countervailing Power* (Rev. ed.; Boston: Houghton Mifflin, 1956).

[5] John K. Galbraith, *The New Industrial State* (Boston: Houghton Mifflin, 1967).

But as Baumol has reminded us,[6] increased realism often must be purchased at a price, and this price may very well be a decrease in the insights into how the microeconomy operates. Moreover, Friedman has contended that the appropriate test of theory is not whether its underlying assumptions conform with the specific details of reality, but rather whether its implications or predictions conform with observable phenomena.[7]

Contemporary theory of the firm distinguishes clearly between firms having power over the market and those tightly constrained by competitive market forces. Surely few would seriously contend that the theoretical predictions inherent in such models are not broadly in conformity with observable phenomena. The familiar dramatic announcements of new prices and newly negotiated wage contracts in highly concentrated industries confronting monopolistic labor unions make it abundantly clear that the participants are not passively responding to the relentless and impersonal forces of the market place. In contrast, the routine daily price quotations on commodities and certain manufactured products are appropriately published in the financial pages as "today's market prices," without attribution to individual companies and as pertaining to a designated hour of the day. Frequently, therefore, a pronouncement to the effect that the behavior of modern large corporate enterprise bears only passing resemblance to that predicted by theoretical models of the firm is simply a matter of misapplication of models. A more accurate statement is that large and complex corporate organizations in possession of considerable discretionary power do not behave in accordance with conventional *competitive*

---

6 William J. Baumol, *Business Behavior, Value and Growth*, pp. 4–5.

7 Milton Friedman, "The Methodology of Positive Economics," *Essays in Positive Economics* (Chicago: University of Chicago Press, 1953), p. 32.

models, but this is a different, and certainly not an entirely novel, proposition.

None of this is to deny the obvious; namely, that models of the firm at their present stage of development are not capable of explaining (or, if one prefers, predicting) with a high order of precision how managers of complex organizations in possession of discretionary power[8] will exercise it. However, some initial steps have been made in this direction. Williamson has developed, and empirically tested, the "expense preference" theory of managerial behavior.[9] In brief, he concludes that managers of firms operating in markets not severely constrained by competitive forces, and in which their interests are separated from those of ownership, will prefer the enlargement of staff and emoluments (discretionary allocations of profits for salaries and perquisites) to additional reported profits. The important contribution of Williamson's analysis is that it explicitly introduces into the theory of the firm the discretionary behavior of management. Discretionary behavior, by definition, is less predictable than that of management constrained to pursue a single uniquely defined course or face extinction.

All this notwithstanding, it is still worthwhile to distill from contemporary microeconomic models the few insights they *do* provide on the multiproduct firm. The relevant models, or theories, may be divided into two broad classes: (1) those concerned with the acquisition process itself; and (2) those concerned with the behavior of the mutiproduct

---

[8] The expression "discretionary power" is perhaps unnecessarily pejorative; power, we are told, corrupts, and absolute power corrupts absolutely. What the term usually describes is the situation where management has options in choosing among alternative courses of action and the firm will at least survive, or possibly even be as well off, irrespective of how the options are exercised.

[9] Oliver E. Williamson, *The Economics of Discretionary Behavior: Managerial Objectives in a Theory of the Firm* (Englewood Cliffs: Prentice-Hall, 1964).

firm, once it has come into existence, with respect to such decisions as pricing, rates of output, and related market variables. Of the two, the acquisition process has been accorded much the more extensive and exhaustive treatment, only a selective portion of which is especially pertinent to diversifying acquisitions.

Studies dealing with the economic incentives and managerial reasons underlying business mergers and acquisitions would comprise a substantial library.[10] A partial list of such incentives and reasons would include, among others, the desire on the part of the acquiring firm to grow, to obtain larger market shares, greater diversity, economies of scale, particular assets, managerial talent, research and development capabilities, tax advantages, synergism, entry into new markets, higher and/or more stable profits and cash flows, and a reduction in risks. A similar but more abbreviated list of the reasons why acquired firms sell would include existing or prospective managerial difficulties, inadequate capital, the desire on the part of management to liquidate, to join a larger, stronger, or more diversified organization, or simply that present management wishes to terminate its involvement with the business.

For the most part, however, these particular buyer and seller motives are subsumed in either the general theory of exchange or the theory of combination: the valuation placed by a potential buyer on a given firm's assets is greater than that placed on them by their present owners, and therefore

---

[10] *Cf.* J. Keith Butters, John Lintner, and William L. Cary, *Effects of Taxation: Corporate Mergers* (Boston: Division of Research, Harvard Graduate School of Business Administration, 1951). For a survey of the historical literature up to and including the Butters, Lintner, and Cary study, see Jesse W. Markham, "Survey of the Evidence and Findings on Mergers," in National Bureau of Economic Research, *Business Concentration and Price Policy*, A *Conference of the Universities-National Bureau Committee for Economic Research* (Princeton: Princeton University Press, 1955), pp. 141–212.

the necessary conditions for exchange are fulfilled; or the anticipated value of the combined assets of any two companies exceeds the sum of their assets operated separately, and therefore the necessary conditions that both parties gain by forming a combination are met.

The recent works of Gort and Mueller,[11] drawing upon the earlier works of Baumol,[12] Penrose,[13] and Marris,[14] have adapted the general theory of exchange to the current wave of acquisitions. For example, Gort contends that economic disturbances generate those differences in valuation that produce acquisitions.

> [Disturbances] alter randomly the ordering of expectations of individuals, with the result that some non-owners move to the right of current owners on the value scale, [and] economic disturbances render the future less predictable, with the result that the variance in valuation increases.[15]

Among the more important disturbances that have altered the pattern of expectations in recent years are rapid technological change, growth, and the pronounced movements in security prices. Gort's statistical analysis of mergers occurring in manufacturing in the period 1951–1959 lends support to his disturbance theory.[16]

Mueller offers an alternative adaptation of the theory of

---

[11] Michael Gort, "An Economic Disturbance Theory of Mergers," *Quarterly Journal of Economics* (November 1969), pp. 624–642; Dennis C. Mueller, "A Theory of Conglomerate Mergers," *Quarterly Journal of Economics* (November 1969), pp. 643–659.

[12] William J. Baumol, *Business Behavior, Value and Growth.*

[13] Edith Penrose, *The Theory of the Growth of the Firm* (Basil Blackwell, 1968).

[14] Robin Marris, *The Economic Theory of Managerial Capitalism* (New York: Basic Books, 1968).

[15] Michael Gort, "An Economic Disturbance Theory of Mergers," p. 627.

[16] *Ibid.*, pp. 631–642.

exchange to the current conglomerate acquisition wave. Some managers, according to Mueller, consistent with Baumol's revenue maximizing thesis,[17] may be growth maximizers. Because they are willing to sacrifice some earnings for growth,[18] they will apply a lower discount rate to a given stream of prospective profits than stockholder-welfare maximizers. Hence, they will place a higher present value on the assets generating the anticipated stream of profits. This, according to Mueller, explains why growth-motivated conglomerates enter into acquisition arrangements calling for a substantially higher valuation of the acquired firm's stock than the price quoted on the stock exchange at the time of the acquisition. Firm growth in recent years has been accomplished primarily through conglomerate acquisitions because they hold out greater opportunities for growth, and because the antimerger statutes have more severely constrained horizontal and vertical acquisitions than diversifying acquisitions.

Applications of microeconomic theory to the managerial behavior of multiproduct firms after they have been created have been confined almost entirely to the familiar problems of short-run equilibrium prices and outputs. However, the insights they provide are not insignificant. The simple logic of marginal analysis supports the general proposition that a conglomerate firm producing strictly independent products would, under conventional profits maximizing assumptions, set prices and rates of output identical with those that would be set if each product were produced by a single-product

---

[17] William J. Baumol, *Business Behavior, Value and Growth,* pp. 45–52.
[18] As evidence Mueller cites Marris' findings that managements' rewards are related more to the size of the companies they manage than to their company's profitability. Marris, *The Economic Theory of Managerial Capitalism,* Chapter 2.

firm.[19] This proposition holds whether the firm possesses market power in any, all, or none of the markets in which it sells. The firm can only *consider* departing from such an optimum pricing rule if it possesses market power. If the firm possesses the requisite market power and departs from the optimum pricing rule, it does so at some sacrifice to profits.[20] If the products are complementary, and the firm possesses at least some market power in both markets, the price of each will be lower than it would be were the products independent;[21] if they are substitutes, under the same market conditions, the price of each would be higher.

The implications the microeconomic theory underlying this proposition holds for public policy are apparent. Non-optimal pricing in a social welfare sense must be attributed to whatever monopoly power conglomerate firms possess rather than to the fact that they are conglomerate; and conglomeration combined with market power results in prices higher than those that would prevail if the products were produced by independent firms only when the products in question are substitutes. Accordingly, although conclusions concerning major policy objectives at this stage of the inquiry must nec-

---

[19] An abbreviated treatment of the model from which this conclusion follows appears in Appendix A. A more detailed treatment may be found in K. Palda, *Economic Analysis for Marketing Decisions* (Englewood Cliffs: Prentice-Hall, 1969), pp. 137–139.

[20] To be sure, firms may elect to make this sacrifice in the present in the interests of more rapid growth or improved prospective profitability in the future, but this would introduce the concept of strategic pricing into the model, a concept which the model in question, as well as determinate microeconomic models generally, do not satisfactorily handle.

[21] Market power (negatively inclined demand schedules) is required in both markets because otherwise the firm must accept the price as given in at least one market. When the latter condition holds, the firm has no incentive to reduce the price in the partially controlled market in order to increase its sales in the competitive market; by assumption, it can sell all it wishes in the competitive market at the prevailing market price.

essarily be highly tentative, the analysis suggests that the
concerns of a rational antitrust policy should be the related
issues of excessive market power and mergers among firms
producing substitute products, and not "conglomerateness,"
or conglomerate mergers, as such.

This modest proposal, with which few students of the
merger issue would in theory disagree, helps reduce the
apparent confusion in what has been written concerning the
conglomerate issue, and anticipates much of the analysis to
follow. As Professor Berry has pointed out,

> If markets *are* unrelated, the conglomerate merger is not a
> device for the creation of market power, just as the market
> power of a corportaion is not to be read directly from the abso-
> lute size of that corporation without reference to its market
> position.[22]

The problem is that conglomerate mergers, as defined for
purposes of assembling factual data, do not necessarily, or
even generally, bring together strictly independent products.
As the data already presented clearly demonstrate, many
recent acquisitions classified as conglomerate have involved
related markets.[23] The appropriate antitrust standard for
assessing the competitive impact of such acquisitions would
appear to be whether these acquisitions augment or tend to
create monopoly in the relevant markets, the standard traditionally employed in merger cases, and the standard contemplated in existing statutes. But where the acquisition involves
strictly independent products this issue does not arise. In
certain cases acquisitions of this type may raise the issue of
corporate bigness or the massing of wealth, but as Professor

---

[22] Charles H. Berry, "Economic Policy and the Conglomerate Merger,"
*St. John's Law Review,* Special Edition (Spring 1970), p. 268.
[23] See Tables 1-5 and 1-6.

Stigler has commented ". . . the antitrust laws are not the weapons with which to deal with non-monopolistic concentrations of wealth." [24]  In short, microeconomic theory points to the necessity of separating out those conglomerate acquisitions involving related markets from those that do not. The former are the appropriate targets of antitrust policy, and existing statutes and case law appear to provide the appropriate standards by which their effects on competition should be assessed.

### ALTERNATIVE HYPOTHESES CONCERNING THE LARGE DIVERSIFIED FIRM

Hypotheses concerning the conglomerate firm's operative mechanics and managerial aspects, and the public policy implications of both, have ranged far beyond the confines of conventional microeconomic theory. Often, those who have advanced them have contended that such extra-theoretical treatises are born of necessity — the theory of the firm in its present state of development is especially inadequate as a framework for analyzing the large diversified firm. While the various hypotheses may individually be intellectually appealing, and each has attracted its own band of adherents, for virtually every hypothesis there is an equally plausible counter-hypothesis. Collectively, therefore, they fall far short of providing either an operative model of diversified firm behavior or appropriate guidelines for public policy.

Professor Corwin Edwards argued that the conglomerate firm defies analysis in terms of traditional theory which is erected on the assumption that firms maximize profits in each of its markets. On the contrary:

---

[24] George J. Stigler, "Mergers and Preventive Antitrust Policy," *University of Pennsylvania Law Review*, Vol. 104 (November 1955), p. 184.

A concern that produces many products and operates across many markets need not regard a particular market as a separate unit for determining business policy and need not attempt to maximize its profits in the sale of each of its products, as has been presupposed in our traditional scheme . . . . It may possess power in a particular market not only by virtue of its place in the organization of that market but also by virtue of the scope and character of its activities elsewhere. It may be able to exploit, extend, or defend its power by tactics other than those that are traditionally associated with the idea of monopoly.[25]

Professor George Stigler commented on Edwards' argument as follows:

The essence of [the conglomerate] firm, as I understand it, is that although the firm need not have an appreciable degree of market control in any one market, yet because of the many markets in which it operates and the large resources it possesses, a power is acquired to sell and buy at preferential terms. I must confess that the exact mechanics by which the total power possessed by the firm gets to be larger than the sum of the parts (in individual markets) escape me, and I am not sure that there are any companies that meet the specifications of the conglomerate firm. There is a certain resemblance between Edwards' concept and the structure of, e.g., duPont, but duPont has monopoly power in many markets, and therefore one does not have to resort to conglomerateness to explain its power and prosperity.[26]

The perceived objectives of the conglomerate firm and the

---

[25] Corwin Edwards, "Conglomerate Bigness as a Source of Power," in *Business Concentration and Price Policy* (Princeton: Princeton University Press, 1955), p. 332.

[26] George J. Stigler, "Mergers and Preventive Antitrust Policy," pp. 183–184.

managerial methods employed to attain them lie at the heart of the issue. First, there is the question of whether conglomerate firms, to some perceptibly different degree than "other" firms, seek maximum profits; second, if there is no perceptible difference between conglomerate and other firms in terms of their respective preoccupation with profits, there is the question of whether conglomerate firms possess and employ certain distinctive managerial techniques for attaining their profits objective.

Professor Joseph Bower has dealt with both aspects of this issue.[27] He concludes that managements of diversified firms are singularly driven by the profits motive. Unlike "steel men" or "knitwear men," they are not constrained by or exclusively committed to "their" industry; instead, they react to a broad range of environmental factors and are unusually alert to profit opportunities wherever they exist. Their instrument of control is multiple profit centers, which means that corporate managements' demands for yearly improvements in earnings applied indiscriminately to all divisions make of the conglomerate firm consummate profits maximizers — often, unbridled profits maximizers.

Clearly, Edwards and Bower, as do others, hold conflicting views on how large diversified firms are managed. The conflicting views in turn give rise to conflicting hypotheses concerning conglomerate firm behavior and its public policy implications. The central antitrust policy issues concerning the conglomerate firm arise out of the firm's alleged special capacity to circumvent and subvert the forces of the marketplace. In brief, the multiproduct firm has open to it the possibility of dissolving the nexus of the product cost and

---

[27] See Joseph L. Bower, "Planning Within the Firm," *American Economic Review*, Vol. 60 (May 1970), pp. 186–194. Also, by the same author, *Managing the Resource Allocation Process: A Study of Corporate Planning and Investment.*

revenue functions on which economic models of firms and markets discussed above have been erected.

The validity of this proposition can be tested only by factual analysis of how conglomerate firms are actually managed; the greater the independent accountability of the various product divisions or profit centers of multiproduct firms, the less valid this proposition becomes. Specifically, the hypotheses that conglomerate firms are singularly given to (1) cross-subsidization, (2) reciprocity in buying and selling, (3) nonprice competition, and (4) the raising of barriers to entry, all clearly presuppose the co-mingling of divisional resources and interdependence among divisions in respect to decisions on important market variables.[28] It is equally evident that these same hypotheses also rest on the assumptions that multiproduct firms possess sufficient market power to yield the monopoly profits requisite to their engagement in interproduct marketing strategies, and that they have incentives to employ such strategies.

## Cross-Product Subsidization

Most of the policy concerns about conglomerate firm behavior are, as will be shown later on, intellectual descendants of the cross-product subsidization hypothesis. Accordingly, the fact that the analytical content of the concept remains virtually undeveloped leaves an especially important void in the theory of conglomerate firm behavior. At a purely descriptive level, the meaning of the term is reasonably clear. A firm engages in cross-subsidization when it employs the revenues earned in one product line to support the activities

---

[28] For discussions of the possible economic effects of conglomerate firms see *Conglomerate Mergers and Acquisitions: Opinion and Analysis, St. John's Law Review*, Special Edition, Vol. 44 (Spring 1970), esp. pp. 9–14, 42–44, 66–80, 90–151, 266–281, 341–377, and 416–438.

pertaining to another. But this does not even define the policy issue, much less resolve it. First, it is not clear whether the concern is with the excess net revenues earned in the "subsidizing" line that makes the cross-subsidization possible, or with the use of these revenues by the "subsidized" product line to engage in activities, or even to continue operating, which it could not finance out of its own revenues. Second, whether it is either of these components of cross-subsidization, or the combination of the two, that comprises the public policy concern, it is clear that they are not confined to conglomerate enterprise; it is not even clear that they are predominantly associated with conglomerate enterprise. And finally, cross-subsidization as a continuing activity cannot be reconciled with the generally accepted theory of the firm.

First is the matter of excess (abnormal) profitability. While the relationship between profitability and "degree of conglomerateness" has not yet been firmly established, it is perfectly obvious that profits in excess of competitive levels are not limited to divisions of highly diversified companies. In fact, reports from the financial world, especially since 1968, have generally headlined the disappointing profits record of some of the more prominent conglomerates. The relevant factual evidence on this point, however, is sufficiently conclusive. An impressive array of studies show that high profitability is associated with a variety of market structure and performance variables; e.g., share of market, advertising intensity, and innovational activities, none of which appear to be uniquely associated with conglomerate firms; moreover, rate of return data by firm and by industry, such as those published periodically by the Federal Trade Commission,[29] show that such relatively undiversified companies

---

[29] *Cf. Report of the Federal Trade Commission on Rates of Return for Identical Companies in Selected Manufacturing Industries, 1958–1967.*

as those engaged in the pharmaceutical, tobacco products (until recently), bakery products, and footwear industries have consistently ranked high on the profitability list. Profitability and conglomerateness, then, are distinctly separate issues.

Second, if the policy concern is that the division subsidized, through its access to "outside" resources, may be maintained beyond its viable economic lifetime were it strictly an independent economic entity, very small businesses rather than conglomerates are the classical textbook case of this particular phenomenon. As the United States Nobel Memorial Prize winner, Professor Paul Samuelson, observed in an early edition of his leading economics textbook, the dominant form of business enterprise in the United States in terms of numbers is the self-owned individual proprietorship. Typically, these firms survive only as long as it takes to exhaust the owners' initial capital, and even then the owners further subsidize their businesses by working long hours and at considerably less than the wages they could earn working in comparable jobs for someone else.[30]

It may very well be true that multiproduct firms continue to operate subsidiaries and divisions, perhaps in some instances for long periods of time, while they are earning below-average profits, or even suffering losses.[31] The economic theory of the firm suggests that *any* firm will maintain operations over the lifetime of the capital invested so long as its total revenues from operations exceed its total variable costs. The issue therefore reduces itself to whether conglomerate firms would be more disposed to violate this managerial rule than single-product firms; without a comprehensive fac-

---

[30] Paul A. Samuelson, *Economics: An Introductory Analysis* (New York: McGraw-Hill Book Company, Inc., 1955), 3rd ed., pp. 74–75.

[31] *Cf.*, Joel B. Dirlam, "Observations on Public Policy Toward Conglomerate Mergers," *St. John's Law Review*, Special Edition (Spring 1970), p. 198.

tual analysis, the answer to this question is not entirely unambiguous. On the one hand, a multiproduct firm earning sufficiently large profits on other operations clearly *could* continue the operation of a division earning total revenues less than its total variable costs, but it would be irrational for it to do so unless the future prospects were for improved profitability, and the short-run subsidization was simply to tide the operation over its period of temporary financial adversity. On the other hand, highly diversified firms are, by definition, less permanently committed to a particular product line than are single-product firms; they would therefore be expected to shift resources out of less profitable operations and into more profitable ones more quickly than single-product firms. On balance, there would appear to be no a priori reason to suppose that conglomerate firms are more disposed than other firms to subsidize unprofitable operations.

The cross-subsidization issue, of course, is more complex than this. It is generally defined broadly enough to include such subordinate issues as "deep pocket" and predatory pricing practices, e.g., the use of revenues earned on some product divisions to support the advertising or to "subsidize" the lower prices of others. Again, it is not clear what special incentives confront multiple-product firms that would induce them to reduce total profits by pursuing these practices. Presumably all firms advertise to the point where marginal revenues from advertising are equal to its marginal costs. Similarly, firms selling in competitive markets have little choice as to the prices they charge, and those selling in oligopolistic markets, according to the conventional economic wisdom, are not especially given to undercutting their rivals' prices. This obviously does not necessarily mean that business firms completely eschew such practices but the annals of business enterprise apparently reveal few, if any, cases where firms have used predatory pricing as a strategic weapon. Moreover, on close inspection of the highly incomplete case record, such predatory practices do not appear to be confined to, or even concentrated in, conglomerate firms.[32] In any case, such predatory practices fall under the jurisdiction of laws prohibiting unfair methods of competition and attempts to monopolize, irrespective of the type of firm engaging in them.

## *Reciprocity*

The creation of reciprocity power, as pointed out earlier,[33] is one of the critical tests the Department of Justice has proposed for prosecuting conglomerate mergers under Section 7 of the Clayton Act. While no systematic quantitative study has been made of the extent to which reciprocity is practiced in American industry,[34] it is generally believed to have been a traditional policy of some firms and used sporadically by many others. Professor Jules Backman recently summarized the available factual evidence on the extent of reciprocity as follows:

> In a 1961 survey of company purchasing agents to which 300 responded, it was revealed that about half of them worked for companies in which reciprocity was "a factor in buyer-seller relationships"; a 1965 survey of *Fortune*'s largest 500 corporations revealed that about 60 percent of them had trade relations men and, by inference, conducted "reciprocal affairs"; and from other scattered sources it appeared that reciprocity was "traditional" in the railroad companies and "widespread" in the tire industry.[35]

[32] Jules Backman, "Conglomerate Mergers and Competition," *St. John's Law Review*, Special Edition (Spring 1970), p. 114, esp. material in fn. 137.

[33] Chapter 1, pp. 3–4.

[34] See George J. Stigler, *Working Paper for the Task Force on Productivity and Competition: Reciprocity* in 115 *Congressional Record*. 6479 (daily edition June 16, 1969).

[35] Jules Backman, "Conglomerate Mergers and Competition," p. 95.

The central issue here, however, is not the pervasiveness of reciprocity but the extent to which facts and a priori logic establish a positive relationship between its practice and conglomerate enterprise. The surveys cited by Backman antedate the conglomerate wave of the 1960s. Moreover, it is doubtful that 60 percent of *Fortune*'s 1965 list of 500 qualify as conglomerates, and the railroads, oil, steel and tire manufacturers, banks, investment underwriting firms, mutual funds, and exchange houses (singled out in the *Fortune* article as businesses especially given to the practice of reciprocity[36]) are not generally regarded as striking representatives of conglomerate enterprises. The available factual evidence, therefore, only tends to confirm that reciprocity is practiced, and that its practice is not confined to, or even especially characteristic of, large diversified companies.

The logic of the case leads to equally ambiguous conclusions. A priori, either of two conflicting hypotheses appear to be equally plausible. The more diversified the company, the larger will be the *number* of markets in which it buys and sells, and hence the larger is likely to be the number of opportunities to practice reciprocity.[37] The opportunities for reciprocity dealings in terms of *volume* depend of course on the percentage of a company's sales made to actual and potential customers who are also actual or potential suppliers. This distinction between numbers and volume might be critical in terms of the strength of the incentives of a firm to practice reciprocity. A firm that deals with a very large number and a wide variety of customers who are also actual or potential suppliers may very well find that its incentives to practice

---

[36] Edward McCreary, Jr., and Walter Guzzardi, Jr., "A Customer is a Company's Best Friend," *Fortune* (June 1965), p. 180.

[37] *Cf.* Lee E. Preston, "A Probabilistic Approach to Conglomerate Mergers," *St. John's Law Review*, Special Edition (Spring 1970), pp. 341–355, esp. pp. 347–353.

reciprocity are weak or nonexistent: the record-keeping required would be unduly burdensome and complicated, the possibilities of alienating some customers are considerable, and no single customer or customer-market accounts for a large enough volume of business lending itself to buyer-seller reciprocity to make the risks worthwhile.

The optimum conditions for the practice of reciprocity would appear to be those where a firm sells a significant percentage of its products or services in a relatively concentrated market consisting of companies who are also important actual or potential suppliers of the firm's inputs. While it may very well be possible to find conglomerate firms operating under these conditions, there are no a priori grounds for concluding that these conditions are more likely to characterize large conglomerate firms than other firms.

The antitrust record on reciprocity dealings points also to this conclusion. The celebrated Federal Trade Commission case against the reciprocity dealings between Consolidated Foods and Gentry's customers who were also Consolidated's suppliers[38] did not involve a highly conglomerate firm; Kennecott Copper, National Steel, Bethlehem Steel, and Pittsburgh Plate Glass,[39] all of which the Department of Justice has recently sued for engaging in reciprocity, would rank low on any ordered list of conglomerates. None of this conclusively refutes the hypothesis that conglomerates beget reciprocity, but the factual, theoretical, and case evidence seriously challenges the validity of any a priori reason for singling out conglomerate acquisitions for antitrust action on these grounds.

---

[38] *FTC* v. *Consolidated Foods Corporation,* 380 U.S. 592 (1965).

[39] U. S. Department of Justice Civil Actions No. 71-119 (January 11, 1971); No. 70-3102 (December 14, 1970); and No. 71-189 (February 26, 1971).

ENTRY BARRIERS, CONCENTRATION, AND COMPETITIVE EFFECTS

The cross-subsidization and reciprocity hypotheses pertain to the managerial aspects of multiproduct enterprise. There has also been considerable theorizing concerning the direct impact of conglomerate enterprise on the structure of American industry. Particularly, many different opinions have been expressed on the possible effects of conglomerate mergers on both the level of concentration of the industries they enter and the overall level of concentration in the economy.

It is emphasized that most of the thrust of the contentions concerning the structural effects of multiproduct enterprise pertain to conglomerate mergers and acquisitions rather than to the managerial aspects of the diversified firm, although the two cannot be clearly divorced. For example, it has been argued that the entry of large diversified firms into industries previously inhabited entirely by small undiversified firms sets the stage for rising concentration in the acquired firm's industry;[40] the acquiring conglomerate can direct its large resources to the objective of enhancing its market share in that industry, and those resources of the acquiring firm in turn become barriers to new entry.

In most actual cases, however, this issue in the final analysis is reduced to certain managerial aspects of the acquiring firm. For example, in *FTC* v. *Procter & Gamble*[41] the court found that "[t]he acquisition may also have a tendency of raising barriers to new entry," [42] but this conclusion was based on Procter & Gamble's presumed ability to command shelf space and use large-scale advertising. The FTC reached

---

[40] *Cf.* Mary Gardiner Jones and Edward J. Heiden, "Conglomerates: The Need for Rational Policy Making," *St. John's Law Review,* Special Edition (Spring 1970), p. 264.

[41] 386 U.S. 568 (1967).

[42] *Ibid.,* p. 579.

the same conclusion, based on the same line of reasoning, in adjudicating General Foods' acquisition of S.O.S.[43] And in *Reynolds Metals Co.* v. *FTC*[44] the increased market share of Arrow Brands subsequent to its acquisition by Reynolds was attributed to retroactive price cuts on Arrow's florist foil[45] — a managerial practice generally associated with predatory pricing, but could possibly be a subtle form of cross-product subsidization. Clearly, the effect conglomerate acquisitions have on the structure of particular markets depends largely on how conglomerate firms are managed, and especially on the managerial rules conglomerate firms use in allocating resources within the firm and in the design of strategies toward particular markets.

The effect also depends on the market position, or positions, of both the acquiring and the acquired firm. The acquisition by a large conglomerate of a firm already in a dominant position in its respective market is likely to have different consequences than those of the acquisition by the same conglomerate of a much less significant firm in the same industry. If the former can be a means of preserving or extending an existent dominant position, the latter can just as surely be a means of challenging such dominance. For example, in reporting on the Department of Justice's suit against the LTV-Jones & Laughlin merger *The Economist* observed:

> Outside Washington a discreet cheer for the suit against Ling was raised in the boardrooms of the big steel companies; . . . A raider like Ling-Temco-Vought is an instant and unwelcome competitor to the established giants . . . .[46]

The impact conglomerate mergers are likely to have on the

---

[43] *General Foods Corporation* v. *FTC*, 386 F.2d. 936, 945 (3d. Cir. 1967).
[44] 309 F. 2d. 223 (D.C. Cir. 1962).
[45] *Ibid.*, p. 230.
[46] "Biting the Hand of Business," *The Economist* (April 5, 1969), p. 35.

overall level of concentration in the economy can be stated in much more precise terms: substantial acquisitions by firms in any size class will increase the relative position of that size class in terms of the size measure used; e.g., if the largest 50 corporations acquire a large number of other firms, other things being equal, their share of total assets, sales, employees, value added, or some other relevant variable, will increase. It is obvious, therefore, that mergers increase the relative size of the acquiring size-group, and that their effect on relative overall concentration in the economy depends on how the total volume of mergers and acquisitions are distributed among firms in various size classes.

## SUMMARY

The theory of the firm falls far short of providing a satisfactory explanatory hypothesis for how large diversified firms operate. Conventional theory establishes a presumption that profits-maximizing conglomerates will produce strictly independent products in the same quantities and sell them at the same prices as single-product firms would in the same market circumstances; they would sell competing products at higher prices and complementary products at lower prices than would single-product firms, provided they possessed the requisite market power in all the markets involved. This does not preclude the possibility that conglomerates, or business firms generally, may forego short-run profits by charging nonoptimum present prices out of long-range strategic considerations, but such a strategy requires only that the firm, whether single-product or conglomerate, possess the requisite market power.

Since contemporary theory provides less than a satisfactory modus operandi of the conglomerate, it also falls short of providing a priori resolutions to many of the current policy issues identified with conglomerate enterprise, especially those issues arising out of the recent upsurge in diversifying mergers and acquisitions. More particularly, it does not provide a basis for determining the tenability of the various conflicting hypotheses concerning such behavioral aspects of the diversified firm as cross-product subsidization, reciprocity dealings, and those that might logically affect market structure. Moreover, the existing factual evidence is much too incomplete to establish a set of workable guidelines for formulating public policy toward conglomerates or toward conglomerate acquisitions and mergers.

# 3. The Research Plan

## DATA GATHERING

THE DATA-GATHERING PROGRAM FOR THIS STUDY was designed to complement the existing storehouse of factual information in ways to permit analysis of certain operational aspects of diversified corporate enterprise heretofore left relatively unexplored. It was also designed so that analysis of the more important policy issues raised by diversifying acquisitions could be extended further than existing data would permit. Accordingly, the two central questions that established the scope of the data-gathering process were (1) what managerial aspects of diversified corporations of public policy import have not yet been satisfactorily analyzed? and (2) what are the ambiguities and deficiencies in existing data relating diversified corporations to the structure and practices of industry one might reasonably hope to remedy with additional data?

Deliberation on the first of these questions led eventually to the formulation of hypotheses concerning the operational aspects of diversified firms, which, for the most part, were logical extensions of the pricing rule for multiproduct firms developed earlier.[1] The rule, restated in abbreviated form,

---

[1] Chapter 2, pp. 30–32; and Appendix C, pp. 187–188.

is that a profits maximizing multiproduct firm should set the price and output of each of its products independently of the prices and outputs of all its other products, provided of course that the products are strictly independent; i.e., the product in question is neither a substitute for, nor a complement of, any of the firm's other products. In general, this independence, or interdependence, might also be expected to hold for such sales-generating activities as advertising and other selling expenses. To be sure, some companies may seek to promote the sales of all their products by advertising in the company's name; and it is very likely that advertising expenditures on one of a company's products may stimulate sales of that company's other products.[2] Nevertheless, in multiproduct market situations where price decisions would be expected to be independent, it would follow that decisions on advertising outlays for particular products would also be relatively independent.

On the other hand, one would expect a high order of interdependence among capital outlay decisions within the diversified firm. Since every firm, however large and however diversified, confronts a cost of capital and operates under a capital constraint, such firms should allocate their available capital among alternative investment opportunities in order to maximize their returns on total investment. This implies that the multiproduct firm's decision to invest capital in one of its product facilities cannot be made independently of its decision to invest in others.[3] In fact, one of the more persua-

---

[2] Such externalities are obviously not limited to interproduct effects within a single company; advertising designed to promote the sales of a company's product may very well stimulate the sales of a competing product.

[3] It would serve little if any useful purpose here to review the issue of whether firms in fact seek maximum profits, or whether the profits-maximizing hypothesis holds greater or less validity for the large multiproduct than for the single-product firm. However, see Joseph L. Bower, "Planning within the Firm," *American Economic Review* (May 1970).

ive arguments made in support of "conglomerate" enterprise
s that it is especially conducive to efficient resource alloca-
ion: Since a "conglomerate" firm operates in many indus-
ries its management is neither dependent upon nor especially committed to any one of them; accordingly, this type
of firm should be relatively unconstrained in allocating capi-
al to its most profitable uses.[4] Much of the same line of
reasoning applies to outlays on research and development.

## FIELD STUDIES

For purposes of testing the validity of the several pertinent
hypotheses, most of which relate to such policy issues as
"cross-product subsidization," reciprocity dealings, and capital allocative efficiency in multiproduct firms, at least two
methods suggest themselves: in-depth field studies of a limited number of conglomerates, and a less extensive statistical
analysis of the relevant corporate universe. Both were used
in this study. In-depth field studies of several large multiproduct firms generally considered to be among the nation's
most obvious "conglomerates"[5] led to the conclusion that the
degree of independence (or interdependence) among product
prices and price-related decisions could be inferred directly
from the organizational structure of the firm itself. In general, when the pricing and related marketing decisions are
made at the division or profit-center levels, rather than at the
corporate management level, it can reasonably be inferred
that such decisions are made independently of those reached
in other autonomous divisions. This inference is reenforced

---

[4] *Ibid.*, pp. 192–193.

[5] The field study included ITT and Textron; the names of other cooperating firms are withheld by request.

substantially when divisional autonomy is combined with a profit-center system of managerial control, especially when the profit center comprises no more than a single product line division. As one corporation president put it, the essential purpose of profit-center or divisional accountability is to hold the managers of such units financially responsible for their performance; this purpose would be defeated if the profits of one unit were compromised through an intercorporate pricing policy in the interests of another, or if corporate management engaged in or fostered reciprocity dealings.

The research results of others generally tend to confirm the findings arrived at through field studies. Berg found that the ratio of general corporate management to total management was discernibly smaller for the true conglomerates than for other large diversified corporations.[6] But more to the point, there is factual evidence that as firms become more highly diversified, such operating decisions as those pertaining to marketing, manufacturing, and purchasing tend to be shifted more toward operating divisions and away from central corporate management. For example, the FTC *Report* concludes that between 1965 and 1968 the 200 largest corporations became more diversified;[7] i.e., the average number of product categories for these companies at the 5-digit, 4-digit, 3-digit and 2-digit SIC levels increased during the four-year period. Studies by the Conference Board show that over the same period, the percentage of divisionalized companies having marketing, manufacturing, and purchasing functions represented at the corporate management level also substantially declined; of the major operating functions studied

---

[6] Norman A. Berg, "Corporate Role in Diversified Companies," Harvard Business School, Division of Research Working Paper HBS 71–2, BP 2.

[7] FTC *Report* (1969), p. 221.

(capital investment decisions were not included), only R&D registered an increase.[8] Among the more striking examples of divisional autonomy, dealt with at some length by Bower,[9] was the exercise of decision-making responsibility on pricing in General Electric prior to the famous electrical equipment price-fixing cases. Ralph Cordiner, then President of General Electric, testified that he was unaware of the price-fixing activities — an assertion that later drew harsh criticism from the presiding judge, not because he doubted its veracity but because he found it repugnant to his views on corporate responsibility.

Conclusions concerning the pricing and price-related practices of diversified corporations based upon the organizational location of the pertinent decision-making functions are subject to several obvious qualifications. Divisions and profit centers often comprise more than a single product. Accordingly, managers of these units, since they must render pricing decisions on more than one product, need not necessarily price all products independently. To the extent that they do not, divisional autonomy obscures intradivisional price interdependence. On the other hand, the mere fact that pricing decisions concerning more than one product are customarily made by a single decision-making unit, whether this be corporate, divisional, or profit-center managers, need not imply that the resulting product price decisions are interdependently reached. Despite these qualifications, however, a survey of a large corporate universe with respect to the

---

[8] *Top Management Organization in Divisionalized Companies;* Studies in Personnel Policy No. 195 (1965); *Corporate Organization Structures;* Studies in Personnel Policy No. 210 (1968); both by the National Industrial Conference Board, Inc.

[9] Joseph L. Bower, "Planning within the Firm," *American Economic Review* (May 1970), p. 193.

location of such decision-making functions as pricing, advertising, R&D and investment outlays, should provide a crude quantitative test of the decision rules derivable from the profits-maximization hypothesis.

Similarly, by the means of appropriate data-gathering techniques, it should be possible to ascertain a variety of other pertinent behavioral characteristics of the diversified firm on which the present state of knowledge is unusually limited and incomplete. The more critical issues on which reasonably reliable data are needed are, among others: the extent to which diversified firms engage in reciprocity dealings; the major changes that acquiring companies make in acquired companies after acquisition, especially in pricing, advertising, research and development, and investment outlays, and in management personnel and techniques.

The data required for subjecting these behavioral and managerial issues to quantitative analysis were obtained from a survey of approximately 600 large United States manufacturing corporations. The initial list of companies receiving the data request after two months of field testing, comprised all those manufacturing companies appearing on the 1969 list of *Fortune*'s largest 500 and, in addition, 100 corporations included on the list of The Associates of the Harvard Business School, but which were not among *Fortune*'s largest 500.[10] From these 600 corporations surveyed, 211 provided enough of the requested data to form the nucleus of the diversified firm data bank. The bank was enriched with selected *Compustat*[11] data for 183 of the 211 corporations, selected multi-

---

[10] The data obtained are described in Appendix C.

[11] *Compustat* is a magnetic tape computer data library containing annual financial information for over 1,000 companies published by Investor's Sciences, Inc., Denver, Colorado, December 13, 1971.

1ational enterprise[12] data for 125, and Charles Berry's diversi-
ication[13] data for 117.  This data bank permitted a variety of
:tatistical analyses presented throughout this volume, includ-
ng several regression models designed to identify some inter-
1cting behavioral and performance characteristics of diversi-
ied firms, and to ascertain the extent to which certain com-
)inations of variables could be related to growth in diversifi-
:ation, especially growth through "conglomerate" mergers
1nd acquisitions.[14]

As a further check on the relative importance of diversify-
ng acquisitions during the 1961–1970 period, each corpora-
.ion included in the survey was requested to report, by year,
he number and value of all acquisitions and the number of
liversifying acquisitions, the latter defined as an acquisition
:hat took the acquiring firm into an entirely new 4-digit SIC
industry, and the percent of their assets and sales as of 1970,
ooth including and excluding the postacquisition growth of
1cquired firms, attributable to such acquisitions.  These data,
;ince they pertain to all acquisitions, including those with
less than $10 million in assets, provided a new basis for mea-

---

[12] The Multinational Enterprise Project of the Harvard Business School is
1 continuing research program under the direction of Professor Raymond
Vernon. See James W. Vaupel and Joan P. Curhan, *The Making of Multina-
*ional Enterprise: A Sourcebook of Tables Based on a Study of 187 Major
U.S. Manufacturing Corporations* (Boston: Division of Research, Harvard
Graduate School of Business Administration, 1969).

[13] Professor Charles Berry of Princeton University supplied his indices of
liversification at the 2-digit and 4-digit SIC levels for all firms included in
:he *Fortune*'s largest 500 for 1960 and 1965. The index is calculated as:

$$D = 1 - \sum_{i=1}^{n} P_i^2$$

where $P_i$ is the ratio of the firm's output in the ith
industry to the firm's total output in n industries.

[14] For the *Compustat* and Multinational Enterprise Project variables, see
also Appendix C.

suring the importance of diversifying acquisitions relative to all acquisitions, and relative to the overall size of the 211 responding companies. They also provided a basis for measuring the effect of various types of mergers on the overall level of concentration in the period 1961–1970.

The data-gathering program was also designed to permit more precise measurement of the impact of diversifying acquisitions during the 1961–1970 period on the structure of the American manufacturing economy. Because existing definitions of "conglomerate" enterprise, and hence of "conglomerate" acquisitions, are not entirely unambiguous, time series of diversifying mergers were compiled under several alternative and, it is believed, equally plausible definitions.[15] This phase of the study consisted of a detailed cataloguing of each acquisition of $10 million or more according to whether it was a "conglomerate" acquisition at the 4-digit, 3-digit, or 2-digit SIC level. For each acquiring and acquired firm, a list of the SIC industries in which they operated prior to the acquisition was constructed from *Fortune's Plant and Product Directory* and *News Front*. By definition, a diversifying acquisition involved two firms without any overlapping SIC industries at the level specified.

Finally, the research plan was designed to address the issue of diversifying acquisitions and market concentration. As indicated earlier, a conglomerate acquisition, strictly defined, has no direct effect on the structure of particular markets; it simply changes the identity of the firms comprising them. Nevertheless, some have contended that the change in identity may very well indirectly affect market structure through eventual increases in the postacquisition market shares of the acquired firms. In both *FTC* v. *Procter & Gamble*[16] and *Gen-*

---

[15] See Chapter 1, pp. 15–17.
[16] 386 U.S. 568 (1967).

*eral Foods Corporation* v. *FTC*,[17] the Commission held that through the additional scale economies and larger advertising outlays from which Clorox and S.O.S. respectively would benefit, each of the two acquired firms would be enabled to exert greater dominance over their actual and potential competitors.

The alleged effects in these two cases perhaps took on a degree of intuitive validity because both of the acquired firms already had the largest share of their respective markets.[18] In general, however, conglomerate acquisitions indirectly affect market concentration in any of three ways: These acquisitions may (depending upon the market position of the acquired firm and the type of postmerger, merger-induced sales growth the acquired firm experiences) increase market concentration, decrease it, or leave it unaffected. The possible indirect effects and the conditions under which they are produced are set forth in Table 3-1.

Consider first the case where the postacquisition sales growth of the acquired firm in its markets is greater than it would have been had it not been acquired. If the acquired firm was already among the four largest firms, and if the growth attributable to acquisition was entirely at the expense of the remaining three largest firms, the familiar concentration ratio would not have been affected by the acquisition; but if any of the growth was at the expense of firms not among the top four, the acquisition would have indirectly increased concentration. If the acquired firm was not among the top four and experienced positive merger-induced growth, the acquisition would have the indirect effect of either re-

---

[17] 386 F.2d. 936 (3d. Cir. 1967), *cert. denied,* 391 U.S. 919 (1968).

[18] The substantive validity of the FTC's argument, however, has been challenged as erroneous. *Cf.* James M. Ferguson, "Anticompetitive Effects of the FTC's Attack on Product-Extension Mergers," *St. John's Law Review* (Spring 1970), pp. 392–415.

ducing the concentration ratio or leaving it unaffected, de
pending upon whether the postmerger sales growth was a

### TABLE 3-1
**Possible Effects of Conglomerate Acquisition
on Market Concentration as Measured
by the 4-Firm Concentration Ratio**

| *(1)* Merger-Induced Sales Growth of Acquired Firm in Relevant Market | *(2)* Premerger Market Position of Acquired Firm | *(3)* Market Status of Firms Affected by *(1)* | *(4)* Effect on 4-Firm Concentration Ratio for Relevant Market |
|---|---|---|---|
| | Among top 4 | All in top 4 | 0 |
| | | Some or all not in top 4 | + |
| > 0 | Not among top 4 | Some or all in top 4 | − |
| | | None in top 4 | 0 |
| | Among top 4 | None affected | 0 |
| 0 | Not among top 4 | None affected | 0 |
| | Among top 4 | All in top 4 | 0 |
| | | Some or all not in top 4 | − |
| < 0 | Not among top 4 | All in top 4 | + |
| | | None in top 4 | 0 |

least in part at the expense of the top four or entirely at the expense of the smaller firms.

If the merger-induced growth of the acquired firm was negative (its postacquisition sales growth was less than it would have been had the acquisition not occurred), the merger would have the indirect effect of increasing concentration only if the acquired firm was not already among the top four and some of its relative loss in sales was picked up by the top four; in any other circumstances, the acquisition would indirectly either reduce concentration or leave it unchanged. Finally, if the postacquisition growth of the acquired firm is the same as it would have been had the acquisition not occurred, concentration is obviously not affected.

It is impossible to establish conclusively the effect an acquisition has on the postacquisition sales of the acquired firm; the sales of acquired firms had they not been acquired cannot be replicated. For this reason, among others, the effect of conglomerate acquisitions on the level of market concentration cannot be inferred from the market position of the acquired firm at the time of acquisition; as already demonstrated, even the acquisition of a dominant firm could conceivably lead to a reduction in the level of market concentration, although inferences to the contrary may have a strong intuitive appeal. The only promising alternative means would therefore appear to be: (1) a comparison of the "before" and "after" acquisition performance of acquired companies, designed especially to ascertain discernible changes in sales performance and the use of such competitive strategies as advertising and R&D effort; and (2) a comparison of the recent trends in concentration of those industries frequently entered by acquisition with the trends in market concentration generally. The survey of large corporations discussed above was designed to permit the first of these comparisons; acquisition data published by the Federal Trade Commission and data on industrial concentration published periodically by the Census of Manufactures made it possible to carry out the second.

For the trend comparison analysis, the acquired firms having $10 million or more in assets were first arranged in a frequency distribution by their principal 3-digit standard industrial classification as reported by the Federal Trade Commission,[19] the narrowest classification the FTC used. Concentration indexes at the 3-digit SIC level were then calculated on a weighted average basis from the 4-digit concentration indexes available from census data for the years 1947, 1958, and 1967. For reasons explained more fully later on, the resulting observable changes in concentration must be interpreted with considerable caution, but they provide a crude measure of the effect diversifying acquisitions may possibly have had on market concentration at the 3-digit SIC level in the 1960s.

For most acquisitions, the 4-digit SIC industries represented by the same acquired firms could be ascertained from the *Fortune's Plant and Product Directory* and *News Front*. These industries were then arranged in a frequency distribution and the changes in concentration for the 4-digit industries most frequently entered were calculated directly from the concentration ratios published by the Census of Manufactures.

---

[19] See the Federal Trade Commission's *Statistical Report No. 7, Large Mergers in Manufacturing and Mining,* 1948–1970 (February 1971).

# 4.

# Diversified Company Management and the Policy Issues

MOST OF THE POLICY ISSUES RAISED by conglomerate acquisitions may be traced to a variety of conflicting hypotheses concerning the business objectives managements of diversified firms pursue, and the means by which they pursue them. In an earlier discussion of these hypotheses[1] it was proposed that neither the a priori logic of the theory of the firm nor factual analysis has yet been carried to the point where the conflicts, and hence the policy issues they have precipitated, can be satisfactorily resolved. This unsatisfactory state of affairs may be attributable in part to an observable overspecialization of professional labor: economists concerned with the public policy issues have generally evidenced little familiarity with the research output of students of business management; and the latter have rarely related their factual studies of management to the public policy issues. The major source of the conflicting hypotheses, however (and of why

---

[1] See Chapter 2, pp. 34 ff.

they remain hypotheses), is simply that the factual analyses of large diversified firms required to sustain the requisite generalizations have yet to be made.

The central policy issue, as discussed at some length earlier,[2] is whether the conglomerate firm possesses market power in excess of the sum of its parts, or, in the language of Edwards, is "able to exploit, extend, or defend its power by tactics other than those that are traditionally associated with the idea of monopoly."[3] Posed in these terms the question suggests two possible sources of market power unique to the conglomerate: (1) that attributable entirely to its intermarket structure, e.g., a firm having a 10 percent share of a dozen or so markets according to the usual methods of computing such shares actually possesses greater market power in each of these markets, say the equivalent of 15 percent, by virtue of its multimarket operations; and (2) that attributable to the tactical weapons or strategies available only to firms engaged in multimarket operations. On close inspection, however, the first is subsumed in the second and, moreover, its validity cannot independently be empirically tested. A firm having 10 percent of each of its various markets, and continuing to behave consistently with its having only 10 percent of each of its markets, i.e., it employs none of the multimarket tactics it allegedly possesses, is conducting itself simply as any other firm. Ultimately, therefore, whatever distinctive market power conglomerate firms may possess must derive from the business tactics and strategies their intermarket structure makes available to them rather than from their shares of particular markets. It is emphasized that this conclusion applies only to the *distinctive* market power inherent in conglomerateness. Obviously, the shares con-

---

[2] *Ibid.*
[3] See Chapter 2, Footnote 25.

glomerate firms may have of particular markets serve as indexes of their market power in those markets, just as they do for business firms generally.

The tactical weapons and strategies with which market power distinctive to conglomerates is generally identified are their alleged special capacity for reciprocity, cross-product subsidization and predatory pricing. Since this identification has never been subjected to systematic study, it is not surprising that students of public policy are in sharp disagreement on the extent to which conglomerates engage in these practices. There is even considerable disagreement over whether business firms of any type engage in them extensively enough to be of great public concern. Donald Turner, former Assistant Attorney General for Antitrust, has observed that the frequent assertions concerning predatory pricing remain wholly unverified.[4] Professor Richard Posner, noting that entrenchment is a contemporary version of predatory price-cutting, asserts that the new theory "uncritically ascribes crucial competitive advantages to size and uncritically denies the possibility that such advantages, if any, may stem from efficiency rather than from power."[5] On the other hand, Professor Robert Brooks apparently subscribes to the theory of the contemporary version to which Posner refers: "Predatory pricing can serve to provide the barriers to entry needed to protect the gains resulting from a successful use of the policy."[6]

The issues of reciprocity and cross-subsidization have been viewed with an equally striking lack of consensus. Professor

---

[4] Donald F. Turner, "Conglomerate Mergers and Section 7 of the Clayton Act," *Harvard Law Review*, Vol. 78 (May 1965), p. 1,340.

[5] Richard Posner, "Conglomerate Mergers and Antitrust Policy: An Introduction," *St. John's Law Review*, Special Edition (Spring 1970), p. 531.

[6] Robert Brooks, Jr., "Price Cutting and Monopoly Power," *Journal of Marketing*, Vol. 25 (1961), pp. 44, 45.

J. Frederick Weston concludes that the cross-subsidization
argument "lacks plausibility on grounds of general economic
theory," [7] while Edwards contends that the practice by diversified firms, whether conscious and deliberate or not, adversely affects their nondiversified competitiors.[8] Professors
Neil Jacoby, Jules Backman, and John Vanderstar all argue
that diversified corporate structure may itself militate against
the practice of reciprocity and cross-product subsidization.[9]
As Backman puts it, "each profit center seeks to maximize its
returns and is not willing to make sacrifices to help other
divisions." [10]

These conflicting opinions on the relationships between
conglomerate enterprise and business practices of public
policy import serve only to document the need to subject
them to factual analysis. Few would deny the need for facts,
but neither would they deny that satisfactory factual analysis
confronts extreme conceptual and practical difficulties. The
most obvious procedure of course would be to classify the
corporate population as conglomerate or nonconglomerate,
and proceed directly through appropriate data-gathering
techniques to ascertain the incidence of such practices within
each class. Aside from the difficulties of designing unambiguous operable classifications, a point developed at some length
earlier, the results would be of questionable validity. Since
such practices as reciprocity dealings, predatory pricing and
cross-product subsidization have been publicly condemned

---

[7] J. Frederick Weston, "The Nature and Significance of Conglomerate
Firms," *St. John's Law Review*, Special Edition (Spring 1970), p. 73.

[8] Corwin D. Edwards, "The Changing Dimensions of Business Power,"
*St. John's Law Review*, Special Edition (Spring 1970), p. 433.

[9] Neil Jacoby, "The Conglomerate Corporation," *The Center Magazine*
(July 1969), p. 49.

[10] Jules Backman, "Conglomerate Mergers and Competition," *St. John's
Law Review*, Special Edition (Spring 1970), p. 118.

as anticompetitive, and hence as either actually or potentially unlawful, such a direct approach would hold out little promise of appealing to the cooperative instincts of responding companies.

An appealing alternative would be a detailed analysis of company records that should reveal the extent and incidence of such practices. Obviously this approach would necessarily be limited to appropriately drawn samples from the conglomerate and nonconglomerate corporate populations, and even then the task in terms of time and resources would take on Gargantuan proportions. But business firms are understandably reluctant to open up their accounting records to researchers seeking evidence on the extent to which they may be engaging in actual or potentially anticompetitive strategies and practices. However, in the early stages of this research several "conglomerates" provided such records, granted access to divisional and/or profit-center periodic (usually monthly) reports,[11] and arranged interviews with members of general management who evaluated them. All of these companies stated that they pursued a policy of divisional independence, and one of the cooperating companies expressly prohibited the practice of business reciprocity and communicated this policy to actual and potential suppliers and customers.

While the study of this small nonrandom sample of firms shows that *some* conglomerates evidently do not engage in cross-product subsidization or reciprocity, the coverage is obviously too limited and too selective to support conclusions concerning conglomerate firms generally. Moreover, it is highly unlikely that such detailed analyses could be performed on sufficiently large samples of companies to establish valid generalizations on the relationships between conglom-

---

[11] See Chapter 3, Footnote 5.

erate enterprise and business strategies and practices. However, results obtained from the several company studies were suggestive of an alternative approach which, while from a methodological point of view has certain shortcomings, has the distinct merit of being operationally feasible.

## Organizational Structure and Managerial Practices

It was suggested earlier that, subject to several important qualifications, meaningful conclusions on certain managerial aspects of large corporations may be adduced from where in the corporate managerial structure the decision is made. Specifically, the more decisions concerning such matters as pricing, advertising, research and development, and capital investment are centered in divisions or production units the more likely they are to be made independently of those made in other divisions and production units. It was further hypothesized that rational pursuit of profits objectives would require independent pricing of products and services in cases where their production costs and market demands were independent, whereas decisions on capital outlays among products within the firm would necessarily reflect interdependence. Hence, within the multiproduct firm it would be expected that pricing and advertising decisions would be significantly more heavily concentrated at the division or operating unit level than capital investment and, to a lesser extent, R&D decisions. The detailed studies of several large conglomerates described above tended to validate the proposition that organizational structure might serve as a reasonably reliable proxy for the managerial strategies and practices with which this research is concerned.

The proposition that certain managerial aspects of corporations may be adduced from their organizational structure can scarcely be considered as novel, or as having found its origins in this study. Malcolm Salter has concluded that corporations experience four successive managerial stages as they develop from the one-man entrepreneur to diverse product and market divisions.[12] In the latter stage, divisional managers are accorded considerable autonomy in the conduct of their respective divisions' operations. Leonard Wrigley[13] found that divisional autonomy was more pronounced in "true" conglomerates (unrelated product firms) than in large diversified firms producing related products, even when both had evolved to the most advanced organizational stage. And Harry Lynch, focusing particularly on the management of conglomerate acquisitions, concluded that:

> . . . there is little integration of the operations of acquired subsidiaries; typically the acquired company continues as a separate operating entity, with the parent corporation assuming operating responsibility only for some staff functions. The parent corporation does, of course, acquire ultimate responsibility for subsidiary performance and, therefore, becomes involved in major decisions which shape the subsidiary's future. However, the parent corporation appears more frequently to provide a "screening" function rather than an "initiating" function in the strategic decision-making process.[14]

The findings set forth in these and similar studies support

---

[12] See his "Stages of Corporate Development: Implications for Management Control," *Journal of Business Policy*, Vol. 1, No. 1 (Autumn 1970), pp. 23–37.

[13] "Divisional Autonomy and Diversification," Unpublished Doctoral Dissertation, Graduate School of Business Administration, Harvard University, 1970.

[14] Harry H. Lynch, *Financial Performance of Conglomerates* (Boston: Division of Research, Harvard Graduate School of Business Administration, 1971), pp. 285–286.

the proposition that as corporations become more complex and diverse, their organizational structure undergoes a predictable metamorphosis. In the process, responsibility for operating decisions tends to gravitate from corporate headquarters to divisional management.

Further, there is persuasive evidence that divisional autonomy may be a more characteristic feature of true conglomerates such as Textron and ITT than of other large diversified firms. Professor Norman Berg, in an analysis of the corporate management of nine large diversified companies of similar size, found striking dissimilarities between the four companies classified as "diversified majors" and the five classified as "conglomerates." His pertinent quantitative findings are shown in Table 4-1. It will be noted that the conglomerates have far fewer corporate executives in total, and no corporate executives in the familiar functions of marketing, manufacturing, purchasing and traffic, and R&D. On the other hand, the conglomerates had a discernibly higher percentage of their corporate executives in the functions of general corporate management, finance, corporate planning, and law. The complete absence of marketing, production, and purchasing executives at the corporate management level is consistent with the hypothesis that pricing, advertising, purchasing, and production decisions are made independently at the divisional manager level, while the relatively large percentage of the conglomerate group's management in the general executive, finance, and corporate planning functions is consistent with the hypothesis that important investment decisions are made at the corporate management level where the prospective returns to alternative uses of capital must be assessed.

An important objective of the HBS Diversified Company Survey[15] was to test these hypotheses with data drawn from

---

[15] See Appendix B.

## TABLE 4-1

**Distribution of Corporate Management
by Function in Diversified Majors and Conglomerates**

| | Diversified Majors | | Conglomerates | |
|---|---|---|---|---|
| Function | Average Number of Corporate Executives | Percent of Total | Average Number of Corporate Executives | Percent of Total |
| General Executive | 4 | 1.3% | 5 | 5.5% |
| Finance | 84 | 27.9 | 51 | 56.0 |
| (Control) | (58) | (19.3) | (23) | (25.3) |
| Legal Secretarial | 20 | 6.6 | 17 | 18.7 |
| Personnel Admin. | 16 | 5.3 | 7 | 7.7 |
| Research & Devel. | 139 | 46.1 | — | — |
| Marketing | 10 | 3.3 | — | — |
| Manufacturing | 3 | 1.0 | — | — |
| Public Relations | 8 | 2.7 | 6 | 6.6 |
| Purchasing & Traffic | 12 | 4.2 | — | — |
| Corporate Planning | 5 | 1.6 | 5 | 5.5 |
| Total Average | 301 | 100% | 91 | 100% |

SOURCE: Adapted from Norman Berg, "Corporate Role in Diversified Companies," HBS Division of Research Working Paper, HBS 71–2, BP 2.

a much larger corporate universe. While in-depth studies of selected small groups of companies provide useful insights on the specific problems to which they are addressed, they seldom provide an adequate basis for generalizations on the corporate universe or its large subclasses. The Survey yielded 211 returns, of which 202 supplied data pertaining to the managerial level at which pricing, advertising, R&D and capital expenditures decisions were made (Table 4-2). The reporting companies, except for 31 companies where it was

## TABLE 4-2

### Location of Managerial Decisions
### Expressed as a Percentage
### of All Reporting Companies

| | | Number of Companies | | |
|---|---|---|---|---|
| *Type of Decision* | *Level of Managerial Decisions* | 57 Con-sumer | 114 Pro-ducer | 202 All |
| | | (*Percentages*) | | |
| Pricing | Other | 3% | 1% | 2% |
| | Profit Center or Operating Unit | 48 | 52 | 51 |
| | Mixed [a] | 19 | 19 | 18 |
| | Corporate | 30 | 28 | 29 |
| | | 100% | 100% | 100% |
| Advertising | Other | 2 | — | 1 |
| | Profit Center or Operating Unit | 42 | 44 | 44 |
| | Mixed [a] | 16 | 22 | 20 |
| | Corporate | 40 | 34 | 35 |
| | | 100% | 100% | 100% |
| R&D Expenditures | Other | 2 | — | 1 |
| | Profit Center or Operating Unit | 15 | 31 | 26 |
| | Mixed [a] | 23 | 29 | 28 |
| | Corporate | 60 | 40 | 45 |
| | | 100% | 100% | 100% |
| Capital Expenditures | Other | 1 | — | 1 |
| | Profit Center or Operating Unit | — | 3 | 4 |
| | Mixed [a] | 18 | 16 | 15 |
| | Corporate | 81 | 81 | 80 |
| | | 100% | 100% | 100% |

[a] Generally Mixed means that the decision is initially made at the lower unit and reviewed by the next highest organizational unit; e.g., a "mixed" decision on price between operating unit and corporate management means that the pricing decision is initially made at the operating unit and reviewed by corporate management.

impossible to do so,[16] were subdivided into producer-goods and consumer-goods companies, primarily for purposes of more refined regression analysis.[17] For 202 of the 211 responding corporations, 29 percent reported that pricing decisions, 35 percent that advertising decisions, 45 percent that R&D decisions, and 80 percent that capital investment decisions, were made at the corporate management level. For the same set of decisions involving only acquired firms (Table 4-3), the respective percentages for 173 of the 211 respondents were significantly lower, suggesting that acquired firms were accorded greater autonomy than divisions resulting from internal expansion or from acquisitions consummated prior to 1961. Only 12 percent of the responding corporations shifted the price-making function from the acquired firm to corporate management; the corresponding figures for advertising, R&D, and capital expenditures were respectively 20 percent, 27 percent, and 61 percent. Only in the case of the R&D decision is there a significant difference between producer-goods and consumer-goods companies; in consumer-goods companies R&D is left to divisional management relatively less than in producer-goods companies, and in the case of acquisitions, 37 percent of the reporting companies shifted this decision from the acquired companies to corporate management.

In interpreting these data it must be borne in mind that they were compiled from the returns of *all* reporting corporations. Some of the largest industrial corporations are obviously not highly diversified, a larger number are only slightly diversified, and an undetermined number are not organized

---

[16] These companies were important in both producers' and consumers' goods but the available data did not show that either was predominant in terms of share of total sales.

[17] See Chapter 6.

## TABLE 4-3

### Location of Managerial Decisions
### For Acquired Companies
### Expressed as a Percentage of All
### Reporting Companies Making
### Acquisitions

| Type of Decision | Location of Managerial Decisions | Number of Companies | | |
|---|---|---|---|---|
| | | 49 Con-sumer | 96 Pro-ducer | 173 All |
| | | (Percentages) | | |
| Pricing | Left with Acquired Firm | 27% | 33% | 30% |
| | Mixed [a] | 63 | 55 | 58 |
| | Moved to Corporate | 10 | 12 | 12 |
| | | 100% | 100% | 100% |
| Advertising | Left with Acquired Firm | 37% | 26% | 28% |
| | Mixed [a] | 43 | 56 | 52 |
| | Moved to Corporate | 20 | 18 | 20 |
| | | 100% | 100% | 100% |
| R&D Expenditures | Left with Acquired Firm | 22% | 12% | 14% |
| | Mixed [a] | 41 | 64 | 59 |
| | Moved to Corporate | 37 | 24 | 27 |
| | | 100% | 100% | 100% |
| Capital Expenditures | Left with Acquired Firm | 4% | 2% | 2% |
| | Mixed [a] | 41 | 34 | 37 |
| | Moved to Corporate | 55 | 64 | 61 |
| | | 100% | 100% | 100% |

[a] Mixed generally means that the decision is initially made at the lower unit and reviewed by the next highest organizational unit; e.g., a "mixed" decision on price between operating unit and corporate management means that the pricing decision is initially made at the operating unit and reviewed by corporate management.

along divisional or operating unit lines. In corporations falling in these categories, all important decisions are very likely made at the corporate level, in some instances because the company is engaged in a single or several closely related products or product lines where the issue of conglomerate interdependent decision making, or "cross-subsidization," is not especially pertinent. Where companies produce related outputs characterized by interdependent demands, the theory of the firm prescribes that they be priced interdependently.

While no attempt was made to reclassify all reporting corporations into single-product, related-product, and conglomerate categories, a satisfactory substitute technique could be employed. Professor Charles Berry has calculated diversification indexes at the 2-digit and the 4-digit level for 460 companies appearing on *Fortune*'s list of the largest 500 for the years 1960 and 1965.[18] One hundred and fourteen, over one-half of the survey companies providing data on where in the company decision making occurred, could be matched with Berry's indexes.

Cross-tabulation of the decision-making location for reporting corporations and various ranges of diversification indexes yielded a few modestly surprising results. In the highly diversified reporting corporations having 2-digit Berry indexes greater than .80 (Table 4-4), neither the pricing nor advertising decision was ever made at the corporation management level, whereas capital expenditure decisions nearly always were; and R&D decisions, while generally left to divisions, were sometimes made at the corporate level. These results are not surprising. It will be noted, however, that scarcely any discernible systematic differences can be detected among the completely undiversified and the intermediate diversification ranges — the pricing and advertising de-

---

[18] Berry's index is defined in Appendix C, B1–B4, and Appendix D.

**TABLE 4-4**

**Cross Tabulations of Decision
Location and Degree of Diversification
(2-Digit Level)
For 114 Reporting Companies**

| Type of Decision | Berry 2-Digit Index, 1965 | | | | | | | Percent of 114 Firms |
|---|---|---|---|---|---|---|---|---|
| | 0.0 | .01–.20 | .21–.40 | .41–.60 | .61–.80 | .81–1.00 | Total | |
| All 114 Firms | 13.1% | 14.9% | 21.0% | 25.6% | 21.0% | 4.4% | 100% | 100% |
| **Pricing** | | | | | | | | |
| Division | 12.7 | 9.5 | 19.1 | 23.8 | 28.6 | 6.3 | 100 | 55.8% |
| Mixed | .0 | 12.5 | 31.3 | 37.4 | 12.5 | 6.3 | 100 | 14.1 |
| Corporate | 20.6 | 26.5 | 11.8 | 26.5 | 14.7 | .0 | 100 [a] | 30.1 |
| | | | | | | | | 100.0% |
| **Advertising** | | | | | | | | |
| Division | 8.3 | 10.4 | 22.9 | 22.9 | 29.2 | 6.3 | 100 | 42.5% |
| Mixed | 4.5 | 9.1 | 13.6 | 40.9 | 22.7 | 9.1 | 100 [a] | 19.4 |
| Corporate | 23.3 | 23.3 | 16.3 | 23.3 | 14.0 | .0 | 100 [a] | 38.1 |
| | | | | | | | | 100.0% |
| **R&D** | | | | | | | | |
| Division | 3.2 | 12.9 | 25.8 | 25.8 | 22.6 | 9.7 | 100 | 27.5% |
| Mixed | 3.2 | 9.3 | 21.9 | 28.1 | 34.4 | 3.1 | 100 | 28.3 |
| Corporate | 26.0 | 20.0 | 12.0 | 26.0 | 14.0 | 2.0 | 100 | 44.2 |
| | | | | | | | | 100.0% |
| **Capital Expenditure** | | | | | | | | |
| Division | .0 | .0 | .0 | 60.0 | 40.0 | .0 | 100 | 4.4% |
| Mixed | 15.0 | 10.0 | 20.0 | 30.0 | 20.0 | 5.0 | 100 | 17.7 |
| Corporate | 13.6 | 17.0 | 19.3 | 23.9 | 21.6 | 4.5 | 100 [a] | 77.9 |
| | | | | | | | | 100.0% |

[a] Do not add to 100% due to rounding.

cisions do not appear to be relegated more to divisions in any monotonically decreasing pattern as diversification increases. Except for the reporting corporations having Berry diversification indexes falling in the .21–.40 class, the percent reporting that pricing decisions were made at the corporate level exceeds the percent of reporting corporations in each class until the 2-digit diversification index reaches .60. The .61–.80 diversification class accounted for 21 percent of all reporting corporations but for only 14.7 percent of the returns indicating that the pricing decision was made at the corporate level. However, there is a discernible tendency for the pricing decision to be shifted downward from corporate management and become a "mixture" of corporate and divisional management as diversification at the 2-digit level increases.[19] The relationship between degree of diversification at the 2-digit level and the location of advertising and R&D decisions follow a similar pattern except, as noted earlier, the closer the decision comes to an investment decision (from pricing to advertising to R&D to capital expenditures), the more it becomes a matter of corporate management.

A similar analysis employing Berry's 4-digit SIC diversification indexes yields a more continuous relationship between diversification and decision location (Table 4-5). In general, the higher the diversification index the more likely are pricing, advertising, and R&D decisions to be made at the division rather than at the corporate management level. For example, reporting corporations falling in the two relatively undiversified classifications having Berry 4-digit diversification indexes of zero and .01–.20 each account for 2.7 percent and 5.9 percent of the responses stating that the pricing decision was made by corporate management. In contrast, highly diversified companies having indexes falling in the .81–1.00 class account for 34.1 percent of all reporting companies and

---

[19] The returns reported as "mixed" are difficult to interpret because they make up a heterogeneous category, ranging from perfunctory submissions of price changes to corporate headquarters by division management to directives from corporate to divisional management that they review their prices.

## TABLE 4-5

### Cross Tabulations of Decision Location and Degree of Diversification (4-Digit Level) For 114 Reporting Companies

| Type of Decision | Berry 4-Digit Index, 1965 | | | | | | | Percent of 114 firms |
| | 0.0 | .01– .20 | .21– .40 | .41– .60 | .61– .80 | .81– 1.00 | Total | |
|---|---|---|---|---|---|---|---|---|
| All 114 Firms | 2.7% | 2.7% | 3.6% | 19.3% | 37.2% | 34.1% | 100% | 100% |
| **Pricing** | | | | | | | | |
| Division | 1.6 | 1.6 | 1.6 | 12.7 | 38.1 | 44.4 | 100 | 55.8 |
| Mixed | .0 | .0 | 6.3 | 18.7 | 43.7 | 31.3 | 100 | 14.1 |
| Corporate | 5.9 | 5.9 | 5.9 | 32.4 | 35.2 | 14.7 | 100 | 30.1 |
| | | | | | | | | 100.0% |
| **Advertising** | | | | | | | | |
| Division | .0 | .0 | .0 | 16.7 | 35.4 | 47.9 | 100 | 42.5 |
| Mixed | 4.5 | 4.5 | 4.5 | 13.6 | 27.3 | 45.6 | 100 | 19.4 |
| Corporate | 4.7 | 4.7 | 7.0 | 25.6 | 46.4 | 11.6 | 100 | 38.1 |
| | | | | | | | | 100.0% |
| **R&D** | | | | | | | | |
| Division | .0 | 3.2 | 3.2 | 12.9 | 29.1 | 51.6 | 100 | 27.5 |
| Mixed | .0 | .0 | 3.1 | 18.8 | 31.3 | 46.8 | 100 | 28.3 |
| Corporate | 6.0 | 4.0 | 4.0 | 24.0 | 48.0 | 14.0 | 100 | 44.2 |
| | | | | | | | | 100.0% |
| **Capital Expenditure** | | | | | | | | |
| Division | .0 | .0 | .0 | 20.0 | 40.0 | 40.0 | 100 | 4.4 |
| Mixed | 5.0 | 5.0 | .0 | 15.0 | 45.0 | 30.0 | 100 | 17.7 |
| Corporate | 2.3 | 2.3 | 4.5 | 20.5 | 36.3 | 34.1 | 100 | 77.9 |
| | | | | | | | | 100.0% |

for only 14.7 percent of the responses stating that the pricing decision was made at the corporate management level. This positive relationship between degree of diversification and apparent divisional autonomy also holds for advertising and R&D decisions. Again, the capital expenditures decision is predominantly centered in corporate management irrespective of the degree of diversification.

This analysis suggests that at some "threshold" level of conglomerateness, responsibility for operating decisions such as those concerned with pricing and advertising is transferred to division management. Companies with diversification indexes greater than .80 at the 2-digit SIC level are highly diversified, and in fact are to a considerable extent the companies often referred to as true conglomerates. This is borne out by the data showing that for this group of companies such operating decisions are virtually never the responsibility of corporate management.

This "threshold" is less apparent in the 4-digit SIC comparative analysis because companies with high 4-digit diversification indexes are spread over a wide range of diversification as measured at the 2-digit level (Table 4-6). Of the 42

### TABLE 4-6

**Forty-Two Responding Companies Having
Berry 4-Digit Diversification Indexes of .80 or
Greater, Classified According to Their Respective
2-Digit Diversification Indexes**

| 2–Digit Diversification Index Range | Number of Companies |
|:---:|:---:|
| 91–100 | 0 |
| 81–90 | 5 |
| 71–80 | 10 |
| 61–70 | 9 |
| 51–60 | 7 |
| 41–50 | 3 |
| 31–40 | 1 |
| 21–30 | 3 |
| 11–20 | 2 |
| 1–10 | 0 |
| 0 | 2 |

responding companies having 4-digit diversification indexes of .80 or greater, two operate in a single 2-digit industry, i.e., they have 2-digit diversification indexes of zero; nearly one-quarter of the 42 companies have 2-digit indexes of .50 or less, and nearly two-thirds have 2-digit indexes of .70 or less. While 2-digit industry classes generally comprise a heterogeneous group of products, it can safely be concluded that 4-digit industries within the same 2-digit class are more similar than 4-digit industries falling in different 2-digit classes. The demands and production costs for similar products are obviously more likely to be interdependent than those for dissimilar products. Hence, consistent with the theory of the firm discussed earlier, it would not be rational business policy to accord divisions producing related products complete autonomy in respect to such operating decisions as those concerning pricing and advertising, even in cases where in the interest of efficient organization or for other administrative purposes, related products are assigned to different divisions. In companies having very high 4-digit diversification but low-to-average 2-digit diversification indexes, operating decisions routinely left to divisions in true conglomerates would logically require substantial participation on the part of corporate management. Accordingly, while the data show that divisional autonomy increases as the 4-digit diversification increases, diversification indexes at this level do not, as in the case of 2-digit indexes, isolate the true conglomerates producing many strictly independent products.[20]

---

[20] Although all the firms falling in the 2-digit diversification index range of .81 to 1.00 in Table 4-4 are obviously highly diversified, i.e., "conglomerate," it should be pointed out that all companies producing completely independent products may not fall in that class interval. For example, three compa-

## CONGLOMERATE ENTERPRISE AND RECIPROCITY

Business reciprocity has loomed large as a policy issue pertaining to conglomerate companies, especially to conglomerate acquisitions. However, hypotheses concerning the connection between the conglomerate and the practice of reciprocity have been highly conflicting, ranging from the uncritical and unqualified assertion that it exists, to Weston's observation that, ". . . if reciprocity has been a practice in American industry the widespread conglomerate development is likely to hasten its diminution rather than increase it." [21] These conflicting hypotheses are likely to persist until the void in the pertinent factual evidence has been remedied. As Stigler has put it, "Systematic quantitative study of the extent of reciprocity has never been made." [22]

It has been urged in the literature[23] that the existence of a trade relations department in a company may at least be highly sugggestive of the practice of reciprocity. The reason for inferring a rough association between the two is that a corporation, especially one that is large and highly diversified, could scarcely practice reciprocity without creating an organizational unit responsible for communicating the relevant supplier and customer information within the company. There appears to be some evidence that trade relations departments have performed this function.

---

nies with outputs divided equally among 3, 5, and 10 2-digit industries would have respectively Berry diversification indexes of .67, .80, and .90. Although in terms of strict independence of products all three qualify as conglomerates, only the last would fall in the .81–1.00 class interval.

---

[21] J. Frederick Weston, "The Nature and Significance of Conglomerate Firms," *St. John's Law Review* (Spring 1970), p. 76.

[22] George J. Stigler, *Working Paper for the Task Force*, p. 6,479.

[23] See Chapter 2, pp. 41–43.

For obvious reasons the use of trade relations departments as a test for the practice of reciprocity can yield results that at best are suggestive rather than conclusive. Trade relations departments may certainly exist for a host of purposes other than that of enabling reciprocity dealings, a conclusion borne out by the field study undertaken as one of the early steps in the design of the HBS Survey. On the other hand, it is equally plausible that some form of sporadic and informal reciprocity may occur without benefit of the services of an organizational unit designed to facilitate its practice.

The HBS Survey requested data on the extent to which responding corporations had such trade relations departments, and on whether they served as a two-way conduit for information on customers and suppliers. This particular request for data generated more than the usual number of inquiries from responding companies concerning the meaning of the questions. While phrased in straightforward factual terms, the questions were evidently interpreted by some respondents — presumably those familiar with the literature on the subject — as equivalent to "Does your firm practice reciprocity?" a question that had been considered and rejected for obvious reasons. In the case of all requests for clarification, the respondent was urged simply to respond factually to the questions as stated. A check of the returns in instances where independent information sources were available confirmed that they did so. Whether the responses as a whole reflect a bias, and how much, is impossible to determine.

Of the 211 responding corporations, 195 provided the requested trade relations data, of which 31, or about 16 percent, maintained trade relations departments; 164, or about 84 percent, did not. The conclusions to be drawn from these data clearly depend upon the extent of the association between the maintenance of trade relations departments and the likelihood that reciprocity is practiced. If the relationship is strong, it can be concluded that reciprocity is practiced, but by a relatively small percentage of the corporate population.

As an additional check on the practice of reciprocity, and on the extent to which a trade relations department might serve as a reasonably reliable surrogate for it, companies were asked to indicate whether they regularly circulated supplier and customer lists to officers responsible for purchasing. While the wording of the question may be considered as having been addressed more pointedly to those yielding to the efforts of suppliers to benefit from reciprocity than to the aggressive use of supplier lists to promote the responding company's sales, it should not materially affect the reliability of the data. Reciprocity, by definition, requires the systematic matching of customer and supplier lists, and no company is likely to make reciprocity sales without engaging in reciprocity buying.

The responses did not lend themselves to entirely unambiguous interpretation. Some companies indicated that lists of suppliers, but not of customers, were circulated to purchasing officers. This of course is a normal business practice having no implications for the practice of reciprocity. While such responses could be classified as not indicative of the practice of reciprocity, the fact that so many responding companies revised the question before answering it suggests that the question was unclear, and hence that the responses may not comport with the information actually sought.

Nevertheless, the additional information supports the conclusion that companies with trade relations departments are much more likely to pursue practices conducive to reciprocity dealings than those without them. A cross-tabulation of the trade relations and information exchange responses revealed that of the 31 companies maintaining trade relations departments about 70 percent responded that they routinely circu-

lated customer and supplier lists to purchasing officers; and
of the 164 reporting that they did not maintain trade relations
departments, nearly 80 percent reported that they did not
routinely circulate customer and supplier lists. The overlap
therefore accounts for approximately 75 percent of all responses to the two questions. While the results suggest that
practices conducive to reciprocity may prevail in some companies without benefit of a trade relations department, and
that some trade relations departments may be entirely inno-
cent of reciprocity dealings, the correspondence between the
two is significant. And although the data do not point conclusively in this direction, they imply that inferences concerning reciprocity based on trade relations departments tend to
understate the extent to which reciprocity may be practiced.
The number of companies reporting that they routinely circulated supplier and customer information exceeded the
number reporting the maintenance of a trade relations department.

The purpose of the analysis, however, was to determine
whether reciprocity is positively associated with conglomerate enterprise. For both producer-goods and consumer-goods
companies the Berry diversification indexes were considerably higher for those corporations reporting no trade relations
departments than for those that did (Table 4-7), thus suggesting, but only suggesting, that "reciprocity" (having a
trade relations department) is less likely to be practiced by
highly diversified than by other corporations. Further, the
data show that the average number of diversifying acquisitions between 1961 and 1970 was substantially higher for
companies having no trade relations departments than for
those that did. It is therefore tempting to draw the conclusion that trade relations departments may be more a concomitant of companies long established in their traditional
product lines than of the diversification process. On the other

## TABLE 4-7

### Analysis of Responses on Trade Relations Department and Degree of Diversification and Diversifying Acquisitions

| | Yes | | No | | |
| | Mean | Standard Devia- tion | Mean | Standard Devia- tion | Difference of Means |
|---|---|---|---|---|---|
| TOTAL (99 firms) | | | | | |
| Berry 2-digit, '65 | .285 | .058 | .450 | .029 | .165 |
| Berry 4-digit, '65 | .630 | .054 | .729 | .019 | .099 |
| Berry 2-digit, '60 | .249 | .054 | .406 | .029 | .157 |
| Berry 4-digit, '60 | .588 | .053 | .688 | .021 | .100 |
| No. Diversifying Aquisitions | | | | | |
| 1961–1970 | 2.71 | .57 | 4.45 | .72 | 1.74 |
| CONSUMERS (31 firms) | | | | | |
| Berry 2-digit, '65 | .276 | .080 | .360 | .060 | .084 |
| Berry 4-digit, '65 | .592 | .067 | .728 | .027 | .136 |
| No. Diversifying Acquisitions | | | | | |
| 1961–1970 | 3.25 | .81 | 3.58 | 1.04 | .33 |
| PRODUCERS (58 firms) | | | | | |
| Berry 2-digit, '65 | .351 | .105 | .468 | .035 | .117 |
| Berry 4-digit, '65 | .658 | .120 | .741 | .021 | .083 |
| No. Diversifying Acquisitions | | | | | |
| 1961–1970 | 2.29 | .92 | 4.51 | .91 | 2.22 |

hand, the ratio of diversifying acquisitions to total acquisitions made in the period 1961–1970 was slightly higher for producer-goods companies, and significantly higher for consumer-goods companies having trade relations departments than for those that did not (Table 4-8). It therefore follows that while companies with trade relations departments tended to make fewer diversifying acquisitions than those

## TABLE 4-8

### Mean Value of Percent Diversifying Acquisitions to Total Acquisitions, 1961–1970, For Selected Subpopulations

|  | *Trade Relations Department* | | | |
|---|---|---|---|---|
|  | *Mean* | | *Number of Firm* | |
|  | *Yes* | *No* | *Yes* | *No* |
| Total, 158 firms | .536 | .382 | 27 | 131 |
| 47 Consumer Goods firms | .682 | .409 | 14 | 33 |
| 86 Producer Goods firms | .400 | .387 | 10 | 76 |

not having such departments, they made relatively even fewer total acquisitions. Again, these relationships sugges that reciprocity is more likely to be practiced by companie: long established in their traditional product lines.

## MANAGEMENT OF COMPANIES MAKING LARGE ACQUISITIONS

The more detailed information obtained from companies making individual acquisitions of $100 million or more in the period 1961–1970 made it possible to subject these companies to special analysis. The field studies undertaken prior to the design of the Survey suggested that acquisitions of this size may have characteristics that distinguish them from acquisitions generally. In view of the fairly rigid prohibitions on horizontal acquisitions developed through case law over the preceding decade, such large acquisitions appeared to have a high probability of falling in the conglomerate class. Accordingly, detailed information on how such important acquisitions were managed after they were acquired was of special interest. Moreover, the Federal Trade Commission, by periodically publishing the annual volume of acquisitions of $100 million or more in assets, had indicated that they might be of unusual public policy significance.

Fifteen of the 211 responding companies reported one or more acquisitions of $100 million or more in the period 1961–1970. Collectively, these companies reported six acquisitions of this size that do not appear on the FTC list. However, the FTC list identified nine additional respondents as having made large acquisitions which they did not report on the Survey returns. The discrepancies between the Survey returns and the FTC list are possibly attributable to the use of different measures of size; responding companies reported on the basis of what they paid for the acquired firm, while the FTC series is based on the book value of assets of the acquired firm at time of acquisition. Wherever possible the nine respondents identified by the FTC under its criterion as having made acquisitions of $100 million or more are included in the following analysis of large company acquirers.

The FTC classified 84 percent of all acquisitions of this size as "conglomerate" at the 4-digit SIC level. However, further analysis revealed that over one-third of such acquisitions had an important horizontal component at the 4-digit SIC level, and an additional 20 percent had an important horizontal component at the 3-digit or 2-digit SIC level. In comparison with all responding companies, the 24 making large acquisitions also made relatively more acquisitions, were more highly diversified, and had larger shares of their 1970 sales and assets attributable to acquisition.[24]

Although the acquiring firms making large acquisitions were generally more diversified than all responding companies, frequency distributions of their Berry diversification indexes indicate that they are not uniformly among the country's most diversified companies (Table 4-9). Nearly one-third of the 24 companies had Berry 2-digit diversification indexes of less than .50. Accordingly, while the group includes

---

[24] See Chapter 6.

## TABLE 4-9
### Diversification of Companies Making Individual Acquisitions of $100 Million or More Compared with All Responding Companies

(In Percent)

| Berry Diversification Index Range | Number of SIC Industries in 1970 | | Number of SICs Entered by Acquisition '61–'70 | | Berry 2-Digit Index—1965 | | Berry 4-Digit Index—1965 | |
|---|---|---|---|---|---|---|---|---|
| | Large Acquisitions $100M and over | All Responding Companies | Large Acquisitions $100M and over | All Responding Companies | Large Acquisitions $100M and over | All Responding Companies | Large Acquisitions $100M and over | All Responding Companies |
| No Response | 17 | 13 | 8 | 11 | 19 | — | 17 | — |
| 0 | — | 2 | 12 | 30 | — | 57 | — | 53 |
| .01– .10 | 12 | 44 | 35 | 47 | 8 | 3 | — | — |
| .11– .20 | 17 | 19 | 21 | 7 | 4 | 3 | — | 1 |
| .21– .30 | 17 | 10 | 12 | 2 | 8 | 6 | 4 | 2 |
| .31– .40 | 4 | 4 | 8 | 1 | — | 3 | — | 1 |
| .41– .50 | 25 | 4 | — | 1 | 12 | 8 | 8 | 4 |
| .51– .60 | 4 | 1 | 4 | — | 20 | 12 | 25 | 19 |
| .61– .80 | — | 2 | — | — | 17 | 6 | 4 | 4 |
| .81–1.00 | 4 | 1 | — | 1 | 12 | 2 | 42 | 16 |
| Total | 100 | 100 | 100 | 100 | 100 | 100 | 100 | 100 |

a large sample of the highly publicized conglomerates it also includes some relatively undiversified companies.

The survey results indicate that two-thirds of the large acquirer companies grant virtual autonomy to the acquired companies in respect to operating decisions; in by far the most typical case the acquiring company management confines itself to an advisory role (Table 4-10). However, in

## TABLE 4-10

### Managerial Policy Questionnaire Responses
(Acquisitions Greater Than $100 Million)

| Question | Acquisitions | Acquirer Companies |
|---|---|---|
| Number of Responses | 30 | 15 |
| I. Which of the following statements most accurately describes the extent to which management of the acquired firm was reorganized: | | |
| 1. Two or more members of top management replaced | 16% | 20% |
| 2. All top management retained | 60 | 73 |
| 3. No response | 24 | 7 |
| Total | 100% | 100% |
| II. Which of the following statements more accurately describes the managerial policy of the company with respect to acquired companies: | | |
| 1. Corporate management assumes significant responsibilities for acquired companies' operating decisions | 16% | 33% |
| 2. Management of the acquired company given virtual independence in operating decision making, but corporate management provides advice and general administrative services | 60 | 60 |

(continued on page 86)

**TABLE 4-10** (*continued*)

| | | |
|---|---|---|
| 3. Management of acquired company made accountable for corporate management only for financial performance; how it is obtained left to acquired company | 24 | 7 |
| Total | 100% | 100% |

III. In general do the accounting methods and practices of acquired firms undergo substantial revision after acquisition?

| | | |
|---|---|---|
| 1. Yes | 10% | 20% |
| 2. No | 90 | 80 |
| Total | 100% | 100% |

| | Yes | No | No Re-sponse | Total Re-sponse |
|---|---|---|---|---|
| IV. Does your company maintain a trade relations department? | | | | |
| Acquisitions Over $100 Million | 21% | 71% | 8% | 24 |
| All Respondents | 14 | 78 | 8 | 204 |

one-fifth of such large acquisitions the acquired firm is likely to undergo more than incidental reorganization; several of its top management are replaced, and its accounting system undergoes substantial revision.

The differences in divisional autonomy with respect to particular operating decisions conform fairly closely to the pattern for all responding companies, except that such decisions are made relatively less often by corporate management of acquirers of large firms (Table 4-11). On the other hand, corporate management appears to have greater responsibility for investment decisions in acquirers of large companies than in all responding companies. Only 8 percent of the acquirers of large companies reported that the pricing decision was shifted from the acquired company to corporate management, about twice this number shifted the responsibility for both

## TABLE 4-11
### Decision-Making Levels and Locations
#### ($100 Million and Over Companies, Compared with All Responding Companies)

| DECISIONS: | Pricing | | Advertising | | R&D | | Capital Expenditure | |
|---|---|---|---|---|---|---|---|---|
| SAMPLE: | $100M | Total | $100M | Total | $100M | Total | $100M | Total |
| LEVELS OF DECISION MAKING | | | | | | | | |
| No Response or Other | 12% | 5% | 12% | 5% | 8% | 4% | 12% | 4% |
| Profit Center | 21 | 20 | 17 | 16 | 8 | 6 | — | 1 |
| Mix | 8 | 3 | — | 2 | — | 2 | — | — |
| Operating Unit | 30 | 20 | 17 | 27 | 21 | 18 | — | 3 |
| Mix | 8 | 14 | 25 | 17 | 38 | 24 | 8 | 15 |
| Corporate | 21 | 28 | 29 | 33 | 25 | 46 | 80 | 77 |
| LOCATION OF DECISION AFTER ACQUISITION | | | | | | | | |
| No Response | 4% | 16% | 4% | 16% | 8% | 16% | 4% | 17% |
| Left with Acq'd Co. | 25 | 23 | 16 | 23 | 12 | 23 | — | 11 |
| Mix | 63 | 50 | 62 | 44 | 63 | 44 | 29 | 48 |
| Moved to Corporate | 8 | 11 | 17 | 17 | 17 | 17 | 67 | 24 |
| Number of Responses | 24 | 205 | 24 | 205 | 24 | 205 | 24 | 205 |

advertising and R&D decisions to corporate management, and nearly all of them shifted the investment decision to the corporate level.

All 15 of the reporting companies making large acquisitions provided detailed data which permitted an analysis of the effects of acquisition on financial performance. Specifically, they provided annually data for acquired companies on profits before and after taxes, advertising and R&D expenditures, new capital outlays, and depreciation and interest charges, for the three years preceding and the three years following the acquisition. Ratios of the "after" to the "before" time periods for the various activities are shown in Table 4-12.

### TABLE 4-12
#### Effects of Acquisition on Financial
#### Performance of Acquired Companies

| Financial Category | Number of Acquisitions | Ratio of 3 Years After Acquisition to 3 Years Before |
|---|---|---|
| Profits before taxes | 18 | 130 |
| Profits after taxes | 18 | 136 |
| Advertising expenditures | 3 | 119 |
| R&D expenditures | 2 | 100 |
| New capital outlays | 15 | 220 |
| Depreciation charges | 21 | 165 |
| Interest charges | 17 | 198 |

NOTE: Based on data supplied by 15 acquiring companies making individual acquisitions of $100 million or more, 1961–1970.

It scarcely needs to be emphasized that comparisons of this sort encounter obvious difficulties. As pointed out above, the accounting methods underwent substantial changes in 20 percent of the acquired companies after acquisition. There are no readily available means whereby the reported data can be recalculated on a strictly comparable accounting basis.

Moreover, intertemporal comparisons are always subject to the qualification that since they, by definition, involve different time periods they involve different economic conditions. However, this problem is somewhat less critical in this analysis since the acquisitions are spread over the years 1961–1967; i.e., the "before" period for some acquisitions is the "after" period for others.

In spite of these qualifications, the data indicate that the acquired companies underwent substantial expansion after acquisition and, on the average, became more profitable. The almost doubling of interest charges after acquisition made it virtually certain that a considerable portion of the postacquisition expansion was financed by debt. The ratios for such activities as advertising and R&D are based on far too few companies to support generalizations of any sort; however, for the few acquired companies covered, the data show that acquisition had little effect on these activities. In general, the results of this analysis are consistent with the earlier findings that corporate management takes a decidedly more active role in investment decisions pertaining to divisions and acquired companies than in those pertaining to their operating activities.

Finally, the responses of large company acquirers to the business reciprocity questions were compared with those for all reporting companies. Five of the 24 large company acquirers, or 21 percent, reported that they maintained a trade relations department, a somewhat higher percentage than that for all responding corporations (Table 4-10). However, the percentage of large company acquirers that routinely circulated customer lists and sales data to purchasing officers was only slightly more than one-half of that for all reporting corporations. As already elaborated at some length, these data obviously fall far short of providing an airtight case on the extent to which corporations practice reciprocity. However, on the issue of whether conditions conducive to reciprocity are positively related to conglomerateness, the data on the 24 companies making large acquisitions are not in conflict with those pertaining to all reporting companies. While all the evidence, on balance, tends to support the conclusion that the more diversified the company the less likely it is to practice reciprocity, in view of its inherent weaknesses a more supportable conclusion is that no positive relationship appears to exist.

## Summary

Developing public policy toward conglomerate acquisitions relies heavily on hypotheses concerning the techniques and methods by which conglomerate companies are managed. Since these hypotheses have never been systematically subjected to empirical tests they derive whatever soundness they have almost entirely from their intuitive appeal, an appeal that is greatly diminished in the company of equally persuasive counter-hypotheses; hence, the need for factual analysis.

Most of the propositions of policy significance concerning the management of conglomerates can ultimately be reduced to the "cross-product subsidization" issue and the issue of competition generally. In the process of commingling its multiproduct operations the conglomerate can, and presumably will, cross subsidize to the detriment of its competitors. Cross subsidization requires the coordination of the relevant decisions among the various divisions producing different products. Coordination, therefore, implies that these decisions are not left essentially to managers of divisions or producing units but require participation on the part of corporate management. This suggests that divisional independence with respect to such operating activities as pricing and advertising should be indicative of the absence of cross-product subsidization.

An application of this test to 204 large manufacturing corporations revealed that, in the highly diversified company, pricing and advertising decisions are left almost entirely to division or operating unit managers. In fact, at the very highest level of "conglomerateness" corporate management is never involved in these decisions but, consistent with the economic theory of the firm, plays a major role in decisions concerning large capital outlays.

Divisional autonomy is also suggestive of the absence of the practice of reciprocity, at least the more extensive forms of reciprocity that transcend individual operating divisions. Information on trade relations departments and their activities, however, made it possible to analyze more directly the relationship between "degree of conglomerateness" and the extent of reciprocity dealings. The results indicated that reciprocity may indeed be practiced by some of the responding companies, but that it clearly was not more likely, and was probably less likely, to be practiced by conglomerates than by corporations generally.

# 5.   Growth by Acquisition and Industry Structure

STUDIES OF MERGER MOVEMENTS HAVE TRADITIONALLY emphasized the impact of mergers on the structure of industry. When the movement consists essentially of mergers among firms in the same or similar industries (i.e., of horizontal mergers), emphasis on its structural effects is a logical concomitant of conventional economic theory. Horizontal mergers involving firms with substantial market shares lead eventually to increased concentration in those markets. When concentration reaches a critical level there is a greater likelihood that conjectural interdependence will dampen the vigor of interfirm competition. For this reason the marshaling of empirical evidence on horizontal acquisitions is essentially a matter of measuring their impact on the structure of the markets involved.

In the case of diversifying acquisitions the primary policy concern shifts from particular markets to overall levels of economic concentration. In its *Report* on the conglomerate merger movement of the 1960s, the Federal Trade Commission sounded an ominous note in addressing this concern:

In unprecedented fashion the current merger movement is centralizing and consolidating corporate control and decision-making among a relatively few vast companies.[1]

In any assessment of the competitive consequences of *particular* diversifying acquisitions, however, as distinct from assessments of merger *movements*, the impact they have on the markets involved is still the critical issue. After all, in enacting Clayton Act Section 7, Congress did not make unprecedented firm growth by acquisition unlawful; the test of legality in any particular acquisition or group of acquisitions by a company is still its probable anticompetitive effects on relevant markets. In applying this test, appropriately designed for adjudicating horizontal mergers, to mergers among firms in different markets, the evidence must inevitably be of a more speculative variety. Since the immediate effect of such mergers and acquisitions is to leave the measurable indexes on the markets involved unchanged, the focus of the inquiry shifts to probable future change. Accordingly, it has been suggested that the entry of large conglomerates into markets by acquisition may eventually lead to increased market concentration, or to the elimination of a potential competitor.

## Conglomerate Acquisitions and Company Growth

The HBS Survey data confirm one of the important statistical findings of the FTC *Report*, namely, that massive diver-

---

[1] FTC *Report* (1969), p. 3. Others have made even direr predictions. For example, Isadore Barmash has reported that, "In the late nineteen-sixties, at the peak of the conglomerate boom, it did not appear inconceivable that the whole of American industry might someday become a single, all-encompassing conglomerate—U.S.A., Inc." (*The New York Times*, Business and Finance Section, November 5, 1972, p. 1.)

sification through acquisition in the 1960s was confined to a very small number of companies. A frequency distribution of the diversifying acquisitions reported by 193 of the reporting corporations reveals that 126, or nearly two-thirds, of the reporting companies made only three or less diversifying acquisitions over the 10-year period; about 84 percent of the companies made eight or less; and only two percent of them made more than 50 (see Table 5-1). The survey data do not include two large companies known to have made a large number of diversifying acquisitions. Reasonable estimates would appear to indicate that widespread diversification through acquisition in the 1960s was confined to about 20 to 25 companies, or about 3 percent of the largest 750 manufacturing corporations.

Of greater significance than the distribution among corporations of the mere number of diversifying acquisitions, however, is the growth in corporate size attributable to such acquisitions. Corporations responding to the HBS Survey were requested to supply data on their overall growth during the 1961–1970 period calculated four different ways:

(1) Sales growth, not including postacquisition growth of acquired firms;
(2) Sales growth, including postacquisition growth of acquired firms;
(3) Asset growth, not including postacquisition growth of acquired firms; and
(4) Asset growth, including postacquisition growth of acquired firms.

In consultations with corporate officials of responding companies it became clear that insistence on segregating the requested data for diversifying and nondiversifying acquisitions would greatly reduce the response rate. Many acquisitions consummated over this period had elements of diversi-

## TABLE 5-1

### Distribution of
### Number of Diversifying Acquisitions
### Made by 193 Reporting Firms
### 1961–1970

| Number of Diversifying Acquisitions | Number of Firms | Percent of Firms |
|:---:|:---:|:---:|
| 0 | 65 | 33.7% |
| 1 | 20 | 10.4 |
| 2 | 20 | 10.4 |
| 3 | 21 | 10.9 |
| 4 | 16 | 8.3 |
| 5 | 8 | 4.2 |
| 6 | 2 | 1.0 |
| 7 | 9 | 4.6 |
| 8 | 8 | 4.2 |
| 9 | 3 | 1.6 |
| 10 | 2 | 1.0 |
| 11 | 3 | 1.6 |
| 12 | 4 | 2.1 |
| 13 | 2 | 1.0 |
| 14 | 1 | .5 |
| 15 | 2 | 1.0 |
| 17 | 1 | .5 |
| 26 | 1 | .5 |
| 28 | 1 | .5 |
| 34 | 1 | .5 |
| 47 | 1 | .5 |
| 53 | 1 | .5 |
| 70 | 1 | .5 |
| Total | 193 | 100% |

fication, horizontality and, quite often, verticality as well.[2] Moreover, it became equally clear at a very early stage of the inquiry that corporate management takes a much broader

---

[2] See Chapter 1.

view of diversification than that of simply extending the corporation's operations into a new 4-digit SIC industry. Company officials who were quite willing to designate those acquisitions involving new 4-digit industries voiced persuasive reasons why such acquisitions should not be regarded as diversifying, and clearly should not be classified as conglomerate, e.g., a container manufacturer acquiring a machine-servicing company to which it had previously contracted the servicing of its container-making machinery. However, officials stated with unanticipated uniformity that they could assemble from existing records the requested data for all acquired companies irrespective of type, because such computations were frequently used for managerial purposes internal to their respective companies. Hence, the growth-by-acquisition data pertain to all acquisitions.[3]

The growth of the responding companies attributable to acquisition expressed as percentages of 1970 sales and assets, both including and excluding the postacquisition growth of acquired companies, is summarized in Table 5-2. As in the case of the distribution of the number of diversifying acquisitions, the typical firm owes a relatively small percent of its 1970 size to acquisitions. The modal percentage class, very pronounced in the case of all four of the alternative measures, is 1%–5%; the mean share of 1970 size for sales and assets, including postacquisition growth, are respectively 23.3% and 21.1%. However, it is evident from the tail of the distribution that a small number of the reporting firms owe much of their 1970 size to acquisition. Whether measured in terms of sales or assets, 13 percent of the reporting companies owed over

---

[3] As will be shown later, the growth attributable to diversifying acquisitions can be approximated from (1) the relationship between the value and number of acquisitions; (2) the average value of diversifying acquisitions compared with the average value of all acquisitions; and (3) the ratio of diversifying acquisitions to all acquisitions.

## TABLE 5-2
### Percent of 1970 Firm Size Attributable to 1961–1970 Acquisitions, Including and Excluding Postacquisition Growth of Acquired Companies

| | Sales | | | | Assets | | | |
| --- | --- | --- | --- | --- | --- | --- | --- | --- |
| | Post-acquisition Growth Not Included | | Post-acquisition Growth Included | | Post-acquisition Growth Not Included | | Post-Growth acquisition Included | |
| Percent | Num-ber | Per-cent | Num-ber | Per-cent | Num-ber | Per-cent | Num-ber | Per-cent |
| 0 | 24 | 14.7% | 24 | 14.7% | 25 | 15.3% | 25 | 15.3% |
| 1– 5 | 35 | 21.5 | 29 | 17.8 | 42 | 25.8 | 27 | 16.6 |
| 6– 10 | 16 | 9.8 | 12 | 7.4 | 23 | 14.2 | 22 | 13.5 |
| 11– 15 | 21 | 12.9 | 14 | 8.6 | 13 | 8.0 | 14 | 8.6 |
| 16– 20 | 12 | 7.4 | 13 | 8.0 | 12 | 7.4 | 11 | 6.8 |
| 21– 25 | 11 | 6.8 | 10 | 6.1 | 7 | 4.3 | 13 | 8.0 |
| 26– 30 | 5 | 3.1 | 11 | 6.8 | 7 | 4.3 | 6 | 3.7 |
| 31– 35 | 9 | 5.5 | 7 | 4.3 | 8 | 4.9 | 4 | 2.5 |
| 36– 40 | 7 | 4.3 | 5 | 3.1 | 8 | 4.9 | 8 | 4.9 |
| 41– 45 | 2 | 1.2 | 5 | 3.1 | 2 | 1.2 | 6 | 3.7 |
| 46– 50 | 7 | 4.3 | 10 | 6.1 | 7 | 4.3 | 7 | 4.3 |
| 51– 55 | 3 | 1.8 | 5 | 3.1 | 2 | 1.2 | 8 | 4.9 |
| 56– 60 | 6 | 3.7 | 3 | 1.8 | 2 | 1.2 | 1 | .6 |
| 61– 65 | 0 | .0 | 7 | 4.3 | 1 | .6 | 3 | 1.8 |
| 66– 70 | 1 | .6 | 3 | 1.8 | 2 | 1.2 | 2 | 1.2 |
| 71– 75 | 0 | .0 | 0 | .0 | 0 | .0 | 1 | .6 |
| 76– 80 | 2 | 1.2 | 1 | .6 | 0 | .0 | 3 | 1.8 |
| 81– 85 | 0 | .0 | 2 | 1.2 | 1 | .6 | 0 | .0 |
| 86– 90 | 1 | .6 | 0 | .0 | 0 | .0 | 0 | .0 |
| 91– 95 | 0 | .0 | 1 | .6 | 0 | .0 | 0 | .0 |
| 96–100 | 1 | .6 | 1 | .6 | 1 | .6 | 2 | 1.2 |
| | 163 | 100.0% | 163 | 100.0% | 163 | 100.0% | 163 | 100.0% |

half of their 1970 size to acquisitions, including their post-acquisition growth, and in the case of four companies acquisitions accounted for over 75 percent. These data again lead essentially to one of the conclusions reached in the FTC *Report:* the acquisition wave of the 1960s, as measured in terms of its effect on firm growth, was largely centered in relatively few companies.

By using the data appearing in Table 5-2, in combination with the computed relationships between the number and the value (the transaction price paid) of all acquisitions, and the number and the value of diversifying acquisitions, a reasonable estimate can be made of the percent of 1970 firm size attributable to diversifying acquisitions. A correlation of the number and value of all acquisitions yielded a coefficient of 0.80, implying a sufficiently high correlation between the two so that the number of acquisitions may serve as a proxy for the value of acquisitions. According to data published by the FTC, between 1960 and 1969 conglomerate acquisitions accounted for 75.6 percent of all acquisitions and for 76.3 percent of the value of all acquisitions. These computations, although each relates to a different corporate universe, made it possible to estimate the share of total 1970 assets attributable to diversifying acquisitions by using the ratio of diversifying to total acquisitions.[4]

Obviously, the magnitude of the estimate depends critically on how a diversifying acquisition is defined. Under the "conglomerate" definition employed by the FTC, approximately three-fourths of all 1961–1969 acquisitions of $10 million or more in assets were of this type. If the data in Table 5-2 were adjusted by this ratio, the modal corporation would attribute only 2.25 percent of its 1970 assets to diversifying acquisitions made in the 1960s, and the mean corpo-

---

[4] For example, if 35 corporations owe 3% of their 1970 asset size to all acquisitions, and if 75 percent of both the number and value of all acquisitions were diversifying acquisitions, then it can be estimated that these 35 corporations owe 2.25 (.75 × 3.0) percent of their 1970 assets to diversifying acquisitions.

ration 15.8 percent (three-fourths of 21.1, the average share of 1970 assets attributable to acquisitions of all kinds for all reporting corporations).

The FTC data, however, overstate the percentage conglomerate acquisitions, as generally defined, were of all acquisitions over the relevant time period. On the basis of data supplied by 193 of the reporting corporations in the HBS Survey, only 35 percent of all acquisitions, irrespective of size, took the acquiring firm into a new 4-digit industry. A rechecking of the FTC list of acquisitions classified as conglomerate shows that well over one-fourth involved firms having one or more important 4-digit industries in common. If one alternatively eliminates from the conglomerate list acquisitions in which both the acquiring and acquired firm had one or more important 3-digit industries in common, and 2-digit industries in common, the FTC list is further reduced respectively by nearly 50 percent and by over 60 percent.[5]

It is obvious, therefore, that the measurable effect of diversifying acquisitions on the present size of large corporations generally — in fact, the measurable size of the 1961–1970 "conglomerate" merger wave itself — varies dramatically according to whether one adopts an all-encompassing or a restrictive definition of what constitutes a "conglomerate" acquisition. Under a restrictive definition — one that requires that the acquisition in question introduces the acquiring firm into an entirely new industry group having little or no relation to its pre-acquisition production and marketing activities: e.g., entry into a new 2-digit SIC industry — the average corporation owes an insignificant percentage of its 1970 asset size to conglomerate acquisitions in the 1960s; about 1 percent for the modal corporation in the survey; and about 6 percent for the mean corporation. However, and this point

─────────

[5] *Cf.* Chapter 1, Table 1-5.

bears repeating, a few of the more aggressive acquirers owe a very large percentage of their 1970 size to diversifying acquisitions made over the immediately preceding decade, both because they made a disproportionately large share of all acquisitions and, as demonstrated earlier, a larger share of their acquisitions were of the conglomerate variety.

## Corporate Size and Net Acquisitions

The foregoing analysis, following the procedures of most such studies,[6] is based on the gross acquisitions made by acquiring companies and groups of companies. Calculations of the effect of acquisitions on company size based on gross acquisitions, however, may be highly misleading, and will almost certainly lead to overstatement of the contribution of acquisitions to firm size. To illustrate, consider the case where a $1 billion corporation acquires a $.5 billion corporation, later divests itself of the acquired company by selling it to a second $1 billion corporation which in turn then sells it to a third $1 billion corporation. A simple calculation of the ratio of acquired assets to total assets over the time period these events occurred would show that each of the three companies, and the three companies as a group, owe 33⅓ percent of their asset size to acquisition. Obviously, the percentages reflect triple counting. If total acquisitions are adjusted by total divestitures to ascertain net acquisitions, the first and second companies owe zero assets to aquisition, the third company 33⅓ percent, and the three companies as a group slightly over 14 percent.

So that the net effect of acquisitions on company size could be more accurately measured, the HBS Survey obtained data

---

[6] *Cf.* FTC *Report* (1969), pp. 43ff; p. 274; pp. 743–745.

on the number and value of divestitures as well as acquisitions made by each reporting firm. Nearly all reporting companies supplied data on the number of divestitures; and most of them supplied the corresponding value of divestitures (Table 5-3). On the basis of data supplied by all reporting

### TABLE 5-3
#### Comparison of Acquisitions and Divestitures

| | All Reporting Firms | | |
| --- | --- | --- | --- |
| | Number of Companies | Number and Value in Millions of Dollars | Percent Divestitures of Acquisitions |
| Number of Acquisitions | 193 | $ 2,412 | |
| Number of Divestitures | 192 | 267 | 11.1 |
| Value of Acquisitions | 188 | $22,749.2 | |
| Value of Divestitures | 189 | 1,515.4 | 6.7 |
| | 187 of Matched Reporting Firms | | |
| Number of Acquisitions | 187 | $ 2,253 | |
| Number of Divestitures | 187 | 263 | 11.7 |
| Value of Acquisitions | 187 | $21,879.0 | |
| Value of Divestitures | 187 | 1,514.7 | 6.9 |

firms, the number and value of divestitures amounted respectively to 11.1 percent and 6.7 percent of total acquisitions. However, some of the responding firms reporting divestitures reported no acquisitions, and some reported acquisitions but no divestitures. Accordingly, the data do not pertain to identical lists of companies. Comparable data for an identical list of 187 responding companies show that the number and vaue of divestitures amounted respectively to 11.7 percent and 6.9 percent of total acquisitions.

Since the Survey covered the largest 1,000 manufacturing corporations, it can be assumed that virtually all of the divested subsidiaries and divisions represented transfers within the relevant corporate universe, i.e., the divestitures are included among the acquisitions of the companies covered in the Survey. However, it is not possible to ascertain which of the reported divestitures were also reported as acquisitions previously made by responding companies in the period 1961–1970, and hence to ascertain the extent to which gross acquisitions overstate growth by acquisition because of double counting. For all responding companies as a group the overstatement in terms of number of acquisitions is probably somewhat less than 10 percent, and in terms of total value of acquisitions somewhat less than 6 percent. The more interesting conclusion the data supports, however, is not that gross acquisition data overstate growth by acquisition, but rather that the volume of divestitures (often overlooked in merger analysis) is much larger than its neglect would imply.

In view of the great disparity in the number and value of acquisitions among companies, the data were analyzed to determine whether there was any discernible relationship between acquisitions and divestitures; i.e., do the most active acquirers also tend to be the most active divestors of divisions, product lines, or previously acquired companies?[7] For this purpose, the acquisitions made by individual companies were correlated with their respective divestitures. The resulting correlation coefficient was +0.24, and significant at the 2 percent level. This suggests that there is a modest tendency for the active acquirers also to be active divestors. Hence, calculations of the acquisition component of firm size based on gross acquisitions significantly overstate the net effect of acquisitions, and tend even more to overstate the net effect of acquisitions on the size of aggressive acquirers.

---

[7] The analysis did not distinguish between voluntary and involuntary (decreed in antitrust proceedings) divestitures.

## Diversifying Acquisitions and Market Concentration

Strictly conglomerate mergers, by definition, have no direct effect on the level of market concentration; in other words, the market shares of the acquired firm are not additive to any of those of the acquiring firm. It has been argued, however, that such conglomerate acquisitions may very well affect the level of market concentration indirectly — the financial and managerial resources of the acquiring firm may eventually enable the acquired firm to increase its market shares. However, the effect of conglomerate acquisitions on market concentration would depend on a number of factors. If the acquired firm were already one of the largest firms, and if its subsequent increase in market share was at least in part at the expense of firms not among the top four, such acquisitions might have the indirect effect of increasing the level of market concentration. If the acquired firm were relatively small, and if the postacquisition growth in market share were partially at the expense of the largest four, such acquisitions might be expected to lead to a decrease in market concentration.[8]

The only available data which may be used to ascertain the indirect effects of conglomerate acquisitions on market concentration are the familiar 4-digit SIC concentration ratios published periodically by the Census of Manufactures. The Federal Trade Commission's list of company acquisitions[9] designates the acquiring firm and the acquired firm at the 3-digit SIC level. The 4-digit SIC industries of the acquired firms on the FTC list can be ascertained from annual issues

---

[8] For a tabular description of the possible effects of conglomerate mergers on market concentration see Chapter 3, p. 56.

[9] FTC, Bureau of Economics, *Statistical Report No. 7, Large Mergers in Manufacturing and Mining.*

of *News Front.*[10] It is possible, therefore, to compare the trend in concentration at both the 3-digit and 4-digit SIC levels of industries into which conglomerate firms entered by acquisition with trends in market concentration for the economy as a whole.

Concentration ratios for 3-digit SIC industries frequently involved in conglomerate acquisitions appear in Table 5-4.

### TABLE 5-4

**Changes in Concentration in 3-Digit SIC Industries Most Frequently Acquired Into in Diversifying Acquisitions in the Period 1947–1967**

| SIC | Concentration Ratio | | | Directional Change 1958 to 1967 |
| --- | --- | --- | --- | --- |
| | *1947* | *1958* | *1967* | |
| 203 | 56 | 31 | 30 | Decrease |
| 221 | — | 25 | 30 | Increase |
| 231 | 9 | 11 | 17 | Increase |
| 261 | — | 46 | 45 | Decrease |
| 262 | — | — | 26 | Increase |
| 281 | 74 | 54 | 42 | Decrease |
| 291 | 37 | 32 | 33 | Increase |
| 331 | 52 | 53 | 49 | Decrease |
| 333 | — | 70 | 64 | Decrease |
| 349 | 25 | 19 | 18 | Decrease |
| 354 | 20 | 21 | 17 | Decrease |
| 355 | 26 | 34 | 27 | Decrease |
| 356 | 56 | 49 | 29 | Decrease |
| 358 | 49 | 51 | 33 | Decrease |
| 361 | 61 | 55 | 48 | Decrease |
| 366 | — | 92 | 92 | No Change |
| 371 | 53 | 68 | 81 | Increase |
| 372 | 72 | 57 | 53 | Decrease |

---

[10] See Chapter 3.

In computing these ratios, the 3-digit SIC industries to which the FTC assigned acquired companies in conglomerate acquisitions were first arranged in a frequency distribution. The 3-digit industries in which acquisitions numbered less than three were eliminated, and wherever possible a weighted concentration index for each of the 18 remaining 3-digit industries was computed from the 4-digit concentration ratios available for the census years 1947, 1958, and 1967.

While the deficiencies in these data for the purpose at hand may be obvious, they merit a brief comment. First, concentration ratios for all the 4-digit industries that comprise each 3-digit industry group are not avaliable from census data; the 3-digit concentration ratios are therefore calculated from incomplete data. Second, the true indirect effect of conglomerate acquisitions may be registered at the 4-digit level, and this effect may be obscured by offsetting movements in the concentration ratios of other 4-digit industries comprising the 3-digit industry group. This deficiency, however, is remedied in the 4-digit SIC analysis presented later on. Third, one can only speculate on the time span in which such indirect effects may reasonably be expected to manifest themselves in the form of changing concentration levels. And, finally, in view of the host of factors that produce changes over time in concentration ratios, it would be naive to attribute such changes entirely to any one factor such as conglomerate acquisitions.

These qualifications aside, if conglomerate acquisitions had a decisive effect on the level of concentration in acquired industries, this effect should have revealed itself sometime during the 1960s when most such acquisitions occurred. While the pattern is far from consistent, there is no evidence that conglomerate acquisitions have produced an increase in the level of market concentration at the 3-digit SIC level, or at least they had not had this effect by 1967. In fact, if one were forced to render a judgment, it would be somewhat

## TABLE 5-5

### Changes in Concentration in 4-Digit SIC Industries Most Frequently Acquired Into in Diversifying Acquisitions in the Period 1961–1970

| SIC | SIC Label [a] | Not Horizontal 1961–1970 | Horizontal 1961–1970 | Concentration Ratio [a] | | | | Changes in Concentration (Percentage Point Difference) | |
|---|---|---|---|---|---|---|---|---|---|
| | | | | 1958 | 1963 | 1967 | 1970 | 1958–1967 | 1963–1970 |
| 2042 | Prepared feeds for animals and fowls | 10 | 1 | 22 | 22 | 23 | 24 | 1 | 2 |
| 2542 | Metal partitions and fixtures | 12 | — | — | 23 | 24 | 19 | | —4 |
| 2621 | Papermills, except building paper | 12 | 8 | — | 26 | 26 | 26 | | 0 |
| 2649 | Converted paper products, n.e.c. [b] | 10 | 2 | — | 23 | 29 | 31 | | 8 |
| 2731 | Book publishing | 11 | 4 | 16 | 20 | 20 | 21 | 4 | 1 |
| 2818 | Industrial organic chemicals, n.e.c. [b] | 18 | 8 | 55 | 51 | 45 | 44 | —10 | —7 |
| 2819 | Industrial inorganic chemicals, n.e.c. [b] | 17 | 12 | 34 | 31 | 27 | — | —7 | —4 [c] |
| 2821 | Plastics, materials, and resins | 12 | 4 | 40 | 35 | 27 | 29 | —13 | —6 |
| 2841 | Soap and other detergents | 13 | — | — | 72 | 70 | 70 | | —2 |
| 2891 | Adhesives and gelatin | 10 | — | — | 28 | 27 | — | | —1 [c] |
| 2899 | Chemical preparations, n.e.c. [b] | 15 | 2 | — | 20 | 19 | 19 | | —1 |
| 3069 | Fabricated rubber products, n.e.c. [b] | 14 | 1 | — | 23 | 21 | 22 | | —1 |

## TABLE 5-5 (continued)

| | | | | | | | | |
|---|---|---|---|---|---|---|---|---|
| 3312 | Blast furnaces & steel mills | 15 | 4 | 53 | 48 | 48 | 47 | —5 | —1 |
| 3323 | Steel foundries | 12 | 3 | 25 | 23 | 20 | 23 | —5 | 0 |
| 3391 | Iron and steel forgings | 10 | 1 | 31 | 30 | 30 | 31 | —1 | 1 |
| 3423 | Hand and edge tools, n.e.c.[b] | 16 | 2 | 19 | 21 | 22 | 25 | 3 | 4 |
| 3429 | Hardware, n.e.c.[b] | 16 | 1 | — | 39 | 38 | 30 | | —9 |
| 3433 | Heating equipment, except electric | 15 | 1 | — | 13 | 22 | 19 | | 3 |
| 3461 | Metal stampings | 17 | 2 | — | — | 39 | 40 | | |
| 3481 | Miscellaneous fabricated wire products | 10 | 2 | 13 | 13 | 11 | 11 | —2 | —2 |
| 3494 | Valves and pipe fittings | 20 | 3 | 17 | 13 | 14 | 14 | —3 | 1 |
| 3499 | Fabricated metal products, n.e.c.[b] | 12 | — | 19 | 16 | 14 | 15 | —5 | —1 |
| 3522 | Farm machinery | 12 | 1 | — | 43 | 44 | 40 | | —3 |
| 3531 | Construction machinery | 16 | 2 | — | 42 | 41 | 42 | | 0 |
| 3537 | Industrial trucks and tractors | 12 | — | 52 | 54 | 48 | 52 | —4 | —2 |
| 3545 | Machine tool accessories | 12 | — | — | 17 | 20 | 21 | | 4 |
| 3548 | Metalworking machinery, n.e.c.[b] | 15 | 6 | — | 25 | 26 | 25 | | 0 |
| 3559 | Special industry machinery, n.e.c.[b] | 18 | 6 | — | — | 13 | 11 | | |
| 3561 | Pumps and compressors | 12 | 8 | — | 23 | 26 | 23 | | —3 |
| 3566 | Power transmission equipment | 12 | 3 | — | 24 | 25 | 25 | | 1 |
| 3569 | General industrial machinery, n.e.c.[b] | 15 | 3 | — | — | 10 | 13 | | |
| 3571 | (N.A.) | 15 | 2 | (N.A.) | (N.A.) | (N.A.) | — | | |
| 3585 | Refrigeration machinery | 17 | 5 | — | 25 | 31 | 31 | | 6 |

## TABLE 5-5 (*continued*)

| Code | Industry | | | | | | | | |
|------|----------|----|----|------|------|------|------|----|-----|
| 3589 | Service industry machines, n.e.c.[b] | 10 | — | — | 14 | 14 | 14 | | 0 |
| 3599 | Miscellaneous machinery except electric | 10 | — | — | 8 | 7 | 7 | | —1 |
| 3611 | Electrical measuring instruments | 12 | 3 | — | 34 | 35 | 38 | | 4 |
| 3621 | Motors and generators | 13 | 5 | 47 | 50 | 48 | 50 | 1 | 0 |
| 3622 | Industrial controls | 16 | 1 | — | 56 | 49 | 47 | | —9 |
| 3643 | Current-carrying wiring devices | 10 | 2 | — | 28 | 32 | 32 | | 4 |
| 3651 | Radio and TV receiving sets | 15 | 2 | — | 41 | 49 | 48 | | 7 |
| 3662 | Radio and TV communication equipment | 24 | 11 | — | 29 | 22 | 19 | | —10 |
| 3679 | Electronic components, n.e.c.[b] | 17 | 8 | — | 13 | 32 | 31 | | 18 |
| 3714 | Motor vehicle parts and accessories | 12 | — | — | — | 60 | 58 | | |
| 3717 | (N.A.) | 15 | 6 | (N.A.) | (N.A.) | (N.A.) | | | |
| 3722 | Aircraft engines & engine parts | 12 | 4 | 56 | 57 | 64 | 68 | 8 | 11 |
| 3729 | Aircraft equipment, n.e.c.[b] | 20 | 9 | — | 38 | 25 | 27 | | —11 |
| 3811 | Engineering and scientific instruments | 23 | 2 | — | 29 | 28 | 26 | | —3 |
| 3821 | Mechanical measuring devices | 19 | 1 | — | 22 | 20 | 21 | | —1 |
| 9998 | (N.A.) | 13 | — | (N.A.) | (N.A.) | (N.A.) | (N.A.) | | |

[a] *1970 Census of Manufactures*, Concentration Ratios in Manufacturing, Part 1, U.S. Department of Commerce, Bureau of the Census.

[b] n.e.c. = not elsewhere classified.

[c] 1963–1967; 1970 data not available.

safer to conclude that such acquisitions may possibly have reduced the level of market concentration over this period. Of the 18 3-digit industry groups, 12 registered decreases between 1958 and 1967, 5 registered increases, and 1 registered no change. However, in view of the uncertainties attending causal relationships and the deficiencies in the data, the safest conclusion is that conglomerate acquisitions appear to have had no discernible effect on the level of market concentration at the 3-digit SIC level over the period 1958–1967.

Concentration ratios at the 4-digit SIC level for industries that figured prominently in conglomerate mergers are presented in Table 5-5. The ratios shown are for those 4-digit industries that were represented ten or more times on the industry breakdown of firms acquired in the period 1961–1970 and which the FTC classified as conglomerate acquisitions. Since industrial concentration is generally identified with horizontal mergers, the frequency with which these same 4-digit industries were involved in horizontal acquisitions over the period 1961–1970 is also shown.

For purposes of analyzing market concentration generally, 4-digit SIC ratios are superior to those at the 3-digit level because they pertain to more homogeneous industries and reduce the problem of aggregation; they have been used as the standard for measuring market concentration levels and trends since the initiation of the Temporary National Economic Committee Studies of the 1930s. However, when used for the purpose of measuring the effects of conglomerate acquisition on market concentration they are deficient in one important respect. A frequency distribution of 4-digit industries entered through diversifying acquisition may show that some were acquired into much more than others. This is true of the frequency distribution of 4-digit acquired industries for diversifying acquisitions consummated in the period 1961–1970, and in fact which served as the basis for identifying the industries frequently involved in these acquisitions. In any given acquisition, however, a particular 4-digit industry may represent a small, even incidental, portion of the acquired firm's total business. Hence, it is possible that 4-digit industries frequently entered through acquisition were simply regarded by the acquiring firms as necessary but incidental concomitants of industry activities that motivated the acquisition. This possibility is substantially reduced in the foregoing analysis of concentration at the 3-digit SIC level.

Nevertheless, the data show that diversifying acquisitions have had no measurable effect on concentration in the 4-digit industries acquired. Of 43 industries represented 10 or more times in diversifying acquisitions in the 1961–1970 period, 20 registered decreases between 1963 and 1970, 16 increases, and 7 registered no change. In three-fourths of the industries the change in concentration, whether an increase or decrease, was less than 5 percentage points. Only three industries, two of which are highly heterogeneous in character, registered dramatic changes in concentration: the electronic components industry, n.e.c., was involved in 17 acquisitions and recorded an increase in concentration of 18 percentage points; aircraft equipment, n.e.c., involved in 20 acquisitions, recorded a decrease of 11 percentage points; and aircraft engines and parts registered an increase of 11 percentage points. On balance, the decreases and increases were of almost the same order of magnitude.

The changes in concentration for industries frequently entered through diversification acquisitions become somewhat more meaningful when compared with changes in concentration for all industries. In his analysis of concentration trends between the census years 1954 and 1966, Professor Joe Bain found that 102 of 195 comparably defined 4-digit industries registered increases, 86 decreases, and 7 registered no change.[11]  A comparison of these changes with those for the period 1954–1963 led Bain to the conclusion that

> . . . from 1954 to 1963 there was a moderate trend toward increased concentration in individual manufacturing industries — and that this trend continued and accelerated from 1963 to 1966.[12]

The application of Bain's method to 4-digit industries that figured prominently in diversifying acquisitions shows that over the period 1963–1970 there was a moderate trend toward decreased concentration in these industries, while for Bain's 195 comparable 4-digit manufacturing industries concentration increased over the period 1963–1966. In view of the host of factors that affect changes in market concentration, and the uncertainties as to the time required for whatever indirect effect diversifying acquisitions have on concentration to manifest itself in the relevant concentration data, these contrasting patterns scarcely warrant a conclusion that such acquisitions reduce market concentration. It is obvious, however, that those consummated between 1961 and 1970 did not increase concentration, or at least had not done so by 1970.[13]

---

[11] Joe S. Bain, "Changes in Concentration in Manufacturing Industries in the United States, 1954–1966: Trends and Relationships to the Levels of 1954 Concentration," *The Review of Economics and Statistics,* Vol. LII, No. 4 (November 1970), pp. 411–416.

[12] *Ibid.,* p. 416.

[13] An attempt to explain in terms of other known behavioral patterns the divergent trends in concentration between all 4-digit SIC industries and those entered through diversifying acquisitions was unsuccessful. Bain (see footnote 11, p. 415) found that between 1954 and 1966 declines in concentration were associated with industries having low concentration. Gilbert's regression analyses led him to conclude that acquisitions between 1965 and 1968 were

It is possible, by making use of an average market share index[14] computed for corporations included in the Harvard Business School's Multinational Enterprise Project, to explore the relationship between the average market shares of a large subset of the HBS Survey corporations and their number of diversifying mergers, their diversification indexes, and their 1961–1970 growth attributable to all acquisitions. The resulting correlation coefficients and their respective levels of significance are shown in Table 5-6. The correlation between the average market share index and all four of the growth-by-acquisition variables is negative but weak and significant only at the 10 percent to 15 percent level. The companies that had relatively low market shares tended to grow more through acquisition in the 1961–1970 period than those with high average market shares, but the tendency is weak and not highly significant. The companies having low average market shares tended to make more diversifying acquisitions in 1961–1970 than those with high average market shares, but again while the correlation coefficient is consistently negative for all firms, consumer-goods firms, and producer-goods firms, it is relatively low and not very significant. However, there appears to be a stronger tendency for average market shares to be negatively correlated with diversification, especially as

---

positively associated with the concentration ratios of acquired firms (David Gilbert, "Mergers, and Diversification and the Theories of the Firm," Unpublished Doctoral Dissertation, Department of Economics, Harvard University, submitted 1971). These patterns suggested that the decline in concentration for the acquired 4-digit SIC industries as a group may be explained by their having had above average concentration ratios at the time of acquisition and, following the pattern set forth by Bain, registered relatively more declines. However, only 10 of the 43 industries included in Table 5-5 had concentration ratios of 40 or greater in 1963.

---

[14] The average market share index was computed by averaging the market shares of individual corporations in 5-digit industries for the year 1964.

## TABLE 5-6

### Correlation Between Average Market Share in 1964 and Sales and Asset Growth by Acquisition, Number of Diversifying Acquisitions, and Degree of Diversification

| Variable Correlated with Market Share Index | Corre-lation Coeffi-cient | Number of Firms | Approxi-mate Signifi-cance |
|---|---|---|---|
| Share of 1970 sales acquired from 1961–1970, excluding postacquisition growth | —.14 | 94 | .100 |
| Share of 1970 sales acquired from 1961–1970, including postacquisition growth | —.13 | 94 | .100 |
| Share of 1970 assets acquired from 1961–1970, excluding postacquisition growth | —.13 | 94 | .100 |
| Share of 1970 assets acquired from 1961–1970, including postacquisition growth | —.12 | 94 | .150 |
| Berry Diversification Index | | | |
| 2-digit level in 1960 | —.15 | 107 | .100 |
| 2-digit level in 1965 | —.15 | 107 | .100 |
| 4-digit level in 1960 | —.23 | 107 | .010 |
| 4-digit level in 1965 | —.19 | 107 | .025 |
| Number of Diversifying Acquisitions | | | |
| All available firms | —.11 | 117 | .150 |
| Consumer-goods manufacturers | —.15 | 35 | .200 |
| Producer-goods manufacturers | —.13 | 66 | .200 |

measured by Berry diversification indexes at the 4-digit SIC level. The correlation coefficients for the average market share index and the 1960 and 1965 diversification indexes are respectively —.23 and —.19, and highly significant.

### Growth by Acquisition and Aggregate Concentration

One of the most popular views on the American economy is that it is dominated by a relatively small number of giant corporations, and that this dominance increases with each passing year — largely through merger. This view is uncritically accepted and widely disseminated by authors of the nonprofessional literature on the subject.[15] FTC reports on mergers and industrial concentration often draw this conclusion, and its 1969 *Report* attributes much of the increase in concentration in the 1960s to the conglomerate merger wave. The *Report* bases its conclusion largely on the coincidence of the upswing in the Federal Trade Commission's conglomerate merger series, both relatively and absolutely, and on increases registered in certain overall concentration indexes after 1947.

When we turn to the factual evidence, however, it does not point uniformly and conclusively to a finding that overall concentration has actually trended upward during the alleged "conglomerate" merger wave, or at least not by very much. Moreover, one can never be certain whether registered changes in the conventional indexes over the relative short time period of a decade or so are reflective of a trend or of cyclical movements that may soon reverse themselves. For example, the FTC *Report* (1969) found that the largest 100 manufacturing corporations increased their share of total corporate assets from 36.1 percent in 1925 to 49.3 percent in 1968, but found that the increase between 1933 and 1962 was only from 44.2 percent to 46.2 percent.[16] Morris Adelman

---

[15] *Cf.* Morton Mintz and Jerry S. Cohen, *America, Inc.: Who Owns and Operates the United States* (New York: Dial Press, 1971), especially pp. 34ff; Senator Estes Kefauver, *In a Few Hands; Monopoly Power in America* (New York: Pantheon Books, 1965).

[16] FTC *Report, Economic Report on Corporate Mergers,* 1969, p. 173.

found that between 1933 and 1960 the share of total manufacturing assets controlled by the largest 117 corporations
actually declined from 45.6 percent to 44.6 percent.[17] Gardiner Means, on the other hand, by assigning to the largest
100 manufacturing corporations all the assets of subsidiaries
in which they held at least a 50 percent common stock interest, found that their share of total assets increased from
40 percent in 1929 to 49 percent in 1962.

More pertinent to this inquiry is Preston's recent analysis
of changes in the 200 largest companies' share of all manufacturing assets.[18] Between 1954 and 1968 their share increased from 50.9 percent to 62.3 percent, or by 11.4 percentage points. Of this total increase, 4.8 percentage points
were attributable to the 141 companies that were among the
largest 200 in both 1954 and 1968 or, as Preston calls them,
the "Surviving Giants." According to Preston, the 102 of
these 141 companies that engaged in large acquisitions accounted for a 5.5 percentage point increase, of which 3.0
percentage points could be traced to assets acquired through
mergers; the 39 nonacquiring giants accounted for —0.7 percentage points. The turnover of 59 companies between 1954
and 1968 accounted for the remaining 6.7 percentage point
net increase, with the new entrants in the list adding 12.6
percentage points, and those they displaced subtracting 5.9
percentage points. In sum, of the total increase of 11.4 percentage points in the share of the largest 200 industrial corporations over the 15-year period, at least 3 percentage points
appear to be attributable to large mergers and the rest to

[17] *Hearings on Economic Concentration Before the Subcommittee on Anti-trust and Monopoly of the Senate Committee on the Judiciary*, 88th Congress, 2nd Session, pt. 1 (1964), pp. 236, 239.
[18] Lee E. Preston, *Giant Firms' Large Mergers and Concentration: Patterns and Policy Alternatives*, Working Paper Series No. 143, State University of New York at Buffalo (July 1972), pp. 4–5.

turnover and internal growth on the part of "Surviving Giants."

As Scherer has pointed out, assets are only one, and not generally regarded as the best, measure of the relative importance of a given number of corporations in the economy. It is known that large corporations are more capital intensive than corporations generally; hence the changes in concentration as measured in terms of assets may simply reflect relative changes in capital intensity.[19] Moreover, the assets of the largest 100 and largest 200 include foreign operations and subsidiaries; any recorded changes in their share of the total may be accounted for by their differential rates of growth in overseas investment. Scherer calculated that the largest 100 manufacturing corporations accounted for only 36 percent of total *domestic* manufacturing assets in 1963, whereas the FTC data show that in the same year they accounted for 46.5 percent of all assets, including foreign assets.[20]

In terms of value added in manufacturing, a more meaningful measure than assets, the shares of the largest 50, 100, and 200 manufacturing corporations for the postwar census years were as indicated in the tabulation on page 117.[21]

It is reasonably certain that the largest manufacturing corporations comprising each of the three size groups increased in relative importance between 1947 and 1954, and that this process continued at a much slower pace thereafter until 1963. But during the 1960s, when the "conglomerate" merger wave was recorded as having occurred, their share of

---

[19] F. M. Scherer, *Industrial Market Structure and Economic Performance* (Chicago: Rand McNally & Co., 1970), pp. 39–41.

[20] FTC *Report* (1969), p. 173.

[21] Betty Bock and Jack Farkas, "The Largest Companies and How They Grew," *The Conference Board Record*, Vol. VIII, No. 3 (March 1971); and *Annual Survey of Manufactures*, Concentration Ratios, 1970.

|        | Largest 50 | Largest 100 | Largest 200 |
| ------ | ---------- | ----------- | ----------- |
| 1947   | 17%        | 23%         | 30%         |
| 1954   | 23         | 30          | 37          |
| 1958   | 23         | 30          | 38          |
| 1963   | 25         | 33          | 41          |
| 1967   | 25         | 33          | 42          |
| 1970   | 24         | 33          | 43          |

total economic activity appears to have remained unchanged. Accordingly, there is no evidence that the recent conglomerate merger wave contributed to increased concentration for the simple reason that no increase appears to have occurred.

It would be premature at this stage of the analysis, however, to reach the more obvious conclusion these data suggest, namely, that the conglomerate merger wave of the 1960s had no measurable effect on overall concentration. Changes in the share of total economic activity accounted for by the largest 50, 100, or 200 companies are affected by several factors, of which acquisitions, or more narrowly, conglomerate acquisitions, is only one. The data required to determine what the overall concentration indexes would have been had the conglomerate merger wave *not* occurred are obviously not available, nor can they be reconstructed. However, available data do provide a basis for forming reasonable judgments concerning the relative importance of factors affecting changes in aggregate concentration.

One of the more incontrovertible features of the manufacturing economy is that in the period 1947–1970 there was considerable turnover of the largest companies, a feature borne out by Preston's analysis. Stated somewhat differently, companies once too small to make the list of the largest 50 or largest 100 grew much more rapidly than those on the original lists and hence replaced them. A Conference Board[22] study found that only 24 of the largest 50 companies in 1947 were still among the largest 50 in 1967; of the 26 that dropped from the list, 17 ranked among the 51st to 100th largest in 1967, and 9 ranked below the 100th largest. In the 10-year period 1958–1967, for which census data more closely coincide with the 1961–1970 data obtained through the HBS Survey, 10 companies numbered among the largest 50 in 1958 had been displaced by others by 1967; 5 of the 10 displaced companies were not even among the largest 100 in 1967. Viewed from the other direction, between 1958 and 1967, 15 companies rose from lower ranks to make the list of the 50 largest, of which 8 ranked between 51 and 100 in 1958, and the remaining 7 were not among the 100 largest.

The slight increase in aggregate concentration that occurred between 1958 and 1967, all of which had taken place by 1963, is therefore attributable to the more rapid growth of those firms not listed among the largest 50 or largest 100 in 1958, than to the growth of those already on the list. As the data in Table 5-7 show, the shares of value added accounted for by the largest 50 and largest 100 companies in 1958 remained virtually unchanged at respectively 23 percent and 30 percent over the 10-year period. However, the largest 50 and largest 100 firms as of 1970 accounted respectively for 24 percent and 33 percent of total value added in manufacture, whereas these same firms had accounted for only 20 percent and 26 percent in 1958. Since those firms that entered the lists of the largest 50 and largest 100 companies necessarily attained larger size in terms of value added than those they displaced, and since the share of value added accounted for by those already on the list as early as 1954 registered virtually no change after that year, the slight in-

---

22 Bock and Farkas, "The Largest Companies and How They Grew," p. 33.

## TABLE 5-7

Shares of Total Value Added by Manufacture
Accounted for by the 50 and 100 Largest Manufacturng
Companies for Census Years 1947–1970

| Year | 50 Largest Manufacturing Companies | | | | 100 Largest Manufacturing Companies | | | |
|---|---|---|---|---|---|---|---|---|
| | In 1947 | In Each Year | In 1958 | In 1970 | In 1947 | In Each Year | In 1958 | In 1970 |
| 1947 | 17 | 17 | 16 | 12 | 23 | 23 | 22 | 18 |
| 1954 | 21 | 23 | 23 | 19 | 27 | 30 | 29 | 25 |
| 1958 | 20 | 23 | 23 | 20 | 27 | 30 | 30 | 26 |
| 1963 | 21 | 25 | 24 | 23 | 28 | 33 | 32 | 29 |
| 1967 | 20 | 25 | 23 | 23 | 27 | 33 | 31 | 31 |
| 1970 | 19 | 24 | 22 | 24 | 26 | 33 | 29 | 33 |

SOURCE: Census of Manufactures, "Concentration Ratios in Manufacturing," Special Report Series, Part 1, MC67(S)2.1, U.S. Bureau of the Census.

crease in aggregate concentration between 1958 and 1963 is entirely attributable to the turnover among the largest 50 and largest 100 companies. Bewteen 1963 and 1970 the increase in value added from this source was almost exactly offset by the decline in the share accounted for by those already on the lists of the largest 50 and largest 100 companies in 1963; hence, aggregate concentration as measured in terms of the largest 100 companies in each year remained unchanged, and as measured in terms of the largest 50 companies it registered a 1 percentage point decline.

Since no increase in concentration occurred in the period of the conglomerate merger wave, the large volume of acquisitions in the 1960s appears to have left the overall structure of the manufacturing economy unaltered. But this does not satisfactorily resolve the issue. While aggregate concentration did not increase during the upswing of the conglomerate merger wave, it is possible that it might have declined had the wave not occurred. In view of the remarkably stable long-run trend in aggregate concentration since the early 1900s,[23] however, there is no strong presumption that the indexes up to 1970 would have been substantially different had the unusually large number of conglomerate acquisitions not occurred. As pointed out earlier, the recent merger wave, while large in absolute terms, involved relatively few unusually active acquiring companies and a very small percentage of the total gross national product.[24] Moreover, both the FTC and HBS Survey data show that between 1948 and 1968 smaller companies grew much more through acquisition than did those numbered among the 100 largest in 1968.[25] However, those firms comprising the smallest 50 on this list owed a substantially larger percent (23.3%) of their 1968 assets to acquisitions than the largest 50 (10%). Some of these companies must have replaced other companies with less total assets. Hence, if it is assumed that they would not have attained such size had they made no acquisitions, it can be concluded that aggregate concentration at the 100-firm level may very well have declined between 1963 and 1970 had the conglomerate merger wave not occurred; since the second largest 100 companies owed an even larger percent of their 1968 size to acquisitions, this conclusion, under the same assumptions, is applicable to concentration at the largest 200-firm level as well.

The most striking consequence of the recent rash of conglomerate acquisitions, however, is the dramatic rise in the

---

[23] *Cf.* Morris A. Adelman, "The Measurement of Industrial Concentration," *Review of Economics and Statistics,* Vol. 33, No. 4 (November 1951), pp. 269–296.

[24] Chapter 1, pp. 00–00.

[25] FTC *Report* (1969), p. 186. The FTC calculations are based on assets rather than value added, and are not corrected for divestitures.

size rank of the aggressive acquirers. Of the 25 companies identified in the FTC *Report* as having made the largest number of acquisitions between 1960 and 1968,[26] 12 became new additions to the list of the largest 100 companies, of which 4 made the list of the largest 50 (Table 5-8). Only

## TABLE 5-8

### Rank Change in Companies Making the Largest Number of Acquisitions, 1960–1968

| Firms That Went From a Rank of Greater Than 51 to a Rank in the Top 50, 1960–1968 | Fortune *Rank* | |
|---|---|---|
| | *1960* | *1968* |
| Ling-Temco-Vought, Inc. | 335 | 22 |
| Union Oil Company of California | 56 | 30 |
| Sun Oil Company | 54 | 28 |
| Gulf & Western Industries, Inc. | — | 34 |
| Occidental Petroleum Corp. | — | 41 |
| Tenneco | — | 16 |

| Firms That Went From a Rank of Greater Than 100 to Top 100 Category, 1960–1968 | *1960* | *1968* |
|---|---|---|
| Ling-Temco-Vought, Inc. | 335 | 22 |
| McDonnell Douglas Corp. | 242  (92) | 62 |
| Signal Companies, Inc. | 126 | 66 |
| U.S. Plywood-Champion Papers, Inc. | 176 | 74 |
| Litton Industries, Inc. | 275 | 67 (55) |
| North American Rockwell | 103 | 58 |
| FMC Corporation | 121 | 89 |
| Textron, Inc. | 132 | 98 |
| Georgia-Pacific Corporation | 128 | 64 |
| Gulf & Western Industries, Inc. | — | 34 |
| Tenneco | — | 16 |
| Occidental Petroleum | — | 41 |

NOTE: Numbers in parentheses based on consolidated returns.
SOURCE: FTC *Report* (1969), pp. 260–261.

---

[26] *Ibid.*, pp. 260–261.

2 of the 12 ranked as high as the 125th largest in 1960, and 6 were not even numbered among the largest 200. The largest of the 4 new additions to the list of the top 50 companies ranked only 335th in 1960; the other 3 were too small to appear on *Fortune*'s largest 500 list. Five of the 11 new entrants to the top 100 are also identified by the FTC as "new conglomerates" — they became large conglomerates through recent acquisitions.[27] The most discernible result of the 1961–1970 conglomerate merger wave is the birth of a new group of large conglomerates. While they do not appear to be sufficiently large or numerous to have measurably affected the level of overall concentration in manufacturing, they have replaced a substantial number of companies that otherwise would have been numbered among the 50 and 100 largest manufacturing corporations in 1970.

This conclusion, borne out by the growth patterns of individual companies over the course of the recent conglomerate merger wave, suggests the hypothesis that acquisition activity was positively related to relative growth rates of companies in 1961–1970, and inversely related to company size. Most recorded acquisitions involved the largest 1,000 companies. If firm growth by acquisition were proportional to company size within the 1,000 largest, we would expect no relationship between growth by acquisition and change in the size rank of firms, and we would expect overall concentration to increase; i.e., if the largest 100 grew proportionately to the largest 1,000, and the largest 1,000 grew more rapidly than all corporations, then aggregate concentration at the largest 100 company level should increase. Hence, the fact that overall concentration in the 1960s appears to have remained virtually unchanged while aggressively acquiring firms became new entrants among the largest 50 and largest

---

[27] *Ibid.*, p. 270.

100 companies suggests that growth by acquisition was positively correlated with company growth and negatively correlated with company size.

The correlation analysis results presented in Table 5-9 tend

### TABLE 5-9

**Correlation Between Growth by
Acquisition and Firm Growth,
Size, and Rank Change, 1961–1970**

| Growth Through Acquisition Measures | Firm Growth, Size, and Rank Change Measures | Coefficient | Firms | Significance |
|---|---|---|---|---|
| Share of 1970 sales acquired from 1961 1970, excluding postacquisition growth | *Fortune* rank change (1961–1969) | .45 | 95 | .001 |
| | Log of sales growth rate (1961–1970) | .52 | 131 | .001 |
| | Log of net sales (1961–1970) | —.41 | 137 | .001 |
| | Number of diversifying acquisitions (1961–1970) | .65 | 157 | .001 |
| Share of 1970 assets acquired from 1961–1970, including postacquisition growth | *Fortune* rank change (1961–1969) | .41 | 95 | .001 |
| | Log of asset growth rate (1961–1970) | .53 | 131 | .001 |
| | Log of net sales (1961–1970) | —.40 | 137 | .001 |
| | Number of diversifying acquisitions (1961–1970) | .64 | 157 | .001 |
| Share of 1970 assets acquired from 1961–1970, excluding postacquisition growth | *Fortune* rank change (1961–1969) | .48 | 95 | .001 |
| | Log of asset growth rate (1961–1970) | .48 | 130 | .001 |
| | Log of assets (1961–1970) | —.40 | 136 | .001 |
| | Number of diversifying acquisitions (1961–1970) | .58 | 157 | .001 |

(*continued* on page 124)

## TABLE 5-9 (*continued*)

| | | | | |
|---|---|---|---|---|
| Share of 1970 assets acquired from 1961–1970, including postacquisition growth | *Fortune* rank change (1961–1969) | .41 | 95 | .001 |
| | Log of asset growth rate (1961–1970) | .46 | 130 | .001 |
| | Log of assets (1961–1970) | —.38 | 136 | .001 |
| | Number of diversifying acquisitions (1961–1970) | .56 | 157 | .001 |
| Number of diversifying acquisitions, 1961–1970 | Log of sales growth rate (1961–1970) | .42 | 149 | .001 |
| | Log of asset growth rate (1961–1970) | .40 | 149 | .001 |

to confirm this hypothesis. Growth by acquisition, as measured in terms of percent of 1970 assets and sales attributable to acquisitions made in the period 1961–1970, is in all cases positively correlated with company relative growth rates and change in rank on *Fortune*'s list of the largest 500, and negatively correlated with the relative size of companies as measured in terms of logs of assets and sales. The correlation coefficients are only moderately high, but significant at the 1 percent level. The stronger correlation of from .56 to .65 between growth attributable to all types of acquisitions and the number of diversifying acquisitions also suggests that diversifying acquisitions contributed substantially to overall company growth through acquisition, and that this contribution varied inversely with size of firm.

## DIVERSIFYING ACQUISITIONS AND POTENTIAL COMPETITION

One of the frequently voiced antitrust concerns over diversifying acquisitions is that they may eliminate *potential* competition by eliminating potential entrants. The premise underlying this argument is that if diversification through acquisition were foreclosed, acquiring firms might very well enter the same industries through internal expansion. Hence, diversifying acquisitions reduce potential competition and, ultimately, actual competition in the markets of acquired firms.

This premise also holds an obvious and important implication for the foregoing analysis of diversifying acquisitions, firm growth, and aggregate concentration. If internal expansion is highly substitutable for growth by acquisition, it would follow that much of the company growth attributable to acquisition would have occurred anyway; companies would have recorded much the same growth had the acquisition route not been open to them and, hence, acquisitions have relatively little effect on the level of aggregate concentration.

The HBS Survey data shed modest light on this issue. Each company included in the Survey was asked, in the case of each diversifying acquisition, whether expansion into the acquired firm's industry by internal expansion had been analyzed and considered as an alternative means of gaining entry. For 79 of the 745 diversifying acquisitions reported by 193 companies for the 1961–1970 period, the acquiring companies stated that internal expansion had been analyzed, and considered as a possible alternative. Internal expansion was therefore given serious consideration in 11 percent of all entries into new 4-digit SIC industries eventually entered by the acquisition route. While there are no means for determining the number of instances in which the acquiring firm would actually have entered through internal expansion had the acquisition route been foreclosed, it very likely would have occurred in fewer than 11 percent of the acquisitions.

It would seem reasonable to conclude from these data that for the vast majority of diversifying acquisitions, internal expansion is not considered as a feasible alternative to acquisition. It would appear to follow, therefore, that the rapid growth registered by the aggressively acquiring companies in the period 1961–1970 is attributable to the large number of acquisitions they made — it would not have occurred had these same firms grown only through internal expansion. These same data also suggest that in by far the vast majority of cases of conglomerate acquisition the acquiring firm is not a potential competitor lurking on the border of the acquired company's market, seriously contemplating entry by the internal expansion route.

However, these conclusions are subject to a modest qualification. The data pertain to the frequency with which internal expansion is considered a likely alternative means of entry into the particular markets of companies actually acquired. Had these acquisitions been frustrated or for some other reason not occurred, the acquiring firms may have either entered *other* markets or expanded in their existing markets through internal expansion. Hence, it is possible that at least a portion of their growth assigned in earlier analyses to diversifying acquisitions would have occurred anyway, and that they lurked on the borders of some unidentifiable markets as potential competitors. These possibilities, however, would not appear to call for a substantial qualification of the conclusions the data more directly support.

# 6. Firm Diversification and Diversifying Acquisitions: An Explanatory Model

THE ANALYSIS IN THE PRECEDING CHAPTERS has dealt primarily with the managerial aspects of diversified enterprise and the structural effects of the recent conglomerate acquisition wave in terms of the major policy issues they have precipitated. Certain statistical relationships developed in the course of this analysis suggest the possibility that an explanatory hypothesis for the diversification process might itself be developed and tested. For example, divisional autonomy over certain critical operating decisions such as pricing and advertising was found to increase as the degree of diversification increased; the existence of a trade relations department was found to vary inversely with the degree of diversification but directly with the number of diversifying acquisitions consummated in 1961–1970; and all growth-by-acquisition measures are positively related to overall corporate growth, and negatively correlated with 1961 relative corporate size.

Other quantitative studies have discovered corroborative relationships. Gilbert[1] found corporate growth to be strongly

---

[1] David Gilbert, "Mergers, and Diversification and the Theories of the Firm," pp. 166–176.

related to growth by acquisition, especially conglomerate acquisition, and negatively related to size and profitability. He concluded that these relationships tend to confirm, at least for conglomerates, the Baumol hypothesis that firms sacrifice profits for growth.[2] Lynch, in his analysis of a large sample of the "new conglomerates," found a consistent pattern between the stock price-earnings ratios of the acquiring and the acquired firms[3] (acquiring firms typically acquired firms having lower price-earnings ratios).

While such stable relationships suggest the possibility of explaining the diversification process in statistical terms, the task is obviously ambitious and, at the outset, encounters the familiar problem of data heterogeneity. Highly diversified firms, even those described by diversification indexes of the same magnitude, possess fundamentally different characteristics which often cannot be satisfactorily quantified. For example, General Electric and Textron have virtually identical Berry 4-digit SIC diversification indexes. Textron is consistently classified as a conglomerate; General Electric rarely if ever is. The reasons for drawing this distinction between the two are essentially qualitative in nature.

For this reason, among others, Rumelt has argued that it may be more productive to classify such firms according to their strategy of diversification rather than their amount of diversification.[4] He found substantially different performance patterns associated with (1) firms engaged in unrelated

---

[2] The Baumol hypothesis is that revenue maximization subject to a profits constraint is more consistent with business behavior than the traditional profits maximization hypothesis. See William J. Baumol, *Business Behavior, Value and Growth.*

[3] Harry H. Lynch, *Financial Performance of Conglomerates.*

[4] Richard P. Rumelt, "Strategy, Structure, and Economic Performance," Unpublished Doctoral Dissertation, Graduate School of Business Administration, Harvard University, 1972.

businesses with no policy of rapid growth by acquisition, (2) firms in unrelated businesses with a policy of rapid growth by acquisition, and (3) firms engaged in diversified activities related to some central skill or strength. The results not only lend validity to his approach, they suggest that even a complete and appropriately selected set of variables may not be capable of satisfactorily explaining diversification expressed in terms of a single quantitative measure. This caveat notwithstanding, an attempt to explain diversification by this means appeared worthwhile.

## LINEAR REGRESSION MODELS AND DIVERSIFICATION

The vast amount of data available in the three data banks[5] made it possible to run simple correlations between most variables the theory of the firm would suggest as relevant to diversification, as well as a very large number for which an economic rationale would, at best, be obscure. From these results linear multiple regression models most likely to "explain" the diversification process were constructed. Both a priori economic logic and the initial correlation results suggested that the measurable effects of advertising and R&D on diversification would differ as between producer-goods and consumer-goods firms. Accordingly, since it seemed desirable to include these two operational activities among the independent variables, the two classes of companies were analyzed separately.

The dependent variables used to represent the diversification process were (1) the number of 4-digit SIC industries

---

[5] *Compustat*, HBS Multinational Enterprise project, and HBS Diversified Company Survey. See Appendix B.

the companies operated in as of 1970; (2) the number of diversifying acquisitions the companies made in the period 1961–1970, and (3) the ratio of diversifying to all acquisitions made in the period 1961–1970. While each of the three measures relate to different aspects of diversification, all would appear to be highly relevant. The number of 4-digit industries in which a company operates may be viewed as a status variable; it measures the amount of diversification the company had attained as of the most recent year for which data are available. Diversification indexes of the type used by Berry[6] would have been preferable to the number of industries, but the *Fortune Plant and Product Directory* data required to calculate them are available only up to 1965. The number of diversifying acquisitions is an activity variable; it measures the extent to which companies diversified by acquisition in the period 1961–1970. However, some firms make acquisitions of all types — horizontal, vertical, and conglomerate. These firms may have ranked high in terms of number of diversifying acquisitions, but the number of such acquisitions may still have been small relative to total acquisitions of all types. Accordingly, the use of both an absolute and a relative measure of diversifying acquisitions appeared to have considerable merit.

The initial operation consisted of performing step-up regressions, that is, stepwise regressions in which the computer was simply programmed to identify, in descending order of the amount of variance in the dependent variable explained, the independent variables that would enter the model. The stepwise regression results for diversification measured in terms of the number of 4-digit industries in 1970 and the selected independent variables are shown in Tables 6-1, 6-2, and 6-3. For all companies combined and for producer-goods

---

[6] See Appendix C.

## TABLE 6-1

### Stepwise Linear Regression Model
### (141 Firms)

*DEPENDENT VARIABLE: Number of 4-Digit SIC Industries in 1970*

| | STEP: 1 | 2 | 3 | 4 |
|---|---|---|---|---|
| **INDEPENDENT VARIABLES:** | | | | |
| Number of 4-Digit SICs Entered | 0.798 | 0.787 | 0.779 | 0.780 |
| Through Acquisition | (15.50) | (19.20) | (18.10) | (17.72) |
| LOG (Assets, 1961) | | 0.362 | 0.371 | 0.372 |
| | | (8.84) | (8.44) | (8.26) |
| Asset Growth Rate | | | 0.027 | 0.027 |
| (1961–1970) | | | (0.59) | (0.57) |
| Return on Assets | | | | 0.014 |
| (1961–1970) | | | | (0.34) |
| ADJUSTED R-SQUARE | 0.634 | 0.764 | 0.763 | 0.761 |

NOTE: Numbers in parentheses are t-statistics associated with the coefficients.

## TABLE 6-2

### Stepwise Linear Regression Model
### (83 Producer-Goods Firms)

*DEPENDENT VARIABLE: Number of 4-Digit SIC Industries in 1970*

| | STEP: 1 | 2 | 3 | 4 |
|---|---|---|---|---|
| **INDEPENDENT VARIABLES:** | | | | |
| Number of 4-Digit SIC | | | | |
| Industries Acquired | 0.818 | 0.844 | 0.856 | 0.858 |
| (1961–1970) | (12.78) | (15.91) | (14.52) | (14.53) |
| LOG (Assets 1961) | | 0.335 | 0.323 | 0.325 |
| | | (6.33) | (5.58) | (5.52) |
| Asset Growth Rate | | | −0.029 | −0.029 |
| (1961–1970) | | | (0.45) | (0.45) |
| Return on Assets | | | | 0.018 |
| (1961–1970) | | | | (0.34) |
| ADJUSTED R-SQUARE | 0.665 | 0.775 | 0.773 | 0.770 |

NOTE: Numbers in parentheses are t-statistics associated with coefficients.

## TABLE 6-3

### Stepwise Linear Regression Model
(41 Consumer-Goods Firms)

| DEPENDENT VARIABLE: *Number of 4-Digit SIC Industries in 1970* | | | | |
|---|---|---|---|---|
| STEP: | *1* | *2* | *3* | *4* |
| INDEPENDENT VARIABLES: | | | | |
| LOG (Assets 1961) | 0.781 | 0.639 | 0.643 | 0.642 |
| | (7.81) | (7.19) | (7.24) | (6.62) |
| Number of 4-Digit SIC Industries Acquired (1961–1970) | | 0.385 | 0.384 | 0.384 |
| | | (4.33) | (4.32) | (4.27) |
| Return on Assets (1961–1970) | | | 0.092 | 0.093 |
| | | | (1.11) | (1.02) |
| Asset Growth Rate (1961–1970) | | | | −0.004 |
| | | | | (0.39) |
| ADJUSTED R-SQUARE | 0.600 | 0.724 | 0.726 | 0.718 |

NOTE: Numbers in parentheses are t-statistics associated with coefficients.

companies, new 4-digit industries acquired between 1961 and 1970 "explain" a large percentage of the variance in the total number of 4-digit industries of those companies in 1970. This result is not surprising. The explained variance increases with the introduction of the 1961 relative asset size variable, but remains virtually unchanged with the successive introduction of a growth rate variable and a rate of return variable. This was not expected. In sum, for all firms combined and for producer-goods firms, the degree of diversification in 1970 was largely explained by their diversifying acquisition activity in the period 1961–1970.

For consumer-goods firms the results are significantly different. The independent variable that explains most of the 1970 diversification is the asset size of the firm in 1961, with the explained variance increasing from 60 percent to 72 percent with the introduction of new 4-digit industries acquired between 1961 and 1970. Again, the successive introduction of asset growth rate and rate of return had an insignificant effect on the explained variance.

Since relatively few firms report either R&D outlays or selling expenses to Compustat, the introduction of these two activity variables into the model requires a substantial reduction in the number of firms. A similar stepwise regression procedure applied to subsets of 36 producer-goods companies and 10 consumer-goods companies indicated that these activities were unrelated to company diversification. In the producer-goods submodel the coefficient of the R&D to sales ratio was small, negative in sign, and statistically insignificant; its introduction as an additional independent variable left the explained variance virtually unchanged (Table 6-4).

## TABLE 6-4

**Stepwise Linear Regression Model
(36 Producer-Goods Firms Reporting
R&D Expenditures)**

| DEPENDENT VARIABLE: *Number of 4-Digit SIC Industries in 1970* | | |
|---|---|---|
| STEP: | 1 | 2 |
| INDEPENDENT VARIABLES: | | |
| Number of 4-Digit SIC | | |
| Industries Acquired | 0.834 | 0.834 |
| (1961–1970) | (8.96) | (8.79) |
| LOG (Assets, 1961) | 0.254 | 0.255 |
| | (2.38) | (2.34) |
| Asset Growth Rate | —0.050 | —0.045 |
| (1961–1970) | (0.46) | (0.38) |
| Return on Assets | 0.041 | 0.041 |
| (1961–1970) | (0.46) | (0.46) |
| R&D Expenses/Sales | | —0.011 |
| (1961–1970) | | (0.12) |
| ADJUSTED R-SQUARE | 0.741 | 0.732 |

NOTE: Numbers in parentheses are t-statistics associated with coefficients.

The introduction of the selling expense variable into the consumer-goods submodel had the same neutral effect (Table 6-5). It will be noted, however, that the regression coefficient

### TABLE 6-5

**Stepwise Linear Regression Model
(10 Consumer-Goods Firms
Reporting Selling Expenses)**

*DEPENDENT VARIABLE: Number of 4-Digit SIC Industries in 1970*

| | STEP: 1 | 2 | 3 |
|---|---|---|---|
| INDEPENDENT VARIABLES: | | | |
| LOG (Assets, 1961) | 0.662 | 0.606 | 0.704 |
| | (3.68) | (3.16) | (1.66) |
| Number of 4-Digit SIC Industries Acquired (1961–1970) | 0.229 | 0.192 | 0.212 |
| | (1.26) | (1.02) | (0.95) |
| Return on Assets (1961–1970) | 0.370 | 0.300 | 0.333 |
| | (2.09) | (1.54) | (1.34) |
| Selling Expense/Sales (1961–1970) | | —0.197 | —0.140 |
| | | (0.91) | (0.44) |
| Asset Growth Rate 1961–1970) | | | 0.112 |
| | | | (0.27) |
| ADJUSTED R-SQUARE | 0.732 | 0.725 | 0.662 |

NOTE: Numbers in parentheses are t-statistics associated with coefficients.

for relative asset size in 1961 increased significantly (from 0.606 to 0.704) with the introduction of asset growth rate into the consumer-goods company model, reflecting the strong negative correlation (—0.77) between growth and size for this small sample of firms. For the larger sample of 41 consumer-goods firms used in Table 6-3 the correlation was also negative, but much weaker (—0.38).

While the stepwise regression approach produced a rather simple and intuitively obvious multivariate model, the model has significant explanatory power and it identified useful relationships for the purposes of designing additional and more sophisticated models. In any open-ended selective procedure where the object is to explain the degree of company diversification as of 1970, it is reasonably clear that the number of industries entered by acquisition in 1961–1970 and the size of the company in 1961 will account for most of the variance before other variables have been drawn into the model. This in itself is a significant although not an entirely surprising finding. It means that recent diversifying acquisitions account for a large portion of the company diversification that presently exists in United States industry.[7] This not only attaches greater importance to ascertaining those factors that explain recent diversifying acquisitions, but also suggests that a variety of alternative explanations of company diversification might fruitfully be explored through regression analysis.

Other empirical investigations have also identified variables associated with the diversification process, which, subject to data restrictions, will be introduced in subsequent analyses. Various studies have found a relationship between diversification and stock price behavior, rate of return, and firm growth.[8] Gilbert found a consistent negative and significant relationship between an industry specialization ratio and merger activity for the period 1961–1968, leading him to conclude that companies already diversified by 1963 accounted

---

[7] The analysis was performed on a PDP-10 time sharing computer operated by Interactive Sciences Corp. of Braintree, Massachusetts, using a set of Bayesian data analysis programs designed by Professor Robert Schlaifer of the Harvard Business School.

[8] *Cf.* the studies by Lynch, Gilbert, and Berry.

for most of the merger activity after 1965.[9]  Others have suggested that diversifying acquisitions in the domestic economy may simply be a regional reflection of recent international diversification and the growth of multinational enterprise and, alternatively, that because of antitrust restrictions international diversification may have become a substitute for diversifying acquisitions in the domestic economy.[10]

## Company Diversification: 1970

Since, as stated above, the number of 4-digit industries acquired in 1961–1970 tended to dominate regression models designed to explain company diversification as of 1970, sets of alternative models omitting this variable were formulated to enlarge on the opportunities for other factors to explain diversification.  For this purpose certain of the 193 variables contained in the data bank were reorganized into four subsets to test the following hypotheses:

> *Variable Subset 1.*  Company diversification in 1970 (its number of 4-digit industries) can be explained in terms of important characteristics of the companies prevailing at the beginning of the period 1961–1971.  The independent variables included were 1961 actual, squared and log values of assets, sales, rate of return on investment, earnings per share, price-earnings ratio, ratio of dividends to earnings, Berry 4-digit diversification index (1960), and dummy variables for product classification as to producer-goods or consumer-goods firms.

---

[9] David Gilbert,"Mergers, and Diversification and the Theories of the Firm," p. 64.

[10] The simple correlation runs referred to earlier revealed a fairly high correlation between Stopford's foreign diversification index and both company diversification in 1970 ($R^2 = .58$) and 4-digit industries acquired between 1961 and 1970 ($R^2 = .505$).

*Variable Subset 2.* Company diversification in 1970 can be explained by the same important company characteristics used in subset 1, but in terms of 1970 values. A trade relations (reciprocity) variable was also included since the HBS Survey had obtained this information as of 1970 from responding companies.

*Variable Subset 3.* Company diversification in 1970 can be explained in terms of the average 1961–1970 values of the variables used in Subsets 1 and 2.

*Variable Subset 4.* Company diversification in 1970 can be explained in terms of company growth between 1961 and 1970 as measured in terms of assets, equity, sales, earnings per share, stock price, price-earnings ratio, and rate of return, in combination with type of product and trade relations department status.

Each of the four hypotheses could be regarded as plausible. If diversification of the scope that occurred between 1961 and 1970 is a logical step in the life cycle of large corporations, it would seem reasonable to postulate that it could be explained in terms of relevant company characteristics that prevailed immediately prior to its occurrence, i.e., 1961. On the other hand, if company diversification takes place concurrently with the ongoing functioning of the corporation, as reflected in changes in its important financial and other measurable characteristics, the explanation may be found in data pertaining either to the final stage of the diversification process (1970) or to the entire period over which it occurred (1961–1970 averages). Alternatively, if diversification simply is a concomitant of company growth, whether a product of "natural" market forces or managerial policies, the explanation may be found in the pertinent growth variables.

Solutions to none of the combinations of variables in Subset 1 satisfactorily explained company diversification in terms of 1961 data. The best adjusted $R^2$ obtained using data from all 129 companies in the sample, which required excluding the Berry 1960 4-digit SIC diversification index from the eligible independent variables,[11] was only 0.228, resulting from the following equation:

| Variable | Beta Coefficient | t-value |
|---|---|---|
| Sales 1961 | +0.254 | 2.49 |
| LOG (Sales 1961) | +0.255 | 2.50 |
| Rate of Return on Assets 1961 | —0.118 | 1.48 |
| Consumer-Goods Dummy | —0.407 | 3.06 |
| Producer-Goods Dummy | —0.201 | 1.53 |
| R-SQUARE | 0.228 | |
| Number of Firms | 129 | |

However, in rerunning the equations using data for only the 93 firms on which Berry indexes were also available the best adjusted $R^2$ decreased to 0.180 before the index was introduced, but increased to 0.324 after its introduction. The square of Berry's index was more significant than the index itself, probably because of its highly skewed distribution and its resulting nonlinear behavior. In the process, log sales and ROA took on slightly added importance, while coefficients for sales and product class were reduced and became statistically insignificant:

---

[11] Berry indexes were available for only 93 of the 129 HBS Survey companies for which data were available for other variables.

| Variable | Beta Coefficient | t-value | Beta Coefficient | t-value |
|---|---|---|---|---|
| Sales 1961 | +0.158 | 1.13 | +0.121 | 0.95 |
| LOG (Sales 1961) | +0.318 | 2.29 | +0.337 | 2.66 |
| Rate of Return on Assets 1961 | —0.146 | 1.48 | —0.125 | 1.35 |
| Consumer-Goods Dummy | —0.147 | 1.47 | —0.054 | 0.58 |
| Berry 4-Digit Index 1960 | | | —0.601 | 1.78 |
| Square (Berry 4-Digit Index 1960) | | | +0.949 | 2.82 |
| R-SQUARE | 0.180 | | 0.324 | |
| Number of Firms | 93 | | 93 | |

The results suggest that diversification is likely to occur in companies already relatively large and diversified, and which are earning less than average rates of return on assets, but in view of the large unexplained variance it is evident that much of the explanation lies elsewhere.

The testing process yielded additional information, however, that proved helpful in the selection of variables for other models. In all equations except those applied to the 93 firms having Berry diversificaiton indexes the coefficient for the consumer-goods dummy variable was negative in sign and statistically significant, implying that consumer-goods firms are generally less diversified than other firms. In virtually all of the equations, sales served as a better measure of size than assets, and rate of return on assets a better measure of profitability than rate of return on investment. Neither the price-earnings ratio nor dividend policy gained significance in the model.

The testing of hypothesis 2 yielded better results, both in terms of explained variance and the identification of more significant variables. The maximum adjusted $R^2$ attained, however, was only .443, with the following variables and coefficients:

| Variable | Beta Coefficient | t-value |
|---|---|---|
| Sales 1970 | +0.170 | 1.63 |
| LOG (Sales 1970) | +0.525 | 4.86 |
| Rate of Return on Assets 1970 | —0.611 | 2.23 |
| LOG (Rate of Return on Assets 1970) | +0.608 | 2.20 |
| Earnings Per Share 1970 | —0.123 | 1.45 |
| Consumer-Goods Dummy | —0.271 | 3.82 |
| Supplier and Price List Dummy | —0.222 | 3.22 |
| R-SQUARE | 0.443 | |
| Number of Firms | 122 | |

Coefficients of all financial performance measures indicated a slight negative relationship between profitability and diversity, and the coefficient for the consumer-goods and reciprocity variables indicated that, other things being equal, consumer-goods firms tended to operate in fewer 4-digit industries than nonconsumer-goods firms, and firms with a potential for reciprocity dealings tended to be less diversified. (The existence of a trade relations department did not enter as significant, but firms that collect and distribute supplier and price information tended to be less diverse.) Again, in all equations, sales provided a better explanation than assets, and ROA a better explanation than ROI.

The testing of hypothesis 3 yielded relatively little new information. As might be expected the results obtained from using 1961–1970 average values tended to fall between those obtained using data for the two terminal years. The highest adjusted $R^2$ for the equations attempted was only 0.298. Again, coefficients for rate of return on assets and the consumer-product dummy variable were consistently negative in sign and significant in all equations in which they entered; the coefficients for size variables tended to be positive and significant, and the relationship between diversification and the two reciprocity proxy variables remained the same as for Variable Subset 2 – the coefficient was negative and significant for "supplier and price list" but statistically insignificant for "trade relations."

The results obtained in testing hypothesis 4 can only be described as having completely failed to develop even modest support for it. The consumer-goods dummy variable and the S and P reciprocity proxy alone explained 14.4 percent of the variance in the diversification variable, and the highest adjusted $R^2$ attained in any of the equations through the successive introduction of 18 growth rate variables was 0.160, a negligible increase.

The foregoing analysis strengthens the earlier conclusion based on the preliminary stepwise regressions: the degree of company diversification existing in 1970 is significantly attributable to diversifying acquisitions consummated over the preceding decade. The testing of alternative hypotheses with four subsets of variables consistently yielded adjusted $R^2$s explaining less than one-half of the variance in the 1970 diversification measure, and the maximum adjusted $R^2$ obtained was 0.44.

In virtually every equation in which they were introduced, the profitability variables yielded coefficients negative in sign while relative size variables, especially log sales, yielded coefficients positive in sign, and both were statistically significant. The introduction of 1960 diversification indexes in an analysis of a smaller sample of companies substantially reduced the unexplained variance in diversification for that smaller sample, but the total explained variance still remained relatively small. Perhaps the most surprising result was the failure of 19 growth rate variables derived from a variety of 1961–1970 growth data to explain even a modest portion of 1970 company diversification. Hence, the analysis provides weak support for the conclusion that relatively large firms, already diversified by 1960, but earning below-average profits, launched diversification programs resulting in their relatively high diversification by 1970. The analysis also provides much stronger support to the conclusion that these firms, in general, registered no greater growth rates than other firms. However, it must be emphasized that these conclusions follow from regression analyses in which all measures of 1961-1970 merger activity were purposely eliminated from the list of independent variables considered and which left over half of 1970 company diversification unexplained.

## COMPANY DIVERSIFICATION AND DIVERSIFYING ACQUISITIONS

The analysis up to this point makes it quite evident that a satisfactory explanation of the state of company diversification in 1970 must explicitly take into account recent diversifying acquisitions. That is, the list of eligible independent variables must be expanded to include measures relating to acquisitions made in the period 1961–1970. However, before opening up the floodgates to admit all variables, it seemed appropriate first to try the opposite approach to that pursued above; in other words, to try to explain company diversification entirely in terms of 1961–1970 acquisition activities.

*Variable Subset 5.* Company diversification in 1970 can be explained in terms of 1961–1970 acquisition activities. The independent variables include number of acquisitions, value of acquisitions, share of 1970 sales, both including and excluding postacquisition growth, attributable to acquisition, the number of diversifying acquisitions, and the number of 4-digit SIC industries acquired.

The correlation coefficient matrix revealed that many of these independent variables were highly correlated with each other and with the dependent variable, thereby raising theoretical problems as well as difficulties of statistical interpretation. However, the object was to find, through the successive introduction and withdrawal of variables, the set that "best" explained company diversification. In the final steps, variables with weaker explanatory power correlated with those having superior explanatory power drop out and, since all the remaining independent variables measure acquisition, both problems, while not eliminated, are substantially reduced.

A scanning of the correlation coefficient matrix showed, as expected, that the dependent variable, the number of 4-digit industries of companies in 1970, was highly correlated with the number of 4-digit SIC industries acquired in 1961–1970 ($r = 0.78$). This of course was simply a matter of correlating A with $A + B$ and finding A to be large relative to B. So that the acquired 4-digit industries' variable would not so reduce the unexplained variance before others had a chance to work, it was forcibly eliminated in some equation constructions. As might have been anticipated, the number of acquisitions, the number of diversifying acquisitions, and the value of acquisitions, each vied for dominance; the maximum adjusted $R^2$ was attained using the number of diversifying acquisitions, but this was only 0.428, and the equation contained four variables that were statistically insignificant. None of the growth-by-acquisition variables or their transformations emerged as significant.

With the introduction of "number of 4-digit industries acquired" the adjusted $R^2$s nearly doubled, attaining a maximum of 0.731, with the following equation:

| Variable | Beta Coefficient | t-value |
|---|---|---|
| Number of 4-Digit Industries Acquired Into | +1.893 | 8.84 |
| Square (Number of 4-Digit Industries Acquired Into) | —1.164 | 4.65 |
| Share of Sales Acquired Including Post-acquisition Growth | —0.398 | 5.38 |
| Square (Number of Acquisitions) | +0.612 | 3.58 |
| Value of Acquisitions | —0.275 | 2.02 |
| Consumer-Goods Dummy | —0.241 | 2.59 |
| Producer-Goods Dummy | —0.221 | 2.30 |
| Trade Relations Department Dummy | —0.133 | 2.42 |
| Supplier and Price List Dummy | —0.057 | 1.09 |
| R-SQUARE | 0.731 | |
| Number of Firms | 110 | |

The consumer-goods and producer-goods dummy variables and the "reciprocity" surrogates appear as significant throughout most of the steps, with their coefficients consistently taking on a negative sign, implying that the more diversified firms tend not to have trade relations departments. However, these variables contribute relatively little to the explained variance.

The analysis supports the conclusion that much of the 4-digit company diversification in 1970 is clearly attributable to the acquisition of 4-digit industries made in 1961–1970, and that the share of 1970 sales attributable to these acquisitions is inversely related to diversification. This apparent anomaly has an explanation. While many companies owe much of their 1970 diversification to acquisitions, the larger the company's total 1970 sales the smaller will be the share of 1970 sales attributable to diversifying acquisitions. Stated somewhat more precisely, for firms with similar values for all other variables, those with the higher share of sales attributable to acquisition tend to have fewer 4-digit industries in 1970.

In view of the reasonably satisfactory results obtained in the Variable Subset 5 analysis, it seemed worthwhile to determine whether the 1961–1970 diversification "wave" resulted from the creation of newly diversified companies, or simply from additional diversification of companies already diversified at the outset of the wave. For this purpose Berry's 1960 4 digit diversification index was introduced as a new independent variable,[12] with the consequent loss of 30 percent of the number of firms in original Variable Subset 5 for which the indexes were not available. In the resulting reduced model, the introduction of Berry indexes increases the adjusted $R^2$ from 0.701 to 0.739, with the coefficient of the square of the index positive and highly significant. Hence, in the model limited to 81 firms, 1970 company diversification is partly explained by the relative degree of diversification of those same companies in 1960. (See tabulation on page 146.) However, it must be understood that these results are based on a subset of the companies used in the previous equation. This may also explain why the effectiveness of some of the variables changes in the reduced model. For example, the coefficient for the "share of sales attributable to acquisition" variable remains negative and becomes more important, and

---

[12] The simple correlation coefficients for number of 4-digit industries in the 1970 and 1960 Berry index, and the index squared, were respectively 0.38 and 0.42.

| Variable | Without Berry Index | | With Berry Index | |
|---|---|---|---|---|
| | Beta Coefficient | t-value | Beta Coefficient | t-value |
| Number of 4-Digit Industries Acquired Into | +1.683 | 6.25 | +1.438 | 5.50 |
| Square (Number of 4-Digit Industries Acquired Into) | —0.912 | 2.71 | —0.769 | 2.42 |
| Share of Sales Acquired Including Postacquisition Growth | —0.366 | 3.36 | —0.320 | 3.14 |
| Square (Number of Acquisitions) | +0.446 | 1.71 | +0.412 | 1.69 |
| Value of Acquisitions | —0.153 | 0.78 | —0.052 | 0.28 |
| Consumer-Goods Dummy | —0.247 | 1.93 | —0.143 | 1.15 |
| Producer-Goods Dummy | —0.204 | 1.58 | —0.164 | 1.34 |
| Trade Relations Department Dummy | —0.169 | 2.53 | —0.139 | 2.18 |
| Supplier and Price List Dummy | —0.090 | 1.41 | —0.086 | 1.39 |
| Berry 4-Digit Index 1960 | | | —0.388 | 1.67 |
| Square (Berry 4-Digit Index 1960) | | | +0.585 | 2.47 |
| R-SQUARE | 0.701 | | 0.739 | |
| Number of Firms | 81 | | 81 | |

the product-type dummy variables fade into insignificance.
When the elimination of 29 companies for reasons of data
availability produce such changes in the solution, there are
reasons for concluding that a variety of patterns characterize
companies in respect to these variables. Or, alternatively, it
confirms earlier findings that diversification-by-acquisition
was heavily concentrated in a subset of the companies included in the larger model. The identity of companies ac-

counting for much of the 1961–1970 diversification wave is further explored in the next section.

## THE GENERAL MODEL WITH ALL VARIABLES

The analysis up to this point has consisted of testing various hypotheses by multiple regression models in which the independent variables were restricted to those more or less defined by each of the hypotheses. Regressions in which 1961–1970 acquisition variables were excluded yielded maximum adjusted $R^2$s no larger than 0.440 — not an insignificant amount of explained variance but scarcely a satisfactory explanation of company diversification. Regressions in which only 1961–1970 acquisition variables were included, except for several identification dummy variables, consistently yielded much larger $R^2$s, with the best model attaining an adjusted $R^2$ of 0.701. The introduction of a 1960 company diversification index into this model increased the adjusted $R^2$ to only 0.739, and in the process nearly 30 percent of the companies were lost.

Completion of the analysis required the design of a set of models in which the independent variables would not be constrained by any one of the various hypotheses. The list of eligible variables to enter the more generalized models was made up of all those that turned out to be significant in any one of the previous models. The results obtained in the final steps of those models yielding the highest adjusted $R^2$s are shown in Table 6-6. The simplified model includes only "number of 4-digit industries acquired" as an acquisition activity variable, while the complex model includes all the acquisition activity variables significant at the 10 percent level in previous models.

## TABLE 6-6

### Generalized Multiple Regressions Using All Significant Variables

*DEPENDENT VARIABLE:* Number of Company 4-Digit Industries, 1970
Complex Model   Simplified Model   Reduced Model

| INDEPENDENT VARIABLES: | (1) Complex Model | | (2) Simplified Model | | (3) Reduced Model | |
|---|---|---|---|---|---|---|
| | Beta Coeffi-cient | t-value | Beta Coeffi-cient | t-value | Beta Coeffi-cient | t-value |
| Number of 4-Digit SICs Acquired | +1.669 | 11.91 | +0.802 | 20.05 | +0.668 | 15.19 |
| Square (Number of 4-Digit SICs Acquired) | −1.087 | 6.59 | | | | |
| Sales 1961 | +0.623 | 3.80 | +0.455 | 3.61 | +0.644 | 3.76 |
| LOG (Sales 1961) | — | | +0.261 | 5.78 | +0.336 | 6.00 |
| Sales 1970 | −0.401 | 2.18 | −0.233 | 1.82 | −0.375 | 2.19 |
| LOG (Sales 1970) | +0.235 | 3.79 | | | | |
| Consumer-Goods Dummy | −0.138 | 3.64 | −0.150 | 4.16 | −0.188 | 4.37 |
| Trade Relations Department Dummy | −0.075 | 1.97 | | | | |
| Supplier and Price Lists Dummy | — | | −0.088 | 2.44 | −0.101 | 2.30 |
| Value of Acquisition | −0.227 | 2.49 | | | | |
| Square (Number of Acquisitions) | +0.610 | 5.50 | | | | |
| Share of Sales Acquired Including Post-acquisition Growth | −0.207 | 3.90 | | | | |
| R-SQUARE | 0.863 | | 0.841 | | 0.780 | |
| Number of Firms | | 116 | | 133 | | 127 |

It is obvious from the high R²s that the more generalized models more fully explain company diversification. The simplified model consisting of only 5 independent variables and a "reciprocity" dummy explain slightly more than 84 percent of the variance. The introduction of additional acquisition activity variables increases the $R^2$ to 0.863 and leaves the signs and magnitudes of the coefficients of other variables virtually unchanged.[13] Both models support the conclusion that the diversifying acquisition and company size variables together explain most of 1970 company diversification. The positive and fairly large coefficient for 1961 size implies that the larger the company in 1961 the more diversified it was likely to be in 1970; the negative and somewhat smaller coefficients for 1970 size variables imply that for firms acquiring the same number of 4-digit industries, the larger their size in terms of 1970 sales the fewer the number of 4-digit industries in which those sales were made. The consumer-goods dummy variable entered the equation and, consistent with all the previous analyses, with a negative sign. One of the "reciprocity" surrogates shows up in both models as very weak but negative in sign. Significantly, none of the profitability, stock price, price-earnings ratios or growth variables entered the equations as statistically significant.

In view of earlier analyses showing that 1961–1970 diversifying acquisitions were heavily concentrated in relatively few companies, the simplified model was rerun eliminating the six "new conglomerates" included in the sample. The new coefficients appearing in Table 6-6, Column 3, indicate that the "acquisitive conglomerates" did in fact exert significant influence on the model. When they were removed, the number of 4-digit industries acquired lost some of its importance, 1961 company size became more important, and the adjusted $R^2$ declined from 0.841 to 0.780.

Finally, the Berry 1960 diversification indexes were introduced and the reduced models, containing only those firms

---

[13] With the introduction of the squared term for "number of 4-digit industries acquired" into the complex model the coefficient for "4-digit industries acquired" increases from 0.802 to 1.669, but the coefficient of the squared term is −1.087. The nonlinear specification of the variable therefore appears to provide a better fit.

for which the indexes were available, rerun to determine their impact on 1970 diversification. Contrary to the results obtained in an earlier analysis, the coefficients of the Berry indexes turned out to be statistically significant and negative in sign, and the adjusted $R^2$ increased from 0.824 to 0.857 in the simplified model, and from 0.862 to 0.887 in the complex model (Table 6-7). This suggests that many of the diversified firms in 1970 were firms that became highly diversified through 1961–1970 acquisitions, and were not the same as the highly diversified companies of 1960.

## Diversifying Acquisitions: 1969–1970

Since diversifying acquisitions emerged so clearly as a dominant factor in 1970 company diversification, it appeared worthwhile, in fact essential, that this activity be singled out for special analysis. For this purpose, following the procedures used in the analysis of company diversification, several variable subsets were identified and analyzed.

It became apparent that in any stepwise regression in which the number of acquisitions was included among the independent variables, it would dominate the results. This was to be expected, since diversifying acquisitions in 1961–1970, as previous analysis had shown, accounted for a significant percentage of total acquisitions. However, so that other variables would have a chance to work, a series of regression models was run in which "number of acquisitions" was eliminated from the eligible dependent variables.

All attempts to explain diversifying acquisitions in terms of 1960–1961 company characteristics met with little success. A variety of regressions using 1961 profitability, size, and diversification measures and their various transformations in combination with product-type dummies as independent

## TABLE 6-7

### The Generalized Models Including
### Berry 1960 Diversification Indexes

*DEPENDENT VARIABLE: Number of Company 4-Digit Industries, 1970*
                        *Complex Model   Complex Model—Identical Firms*

| INDEPENDENT VARIABLES | Beta Coefficient | t-value | Beta Coefficient | t-value | Beta Coefficient | t-value |
|---|---|---|---|---|---|---|
| Number of 4-Digit SICs Acquired | +1.669 | 11.91 | 1.699 | 9.50 | +1.568 | 9.32 |
| Square (Number of 4-Digit SICs Acquired) | −1.087 | 6.59 | −1.192 | 4.92 | −1.127 | 5.05 |
| Sales 1961 | +0.623 | 3.80 | +0.705 | 3.18 | +0.591 | 2.93 |
| Sales 1970 | −0.401 | 2.18 | −0.452 | 1.82 | −0.375 | 1.67 |
| LOG (Sales 1970) | +0.235 | 3.79 | +0.209 | 2.75 | +0.228 | 3.30 |
| Consumer-Goods Dummy | −0.138 | 3.64 | −0.123 | 2.62 | −0.058 | 1.29 |
| Trade Relations Department Dummy | −0.075 | 1.97 | −0.084 | 1.79 | −0.071 | 1.70 |
| Value of Acquisitions | −0.227 | 2.49 | −0.261 | 1.81 | −0.209 | 1.61 |
| Square (Number of Acquisitions) | +0.610 | 5.50 | +0.749 | 3.92 | +0.739 | 4.26 |
| Share of Sales Acquired Including Post-acquisitions Growth | −0.207 | 3.90 | −0.153 | 2.28 | −0.149 | 2.44 |
| Berry 4-Digit Index 1960 | | | | | −0.440 | 2.62 |
| Square (Berry 4-Digit Index 1960) | | | | | +0.579 | 3.34 |
| R-SQUARE | 0.863 | | 0.862 | | 0.887 | |
| Number of Firms | 116 | | 76 | | 76 | |

variables yielded insignificant $R^2$s. Reformulations of the
model by successively introducing and eliminating size and
profitability growth measures, retaining those that worked
best, led to the results shown in Table 6-8.

## TABLE 6-8

### Exploratory Stepwise Regression Model

*DEPENDENT VARIABLE: Number of Diversifying Acqisitions, 1961–1970*

| | | | | | | | | | | | | | |
|---|---|---|---|---|---|---|---|---|---|---|---|---|---|
| Adjusted R-SQUARE | .428 | .434 | .439 | .443 | .423 | .398 | .374 | .350 | .323 | .269 | .200 | .202 | .112 |
| Share of Assets Acquired Including Postacquisition Growth/Asset Growth | 2.19 | 2.20 | 2.19 | 2.18 | 2.13 | 1.31 | 1.25 | 1.27 | 1.39 | 1.19 | .93 | .84 | .34 |
| Square (Share of Assets Acquired Including Postacquisition Growth/Asset Growth) | −1.38 | −1.39 | −1.37 | −1.38 | −1.35 | −.88 | −.83 | −.87 | −.93 | −.84 | −.65 | −.58 | |
| Share of Assets Acquired Including Postacquisition Growth/Asset Average | −.78 | −.78 | −.78 | −.81 | −.70 | −.87 | −.82 | −.82 | −1.17 | −.84 | −.08 | | |
| Square (Share of Assets Acquired Including Postacquisition Growth/Asset Average) | .80 | .80 | .80 | .82 | .73 | .72 | .69 | .70 | .91 | .73 | | | |

## TABLE 6-8 (*continued*)

| Variable | | | | | | | | | |
|---|---|---|---|---|---|---|---|---|---|
| Asset Growth | (.85) | (.83) | .65 | .49 | .49 | .30 | .31 | .31 | .28 |
| LOG (Assets 1961) | (.64) | (.62) | .31 | .30 | .28 | .24 | .24 | .24 | |
| Consumer-Goods Dummy | −.16 | −.16 | −.16 | −.17 | −.17 | −.17 | | | |
| Square (Price/Earnings Growth) | −.18 | −.18 | −.18 | −.19 | −.13 | | | | |
| Share of Assets Acquired Including Post-acquisition Growth | −.68 | −.68 | −.66 | −.63 | | | | | |
| Square (ROA Growth) | (.13) | .16 | .16 | | | | | | |
| Square (Asset Growth) | (−.25) | (−.24) | (−.15) | | | | | | |
| LOG (Assets 1970) | (−.29) | (−.28) | | | | | | | |
| ROA Growth | (.03) | | | | | | | | |

NOTE: ( ) means not significant at the 10% level.

It will be noted that the maximum adjusted $R^2$ attained was 0.443, and the model is difficult to interpret in economically meaningful terms. The size of the coefficients for the several squared terms imply that the relationships, if any, are not linear, and the asset growth transformations are cumbersome. However, the results suggest that the share of 1970 assets attributable to acquisition as a percent of total asset growth between 1961 and 1970 is positively and significantly related to the number of diversifying acquisitions, but that this share normalized for asset size of firm is inversely related to the number of diversifying acquisitions. The coefficients for share of assets acquired (including postacquisition growth), and the price-earnings growth variables are both negative in sign and significant, and that of the relative 1961 size variable positive and significant. The results suggest, but only suggest, that 1961–1970 diversifying acquisitions were made more frequently by companies already large in 1961 than by smaller firms, that the more aggressive acquirers experienced relatively low price-earnings ratios, and that 1970 assets attributable to 1961–1970 acquisitions as a percent of total 1961–1970 asset growth, were inversely related to the number of diversifying acquisitions.

The failure of even the "best" and relatively complex model to explain as much as one-half of the 1961–1970 diversifying acquisition process without explicitly introducing an acquisition variable is itself significant. It strongly suggests that diversifying companies are characterized by diverse size and performance measures that fall into no consistent pattern.

The statistical results were also very likely affected by the constraint that the time period to which the data pertain necessarily imposed. If companies, especially those companies with high growth-rate objectives, eventually enter a stage in their life cycle characterized by growth through diversifying acquisitions, analyses confined to a particular decade (1961–1970) necessarily catch firms in different phases of their growth cycle. This may explain why various 1960–1961 size, diversification, and profitability measures alone, and in combination with 1961–1970 growth and performance measures, fall far short of explaining the diversification-through-acquisition process. While the "conglomerate" merger wave is identified with the 1960s, many companies launched diversification programs earlier, and those that launched them in the 1960s evidently did not step off in unison in 1960–1961. The foregoing analysis therefore relies on data pertaining to companies in different phases of growth by diversification. This suggests that an analysis based on data pertaining to similar company diversification stages rather than to a given time period may yield more satisfactory explanations of the diversifying acquisition process.[14]

The inconclusiveness of the analysis is largely overcome, in a purely statistical sense, when a measure of acquisition activity is included among the independent variables. However, if total acquisitions are used, the statistical conclusiveness is attained at a considerable cost in new and meaningful economic information. Previous analysis has shown that diversifying acquisitions comprise about 35 percent of the total acquisitions made by companies covered in the HBS Survey; simple correlations between the two yielded a highly significant and positive coefficient of 0.783. The relatively high correlation is attributable to the fact that over one-third of all acquisitions *are* diversifying acquisitions, and that those companies most active in making diversifying acquisitions are also generally the most active in making other types of acquisitions. It is for the latter reason that nondiversifying

---

[14] This approach is contemplated in a companion volume to this study, to appear later. The comprehensiveness of the company data requirements and the conceptual difficulties scarcely need to be emphasized.

acquisitions were introduced into the regression models to see whether they would shed additional light on the diversifying acquisition process.

Following the procedure used in analyzing the degree of diversification in the previous section, a large number of experimental model specifications, drawing on the most promising variables, were solved for purposes of determining those independent variables that yielded important and significant coefficients. These variables were then tested in alternative combinations to ascertain the set of significant variables that yielded the highest $R^2$. The final results are shown in Table 6-9.

(1) Model A includes all 108 HBS Survey corporations for which there were no missing values for any of the variables.

(2) Model B includes the 100 firms used in A which remained after the elimination of 8 firms which could not be classified as consumer-goods or producer-goods companies, all of which were petroleum or pharmaceutical companies.

(3) Model C includes the 68 producer-goods firms included in A.

(4) Model D includes the 98 firms used in A which remained after the elimination of the 10 firms that made individual acquisitions in excess of $100 million.

(5) Model E includes only those firms which reported the "number of 4-digit SIC industries entered through acquisition during the 1961–1970 period." It was constructed only for purposes of comparison with Model F.

(6) Model F is the same as Model E with the elimination of the 2 firms reporting more than 33 4-digit SIC industries entered through acquisition.

It will be observed that the inclusion of the acquisi-

## TABLE 6-9

### Linear Regression Models of Diversifying Acquisitions for Various Sets and Subsets of Firms

DEPENDENT VARIABLE: Number of Diversifying Acquisitions, 1961–1970

| | A | B | C | D | E | F |
|---|---|---|---|---|---|---|
| Number of Firms | 108 | 100 | 68 | 98 | 100 | 98 |
| Adjusted R-SQUARE | 0.746 | 0.718 | 0.815 | 0.619 | 0.752 | 0.599 |
| Consumer-Goods Dummy | −0.108 | −0.123 | | −0.148 | −0.102 | −0.133 |
| | (2.16) | (2.24) | | (2.32) | (1.96) | (2.02) |
| Number of Nondiversifying Acquisitions | +0.641 | +0.658 | +0.758 | +0.112 | +0.652 | +0.217 |
| | (12.80) | (12.18) | (14.05) | (1.62) | (12.80) | (3.10) |
| Share of 1970 Assets Including Post-acquisition Growth/1970 Assets | −0.979 | −1.034 | −0.941 | −1.057 | −0.998 | −1.210 |
| | (6.40) | (6.01) | (4.88) | (5.12) | (6.31) | (5.76) |
| Square (Share of 1970 Assets Including Postacquisition Growth/1970 Assets) | +0.861 | +0.919 | +0.852 | +0.923 | +0.889 | +1.067 |
| | (6.33) | (6.00) | (5.10) | (4.88) | (6.21) | (5.64) |
| Share of 1970 Assets Including Post-acquisition Growth/Assets Growth Rate | +1.189 | +1.242 | +0.901 | −1.686 | +1.155 | +1.543 |
| | (9.74) | (8.89) | (4.69) | (10.01) | (9.40) | (9.24) |
| Square (Share of 1970 Assets Including Post acquisition Growth/Asset Growth Rate) | −0.817 | −0.871 | −0.247 | −1.206 | −0.813 | −1.103 |
| | (7.42) | (6.91) | (1.45) | (8.00) | (7.19) | (7.28) |
| Square (Price-Earnings Ratio Growth) | −0.149 | −0.157 | −0.174 | −0.221 | −0.150 | −0.203 |
| | (2.92) | (2.81) | (3.11) | (3.36) | (2.89) | (3.03) |
| Return on Assets Growth Rate | −0.337 | −0.133 | −0.093 | −0.420 | −0.342 | −0.449 |
| | (2.32) | (0.62) | (0.21) | (2.16) | (2.23) | (2.28) |
| Square (Return on Assets Growth Rate) | +0.425 | +0.100 | +0.049 | +0.522 | +0.437 | +0.565 |
| | (2.93) | (0.47) | (0.21) | (2.71) | (2.89) | (2.91) |

NOTES: See below for definition of model subsets. Numbers in parentheses are t-statistics associated with the coefficients.

tion variable "total acquisitions — diversifying acquisitions" [15] among the independent variables resulted in a spectacular increase in the adjusted $R^2$s, from 0.440 for the earlier model that excluded it to 0.746 in model A; the elimination of this variable from model A would result in a reduction in the adjusted $R^2$ to 0.346. It is clear, therefore, that the companies making most of the diversified acquisitions also account for a large share of the nondiversified acquisitions.

The remaining explained variance is so spread over the rest of the variables, and the likely interaction among some of these variables so strong, that none of them emerge as dominant. The transformed variables' share of 1970 asset growth, and their respective squared terms, together account for nearly one-fourth of the explained variance, but their obvious interaction makes it difficult to sort out the effect of any one of them. Moreover, the significance of the squared term in each case suggests that the relationship between them and number of diversifying acquisitions is nonlinear. However, the coefficient for the ratio of the share of acquired assets to total assets is significant and negative in sign, implying that, all other factors held constant, the larger the number of diversifying acquisitions the smaller this ratio is likely to be; the coefficient for the ratio of acquired assets to total asset growth is equally significant but positive in sign, implying that the larger this ratio the larger the number of diversifying acquisitions is likely to be. Again, as in previous models, the rate of return on assets coefficient is statistically significant and negative in sign.

These relationships remain substantially the same for model B, which means that the 8 companies that could not

---

[15] Expressed as "nondiversifying acquisitions." The diversifying acquisitions were eliminated since they *are* the dependent variable. The use of total acquisitions in model A yielded an $R^2$ of 0.807.

be classified by product class were not discernibly different, in respect to these variables, from the other 100 companies used in model A. Similarly, the conformity of model C, constructed from the 68 producer-goods companies, to the same pattern means that no clear distinction can be drawn between these companies and consumer-goods companies. However, in model D with the elimination of the 10 companies making individual acquisitions of $100 million or more, the influence of number of nondiversifying acquisitions was significantly reduced and the adjusted $R^2$ declined from 0.746 to 0.619, which supports the earlier conclusion that much of the "conglomerate" merger wave was attributable to the acquisitions of a relatively small number of companies. A comparison of models E and F offers even more striking support to this conclusion. In eliminating only the two most acquisitive conglomerates from E, the adjusted $R^2$ declines from 0.752 to 0.599, and the number of nondiversifying acquisitions variable loses much of its importance.

## Summary

The principal conclusions to be drawn from the results obtained through regression analysis are not especially surprising: a very large portion of company diversification in 1970 is directly attributable to the diversifying acquisitions those companies consummated over the 10-year period 1961–1970; and the number of diversifying acquisitions are in turn largely explained by the total acquisition activity of those same companies.

There is a significant difference, however, between producer-goods and consumer-goods companies in this regard; the latter owe much less of their 1970 product diversity to 1961–1970 acquisitions and much more to their 1961 relative size, which may very well indicate that they had already attained much of their diversity by 1961. In virtually all diversification and diversifying acquisition models the coefficient of the consumer-goods dummy variable becomes significant and negative in sign, implying that consumer-goods companies are relatively less diverse and participated less heavily than other companies in diversifying acquisitions in 1961–1970.

Growth by acquisition, as measured in terms of percentages of 1970 assets and sales attributable to 1961–1970 acquisitions, is directly related to both 1970 diversification and to 1961–1970 diversifying acquisitions, but inversely related to company size. The emergence of these relationships serves more to enhance the general appropriateness of the various models than to increase the state of knowledge concerning company diversification and the conglomerate acquisition process. That growth by acquisition was inversely related to company size had already been established by much simpler and more direct means.

In almost all models in which profitability and price-earnings ratios entered as statistically significant, they took on a negative sign. This inverse relationship between profitability and both 1970 company diversification and the volume of 1961–1970 diversifying acquisitions is consistent with any one of several hypotheses: It may, as Gilbert[16] has proposed, indicate that acquisitive conglomerates sacrifice profitability for growth; it may mean that companies earning relatively low rates of return in their present industries are the most active acquirers of companies in other industries; or, alternatively, it may simply mean that diversification through acquisition in 1961–1970 was not generally an especially profitable activity.

---

[16] See Footnote 9, this chapter.

A comparison of models including and excluding the small number of highly acquisitive conglomerates confirmed the conclusion established earlier that the 1961–1970 diversifying acquisition wave was heavily concentrated in relatively few firms. When these companies were excluded the explained variance in company diversification and number of diversifying acquisitions decreased dramatically, and in some equations the coefficients for other independent variables changed significantly. This suggests that the 1961–1970 conglomerate merger wave may consist of two distinct components — "normal" diversifying acquisitions motivated only by a constrained diversification program, and those resulting from an aggressive strategy of diversification.

All the regression models designed to explain both company diversification and diversifying acquisitions in terms of variable sets characterizing companies at the beginning of the 1961–1970 acquisition period met with little success. This may mean that the conditions conducive to diversifying acquisitions are so varied and so complex that they defy systemization, or that these conditions, if they in fact define the beginning of a corporate life cycle phase of diversification, are present in different companies at diffreent times. Hence, it is possible that the 1960–1961 measures of these conditions pertained to different phases of a corporate life cycle.

The results of the regression analysis, however, derive almost as much importance from what they did not establish as from relationships they affirm. At the outset of the analysis it was assumed that R&D would be related to the acquisition activities of producer-goods firms, and that advertising would be related to the acquisition activities of consumer-goods firms. This was an important consideration in the decision to divide HBS Survey responding companies into these two classes for separate analysis. Yet neither of these two variables became significant in the various models. Similarly, the two reciprocity dummy variables, trade relations departments and the internal dissemination of sales and customer lists, attained significance in only a few of the numerous models, and in each case they were found to be inversely related to diversification and diversifying acquisitions.

# 7. The Policy Implications

THE MODERN CORPORATION, BY COMMON CONSENSUS, has yet to be assimilated into economic theory. As Galbraith has put it, "The theory of the firm makes little distinction between a Wisconsin dairy farm and General Motors Corporation except to the extent the latter may be thought more likely to have some of the technical aspects of monopoly." [1] Since corporate enterprise accounts for three-fifths of our total economic life, it is disturbingly apparent that our understanding of how the contemporary United States economy functions is seriously deficient.

If this knowledge gap exists in respect to the modern corporation generally, it is even more apparent in the case of the highly diversified corporation, a more complex form of business enterprise that, while not of recent origin, is in its ascendancy. According to data recently released by the Federal Trade Commission, 181 of the 200 largest manufacturing corporations operate in at least 10 distinguishable product markets.[2] These large companies account for 50 percent of

---

[1] John Kenneth Galbraith, *A Contemporary Guide to Economics, Peace and Laughter* (New York: The New American Library, Inc., 1972), pp. 19–20.
[2] FTC *Report* (1969) p. 224.

163

total corporate manufacturing assets and profits, and for about two-fifths of total value added in manufacturing. Our lack of knowledge concerning the operative mechanics of enterprises comprising such an important component of our total economic activity — and the consequent conflicting policies proposed for their governance — is obviously not a trivial matter, either for those who govern or those who are governed.

This study was not designed to resolve the broad issues of social, political, and economic policy posed by the ascending importance of the large diversified corporation, although hopefully even these ambitious objectives are served by factual analysis. Rather, it was addressed to the more immediate and limited issue of what conglomerate enterprise portends for antitrust policy which, not withstanding the recent imposition of price and wage controls, remains our basic and continuing public policy toward the corporate economy.

This, as already emphasized, is no trivial issue. On the one hand the highly diversified firm has been perceived as a special form of monopoly requiring a radical enlargement of the scope of traditional principles of antitrust, especially those legal and economic guideposts applied to corporate mergers, the vehicle by which much product diversification has been accomplished. On the other hand an equally plausible case, in terms of its logical appeal, has been made for directing antitrust toward the prevention and dismantling of intolerable market power as traditionally defined. In pursuit of this objective "conglomerateness" as such is not only neutral, it is irrelevant; intolerable market power is simply unlawful, irrespective of the diversity of its corporate residence.

The theory of the firm, either the traditional or behavioral version, lends support to the conglomerate neutrality thesis. Whether the goal of the firm is profits maximization or revenue maximization subject to a predetermined profits constraint, rational corporate management would view each of its product markets independently if in fact such markets were independent; that is, if none of its products were perceived to be either substitutable or complementary. The conglomerate issue arises in large measure, however, out of the alleged inadequacies of the theory of the firm as a basis for public policy toward conglomerate enterprise. The modern corporation, and especially the modern conglomerate, is far too complex an organization to be cast in the procrustean mold of marginal revenue — marginal cost nexuses. The utility surfaces, or horizons, to which corporate management react are in large measure shaped by long-range strategic considerations, at least some of which are divorced from the interests of those who in legal theory represent ownership, i.e., the stockholders.[3]

Accordingly, it is argued, corporate management may engage in practices that vitiate the received wisdom. Particularly, managers of conglomerate enterprise may engage in cross-product subsidization, business reciprocity, practices that frustrate or circumvent actual and potential competition, or pursue courses of conduct entirely incongruent with the received theory on which antitrust policy ultimately rests. In short, the behavior of conglomerate enterprise is potentially at variance with that which the traditional theory of the firm predicts, and herein lies its principal threat to a workably competitive market economy.

When unfettered by constraints the theory of the firm imposes, speculations on the significance of conglomerate enterprise range widely, and not all are condemnatory. Some have extolled its positive and distinctive merits. For example, it has been urged that large diversified firms may engage

---

[3] *Cf.* Adolf A. Berle and Gardiner C. Means, *The Modern Corporation and Private Property* (New York: Harcourt, Brace and World, Rev. Ed., 1968).

more heavily, and more efficiently, in research and development. Industrial research, by definition, confronts heavy
risks that inhibit its undertaking. When firms operate on
many industrial fronts this risk is substantially reduced.
Some have suggested that the process of diversification may
in fact hold down levels of market concentration below those
levels that would otherwise prevail; to the extent firms may
realize growth by invading new markets, they may be less
disposed aggressively to enlarge their shares of the markets
in which they already operate.

Significantly, speculations on both sides emphasize the
conglomerate's distinctive features, particularly its special
power either to circumvent or enliven the competitive forces
of the marketplace, the preservation of which has been assigned to our antitrust policy. It is to this issue, the antitrust
implications of the 1961–1970 diversifying acquisition wave,
that this study has been directed.

Since the central antitrust issues evolve ultimately around
how conglomerate enterprise is managed, its primacy in any
factual analysis directed toward these issues would appear
to call for no special explanation. In fact, and policy issues
aside, the managerial aspects of highly diversified corporations merit analysis purely out of theoretical imperatives.
Microeconomic theory — the only determinative theory of
the market economy — is erected on postulations of rational
and predictable behavior of the firm. In the models that
comprise this theory "the firm" is identified with a single centralized decision-making entity, the entrepreneurial function.
The predicted outcome in such models, however, depends on
the assumptions made concerning the perceived objectives
of the firm, and the means by which they are attained. As
already elaborated at some length throughout this study,
under the conventional assumption of short-run profits objectives there is little reason to infer that large multiproduct

firms would behave differently from other firms in respect to their particular markets. Under different assumptions, e.g., if the single decision-making entity strategically employs the proceeds from some markets to attain certain long-run objectives in others, the outcome might be materially different. Hence, factual analysis of how conglomerate enterprise manages itself in respect to its various markets should provide a basis for the needed refinements in the theory of the firm itself.

## STRUCTURAL IMPACT

While most published statistics on recent mergers and acquisitions have exaggerated the extent to which they were conglomerate, there can be little doubt that the 1960s witnessed a pronounced upturn in the volume of diversifying acquisitions. It may be quixotic to attribute to this acquisition wave the origins of a new form of corporate enterprise, but it clearly produced a group of companies significantly more diversified than their predecessors, and substantially increased the product diversity of corporate enterprise generally. An analysis of data provided by over 200 corporations revealed that diversifying acquisitions consummated in 1961–1970, more than any other single factor, accounted for the level of company diversification prevailing in 1970.

The large volume of diversifying acquisitions was spread highly unevenly over the corporate population. While a scant 2 percent of all reporting companies made more than 30 diversifying acquisitions in 1961–1970, nearly two-thirds made 3 or less, and 84 percent made 8 or less. Since the diversifying acquisition wave was so heavily concentrated in a relatively small number of companies, these companies tended to dominate the quantitative analyses at virtually every turn, especially the multiple regression analysis designed to explain company diversification and the diversifying acquisition process. This suggests that the conglomerate acquisition wave of the 1960s was very likely an aggregation of two distinct and dissimilar components: those "normal" diversifying acquisitions motivated only by conventional business objectives sought through a selective and highly constrained diversification program, and those associated with an aggressive diversification strategy. The latter involved relatively few acquiring companies but accounted for a disproportionately large share of the diversifying acquisitions. Had it not been for the acquisitive conglomerates, the 1961–1970 wave may possibly have passed unnoticed, and it is highly improbable that it would have attracted the attention it has received.

In spite of its size, the wave of diversifying acquisitions has left the structure of the manufacturing economy essentially undisturbed. Indexes of aggregate concentration, measured in terms of value added, at the largest 50, 100, and 200 industrial corporations level, which had registered increases in the 1950s, remained extremely stable throughout the 1960s while the conglomerate merger wave was in progress. Why, contrary to expectations and to widely held beliefs, aggregate concentration did not register an increase over this period is attributable to several factors. First, as already indicated, a large portion of the acquisitions was made by relatively few firms, according to the Federal Trade Commission, 25. Between 1960 and 1968, 12 of these companies became new additions to the list of the largest 100 companies, half of which were not among the largest 200 in 1960, and 3 were too small to appear on *Fortune*'s list of the largest 500. Hence, much of the growth by acquisition did not occur within the largest 100 companies, but involved much smaller firms that eventually replaced other large firms among the largest 100. Second, while a few aggressive conglomerates acquired many companies, the diversifying acquisitions accounted for a very small fraction of total manufacturing assets. Finally, the level of aggregate concentration is obviously affected by many factors other than diversifying acquisitions. For example, well over half of the companies reporting acquisitions for the 1961–1970 period owed less than 7.5 percent of their total 1970 assets to diversifying acquisitions. For the vast majority of manufacturing firms, their 1961 size and internal expansion thereafter explain very nearly all of their 1970 relative size. Estimates show that the outworking of these factors would have resulted in a slight decline in overall concentration in the 1960s had the more acquisitive conglomerates made no acquisitions, but only if it is assumed that they would not have made up the difference through internal expansion. This qualification aside, the conglomerate merger wave appears to have had no measurable effect on the overall structure of the manufacturing economy.

Strictly conglomerate acquisitions, by definition, have no direct effect on the level of market concentration; the market shares of the acquiring and the acquired firms are not additive. It has been argued, however, that conglomerate acquisitions may affect the level of market concentration indirectly. The financial and managerial resources of the acquiring firm, abetted by its extraordinary opportunities to engage in cross-product subsidization, reciprocity dealings, and similar trade practices, may enable it eventually to increase its shares in the acquired markets. Whether this would increase market concentration in the process would, of course, depend on the initial rank of the acquired firm and on the size of the firms whose market shares were correspondingly reduced.

The only data available for measuring changes in concentration in markets are the 4-digit SIC concentration ratios published periodically by the Census of Manufactures. The most recent year for which such data are available is 1970.

These data may be aggregated to obtain weighted average concentration ratios for 3-digit SIC industries, the most refined industry level for which the Federal Trade Commission has identified acquired companies for the 1961–1970 period.

For purposes of this analysis all 1960–1967 acquisitions were arranged in a frequency distribution by 4-digit and 3-digit industries. Those industries acquiring companies had frequently entered through acquisition were considered to be the industries most likely to have been affected by the "conglomerate" factor. The changes in concentration in these industries were then compared with changes in concentration in the manufacturing economy generally.

The results show that diversifying acquisitions have had no measurable effect on concentration in either the 3-digit or 4-digit industries acquired — or at least they had not had any such effect by 1970. The acquired industries actually registered more decreases than increases, and as a group registered a decline in concentration, while manufacturing generally showed a slight increase.

It may reasonably be argued that the time span required for diversifying acquisitions to affect the structural measures of the manufacturing economy is a longer one than the analysis covered. While the question "How long is long enough?" has legitimacy it has no unequivocal answer; and reasonable men will respond differently. Until much more is known about the postacquisition management of acquired companies, the answer remains a matter of judgment.

The facts, however, speak for themselves. Diversifying acquisitions we have come to call the conglomerate merger wave of the 1960s have had no measurable effect on either the overall structure of the economy, or on the individual markets the acquisitions most frequently involved. They did have the effect of creating some two dozen new and highly diversified companies, and of increasing the level of diversification in manufacturing companies generally. But in the process the overall size distribution of firms, and the level of concentration in the markets in which they operate, were not measurably affected.

### CONGLOMERATE MANAGEMENT AND TRADE PRACTICE ISSUES

Trade practices, unlike industrial structure, are not susceptible to quantitative measurement, at least not by direct means. The concern most often expressed in connection with conglomerates is their alleged special capacity for cross-product subsidization and reciprocity dealings. Students of industrial organization have not designed quantitative indexes for these practices, at least not yet. In fact, these matters have never been subjected to systematic study. Accordingly, it is not surprising that in antitrust circles they have generated considerable disagreement.

It should be possible, however, to draw meaningful conclusions concerning the incidence and extent of practices such as these from where in the company decisions on them are made, and who makes them. That is, the more these decisions are centered in corporate divisions and product units, the more they are likely to be made independently of those made by other divisions and production units of the same company. It is highly unlikely, for example, that a division given complete autonomy over its pricing policy will compromise its own financial performance in order to subsidize another autonomous division's product. Moreover, divisional autonomy, when combined with profit-center accounting and control, and a system of managerial rewards based on financial performance, is an impediment to the practice of reciprocity and cross-product subsidization across divisions.

The decisions this study analyzed for purposes of ascertaining the extent of divisional autonomy in diversified firms were those pertaining to pricing, advertising, R&D, and capital outlays. These, in that order, graduate from current operating to long-run investment decisions. The theory of the firm established an a priori case for independent pricing when the products are strictly independent, and for interdependence in regard to capital outlays. The analysis testing this proposition consisted of comparing the degree of divisional autonomy in respect to the four types of decisions with the degree of company diversification. As an additional check on conglomerate reciprocity, the incidence of trade relations departments was also compared with the degree of company diversification.

The results of the analysis, at least from a purely statistical point of view, are unequivocal. In highly diversified firms pricing and, to a lesser extent, advertising, are left almost entirely to divisions and production units, while decisions on capital outlays are generally made by corporate management. In most relatively undiversified firms general management assumes responsibility for all four types of decisions. It may be of some significance that modestly diversified companies more closely resemble the relatively undiversified than the highly diversified companies. There apparently is a threshold level of diversification at which pricing and, to a large extent other operating decisions, are made a matter of divisional autonomy.

Further analysis of the data revealed that the presence of trade relations departments varied inversely with diversification. For both producer-goods and consumer-goods companies, the diversification index was considerably higher for those firms reporting no trade relations departments than for those who did. This relationship persistently showed up in the numerous regression equations designed to explain company diversification and diversifying acquisitions. In only three of the several hundred equations did the "reciprocity" (trade relations) variable turn out to be statistically significant, and in each case it was inversely related to company diversification.

In the case of most conglomerate acquisitions challenged under the Clayton Act, Section 7, the acquiring firm has been defined as a potential competitor of the acquired firm — in familiar antitrust language, it has been lurking on the border of one or more of the acquired firm's markets as a potential competitor. The evidence suggests that this applies to a relatively small number of conglomerate acquisitions. For only 11 percent of the 745 diversifying acquisitions made by 193 companies did the acquiring company report that it seriously considered entry into these same markets by internal expansion.

Obviously, data such as those must be interpreted with considerable caution. It is quite possible that no serious consideration was given to internal expansion because, over most of the period 1961–1970, the acquisition route was perceived to be open. On the other hand, even events given serious consideration do not always materialize. There is no way of determining the extent to which these uncertainties counteract each other. However, in view of the small percentage of instances in which acquiring companies considered internal expansion as an alternative, it would seem reasonable to conclude that conglomerate acquisitions seldom remove a potential competitor from the acquired company's markets.

There are, of course, other alternatives for entry into those markets the acquiring company in fact entered through acquisition. Firms acquire other firms for a variety of reasons and, in the case of acquisitive conglomerates, the particular markets involved often are not a primary consideration. There is some evidence that the new conglomerates assign a high priority to growth, even at the expense of immediate profitability. Accordingly, had the acquisition route been foreclosed it is highly probable that in the 1960s these firms may have entered markets through internal expansion that differed from those they acquired, or directed their expansion to their existing markets.

One thing is clear; the road to company diversification is complex and varied, conforming to no consistent and predictable pattern. Numerous alternative regression models tested with data rich in variety and coverage revealed that the process of diversification neatly conforms to no systematic and predictable pattern. These models confirm that much of the company diversification prevailing in 1970 is attributable to the "conglomerate" acquisitions of 1961–1970, and that this wave consisted of two distinct components: one comprising the aggressively acquisitive companies pursuing a strategy of growth through diversification, and another made up of companies pursuing more conventional, and far more constrained, programs of diversification. The two types of companies appear to conform reasonably well with what business analysts have begun to distinguish as the "conglomerates" and the "diversifieds."

When it comes to explaining the diversification process itself — to identifying the underlying factors common to those companies that engaged in the process — the data stubbornly refuse to yield a consistent pattern. For all companies, diversifying acquisitions are positively correlated with various company growth-by-acquisition measures and nondiversifying acquisitions, and negatively correlated with relative company size. It may be inferred that growth was the proximate, if not the ultimate, goal. But when the more aggressive acquirers are eliminated, these relationships are substantially weakened, highlighting the extent to which these firms dominate the results. It is evident, therefore, that for most companies making diversifying acquisitions over the period 1961–1970, the acquisitions accounted for very little of their total growth.

The strong relationship between diversifying and non-diversifying acquisitions for the aggressive acquirers would appear to have important policy implications. These companies, while diversifying through acquisition, also made numerous horizontal and vertical acquisitions as well. Aside from the fact that they can scarcely be regarded as presenting novel antitrust issues, the nondiversifying acquisitions accounted for a substantial portion of the aggressive acquirers' growth.

## THE POLICY IMPLICATIONS: A SUMMARY

The object of this study has been to subject to factual analysis issues concerning conglomerate enterprise about which there has been much speculation—and much disagreement. More particularly, the analysis has been directed toward those unique features that allegedly inhere in large diversified companies, and which give such companies a special power to immobilize or circumvent the forces of the competitive marketplace. For this reason it has been urged that either our present antitrust standards must be radically stretched, possibly warped, to cope with the sources of this power, or there is need for a new policy to accomplish this purpose. The marshaling of the available facts pertinent to conglomerate enterprise in this context is not expected satisfactorily to resolve this issue, but hopefully it will narrow the area of debate and reduce the necessity for speculation.

If the facts on which this analysis has been based are reliably indicative of the corporate universe — and there are no reasons to believe they are not — there is little if any evidence that diversified companies, simply because of their diversification, present special problems beyond the reach of our anti-trust policy as presently administered. As companies reach a threshold of diversification, such matters as pricing and related market activities increasingly are made a matter of divisional autonomy. This means that in day-to-day operations divisions of conglomerates function very much the same as undiversified companies. Moreover, the evidence is fairly persuasive that highly diversified companies are certainly no more, and may even be less, given to the practice of reciprocity than large corporations generally. Hence, the facts support the unspectacular conclusion that while conglomerates may organize themselves differently, their behavior in markets in which they operate is indistinguishable from other large companies.

It would also appear to follow from these same facts that the decision-making processes of conglomerate enterprise call for no serious modification of the conventional microeconomic theory of the firm. If, as this analysis tends to confirm, the short-run operating decisions pertaining to such matters as pricing, advertising, and, by inference, rates of output, are left to divisional management, these decisions are not contingent upon those made in other company divisions. In sum, in respect to the essential variables on which they are erected, the conventional short-run models are as applicable to a conglomerate division as to a "typical" firm.

Moreover, the rise of conglomerate enterprise (largely through acquisition) in the decade of the 1960s has surprisingly had little if any measurable effect on the overall structure of the manufacturing economy, or on the particular markets diversifying companies have entered through acquisition. Aggregate concentration, of dubious antitrust significance in any case, has remained virtually unchanged; and changes in concentration in the invaded markets have been marked more frequently by decreases than by increases, a pattern indicative of slightly less monopoly growth but statistically not distinguishable from that of markets generally.

We are led then to the conclusion that highly diversified firms (or, if one prefers, conglomerates) present no special antitrust problems, and require no special antitrust policy. The decade of the 1960s witnessed the spectacular rise of about 25 new conglomerates, and a significant increase in overall company diversification. But in the marketplace they appear to behave no differently from other firms. Accordingly, our present policy would appear to lose none of its effectiveness if directed toward preventing and dismantling intolerable market power without special regard to the product diversity of its corporate residence.

Lest this prescription be vastly misunderstood, it should be reiterated carefully and emphatically that it is an *antitrust* policy prescription. One scarcely needs to be a professional observer of the American economy to be aware of the enormous size to which corporations have grown. As a rough indication of the trend, the first billion-dollar manufacturing corporation in the United States was born in 1901; firms of this size now number well over 100, the largest of which is approaching assets of $20 billion. As has often been pointed out, each of the largest 5 U.S. corporations generate goods and services valued in excess of the gross national product of any one of the small countries making up a majority of the United Nations. Many of these large companies, about 200 by actual count, are multinational in scope, and the conduct of their affairs may at times present a challenge to national sovereignty.[4] The recent growth-oriented conglomerates have added to their number. These, however, are entirely different matters. If corporate bigness and multinational opera-

---

[4] *Cf.* Raymond Vernon, "Multinational Enterprise & National Sovereignty," *Harvard Business Review* (March–April 1967), pp. 156–172.

tions, which are often one of its concomitants, raise serious political and geopolitical issues, bigness merits serious analysis in these terms. But the scope and thrust of antitrust have rationally been concerned with efficiency in the allocation of resources in the domestic economy. Conglomerate companies, even the new conglomerates, fall within the ambit of this concern; however, the test of their legitimacy should not be how big they are or how many products they produce, but how much market power, as conventionally measured, they possess.

Appendixes
References
Index

# APPENDIX A.
## The Multiproduct Pricing Model

Contemporary price models pertaining to a single-product firm confronting definable cost and revenue schedules may readily be adapted to multiproduct operations.[1] An appropriate starting point is the conventional, and simplest, case where a firm produces more than one product $(i, j \ldots, n)$, the marginal costs of producing one is independent of the marginal costs of producing any one of the others, and the firm is a strict profits maximizer; i.e., it engages in no strategic price maneuvers such as purposely charging nonoptimum (nonprofits maximizing) prices in the present period in order to attain such possible long-range objectives as growth, increased revenues, or a larger market share in future time periods. If we further simplify the problem by assuming

---

[1] Cf. K. Palda, *Economic Analysis for Marketing Decisions,* pp. 137–141; Martin J. Bailey, "Price and Output Determination by a Firm Selling Related Products," *American Economic Review,* Vol. 44 (March 1954), pp. 82–93; Thomas H. Naylor and John M. Vernon, *Microeconomics and Decision Models of the Firm* (New York: Harcourt, Brace & World, 1969), pp. 123–127.

that the firm produces only two products, *i* and *j*, its basic profit-maximizing equation may be stated as:

(1)   $\pi = q_iP_i + q_jP_j - c\,(q_i,q_j)$, from which it follows that

(2)   $\dfrac{\delta\pi}{\delta q_i} = \dfrac{\delta\pi}{\delta q_j} = 0$

that is, the firm maximized profits $(\pi)$ by producing both products up to where the marginal profitability of each is equal to zero. The corresponding marginal revenue-marginal cost equalities are:

(3)   $P_i + q_i\dfrac{\delta P_i}{\delta q_i} + q_j\dfrac{\delta P_j}{\delta q_i} = \dfrac{\delta c}{\delta q_i}$

$P_j + q_j\dfrac{\delta P_j}{\delta q_j} + q_i\dfrac{\delta P_i}{\delta q_j} = \dfrac{\delta c}{\delta q_j}$

Transposing terms, the respective price equations become:

(4)   $P_i = \dfrac{\delta c}{\delta q_i} - q_i\dfrac{\delta P_i}{\delta q_i} - q_j\dfrac{\delta P_j}{\delta q_i}$

$P_j = \dfrac{\delta c}{\delta q_j} - q_j\dfrac{\delta P_j}{\delta q_j} - \dfrac{{}_i\delta P_i}{q\delta q_j}$

The terms in the price equations lend themselves to an economic interpretation. The cross derivatives $\dfrac{\delta P_j}{\delta q_i}$ and $\dfrac{\delta P_i}{\delta q_j}$ define the interdependence of the quantity demanded of i(j) and the price of j(i); the derivatives $\dfrac{\delta P_i}{q_i}$ and $\dfrac{\delta P_j}{q_j}$ are the slopes of the partial equilibrium demand schedules for i and j. The algebraic sum of the derivative and cross derivative in each price equation therefore measures the difference between the price of each product and its marginal costs. But the cross derivative also defines the effect of "conglomeration"; that is, the effect on price of having the same firm produce both products. If the demand schedules for i and j are strictly independent, the two products are neither complementary nor substitutable, then $q_j\dfrac{\delta P_j}{\delta q_i} = 0$; $q_i\dfrac{\delta P_i}{\delta q_j} = 0$, and the effect of "conglomeration," irrespective of the firm's share of each market, is zero. It may be further noted that in the special

case where the firm operates under conditions of perfect competition (confronts a demand schedule with zero slope), the derivatives ($\delta P_i$ and $\delta P_j$) are also equal to zero, and $P_i = \delta c$ and $P_j =$
$\overline{\delta q_i}$ $\overline{\delta q_j}$ $\overline{\delta q_i}$
$\delta c$. If products i and j are complementary, in the price equations
$\overline{\delta q_j}$
$\delta P_j > 0$ and $\delta P_i > 0$, this implies that the resulting prices would be
$\overline{\delta q_i}$ $\overline{\delta q_j}$
lower than if the two products were produced independently. If they are substitutable, the cross-derivatives are both negative, implying that the resulting price would be higher than if the two products were produced independently.

It follows from the foregoing simple model that a conglomerate firm producing totally independent products, under conventional profits maximizing assumptions, will set prices and rates of output identical with those that would result if each product were produced by an independent firm. Moreover, even when the product demand schedules which the conglomerate firm confronts are interdependent, the price and output effects of conglomeration are attributable to the *combination* of market power *and* conglomeration, and not simply to the fact that the firm is a conglomerate. Finally, the combination of market power and conglomeration is likely to lead to higher prices and lower rates of output than single-product firm market organization only when the products in question are substitutes, i.e., when the cross derivatives $\delta P_i$ and
$\overline{\delta q_j}$
$\delta P_j$ are negative.
$\overline{\delta q_i}$

# APPENDIX B.
## The Diversified
## Company Survey

The quantitative data required for analysis of what might be broadly defined as the managerial characteristics of diversified and diversifying companies, as well as the impact of the diversification process on the structure of the American economy, were obtained mainly from the Diversified Company Survey, Compustat, and the Multinational Enterprise Project data bank. Compustat data are generally familiar to financial analysts, and a description of the Multinational Enterprise Project data bank is fully described elsewhere.[1]

The companies comprising the initial list covered by the HBS Survey included all manufacturing companies appearing among *Fortune*'s 1970 largest 500 corporations, and an additional 100 companies on the list of Associates of the Harvard Business School, but not among the largest 500 corporations. The number of corporations supplying the requested data, by size group, is

---

[1] See James W. Vaupel and Joan P. Curhan, *The Making of Multinational Enterprise.*

184

shown in Exhibit B-1. It will be observed that the response rate for each size group rank of 100 among *Fortune*'s largest 500 corporations was fairly uniform, ranging from 25 percent for the corporations ranking in the 201–300 largest, to 41 percent for the largest 100. The approximately 100 data requests sent to the 501–1000-size group yielded 44 returns. Responses from corporations making individual acquisitions of $100 million or more in assets are shown separately; these companies were asked to supply additional data on acquisitions of this size (see HBS Diversified Firm Survey Variables A71–A74, Appendix C) so that they could be subjected to more detailed analysis.

## EXHIBIT B-1

### CORPORATE SURVEY RETURNS BY SIZE RANGE OF COMPANY

| Rank Range | Number of Corporations Reporting No Acquisitions of $100 million or more | Number of Corporations Reporting Acquisitions of $100 million or more | Total | Percent of Reporting Companies |
|---|---|---|---|---|
| 1– 100 | 31 | 10 | 41 | 19% |
| 101– 200 | 32 | 2 | 34 | 16 |
| 201– 300 | 23 | 2 | 25 | 12 |
| 301– 400 | 31 | 1 | 32 | 15 |
| 401– 500 | 34 | 1 | 35 | 17 |
| 501–1000 and Anonymous | 44 | — | 44 | 21 |
| Totals | 195 | 16 | 211 | 100% |

# APPENDIX C.

## Variables in the Data Bank

HBS DIVERSIFIED FIRM SURVEY

| Code | Description |
| --- | --- |
| A1–A10 | Total number of acquisitions by year (for years 1961–1970) |
| A11–A20 | Value of acquisitions by year defined as amount the acquiring company paid in cash and/or other assets (for years 1961–1970) |
| A21–A30 | Total number of divestitures by year (for years 1961–1970) |
| A31–A40 | Value of divestitures by year (for years 1961–1970) |
| A41–A50 | Number of diversifying acquisitions by year, defined as one that puts the acquiring company into a 4-digit SIC industry in which it did not previously compete (for years 1961–1970) |
| A51–A60 | Number of acquisitions reported where internal expansion was seriously considered as an alternative means of diversification by year (for years 1961–1970) |

A61   Share of the firm's total 1970 sales accounted for by acquisitions during the 1961–1970 period, not including postacquisition sales growth of the acquired companies

A62   Share of the firm's total 1970 sales accounted for by acquisitions during the 1961–1970 period, including postacquisition sales growth of the acquired companies

A63   Share of the firm's total 1970 assets accounted for by acquisitions during the 1961–1970 period, not including postacquisition asset growth of the acquired companies

A64   Share of the firm's total 1970 assets accounted for by acquisitions during the 1961–1970 period, including postacquisition asset growth of the acquired companies

A65   Total number of 4-digit SIC industries in which the firm competed as of 1970 (or 1969 if more convenient)

A66   Total number of 4-digit SIC industries which the firm entered through acquisition during the 1961–1970 period

A67   Managerial level at which decisions on price are made (corporate, operating unit, profit center, other)

A68   Managerial level at which decisions on advertising and promotion are made (same as A67)

A69   Managerial level at which decisions on research and development are made (same as A67)

A70   Managerial level at which decisions on major capital expenditures are made (same as A67)

A71   General company policy or practice with respect to pricing decisions in acquired companies (left entirely with management of acquired company; left primarily with acquired company's management but worked out in consultation with corporate management; or moved to corporate management, or some managerial level having broader responsibilities than the acquired company management)

A72   General company policy or practice with respect to

188                                                          *Appendix C*

advertising decisions in acquired companies (same as A71)

A73     General company policy or practice with respect to research and development decisions in acquired companies (same as A71)

A74     General company policy or practice with respect to major capital expenditures in acquired companies (same as A71)

A75     Existence of a trade relations department in the firm (yes or no)

A76     Existence of dissemination of information on sales, purchases, or lists of suppliers to employees responsible for purchasing (yes or no)

CHARLES BERRY DATA

B1   Berry 2-digit SIC index of diversification—1960 (calculated as one minus the sum of the squares of the portion of the firm's employment in each 2-digit SIC industry; i.e., from

$$B1 = 1 - \sum_{i=1}^{n} (P_i^2),$$ where $P_i$ is the percentage of the com-

pany's employment in the ith industry)

B2   Berry 4-digit SIC index of diversification—1960 (calculated as in B1)

B3   Berry 2-digit SIC index of diversification—1965 (calculated as in B1)

B4   Berry 4-digit SIC index of diversification—1965 (calculated as in B1)

COMPUSTAT DATA
(For Years 1961, 1965, 1970, and the 10-Year Total 1961–1970)

C1–C4     Total assets or liabilities
C5–C8     Common equity
C9–C12    Net Sales
C13–C16   Operating income

C17–C20  Depreciation and amortization
C21–C24  Fixed charges (interest)
C25–C28  Income taxes
C29–C32  Net income (before netted nonrecurring)
C33–C36  Common dividends
C37–C40  Stock price—high
C41–C44  Stock price—low
C45–C48  Dividends per share
C49–C52  Capital expenditures
C53–C56  Investment and advances to subsidiaries
C57–C60  Intangibles
C61–C64  Total invested capital
C65–C68  Incentive compensation expense
C69–C72  Selling and advertising expense
C73–C76  Research and development expense
C77–C80  Potentially diluted earnings per share
C81–C84  Earnings per share as reported

HBS MULTINATIONAL ENTERPRISE PROJECT

D1   Average concentration of domestic products (calculated as an average of 4-firm concentration ratios for the 4-digit SIC industries in which the firm competed, weighted by the share of domestic shipments)

D2   Average market share (calculated as the total firm's sales divided by the total shipments of all 5-digit SIC product-markets in which the firm competed)

D3   Growth in sales (1955–1964)

D4   Growth in value-added for domestic products (1947–1963)

D5   Return on investment (1964)

D6   Average return on investment (1960–1964)

D7   Average markup (1960–1964)

D8   Average price/earnings ratio (1962–1964)

D9   Number of 2-digit SIC industry groups in which the firm competed in 1964

D10  Number of 3-digit SIC industry groups in which the firm competed in 1964

D11   Number of 5-digit SIC product-markets in which the firm competed in 1964

D12   Average correlation between products (computed as average of the Pearson correlation coefficients for all parts of 5-digit product-markets) where the coefficient was based on the number of instances the companies studied manufactured both, one, or none of the products

D13   Effective diversification index (calculated as D11 x D12)

D14   Stopford's index of domestic diversification (calculated as the sales of the firm outside the major product line, expressed as a percentage of the sales, for domestic products and sales only)

D15   Stopford's index of foreign diversification (calculated as the sales of the firm outside the major product line, expressed as a percentage of the total sales, for all countries in which products are sold)

D16   Corporate funded research and development expressed as a percentage of sales (1964)

D17   Corporate funded research and development expressed as a percentage of value-added (1964)

D18   Scientists and engineers expressed as a percentage of total number of employees (1962)

D19   Advertising expenses expressed as a percentage of sales (1965)

D20   Advertising on national magazines, newspaper supplements, and network television and radio expressed as a percentage of sales (1965)

D21   Crude materials input expressed as a total of inputs (1958)

D22   Primary 3-digit SIC industry group in 1966

D23   Organizational stage (measured by John Stopford)

D24   Number of foreign countries manufactured in at end of 1963

FORTUNE MAGAZINE

F1   Rank by sales among the largest 500 publicly held mining and manufacturing firms in the United States (1961)

F2    Rank by sales among the largest 500 publicly held mining and manufacturing firms in the United States (1964)

F3    Rank by sales among the largest 500 publicly held mining and manufacturing firms in the United States (1969)

RESEARCH STAFF EVALUATION

(Based on the *Fortune Plant and Product Directory,* 1965)

E1    Consumer-goods manufacturer (yes or no)

E2    Producer-goods manufacturer (yes or no)

TRANSFORMATIONS [1]

| | |
|---|---|
| $X1 = A1 + A2 + \ldots + A10$ | Number of Acquisitions, 10-year total |
| $X2 = A11 + A12 + \ldots + A20$ | Value of acquisitions, 10-year total |
| $X3 = A21 + A22 + \ldots + A30$ | Number of divestitures, 10-year total |
| $X4 = A31 + A32 + \ldots + A40$ | Value of divestitures, 10-year total |
| $X5 = A41 + A42 + \ldots + A50$ | Number of diversifying acquisitions, 10-year total |
| $X6 = A51 + A52 + \ldots + A60$ | Number of diversifying acquisitions for which internal development was considered, 10-year total |
| $X7 = (C17 + C21 + C25 + C29)/C1$ | Return on assets, 1961 |
| $X8 = (C18 + C22 + C26 + C30)/C2$ | Return on assets, 1965 |
| $X9 = (C19 + C23 + C27 + C31)/C3$ | Return on assets, 1970 |

---

[1] In addition to the transformations listed here, the square and logarithm of all variables listed in this appendix were available for use in any calculation or model and many square or logarithm transformations were used.

| | |
|---|---|
| $X10 = (C20 + C24 + C28 + C32)/C4$ | Return on assets, 10 years |
| $X11 = C29/C61$ | Return on investment, 1961 |
| $X12 = C30/C62$ | Return on investment, 1965 |
| $X13 = C31/C63$ | Return on investment, 1970 |
| $X14 = C32/C64$ | Return on investment, 10 years |
| $X15 = (C37 + C41)/2$ | Average stock price, 1961 |
| $X16 = (C38 + C42)/2$ | Average stock price, 1965 |
| $X17 = (C39 + C43)/2$ | Average stock price, 1970 |
| $X18 = (C40 + C44)/2$ | Average stock price, 10 years |
| $X19 = X15/C81$ | Price/earnings ratio, 1961 |
| $X20 = X16/C82$ | Price/earnings ratio, 1965 |
| $X21 = X17/C83$ | Price/earnings ratio, 1970 |
| $X22 = X18/C84$ | Price/earnings ratio, 10 years |
| $X23 = C3/C1$ | Total asset growth rate, 10 years |
| $X24 = C7/C5$ | Common equity growth rate, 10 years |
| $X25 = C11/C9$ | Net sales growth rate, 10 years |
| $X26 = C31/C29$ | Net income growth rate, 10 years |
| $X27 = C83/C81$ | Earnings per share growth rate, 10 years |
| $X28 = X17/X15$ | Stock price growth rate, 10 years |
| $X29 = X21/X19$ | Price/earnings ratio growth rate, 10 years |
| $X30 = X9/X7$ | Return on assets growth rate, 10 years |
| $X31 = X13/X11$ | Return on investment growth rate, 10 years |
| $X32 = C45/C81$ | Dividend ratio, 1961 |
| $X33 = C46/C82$ | Dividend ratio, 1965 |
| $X34 = C47/C83$ | Dividend ratio, 1970 |
| $X35 = C48/C84$ | Dividend ratio, 10 years |
| $X36 = A5/A1$ | Fraction of acquisitions which were diversifying, 10 years |

| | |
|---|---|
| $X37 = A1 — A3$ | Net number of acquisitions, 10 years |
| $X38 = A2 — A4$ | Net value of acquisitions, 10 years |
| $X39 = A2/A1$ | Average value of an acquisition, 10 years |
| $X40 = A1/C4$ | Number of acquisitions normalized for size, 10 years |
| $X41 = X37/C4$ | Net number of acquisitions normalized for size, 10 years |
| $X42 = A2/C4$ | Value of acquisitions normalized for size, 10 years |
| $X43 = X38/C4$ | Net value of acquisitions normalized for size, 10 years |
| $X44 = A61/C72$ | Share of sales acquired excluding postacquisition growth divided by sales, 10 years |
| $X45 = A62/C72$ | Share of sales acquired including postacquisition growth divided by sales, 10 years |
| $X46 = A63/C4$ | Share of assets acquired excluding postacquisition growth divided by assets, 10 years |
| $X47 = A64/C4$ | Share of assets acquired including postacquisition growth divided by assets, 10 years |
| $X48 = A61/X25$ | Share of sales acquired excluding postacquisition growth divided by sales growth rate, 10 years |
| $X49 = A62/X25$ | Share of sales acquired including postacquisition growth divided by sales growth rate, 10 years |

$X50 = X49 — X48$      Growth of share of sales acquired divided by sales growth rate, 10 years

$X51 = A63/X23$      Share of assets acquired excluding postacquisition growth rate divided by asset growth rate, 10 years

$X52 = A64/X23$      Share of assets acquired including postacquisition growth rate divided by asset growth rate, 10 years

$X53 = X52 — X51$      Growth of share of assets acquired divided by assets growth rate

$X54 = C72/C12$      Selling and advertising expense as a share of net sales, 10 years

$X55 = C76/C12$      Research and development expense as a share of net sales, 10 years

$X56 = X1 — X5$      Number of nondiversifying acquisitions

# APPENDIX D.
## General Description of Data Bank

| Fortune Rank—1969 | HBS Survey Responses | Compustat Variables | Berry Data | HBS Multi-National Project Data (HBS-MNP) |
|---|---|---|---|---|
| 1–100 | 41 | 41 | 34 | 38 |
| 101–200 | 34 | 34 | 31 | 32 |
| 201–300 | 25 | 24 | 22 | 20 |
| 301–400 | 32 | 29 | 20 | 22 |
| 401–500 | 35 | 30 | 10 | 13 |
| Not on 500 | 37 | 25 | | |
| Anonymous | 7 | | | |
| | 211 | 183 | 117 | 125 |

NOTE: Not all companies have complete data in any of the above categories; therefore, no individual variable may have the number of responses indicated above. Furthermore, not all 117 companies with Berry data will have Compustat or HBS-MNP data; therefore, calculations involving more than one category may eliminate some companies. Companies were included in the Compustat, Berry, and HBS Multinational Project data only if they had HBS Survey responses.

# APPENDIX E.
## Companies Responding to HBS Diversified Firm Survey

AMP Incorporated
Air Products and Chemicals, Inc.
Akzona Incorporated
Alcan Aluminum Limited
Allegheny Ludlum Industries
American Airlines, Inc.
American Can Company
American Cyanamid Company
American Petrofina, Inc.
American Smelting and Refining Company
The Anaconda Company
Anchor Hocking Corporation
Armco Steel Corporation
The Armstrong Rubber Company
Avon Products, Inc.

Bath Industries, Inc.
The Bendix Corporation
The Black & Decker Manufacturing Company
Blue Bell, Inc.
Boeing Company
Borg-Warner Corporation
Broadway-Hale Stores, Inc.
Brockway Glass Company, Inc.
Brunswick Corporation
Burroughs Corporation

Cabot Corporation
Cameron Iron Works, Inc.
Campbell Taggart, Inc.
The Carborundum Company
Carnation Company
Carpenter Technology Corporation
Carrier Corporation
Caterpillar Tractor Company
Celanese Corporation
Cessna Aircraft Company
Chrysler Corporation
Clark Equipment Company
Colorado Interstate Corporation
ConAgra, Inc.
Control Data Corporation
Cooper Industries, Inc.
Cox Broadcasting Corporation
Cummins Engine Company, Inc.

Dan River Inc.
Dana Corporation
Deere & Company
DeKalb AgResearch, Inc.
Dennison Manufacturing Company
Diamond Shamrock Corporation
Dillingham Corporation

R. R. Donnelley & Sons Company
E. I. duPont de Nemours & Company

Eagle-Picher Industries, Inc.
Eaton Corporation
Peter Eckrich and Sons, Inc.
Emerson Electric Company
Emery Industries, Inc.
Ethyl Corporation

Farmers Union Central Exchange
Fibreboard Corporation
Fuqua Industries, Inc.

General Foods Corporation
General Mills, Inc.
General Motors Corporation
General Signal Corporation
The B. F. Goodrich Company
Grumman Corporation
Gulton Industries, Inc.

Hammermill Paper Company
Handy & Harman
The Hanna Mining Company
Hart Schaffner & Marx
Hoerner-Waldorf Corporation
Hoffman-LaRoche Inc.
Honeywell Inc.
Hoover Ball and Bearing Company
George A. Hormel and Company
Hygrade Food Products Corporation
Hyster Company

Industrial Nucleonics Corporation
Inland Steel
International Business Machines Corporation

International Harvester Company
International Telephone & Telegraph Corporation
Iowa Beef Packers, Inc.

Jewel Companies, Inc.
Johns-Manville
Johnson and Johnson
Johnson Service Company

Kaiser Aluminum & Chemical Corporation
Kaiser Steel Corporation
Keebler Company
The Kendall Company
Kimberly-Clark Corporation
S. S. Kresge Company

Lear Siegler, Inc.
Eli Lilly and Company
Thomas J. Lipton Inc.
Lockheed Aircraft Corporation
The Lubrizol Corporation

MacMillan Bloedel Limited
R. H. Macy & Company, Inc.
Magnavox Company
Oscar Mayer & Company
McLouth Steel Corporation
Medusa Portland Cement Company
Melville Shoe Corporation
Merck & Company, Inc.
Midland-Ross Corporation
Minnesota Mining and Manufacturing Company
Mobil Oil Corporation
Murphy Oil Corporation

National Presto Industries, Inc.
National Service Industries, Inc.

Norlin Corporation
Norris Industries, Inc.
Northern Natural Gas Company

Occidental Petroleum Corporation
Olivetti Corporation of America
Omark Industries, Inc.
Outboard Marine Corporation

PPG Industries
Panhandle Eastern Pipe Line Company
Parke-Davis & Company
J. C. Penney Company, Inc.
The Perkin-Elmer Corporation
Pet Incorporated
Phelps Dodge Corporation
Philip Morris, Inc.
Pitney-Bowes, Inc.
Polaroid Corporation

The Quaker Oats Company

Raytheon Company
Reichhold Chemicals, Inc.
Republic Steel Corporation
R. J. Reynolds Industries, Inc.
Reynolds Metals Company

SCM Corporation
St. Joe Minerals Corporation
Sanders Associates, Inc.
F. & M. Schaeffer Corporation
Scovill Manufacturing Company
Joseph E. Seagram & Sons, Inc.
Simmons Company
Simpson Timber Company
A. O. Smith Corporation

Smith Kline & French Laboratories
Spencer Foods, Inc.
Sperry and Hutchinson Company
A. E. Staley Manufacturing Company
Standard Oil Company of California
Stauffer Chemical Company
Stokely-Van Camp, Inc.
Sun Oil Company
Supermarkets General Corporation
Sybron Corporation

Tenneco Inc.
Texas Instruments, Inc.
Textron Inc.
Thiokol Chemical Corporation
The Trane Company
Trans Union Corporation
Trans World Airlines, Inc.

Union Oil Company of California
United Merchants and Manufacturers, Inc.
U. S. Plywood-Champion Papers Inc.

Varian Associates

Wallace-Murray Corporation
Warnaco, Inc.
Warner & Swasey Company
West Point Pepperell, Inc.
Western Gear Corporation
Western Publishing Company, Inc.
Whirlpool Corporation
Wyman-Gordon Company

Total Identified Companies = 175
Anonymous Companies    = 36
Total Answering Survey   = 211

# REFERENCES

Adelman, Morris A., "The Measurement of Industrial Concentration," *The Review of Economics and Statistics*, Vol. 33, No. 4 (November 1951).

Backman, Jules, "Conglomerate Mergers and Competition," *Conglomerate Mergers and Acquisitions: Opinion and Analysis, St. John's Law Review*, Special Edition, Vol. 44 (Spring 1970).

Bailey, Martin J., "Price and Output Determination by a Firm Selling Related Products," *American Economic Review*, Vol. 44 (March 1954).

Bain, Joe S., "Changes in the Concentration in Manufacturing Industries in the United States, 1954–1966: Trends and Relationships to the Levels of 1954 Concentration," *The Review of Economics and Statistics*, Vol. LII, No. 4 (November 1970).

Barmash, Isadore, *The New York Times*, Business and Finance Section, November 5, 1972.

Baumol, William J., *Business Behavior, Value and Growth*, Revised Edition. New York: Harcourt, Brace & World, Inc., 1967.

Berg, Norman A., "Corporate Role in Diversified Companies," Harvard Business School Working Paper, HBS 71–2, BP2.

Berg, Norman A., "Strategic Planning in Conglomerate Companies," *Harvard Business Review* (May-June 1965).

Berle, Adolf A., *The Twentieth Century Capitalist Revolution*. New York: Harcourt, Brace & World, Inc., 1954.

Berle, Adolf A. and Gardiner C. Means, *The Modern Corporation and Private Property*, Revised Edition. New York: Harcourt, Brace & World, Inc., 1968.

Berry, Charles H., "Economic Policy and the Conglomerate Merger," *Conglomerate Mergers and Acquisitions: Opinion and Analysis, St. John's Law Review*, Special Edition, Vol. 44 (Spring 1970).

Bock, Betty, "Notes on Problems of Identifying Merger Patterns." Unpublished paper, 1968.

Bock, Betty and Jack Farkas, "The Largest Companies and How They Grew," *The Conference Board Record*, Vol. VIII, No. 3, (March 1971).

Bower, Joseph L., "Management Decision Making in Large Diversified Firms." Draft of a paper presented to the *Large Diversified Firm Conference*, Harvard Graduate School of Business Administration (November 14–16, 1971).

Bower, Joseph L., *Managing the Resource Allocation Process: A Study of Corporate Planning and Investment*. Boston: Division of Research, Harvard Graduate School of Business Administration, 1970.

Bower, Joseph, "Planning Within the Firm," *American Economic Review*, Vol. 60 (May 1970).

Brooks, Robert, Jr., "Price Cutting and Monopoly Power," *Journal of Marketing*, Vol. 25 (1961).

Butters, J. Keith, John Lintner, and William L. Cary, *Effects of Taxation: Corporate Mergers*. Boston: Division of Research, Harvard Graduate School of Business Administration, 1951.

Chandler, Alfred D., Jr., *Strategy and Structure: Chapters in the History of the American Industrial Enterprise*. Cambridge: Massachusetts Institute of Technology Press, 1962.

Compustat. Magnetic tape computer data library. Denver, Colorado: Investor's Sciences, Inc., December 13, 1971.

Dirlam, Joel B., "Observations on Public Policy Toward Conglomerate Mergers," *Conglomerate Mergers and Acquisitions: Opinion and Analysis, St. John's Law Review*, Special Edition, Vol. 44 (Spring 1970).

*The Economist,* "Biting the Hand of Business" (April 5, 1969).

Edwards, Corwin D., "The Changing Dimensions of Business Power," *Conglomerate Mergers and Acquisitions: Opinion and Analysis, St. John's Law Review,* Special Edition, Vol. 44 (Spring 1970).

Edwards, Corwin D., "Conglomerate Bigness as a Source of Power," in National Bureau of Economic Research, *Business Concentration and Price Policy, A Conference of the Universities-National Bureau Committee for Economic Research.* Princeton, New Jersey: Princeton University Press, 1955.

FTC *Report.* See U.S. Federal Trade Commission, Bureau of Economics, *Economic Report on Corporate Mergers.*

Ferguson, James M., "Anticompetitive Effects of the FTC's Attack on Product-Extension Mergers," *Conglomerate Mergers and Acquisitions: Opinion and Analysis, St. John's Law Review,* Special Edition, Vol. 44 (Spring 1970).

Friedman, Milton, "The Methodology of Positive Economics," *Essays in Positive Economics.* Chicago: University of Chicago Press, 1953.

Galbraith, John Kenneth, *American Capitalism: The Concept of Countervailing Power,* Revised Edition. Boston: Houghton Mifflin, 1956.

Galbraith, John Kenneth, *A Contemporary Guide to Economics, Peace and Laughter.* New York: The New American Library, Inc., 1972.

Galbraith, John Kenneth, *The New Industrial State.* Boston: Houghton Mifflin, 1967.

Gilbert, David, *Mergers, and Diversification and the Theories of the Firm.* Unpublished Doctoral Dissertation. Department of Economics, Harvard University, Cambridge, 1971.

Gort, Michael, "An Economic Disturbance Theory of Mergers," *Quarterly Journal of Economics* (November 1969).

Hall, R. L. and C. J. Hitch, "Price Theory and Business Behavior," *Oxford Economic Papers,* Vol. 2 (May 1939).

Harvard Business School Diversified Firm Survey. See Appendixes C and E.

Hilton, Peter, *Planning Corporate Growth and Diversification*. New York: McGraw-Hill Book Co., 1970.

Jacoby, Neil, "The Conglomerate Corporation," *The Center Magazine* (July 1969).

Jones, Mary Gardiner and Edward J. Heiden, "Conglomerates: The Need for Rational Policy Making," *Conglomerate Mergers and Acquisitions: Opinion and Analysis, St. John's Law Review*, Special Edition, Vol. 44 (Spring 1970).

Kefauver, Senator Estes, *In a Few Hands: Monopoly Power in America*. New York: Pantheon Books, 1965.

Lester, R. A., "Shortcomings of Marginal Analysis for Wage-Employment Problems," *American Economic Review*, Vol. 36 (March 1946).

Lynch, Harry H., *Financial Performance of Conglomerates*. Boston: Division of Research, Harvard Graduate School of Business Administration, 1971.

Machlup, F., "Marginal Analysis and Empirical Research," *American Ecnomic Review*, Vol. 36 (September 1946).

Machlup, F., "Theories of the Firm: Marginalist, Behavioral, Managerial," *American Economic Review*, Vol. 52 (March 1967).

Markham, Jesse W., "Antitrust and the Conglomerate: A Policy in Search of a Theory," *Conglomerate Mergers and Acquisitions: Opinion and Analysis, St. John's Law Review*, Special Edition, Vol. 44 (Spring 1970).

Markham, Jesse W., "Survey of the Evidence and Findings on Mergers," in National Bureau of Economic Research, *Business Concentration and Price Policy, A Conference of the Universities-National Bureau Committee for Economic Research*. Princeton, New Jersey: Princeton University Press, 1955.

Marris, Robin, *The Economic Theory of Managerial Capitalism*. New York: Basic Books, 1968.

McCreary, Edward, Jr., and Walter Guzzardi, Jr., "A Customer is a Company's Best Friend," *Fortune* (June 1965).

McLaren, Richard W., "Antitrust—The Year Past and the Year Ahead." An address before the New York State Bar Association, Antitrust Law Section, New York City, January 29, 1970.

Mintz, Morton, and Jerry S. Cohen, *America, Inc.: Who Owns and Operates the United States.* New York: Dial Press, 1971.

Mueller, Dennis C., "A Theory of Conglomerate Mergers," *Quarterly Journal of Economics* (November 1969).

National Industrial Conference Board, Inc., *Corporate Organization Structures.* Studies in Personnel Policy No. 210 (1968).

National Industrial Conference Board, Inc., *Top Management Organization in Divisionalized Companies.* Studies in Personnel Policy No. 195 (1965).

Naylor, Thomas H. and John M. Vernon, *Microeconomics and Decision Models of the Firm.* New York: Harcourt, Brace & World, 1969.

*The New York Times,* "Antitrust Strategist," Financial Section, November 12, 1972.

*News Front,* Leading U.S. Corporations. New York: *Year, Inc.,* Various Years.

Palda, K., *Economic Analysis for Marketing Decisions.* Englewood Cliffs, New Jersey: Prentice-Hall, 1969.

Penrose, Edith, *The Theory of the Growth of the Firm.* Oxford, England: Basil Blackwell, 1968.

Posner, Richard, "Conglomerate Mergers and Antitrust Policy: An Introduction," *Conglomerate Mergers and Acquisitions: Opinion and Analysis, St. John's Law Review,* Special Edition, Vol. 44 (Spring 1970).

Preston, Lee E., *Giant Firms, Large Mergers and Concentration: Patterns and Policy Alternatives.* Working Paper Series No. 143, State University of New York, Buffalo (July 1972).

Preston, Lee E., "A Probabilistic Approach to Conglomerate Mergers," *Conglomerate Mergers and Acquisitions: Opinion and Analysis, St. John's Law Review,* Special Edition, Vol. 44 (Spring 1970).

Rumelt, Richard P. "Strategy, Structure, and Economic Performance." Unpublished Doctoral Dissertation, Harvard Graduate School of Business Administration, Boston, 1972.

Salter, Malcolm, "Stages of Corporate Development: Implications for Management Control," *Journal of Business Policy*, Vol. 1, No. 1 (Autumn 1970).

Samuelson, Paul A., *Economics: An Introductory Analysis*, 3rd Edition. New York: McGraw-Hill Book Co., 1955.

Scherer, F. M., *Industrial Market Structure and Economic Performance*. Chicago: Rand McNally & Co., 1970.

Stigler, George J., "Mergers and Preventive Antitrust Policy," *University of Pennsylvania Law Review*, Vol. 104 (November 1955).

Stigler, George J., *Working Paper for the Task Force on Productivity and Competition: Reciprocity* in 115 Congressional Record, 6479 Daily edition (June 16, 1969).

Turner, Donald F., "Conglomerate Mergers and Section 7 of the Clayton Act," *Harvard Law Review*, Vol. 78 (May 1965).

U.S. Congress, House of Representatives, "Amending an Act Entitled 'An Act to Supplement Existing Laws against Unlawful Restraints and Monopolies, and for other Purposes,' Approved October 15, 1914," Report 1191, 81st Congress, 1st Sess. (August 4, 1949).

U.S. Congress, Senate, "Hearings on Economic Concentration before the Subcommittee on Antitrust and Monopoly of the Senate Committee on the Judiciary," 88th Congress, 2nd Sess., Pt. 1 (1964).

U.S. Department of Commerce, Bureau of the Census, *Annual Survey of Manufactures*. Washington: U.S. Department of Commerce, Bureau of the Census, 1970.

U.S. Department of Commerce, Bureau of the Census, *1967 Census of Manufactures*. Washington: U.S. Department of Commerce, Bureau of the Census, 1967.

U.S. Department of Commerce, Bureau of the Census, *1970 Census of Manufactures*, "Concentration Ratios in Manufacturing," Special Report Series, Part 1, MC67(S)2.1. Washington: U.S. Department of Commerce, Bureau of the Census, 1970.

U.S. Federal Trade Commission, Bureau of Economics, *Current Trends in Merger Activity, Statistical Reports*, No. 4, 6, 8, & 10.

Washington: U. S. Government Printing Office, 1969, 1970, 1971, 1972, respectively.

U. S. Federal Trade Commission, Bureau of Economics, *Economic Papers, 1966–69*. Washington: U.S. Government Printing Office, 1970.

U.S. Federal Trade Commission, Bureau of Economics, *Economic Report on Corporate Mergers*. Washington: U.S. Government Printing Office, 1969.

U.S. Federal Trade Commission, Bureau of Economics, *Statistical Reports No. 5, 7 and 9, Large Mergers in Manufacturing and Mining, 1948–69, 1948–70, 1948–71*. Washington: U.S. Government Printing Office, 1970, 1971 and 1972, respectively.

U.S. Federal Trade Commission, *Report on Corporate Mergers and Acquisitions*. Washington: U.S. Government Printing Office, May 1955.

U.S. Federal Trade Commission, *Report of the Federal Trade Commission on Rates of Return for Identical Companies in Selected Manufacturing Industries, 1958–1967*. Washington: Federal Trade Commission, 1967.

Vaupel, James W. and Joan P. Curhan, *The Making of Multinational Enterprise: A Sourcebook of Tables Based on a Study of 187 Major U.S. Manufacturing Corporations*. Boston: Division of Research, Harvard Graduate School of Business Administration, 1969.

Vernon, Raymond, "Multinational Enterprise and National Sovereignty," *Harvard Business Review* (March-April, 1967).

Weston, J. Frederick, "The Nature and Significance of Conglomerate Firms," *Conglomerate Mergers and Acquisitions: Opinions and Analysis, St. John's Law Review*, Special Edition, Vol. 44 (Spring 1970).

Williamson, Oliver E., *The Economics of Discretionary Behavior: Managerial Objectives in a Theory of the Firm*. Englewood Cliffs, New Jersey: Prentice-Hall, 1964.

Wrigley, Leonard, "Divisional Autonomy and Diversification." Unpublished Doctoral Dissertation. Harvard Graduate School of Business Administration, Boston, 1970.

## Antitrust Cases

*FTC* v. *Consolidated Foods Corporation,* 380 U.S. 592 (1965).

*FTC* v. *Procter & Gamble,* 386 U.S. 568 (1967).

*General Foods Corporation* v. *FTC,* 386 F. 2d., 936, 945 (3d. Cir. 1967).

*Reynolds Metals Company* v. *FTC,* 390 F.2d. 223 (D.C. Cir. 1962).

U.S. Department of Justice Civil Actions No. 71-119 (January 11, 1971); No. 70-3102 (December 14, 1970); No. 71-189 (February 26, 1971).

# Index

# ABSTRACT

# Conglomerate Enterprise and Public Policy

*During the decade of the 1960s there was a dramatic increase in conglomerate mergers. Unlike the combinations and mergers in earlier periods of American business history, these mergers were not vertical or horizontal within individual industries, but rather diversified among various industries. For instance, a tobacco company might expand into manufactured foods; or a pharmaceutical company into optical equipment.*

*Among antitrust students and practitioners, and in the business press, there was much debate as to whether these conglomerate mergers required new law or simply an enlargement and modification of the existing antimerger statute.*

*The purpose of this study was to develop and analyze the facts pertinent to the impact that conglomerate mergers and acquisitions have had on public policy.*

*The author, Jesse W. Markham, is Charles E. Wilson Professor of Business Administration, Harvard University.*

The dramatic increase in conglomerate mergers during the decade of the 1960s rekindled the concerns of public policy with this very special form of big business. Unlike the waves of combinations and mergers identified with earlier periods in American business history, these mergers did not bring under the control of a few corporate roofs entire industries, or even dominant shares of particular markets. Rather, they were the means by which, among others, a communications equipment company expanded into such diverse businesses as bread baking, automobile rental services, and home-building; a tobacco company into manufactured foods; a pharmaceutical company into optical equipment; an industrial machinery company into textiles; and an electronic equipment company into aircraft manufacturing, and eventually into steel. In short, the instant effect (and apparent objective) of such mergers and acquisitions was widespread company diversification rather than market control.

Since diversifying acquisitions did not conform to the earlier patterns from which the nation's antimerger policy had evolved, and toward which it had in recent years been applied with considerable clarity and effectiveness, a discernible gap existed between the basic tenets of the law and the business phenomenon the law was designed to govern. The situation was somewhat like that of hunters pursuing the fox with a pack of hounds well after the fox had turned into a herd of whales. The gap generated considerable debate before pertinent congressional committees, among antitrust students and practitioners, and in the business press, as to whether conglomerate mergers required new law or simply an enlargement and modification in application of the existing antimerger statute.

The succession of chief antitrust law enforcement officials in the 1960s held different views on the issue. The Honorable Donald F. Turner, Assistant Attorney General for Antitrust from 1965 to 1968, argued that, except in special circumstances, conglomerate acquisitions did not substantially lessen competition by application of the usual tests for making this determination in merger cases. The Honorable Richard A. McLaren, the Assistant Attorney General throughout most of President Nixon's first term, contended that they did. His successor, Assistant Attorney General Kauper, holds a similar view.

The reasons for challenging conglomerate mergers have necessarily been more speculative in character than those employed in cases of horizontal and vertical mergers. Unlike the latter, strictly conglomerate acquisitions have no immediate impact on the structure of the particular markets involved; the market shares before and after such acquisitions are the same, only they are held by different companies. Nevertheless, it was contended that they adversely affected competition because they may:

(1) Eliminate a *potential* competitor
(2) Enhance the possibilities for the practice of business reciprocity
(3) Lead to competitive forebearance
(4) Result in cross-product subsidization
(5) Increase aggregate concentration, and ultimately
(6) Lead to increases in market concentration

Since for each hypothesis offered in support of any of these possible consequences there exists an equally plausible counter-hypothesis, their resolution is ultimately an empirical matter. The purpose of this study was to develop and analyze the facts pertinent to these issues.

The factual data supplied by 211 corporations, most of which were on *Fortune's* 1970 list of the largest 500, provided a basis for most of the analysis. These data, in conjunction with 1965 company diversification indexes computed by Professor Charles Berry of Princeton University, financial data available from Compustat, the Federal Trade Commission's periodic compilations of large mergers, and the Harvard Business School's Multinational Project data bank, provided a more comprehensive basis for additional analyses, including the employment of multiple regression techniques.

The author concludes that the speculative grounds on which conglomerate acquisitions are currently being challenged are of highly dubious validity. He is careful to point out that the growth in size and number of what has come to be called "giant" corporations may be a legitimate concern of public policy. However, it would be inappropriate to stretch, perhaps to warp, contemporary antimerger policy to fit conglomerate mergers in the interests of meeting this concern.

(Published by Division of Research, Harvard Business School, Soldiers Field, Boston, Mass. 02163. LC 73-75882; ISBN 0-87584-104-X. xviii + 218 pp.; $9.00; 1973.)